I0660521

THIS BOOK
BELONGS TO

THE ROYAL TIMELINE OF OZ

WWW.OZTIMELINE.NET

The **LOST TALES** of **Oz**

THE LOST TALES OF OZ

COPYRIGHT ©2018 THE ROYAL PUBLISHER OF OZ

ILLUSTRATIONS COPYRIGHT © ERIC SHANOWER

ALL RIGHTS RESERVED

FIRST TRADE PAPERBACK PRINTING—AUGUST 2018

10 9 8 7 6 5 4 3 2 1

ISBN 978-0-9911991-6-7

THE ROYAL PUBLISHER OF OZ
1085 FRANCES DR.
VALLEY STREAM, NEW YORK
11580-2124

www.oztimeline.net

The Royal Publisher of Oz is a trademark of Joe Bongiorno

The Royal Publisher of Oz uses Bullzip PDF creator

THE LOST TALES OF OZ

EDITED BY

JOE BONGIORNO

FOUNDED ON AND CONTINUING THE FAMOUS OZ STORIES
BY

L. FRANK BAUM

"ROYAL HISTORIAN OF OZ"

ILLUSTRATED BY
ERIC SHANOWER

In appreciation of my co-editors

PAUL DANA

MARCUS MEBES

ANDREW HELLER

Without whose dedication and hard work this book
would be much poorer

Thanks too to Richard Terrone for his tireless
assistance, eye drops, and tea.

Thanks also to the illustrator and authors who
contributed their amazing work to this book.

In memory of Margaret Berg, Robin Olderman, Sam
Sackett, and Richard Paul Smyers, who crossed the
Shifting Sands too soon, but remain in our hearts.

This Book Is Dedicated To L. Frank Baum,
Who Started It All, And To The Many Old
And New Fans Who Continue To Love Oz!

TO THE READERS

It's hard to imagine that it's been 120 years since Dorothy Gale first embarked on her journey through Oz, and nearly as long since L. Frank Baum chronicled that first adventure and the many fantastic tales that followed.

The sad passing of the original Royal Historian did little to stop the stories from coming or dampen the enthusiasm of fans eager to journey to that mysterious and faraway land, and the torch soon passed to another, and then another after that, until the present day when there seems to be as many Royal Historians as there are fans! Thus, the saga that Baum started so long ago continues to flourish and grow. And why shouldn't it? After all, of the many magical realms that exist in the dimensions beyond, Oz has some of its most beloved characters!

In this grand anthology of lost tales, you'll find heroes and villains, (and a few who are somewhere in between), scarecrows, woozies and witches, living victrolas and floating cities, talking animals of all kinds, fairy queens and enchantments, ogres and evil spirits, and some secrets too dark to tell. Here are tales of shadow and light, and some tales that have been hidden for far too long...

You are not alone in seeking out the mysteries of Oz, for Dorothy and her friends are seekers too, and there is much yet to be revealed of the distant past and those that walked the hidden forests, dark valleys and underground lairs, so that even now a vigilant watch is kept over those who would try to take Oz from those who love it most, you and me...

JOE BONGIORNO
ROYAL PUBLISHER OF OZ

TABLE OF CONTENTS

PROLOGUE

THE LOST HISTORIES

With such a wet and blustery Tuesday afternoon in the Emerald City, Betsy Bobbin and her best friend, Trot Griffiths, were feeling restless.

"It's silly to waste the day, Trot," Betsy urged. "Let's find Dorothy and explore the library!"

"I'd hoped go sailing with Cap'n Bill today," Trot grumbled, "but there's not much chance of that. Ok, let's go."

After a short time, they came across Toby Blunderbuss Jr., the Royal Guard of Oz, and asked him if he'd seen Dorothy anywhere. He hadn't, but he directed them to Herby the Medicine Man, who said he'd spotted Dorothy heading to the library a short time earlier.

"That's a nice coincidence," said Betsy.

"I should've realized," Trot huffed. "Dorothy spends a *lot* of time there these days!"

The Royal Library was a sprawling, five-story building directly adjacent to the palace, and was even bigger inside than it appeared from the outside. It was so large that it was easy to get lost in, despite the floor plans posted on the walls at every level and entrance. The Oz sections were color coded by subject matter, while separate sections existed for the magical countries beyond Oz, including the various island nations of the Nonestic Ocean. There were even books from and about the Great Outside World.

Having been there many times before, both girls were familiar with the layout. As the collection was constantly growing, they always managed to find something new and different on every visit. This would not be possible in our world, where there is a physical limit on the number of books even the biggest library can hold, but the Royal Library of Oz had been designed by Glinda the Good and the Wizard of Oz as a magical building, capable of expanding to accommodate an infinite number of books.

The girls passed by the sprawling fiction section, with an area designated for Oz. "We could read some of these," Betsy suggested. "The *Wicked* series has been popular in the outside world."

"I don't see the point," said Trot. "The real stories are so much more fun than these mixed-up, made-up things."

"*Some* would say you're just being closed-minded."

"*Some* would," Trot mimicked, "but I want to read something different today."

"Ok, well, we've read most of the Classics, I think," Betsy agreed. "The Western ones anyway. Did you know there's a magical translator for the non-English ones?"

"No, not like that," said Trot. "Something *different*."

"Well, we're sure to find something *interesting*, at the very least" said Betsy. If there was one thing they were certain of, it was that.

"Who decides what makes a book a Classic anyway?" Trot asked, wrinkling her brow.

Betsy rolled her eyes: "Educators who know a lot more about literary merit than their students."

"In theory, and don't roll your eyes at me! I mean, I know there's educational and artistic value to some of it but *I* think young people should have a bigger pool to choose from..."

Having heard this particular rant from her before, Betsy let Trot prattle on. It's not that she disagreed, but Trot had a greater idealistic streak than Betsy, whose passion for societal change was tempered by the reality that the outside world was unlikely to become as egalitarian as Oz.

They wandered more or less aimlessly through the labyrinthine corridors for a while without striking upon that one thing to spark Trot's interest. Finally, after a considerable distance, they came upon a section called "Other Fairylands," which took up several aisles.

"What do you think?"

"I like this section," declared Trot, "and I want to read those Narnia and Prydain books again..."

"There are lots of good stories here, but wait! What's *this*?" Betsy asked, looking down an aisle between rows of shelves. They walked closer to inspect the sign. "I've never seen this before. Have you?"

"The Lost Histories of Oz," Trot said, reading the sign. "*That* definitely sounds interesting!"

"Do I hear two noisy girls?" asked a voice from the other side of a bookshelf. They peered around the corner and saw the familiar and smiling face of the head of the Rare Books Department, Miss Ann Tiquarian. She was a middle-aged woman with large eyes, a pretty nose, and greyish-black hair that ringed her face. Spectacles dangled from a gold chain around her neck

"Oh! We're sorry if we bothered anyone, Miss Quarian," Trot apologized in an undertone.

The librarian's smile only broadened. "I was only teasing," she said. "What kind of librarian would I be if I didn't tell everyone to keep quiet? As it is, there really aren't many people here to disturb. Have you come to find Dorothy or reading material of your own?"

"I almost forgot we came looking for her," said Betsy. "But yes, we came to take out books. Can you tell us when this section appeared?"

"We didn't even know it was here," Trot added.

"That's because it wasn't," Miss Tiquarian answered. "You've discovered our new Lost Histories section! We've been gathering them for some time, but we don't like to place any book until we can verify where it ought to really go, especially now that the Wizard's given us these..." She pointed to the spectacles that hung around her neck. "They can detect falsehoods."

"*That* must come in handy," Trot said.

"It does! In the case of any title that purports to be the history of our land, part of *our* job is make sure they're authentic! We don't allow untruths to be taught here!"

"Are there false histories of Oz?" asked Trot, incredulous at the idea.

"All the ones in the 'Oz fiction' section. Bunkum Hill's been publishing this kind of thing for years, and some of the book trees in Oogaboo grow fiction. But there's also quite a bit coming in from the outside world these days."

"I never understood it," said Trot. "We have thousands of exciting adventures that happen for real in Oz. Why bother making something up?"

"Mostly for fun," said the librarian. "Not everyone's a historian. We filter through a lot of books from the outside world that are *not* so harmless."

"Don't get Trot started," said Betsy playfully.

"You mean things that are accepted as true that are actually false," grumbled Trot.

"And the other way around, I'm sure," added Betsy.

The librarian looked at the two girls, recalling that their appearance, just likes hers, belied their true ages. "You know how the magic of Oz has made our world... well, *interesting?*" The girls nodded. "Well, it's that way not so much for our amusement, but to keep things growing and flourishing, especially people. In the outside world interest is generated for the opposite reason, to sell ideas that aren't true and things that are useless, and to keep people distracted. It's my job to see that such falsehoods—no matter what they are—don't creep into Oz. Lies are a kind of rot that's very hard to get rid of once they seep in."

"My mother was a lot of things," Trot said pensively, "but a liar was never one of them. I think that's what I liked best about Cap'n Bill when I was a kid. No matter how hard the truth was, he always told it. He didn't treat me like a fragile flower, or try to dress up the truth in a comforting lie."

"My mother wasn't like that at all," Betsy said, "but I understand now that she was just trying to protect me from things that even she couldn't handle."

"I, for one, am glad I don't live there anymore."

"Me too," Betsy concurred. "When I came to Oz, as scared as I was, I never looked back."

"Don't be too hard on the outside world," Miss Tiquarian said. "To paraphrase a senator from your former state of California, 'truth is the first casualty of war,' which is why despite the fact that most people want truth, they're besieged by falsehoods."

"It's no wonder they're in such a state," said Trot. "But how are you getting all these books from all over?"

"We have teams who make trips into the various quadrants and even to the fairylands outside of Oz, where they go in search of books they can copy and bring back. And though he has his own extensive collection, Professor Wogglebug still supplies us with material from his midnight trips to libraries in the outside world. In the old days, back when we lived in Ozmara, the old capital, before the Wizard came, King Pastoria II would give us a stipend to buy out estates that had large collections.

"Also, some books grow on trees, like those in Oogaboo, Story Blossom Garden, and the Reading Tree. We've also acquired some that were a bit of an enigma to us."

"What do you mean?" asked Trot.

"It seems that some books were never actually published... they just *appeared* here. In one instance, we found a cache of manuscripts that came from the desk drawer of a writer who'd passed away. From what we can see, he never even tried to publish them. There's a manuscript that I'm examining now that's still being written! Every few weeks there's new material added to it."

Betsy and Trot looked at each other. "How's that possible?" Betsy asked.

"Honestly, I don't know," the librarian admitted. "Oz is a strange and magical place, and even those of us who've been around as long as I have don't understand it all. But I have some hypotheses."

"Don't keep us in suspense!" urged Trot.

Miss Tiquarian smiled. "Most of the wild and fascinating things that have happened in Oz have yet to be recorded. We have Royal Historians here in Oz, as well as in the outside world, some of whom have gotten their information from the Wizard, Dorothy, Ozma, even you two… But then there are the anomalies…"

"Such as?" Betsy inquired.

"Look at these." The librarian extended her arm to indicate the huge section containing the Royal Histories of Oz. "These have all been authenticated as real histories. Yet, most were never written by those who saw the events firsthand, nor were they directly told to anyone in the outside world."

"Suggesting?" asked Trot.

"Think about it," she insisted.

"Ok," said Betsy, rising to the challenge. "Fairies must have had a hand in it."

"If that's true," Trot started, brow furrowed in thought. "Then they must want these stories told. Why else bother?"

"Perhaps these stories were *meant* to be written, just as you were *meant* to come here," said Miss Tiquarian with a wink, knowing Trot had been marked by the fairies at birth. "No story is ever lost for long…"

"I like that idea," nodded Betsy. "I've always suspected that magical forces would the imagination and dreams of some to write down our history."

"And the histories of other worlds too, apparently" the librarian concurred. "Oz is far from the only realm beyond the outside world. What it doesn't explain is why some tell accurate tales they could never have known, while some only ever see through a glass darkly, if at all."

"That falls to the receptacle," said Betsy.

"The *what?*" demanded Trot.

"I think she means the writer herself," Miss Tiquarian said, "the one who receives the vision. 'Not all who are called respond,' to paraphrase the Great Teacher."

"And those stories get lost," reflected Trot.

"Well, I'd like to believe they emerge sooner or later," declared Miss Tiquarian. "But 'Lost Histories' makes for a catchy name, and we librarians are allowed a bit of fun too."

"But wait a minute," Trot started again. "Why?"

"What do you mean, 'why'?" Betsy asked. "There's probably a History Fairy or some such thing sitting in a palace in the Land of An directing writers to compose stories."

"Yes, but *why*? Why involve anyone at all? Why not just write it herself? There has to be a reason besides that," Trot argued. "Otherwise, what's the point of it all?"

"You may want to ask your friend Dorothy that," Miss Quarian said with a smile. "She seems to be fascinated by those kinds of question as well. She's in the ancient history section. I can give you directions if you'd like."

"No need," Betsy responded. "I know exactly where she is."

"Well, let's go find her then. Thank you, Miss Quarian. I know what I'll be reading today!" Trot exclaimed.

"I'm glad to hear it, and don't be surprised if you find yourselves in some of those," she said as she walked out, indicating the growing bundle going into each basket.

Trot and Betsy knew, of course, they'd been in Oz books before, some written by Mr. Baum and others by his successors, but it still amazed them each time an adventure of theirs emerged in a book.

Adding a few more books to the tall stack already in their baskets, they walked down a flight of stairs, through several long and twisty corridors, all lined with volumes of varying shapes and sizes.

Finally, they came to a large room with numerous bookcases and tables. With its recessed lighting and old stone walls made up of large granite blocks, it was no surprise to see that the "Ancient History" section of the library looked ancient itself.

"I don't see her," said Trot.

"There's an alcove some corridors down," Betsy pointed.

"Leave it to Dorothy to find a spot that's not even on the library map."

"That's because there's always so much going on in the Emerald City. It can be hard to study without distractions."

Dorothy sat at a medium-sized table, furiously scribbling notes on a pad of paper. An ornate lamp cast a brilliant light on an untidy heap of books, manuscripts, scrolls, pens and notebooks in front of her. A half-empty cup of loose tea and a small plate containing the remnants of a sandwich had been pushed off to one side to make room. She was so focused on notetaking she didn't notice the appearance of her friends until Trot spoke.

"Well, there you are! I bet I can guess what you're working on."

"The neverending project," Betsy said.

"Oh, hi girls," Dorothy said, looking up from her notes. "I didn't even hear you come in."

"It's a good day for staying inside," remarked Betsy.

"Is it?" Dorothy asked. "I haven't been out today."

"You haven't been out all week," Toto growled from under the table, where he had been napping.

"Oh, hi Toto," said Trot. "I didn't know you were here."

"I like it here," he said. "No cats!"

Dorothy laughed, "Toto, you love cats as much as I do! Besides, there are plenty of cats napping throughout the library!"

"Hmmm," he softly growled, "if you say so."

"So what are you working on today?" Betsy asked.

"The Erbs," Dorothy answered.

"Aren't you in the wrong section then?" asked Trot, with a smirk. "Cooking's two floors up."

"Har, har," Dorothy barked in a mirthless parody of a laugh. "You know who I mean."

"How many years have you been working on this now?" asked Betsy.

"Adventures keep getting in the way," she said sheepishly. "But I really want to finish it, you know... Once I sink my teeth into something, I don't want to it let go."

"Like a dog with a bone," remarked Trot.

"Hey, I resent that," Toto barked from under Dorothy's chair. "You wouldn't have happened to have brought any?"

"No we didn't, sorry," said Betsy.

"That's all right, but if you find yourself near Giriffic Park or Dogwood, be sure to bring me some," he said before resuming his nap.

"Pay him no mind," said Dorothy. "The palace chef brings him a dogbone every day fresh from the gardens."

"So, explain to me again why you're studying such horrible subjects," Trot said.

"Because they're important, for one," Dorothy answered. "The Erbs played a crucial role in the earliest history of Oz, a history that we still barely know."

"You know," began Betsy, "we just grabbed a bunch of stories from a new section called 'The Lost Histories of Oz.' There's bound to be something in here that will help."

"No doubt," said Dorothy, intrigued. "Every new story is helpful. It's like they contain pieces to the larger puzzle that's Oz."

"We also ran into Miss Quarian," said Trot, "and she says some were never even published, and that fairies might be involved. She seems to think you'd know how and why there are always new stories being written about Oz."

"That's just it. I don't. No one does, not even Ozma, and she's one of the fairies. Isn't it funny that the three of us have lived here for over a century each, and there's still so much we don't know? The second Royal Historian said that I discovered Oz, and that's obviously not true, except in the sense that with my arrival and Mr. Baum's book about it, *the world outside* discovered Oz through me."

Betsy and Trot looked at each other. Finally, Betsy said, "Are you implying that the world was *supposed* to discover Oz at some point, and that you were *supposed* to come here? Not to sound like Trot, but why would that be?"

"Maybe... maybe all of our adventures are part of a bigger picture," added Dorothy. "As to the outside world, don't you already know the answer to that?

"No," said the girls flatly.

"We're from that world. Do you remember what it was like when we lived there?"

"Yeah, miserable," said Trot, "well, except when I was with Cap'n Bill."

"Sad..." added Betsy, "and lonely too."

"Yep. For me it was grey and depressing," Dorothy said. "And that's how it is for a lot of kids. Plenty of adults too. So, what did our stories do when they're published there?"

"Oh!" Betsy piped up. "I see what you're saying now."

"They brought joy, excitement and hope to those who read them," Dorothy explained. "Mr. Baum told me that when I still lived in Kansas, and he it knew firsthand from all the letters he got and the people he met."

"It's true," opined Trot. "Each story is like a voyage to another place, even if it's just for a short time."

"Since we live in that *other* place, I want to know all I can about it. Ancient texts and some books that the outside world calls fantasy all bear out a pattern of evidence. Erbs, fairies and dragons, giants, monsters and men? How does it all fit in? I keep discovering new things all the time. The problem is there are so many fascinating threads, and each leads to another, and that leads to ten more. It's a challenge focusing on any one part of it."

"Well, if it involves the Erbs, it's going to be a horror story," Trot commented.

"I'm afraid you may be right at that," Dorothy agreed.

"I love scary stories," said Betsy.

"*Really?*" gibed Trot. "You didn't seem to like it when that beast was attacking us in Merryland!"

"That was different," said Betsy.

"Or the time the Flower People tried to plant us in the ground!"

"I know, but..."

"Or that time on your birthday..."

"Yes, Trot, I get the point!" said Betsy, restraining her annoyance. "What I meant to say was that I like to *read* scary stories."

"Oh, well why didn't you say so?" Trot teased. "Personally, I like mysteries best."

"Well, if it's scary stories and mysteries you like, I've got just the one for you!" The girls each grabbed a chair and sat on either side of Dorothy as she flipped through the pages to the beginning of the manuscript. Even Toto snuggled closer to Dorothy as she leaned over the pages and began to read...

THE GREAT AND TERRIBLE OZ MYSTERY

by Michael O. Riley

CHAPTER I
THE MYSTERY GAME

No one in the famous Emerald City of Oz will ever forget the spectacular ending to Ojo's adventure. But the beginning of the adventure was so unremarkable that no one noticed. All that happened was that Dorothy loaned her friend Betsy Bobbin a new story book.

Mary Louise Solves a Mystery was the title of that exciting story. Betsy enjoyed it and passed it on to Trot, who then gave it to Button Bright. Button-Bright, in turn, loaned it to his best friend, Ojo. This little boy and his uncle lived in a cottage outside the walls of the Emerald City.

Ojo had never read a mystery story before, and he was as enchanted by it as if the Wizard had put a spell on him. His mind was filled with nothing but puzzles and clues, and he decided that he would become a great detective. Ojo even invented a game for them all to play—the Mystery Game.

Besides Ojo, the main players were the aforementioned children from the Great Outside World who resided in Oz. According to the rules, each child was allowed one helper because fictional detectives always have assistants. Dorothy's was her dog, Toto; Betsy's was her mule, Hank; Trot's was the square Woozy; Button-Bright's was Billina, the Yellow Hen; and Ojo's was Tik-Tok, the clockwork man. The object of the game was to see which of the detective teams could solve the mystery first. Some of their other friends participated by inventing the mysteries, complete with elaborate plots and clues, for the children to solve.

Eventually, all the famous celebrities who lived in the Emerald City were drawn into the game. Even Ozma enjoyed playing when she could take the time away from her duties as Ruler of Oz. The citizens of the City grew accustomed to seeing various members of Ozma's court being shadowed by the children and their assistants. Hank, unfortunately, was very bad at shadowing a suspect. He was just too big to be inconspicuous. Scraps and the Scarecrow had great fun leading them on merry chases, and because neither of them ever got tired, they could always outlast the children. The citizens, too, were amused by the children's attempts at interrogation, and they happily answered question after question put to them by the curious youngsters.

It is impossible to say just how long the Mystery Game would have remained the palace favorite because preparations for an important state function drew the main players away long before anyone lost interest in it. Even in Oz, the most wonderful fairyland in the world, the children had duties to attend to, and this event promised to be one of the most spectacular ever held there.

It was Ozma's idea. The Emerald City "is the most splendid as well as the most beautiful city in any fairyland" the Royal Historian has told us. Everyone knows that, but Ozma, being kind hearted and considerate, often worried that the Wizard of Oz was not given enough credit for causing the city to be built in the first place. Therefore, she decided to hold a Grand Festival to honor both the founding of the City and its founder.

Everyone in the City thought this was a wonderful idea. Those in other parts of Oz who had known the Wizard in his early years were invited, including Glinda who immediately agreed to take part, as well as to the former Good Witch of the North and the powerful King of the Winged Monkeys. Ozma expected most to accept, but the Winged Monkeys kept very much to themselves since the magic Golden Cap had been restored to them. Glinda feared that they still harbored distrust of the Oz people. Otherwise, everyone from the Wizard's past would likely attend—except, of course, the two Wicked Witches whom Dorothy accidentally destroyed on her very first visit to Oz.

Dorothy left the Mystery Game first because, being a Princess of Oz, she had to help Ozma plan this great celebration. Then Trot, Betsy, and Button Bright had to stop playing so that they would have time to rehearse the song Professor H. M. Woggle-Bug, T. E. had written for them to sing for the Wizard.

Ojo, too, had a part in the ceremonies. He was to march with the Wizard's other close friends in the procession that would start at the Royal Palace and end outside the City walls in the Balloon Meadow, so named because it was the spot where the Wizard's balloon had first touched down in Oz. With all the exciting preparations for the Festival, it would have been easy for Ojo to have forgotten his ambition to be a detective had not something happened during the last pretend mystery that made the game all too real. In the questioning Ojo had done around the city, some very disturbing facts had emerged—facts that caused Ojo to make a terrifying discovery.

CHAPTER II
A REAL MYSTERY

"Now, Omby—I mean, Mr. Amby—you say you saw the counterfeiters hide the fake emeralds in the empty bird house in the tree outside

Trot's window?" Ojo asked as he opened his notebook and moistened the point of his pencil with his tongue.

"Yes, sir, the Greenbird family who live two branches up can confirm what I saw," Omby Amby said in his best witness manner. Ojo and Tik-Tok had found him having milk and cookies with the jolly little Guardian of the Gates, and because the boy wanted to question them both and also because he was hungry, Ojo happily accepted the invitation to join them. Tik-Tok did not need food, but he was always content to sit at the table and talk with those that did.

Omby Amby—otherwise known as the Soldier with the Green Whiskers—enjoyed playing the Mystery Game, and he had an important part in the current one that was titled "The Case of the Curious Counterfeiters." It had been thought up by the Shaggy Man, who was very good at creating interesting problems for the young detectives to solve.

"When did you observe this?"

"It was last Thursday morning, sir. I was walking in the palace garden when a sound in the tree outside Trot's suite caused me to look up. I was surprised to see three suspicious looking men up in the tree, putting something sparkling into the empty bird house."

"Why did you think them sus-pi-cious look-ing?" Tik-Tok asked in his slightly metallic voice.

"Well, sir, they were in a tree—all three of them," Omby Amby said, suppressing a smile, "a tree in the private gardens of the palace—and they were dressed in the costumes of the Quadling Country."

"I'm sure those must have been the same men I saw coming into the city the day before," the Guardian of the Gates put in excitedly after a quick look at his script. "Those men were dressed in Quadling clothes, and they kept their heads down so that the brims of their hats hid their faces. I didn't think much about it at the time, except that they were not very cordial."

"Now, Mr. Guardian, just be patient. I will take your statement soon, but first I need to finish with the first witness," Ojo said trying to look like a stern, no-nonsense detective. "What did you do then, Mr. Amby?"

"When I heard them descending from the tree, I quickly hid in the shrubbery to see what they were up to. I had every intention of following them; however, my beautiful whiskers got entangled in a rose bush. By the time I got free, the men had disappeared."

"Then, that's all you can tell me about the mystery?" Ojo asked, reaching for another cookie.

"Yes, that is everything I know—about the fake emeralds."

The trained detective was quick to notice a hesitation and a change in the witness's tone. He also noticed a quick, enigmatic glance pass between Omby Amby and the Guardian the Gates. "*Is* there something else you would like to tell me?"

"Actually, Ojo, there is," Omby said in his normal voice, "but it doesn't have anything to do with the pretend mystery. It's a real one, though the pretend one made us decide we should do something about it." And then, as if he wanted to get it over in a hurry, the words came out in a rush, "We think there's *something* haunting the palace!"

Omby's tone, more than the word "something," made chills run up Ojo's back, and the chills continued down both Ojo's arms when the Guardian of the Gates added, "something evil!"

"What do you mean?" Ojo asked in a hushed, breathless voice.

Again the two men looked at each other, and after a long pause, Omby began, "This has gone on for a long time—"

"Why have you not said an-y-thing be-fore now," interrupted the always logical Tik-Tok.

"Because we thought we knew what it was. We never thought there was anything to worry about—until recently. Things have changed."

"Why not tell Ozma about this? She would do something," Ojo suggested.

"We can't. We don't know whom to trust. I don't even know if we're doing the right thing in telling you, but at least, we know you arrived in the Emerald City long after this started."

"So give me some details," Ojo urged.

"No, we can't say anything more. It's Jellia Jamb that you need to talk to. She's been right there on the spot."

It was clear that the two men were not going to give him any more information. Omby Amby offered Ojo the last of the cookies, but the boy had lost his appetite.

CHAPTER III
JELLIA'S STORY

Ojo and Tik-Tok found Jellia Jamb arranging flowers in the great hall of the palace.

"Hello, Detective Ojo and Detective Tik-Tok," she said smiling. "I was wondering when you would get around to me."

"Yes, we do have some questions Jellia."

"Well, it was last Thursday morning," she began in a well-rehearsed voice, "and I had just put some fresh flowers on the table in Trot's bedroom when I happened to glance out the window—"

"No," Ojo interrupted. " It's not the pretend mystery we want to know about. We've already talked to Omby and the Guardian of the Gates. It's the *real* mystery here in the palace."

Jellia's pretty face turned pale, but she did not really seem surprised. "We can't talk here," she said quietly.

She led them out into the garden and to a green marble bench that had carved arms and a high back so that they were effectively shielded from view from the direction of the palace. The bench was situated in the middle of a lovely green lawn with no bushes or trees close by.

"I don't want to be overheard," she said, looking anxiously all around them, "although I don't know what powers this thing has. We'll have to take our chances here."

By this time Ojo's curiosity could not be contained, and his questions tumbled out. "What is this all about, Jellia? When did it start? Who knows about it? What can we do? Why haven't you told Ozma or the Wizard or Glinda?"

"Calm down, Ojo," Jellia urged. Then, taking a deep breath, she began, "I can answer most of your questions by telling you everything from the beginning, but as to who knows about this thing, only Omby Amby, the Guardian of the Gates, and me—that we know of.

"I don't know exactly when it all began, but mysterious things have been going on here for a very long time—in fact, since the City was first built."

"The Emerald City?" Ojo exclaimed in disbelief. He looked around at the beautiful gardens, cool fountains, and magnificent buildings all sparkling in the bright sunshine and outlined against the deep blue sky, and he could not imagine a more serene and happy place.

"Yes, right here. You forget that it was built and ruled for a long time by a mighty Wizard. Of course, mysterious things happened here. Great magic workers like our Wizard are not bound by the same rules as the rest of us."

"But Jel-li-a, when Dor-o-thy first came to Oz, she proved that the Great Oz was just an or-di-nar-y man from the out-side world. He did not know an-y re-al ma-gic," Tik-Tok argued.

"But maybe that's just what he wanted everyone to think," Jellia said with a toss of her head. "Some of us have never believed that story. We who worked in the palace were closer to him than anyone else. We saw things."

"Even the Wizard says that his magic was only humbug then," Ojo pointed out.

"I don't know about that. All I know is that when the Wizard was our Ruler, there was magic abroad in the City. He wasn't seen often, but when he was, it was always in strange and wonderful forms—sometimes a lady, sometimes a fearsome beast, and sometimes he appeared as an ordinary man. We in the palace knew that all those forms were just disguises to hide his true shape—we knew that he wasn't a man at all!"

"But *how* did you know?"

"Oh, we just knew," Jellia said stubbornly.

"Jellia," Ojo said patiently, "those *were* only circus disguises. The Wizard still keeps them in his rooms. He's shown them to me himself—the great head, the lady costume, and the beast outfit—even the material to make the fireball. They weren't magic disguises."

Jellia remained unconvinced. "We didn't know what the Wizard's true shape was, but we loved him because he was a good ruler," she said hotly. "Maybe he hadn't learned that kind of shape changing magic then, but you don't wear a disguise unless you want to hide your true identity. Now, he probably doesn't need to bother with such primitive methods."

"All right, all right," Ojo said, "let's not argue. Go on with your story."

With a sigh, Jellia brushed a tear from her eye. "I *know* that the City was a place of magic when the Wizard was here because when he went away, so did that feeling. It became just a normal city when the Scarecrow ruled it. Then when Ozma became queen, she filled the Emerald City with magic again, but her magic is all sunshine and laughter—there's nothing mysterious about it.

"After the Wizard left, I no longer saw strange shapes in the halls of the palace—at least, I didn't for a very long time."

"You're seeing strange shapes there again? Was that what Omby was talking about?" Ojo demanded.

"Yes."

"What do these shapes look like?"

"Sometimes like a shimmer of gray light, but often it takes the form of a person."

"But how can you know that a person you see is really this *thing*?"

"It's my duty, Ojo, to know who lives in the palace and who visits it. When I see a stranger in a place where guests are not allowed, I'm certain this must be one of the shapes this thing has taken. And then, too, very often I see a person that I do know in two different places at the same time—Omby and the Guardian of the Gates have had this experience, also."

"I don't understand what you mean," Ojo said, puzzled.

"Well, for example, do you remember last Thursday that I spoke to you and Button-Bright when you were on your way out to Farmer Bern's to play in the hay barn?"

"Yes, I remember that. You told us that we should take a picnic lunch with us so that we would have more to eat than just apples from the farmer's trees."

"And did you really go to Farmer Bern's, and was Button Bright with you all the time?"

"Yes, of course. We go there often, and Button-Bright was never out of my sight that day," Ojo answered wondering what Jellia was getting at.

Jellia then gave him a triumphant look and said, "Not ten minutes after I saw you two on your way out of the City, I came across Button-Bright—or something that looked like Button-Bright—in the hall near the Wizard's laboratory. Now explain that!"

"I can't," Ojo exclaimed with a shiver.

"Whom else have you seen dou-bles of?" Tik-Tok asked.

Jellia looked miserable as she answered, "That's what is so awful. Among the three of us, we've seen doubles of almost everyone—even Dorothy—even Glinda! You see why we don't know who to trust."

"But you are trust-ing us," Tik-Tok observed.

"That's because—as far as we can tell—all the shapes it has assumed have been of flesh and blood creatures. That's why we couldn't go to any of the other detective teams. When you are with Ojo, we know he must really be Ojo, so we decided to take a chance. We need your help."

"Real mysteries aren't as much fun as pretend ones," said a much sobered Ojo. He was beginning to realize the seriousness of the situation. Oz had been threatened by enemies before—the original Wicked Witches, old Mombi, and Ugu the Magician to name some of the most infamous. There also had been enemies from outside Oz: the foolish Whimsies, the terribly strong Growleywogs, the supremely evil Phanfasms, and the most persistent of them all, the greedy and vengeful Nome King. These last had once banded together and reached the palace garden through a tunnel, only to be defeated by the water of the Fountain of Oblivion. None, though, had ever established a foothold in the Royal Palace itself. Ojo was beginning to share Jellia's fear.

"When did you first become aware of these shapes?" Ojo asked.

"Well, as I said, we saw wondrous shapes when the Wizard was our Ruler, but you mean when did we start seeing them again," Jellia corrected. "We can't agree on that—the Guardian of the Gates would put the time earlier than I would, and Omby would put it later. The nearest we can pinpoint it is somewhere between the time Dorothy brought the Wizard back here to live and shortly after Glinda cut Oz off from contact with the outside world."

"But Jel-li-a, do you re-a-lize what you are say-ing? You real-ly think this thing is the Wiz-ard," Tik-Tok stated.

"Our wonderful, dear Wizard!" Ojo exclaimed in shock.

At this, Jellia burst into tears, and choked with sobs she gasped, "We did. We did! Oh, how could we ever have thought anything so awful! What would the Wizard think of us if he knew!"

"You mean you don't think so now?" Ojo asked.

"Oh no! There was a happy, benevolent atmosphere in the City when he was Ruler. We were proud to be ruled by such a Wonderful Wizard who could take on all kinds of shapes. He was Great and Terrible, but he was also very, very good.

"When we first began to see this thing, we *did* think it was the Wizard—the Wizard going about in different shapes to avoid being bothered by people. He is so kind that he can never say no to anyone. Then one day, about a month ago, I saw a double of the Shaggy Man near the Wizard's rooms. I knew it wasn't really the Shaggy Man because I had just left him in the kitchen filling his pockets with apples. I wanted to let the Wizard know that I knew his secret and that it would be safe with me. I touched the Shaggy Man shape on the arm to get its attention.

"Ojo, just that quick touch made me turn cold all over, and my hand felt numb. But that wasn't the worst. I looked into its eyes, and what looked back was *evil*. I just ran away as fast as I could. That's when we knew it couldn't be the Wizard. We know our dear Wizard too well to believe that he could be evil."

"What is it, then, and why is it here," Ojo wanted to know.

"We don't know what it is. But it's most often seen around the Wizard's rooms. We're afraid it is after the Wizard's magic!"

"I'm beginning to understand," Ojo said, "but why haven't you told Ozma instead of us?"

Jellia turned frightened eyes to Ojo, "When we thought it was the Wizard, it wasn't our business to tell Ozma. We still love and respect him as our first Ruler. But then, once we decided that it couldn't be the Wizard, we didn't dare tell the others because it could have been any one of them! We've seen a double of Ozma, too!

"For a long time, we didn't see it very often, if at all, and we thought it finally left for good. But suddenly, in the past few weeks, it returned, and the number of sightings has only increased. We're afraid that means something is about to happen. That's why we decided to tell you.

"But what can *I* do?"

"You can prove that you are a brave detective," Jellia said. "We have a plan."

CHAPTER IV
THE DISCOVERY

For the past several weeks, Jellia explained to Ojo and Tik-Tok, the Wizard had been spending the hours after lunch in his private garden, giving orders that no one was to disturb him there. It was also during this time of day that the thing haunting the palace was most often seen.

Jellia and Omby believed that this was no coincidence. Therefore, their plan was simple. They proposed that Ojo hide himself in the Wizard's suite the next afternoon to see what he could learn. Unfortunately, the ticking noise of Tik-Tok's machinery made it impossible for him to hide anywhere outside of a clock factory, so he would have to wait for Ojo at Unc Nunkie's cottage outside the City walls.

The Wizard's rooms were among the most beautiful in the palace because he had designed them himself when he caused the City to be built. A small foyer led into a large, comfortable living room. On one side of the living room, through an archway hung with green satin draperies, was the dining room, and on the other side a door led to the well-appointed bedroom. All of these rooms had beautiful sunny views of the palace gardens. There was also a bathroom with a marble bath the size of a small swimming pool, and beyond the bedroom was the largest of the rooms, the Wizard's laboratory. This was the place where he had once created his circus tricks to fool his subjects and enemies, and where now he practiced real magic.

It was with a rapidly beating heart and shaking knees that Ojo entered the Wizard's suite the next afternoon. He had an uneasy feeling that a real detective would not be so frightened. After looking quickly into all the other rooms to make certain that they were empty, Ojo headed to the Wizard's laboratory. This was one of his favorite places in the palace, and he was soon lost in wonder at the things he saw. Ojo did not think the Wizard would mind his being there because the

Wizard often showed him his experiments. Ojo especially enjoyed looking at the beaker of liquid emeralds from which the Wizard hoped to make emerald cloth for Ozma.

The far side of the room was lined with storage closets, most of them open. Ojo recalled the stories he had heard of the Wizard's early days as he moved past them. In one was the great head that had so frightened Dorothy on her first visit to Oz, in another was the beast costume, and in another were the wig and outfit of the lady. The closet next to that one was locked, but the key was still in the lock. Ojo knew that as a detective he should investigate that closet, but as the Wizard's friend, he did not feel that it would be right to do so.

Ojo loved the Wizard as just about everyone did, and he had been told the story of how Glinda taught the humbug magician to be a real wizard when he returned to Oz to live. Ojo himself had heard her say that she had never had a brighter pupil or one who learned faster. But then Ojo also thought to himself, "If I am to be a good detective, I should question everything and everybody and not take anything for granted. Is that really what happened, or did the Wizard already know some magic? After all, I've also heard Glinda say that in some areas of magic, the Wizard actually excels her! How could that be when she is the greatest magic worker in Oz—and probably the whole world?"

He turned the key and unlocked the door, but he still hesitated about opening it. Ojo suddenly felt very sad and much of his joy in detecting drained away. "I don't think I want to continue the Mystery Game," he said to himself. "It's making me suspect and distrust my closest friends."

Ojo's good instincts would have won out, but just as he reached up to re-lock the closet door, he heard a noise in one of the outer rooms. He whirled around to face the door opposite and heard the noise again, a frightening, ugly, snuffling sound. It seemed to be coming towards the laboratory. Almost without thinking, Ojo reached behind him and opened the closet door just enough to back in, always keeping his eyes on the door to the laboratory. He pulled the door almost closed, leaving just a crack that gave him a view of the room.

He also had a good view of the entrance to the laboratory opposite, and in a moment, he became aware of something framed in the doorway. It was not a solid shape; he could see vague outlines of the furniture in the bedroom through it, but there definitely was something there—something shimmering like a combination of fog and steam. If that were not bad enough for the boy trapped in the laboratory, the thing's outline kept changing, and Ojo saw hints of all kinds of repulsive things. As he watched, he got a suggestion of fur at one moment and of scales at another. He thought he saw a tail, but then it was gone, and he was sure he glimpsed long, sharp claws. But worst of all was when two—then three—yellow eyes looked out of the grayness for an instant.

Ojo tried to be brave, but he could not completely suppress a gasp when those eyes appeared. Faint as the sound had been, the thing in the doorway heard it. Ojo's heart almost stopped beating, and time seemed to stop. Finally, to his great relief, the thing turned and glided back into the other room. Soon he heard the faint click of the outer door closing.

The boy pushed open the closet door, mopped his face with his handkerchief, and took the first full breath he had taken for several minutes. But Ojo did not have the time to recover from one shock before he had another. When he turned to re-lock the closet door, he found himself staring into the grotesquely grinning face of the Wizard!

It took Ojo only an instant to see that this empty-eyed face was not actually the Wizard, but only a mask made of rubber and paint, hanging above a suit of clothes like the Wizard always wore. Ojo smiled at his fear when he realized that this was just another of the Wizard's disguises, and he thought it funny that the disguise even had hands made of the same rubber material, hands exactly like those of the kindly Wizard.

But Ojo stopped smiling as the full implications of this disguise gradually dawned on him. His eyes widened in horror, and his hands shook so badly that he was barely able to re-lock the closet before rushing out of the Wizard's suite and out of the palace. He ran through the city as fast as his fear and his legs would take him and did not even pause when the Guardian of the Gates called out to him. Ojo stopped only when he reached the little cottage outside the walls of the city where he lived with his beloved Unc Nunkie.

Tik-Tok and Unc Nunkie were sitting by the window. Tik-Tok was telling the old man about his former home in Ev when the crash of the front door slamming startled them. Suddenly, Ojo burst into the room, threw himself into his uncle's arms, and sobbed, "Help me, Unc Nunkie! Help me!"

CHAPTER V
THE MAGIC POWDER

When he had calmed down, Ojo told his uncle and Tik-Tok everything that had happened in the laboratory. He concluded, in a heartbroken tone of voice, "It looks like Jellia's first suspicion was right. The Wizard isn't a man at all, but some evil magical being who takes the form of a man."

"So you think what you saw in the lab-o-ra-to-ry was the Wiz-ard?" Tik-Tok asked in his mechanical voice.

"I don't want to," Ojo answered miserably, "but what else can I think? Jellia said that she often saw the Wizard in different shapes when he was Ruler of the City—"

"Costumes," corrected Unc Nunkie, who was a man of few words.

"All right, disguises, then. But she was there, and she believes that he was hiding his true shape, even when he appeared as a man. Then there is the fact that there were no more sightings after he left—none until sometime after he returned to Oz."

"The Wiz-ard is free to go an-y-where in the Pa-lace he wants to," Tik-Tok pointed out. "Why would he be tak-ing on dif-fer-ent shapes now?"

"Ruler?" Unc Nunkie contributed.

"You may be right, Unc. In the beginning he was the Ruler, but when he returned he wasn't any longer. Maybe he wants his power back—maybe he's plotting to take it back, and he's taking all these shapes to be able to spy on Ozma and the others."

"Do not get car-ried a-way, O-jo," Tik-Tok cautioned. "Some of what you say is lo-gi-cal, but much of it is not. We know that some-thing un-known is in the pa-lace, and we know that the Wiz-ard pos-sess-es a cos-tume and mask of him-self as he ap-pears to us. While I can-not think of a lo-gi-cal ex-pla-na-tion for the dis-guise, that still does not mean that what-ev-er is in the pa-lace and the Wiz-ard are the same be-ing. A-gainst your ev-i-dence, we have to place all our ex-pe-ri-ence of the Wiz-ard."

"You're right, Tik-Tok," Ojo said, calming down a little. "The Wizard saved Unc Nunkie from being a marble statue, and he has been a good friend to us ever since. That's why it's so disturbing to think that he may not be what he seems. If we only knew what to do!"

Tik-Tok's mechanical brains whirred rapidly for a moment before he said, "Wheth-er or not this thing is the Wiz-ard, we know some-thing is there. Some-thing a-lien, I would guess from Ojo's des-crip-tion of it. There-fore, we cannot do noth-ing. What we need is ad-vice from some-one who knows a lot about ma-gic—the Wiz-ard's kind of ma-gic."

"Glinda will be here next week for the Festival, but Jellia has seen a double of her, too. Do you think we should take the chance and ask her?"

"Too dangerous," Unc Nunkie said, and then, in what was a long speech for him, added, "Dr. Pipt."

Dr. Pipt had once been known as the Crooked Magician and had been able to do some wonderful things. He had invented the famous Powder of Life that had brought Jack Pumpkinhead, the Patchwork Girl, and the Glass Cat to life. It had also been his Liquid of Petrifaction that had turned Ojo's uncle into a marble statue.

"But Ozma took has magical ability away from him and took the crooks out of his body."

"E-ven though he can-not prac-tice ma-gic now, he still has his mem-o-ries and ex-per-ience. Yes, I think it would be a good i-de-a for us to go to him," Tik-Tok said. "If we go to-day, we can be back be-fore the Fes-ti-val, and we will know more what to tell Glin-da."

They decided to leave immediately. Unc Nunkie would stay at the cottage in case anyone asked about Ojo and Tik-Tok. They did not want Ozma, and especially the Wizard, to get the idea of looking for them in the Magic Picture. They hoped that with all the flurry of preparations for the Festival, no one would think of them.

Ojo's uncle packed a basket of food for him. Tik-Tok, of course, needed no food, but Ojo wound his movement, speech, and thoughts, as well as applying a little oil here and there. With these preparations made, they started on their way.

Dr. Pipt and his wife lived in the Munchkin Country, several hours from where Ojo and his uncle once lived, and the southern Yellow Brick Road would take them there. It was a beautiful sunny afternoon, and Ojo and Tik-Tok walked along briskly. Most of the land around the Emerald City was rolling farmland, rich and well cared for. A cool stream could be seen flashing in the sunlight or heard singing over rocks as it passed through wooded areas. Well-tended fences lined the road, as did fruit trees and colorful flowers. If the purpose of their trip had not been so serious, Ojo would have found joy in all the sights and sounds around them.

Soon they passed the house and barn of Farmer Bern, and Ojo thought of the fun he always had there with Button-Bright. His best friend was the first person he had thought of when he fled the palace, but because Jellia had seen a double of Button-Bright, Ojo was afraid to go to him. He did not know whom in the palace to trust. Jellia would never believe anything bad about the Wizard, even though it was her earlier suspicion that had first given Ojo the idea. He was distressed that these people he thought he knew so well suddenly seemed like strangers, and he did not like the thoughts that kept pushing their way into his mind.

"You know, Tik-Tok," he said finally, "Dr. Pipt *could* have restored Unc Nunkie when he was a statue. I had found all the ingredients for the magic potion. But it was the Wizard who performed the magic. And, too, Ozma may have decreed that Dr. Pipt's magic power be taken away from him, but it was the Wizard who took it—and who took the crooks out of his body. In fact, the Wizard has taken the magic away from a good many magic workers in Oz. I know that there is a law against practicing magic illegally, but the result is that the Wizard has almost become the most powerful magician in Oz. There are only a few other Magic Workers who are probably greater than he is."

Tik-Tok did not answer, but it was evident that he was thinking. The two walked rapidly along the Yellow Brick Road with only the songs of the birds and the distant lowing of cattle to break the silence.

Ojo's first trip along this road had been filled with many dangerous adventures, but since that time the road had been put into better repair and its course altered in a few places to avoid trouble spots. He and Tik-Tok were able to make this journey without encountering anything more than the minor inconveniences of finding places for Ojo to sleep and keeping all three of Tik-Tok's mechanisms wound at the same time. The urgency of their mission made them keep to a fast pace, and so, by late afternoon of the third day, they had reached Dr. Pipt's.

The famous Magician and his wife, Margolotte, were very glad to see Ojo, who was a favorite of theirs. While

Margolotte bustled around preparing a hot meal for the hungry boy, Ojo and Tik-Tok told them the reason for their visit.

Dr. Pipt had wide experience with all kinds of magic workers, and he was not ready to assume, without further evidence, that the being Ojo had seen was an evil one. He did, though, believe that it was powerful. "Great power gives off great energy," he explained, "and that energy is such a disturbance to the normal order of things that it is often difficult to tell if it is a good or a bad power. This thing may be the Wizard and be evil. It could also be the Wizard and be good—remember that long ago the Great Oz was thought to possess a terrifying goodness beyond the comprehension of his subjects. Either way, we need to ensure the safety of Ozma and our other friends—and of all Oz. And the first thing we need to know is what its true shape is, because this thing may also be something entirely unknown to us."

Ojo was encouraged by the Doctor's use of "we" because it indicated another ally, but he had to protest, even though his mouth was full of apple pie, "But I've already seen it without its disguise. I saw it in the laboratory."

"I think not," Dr. Pipt said slowly. "We know that the thing can assume different shapes, but it sounds to me like it cannot achieve complete invisibility. That is not uncommon for shape shifters. It is likely that the nearest it can come to invisibility is a kind of translucency that is achieved by rapidly changing from one shape to another. What you were seeing was the blurring together of all those shapes as one changed into another."

"That makes sense," Ojo agreed. "I did get hints of many different forms, but they were all horrible."

"Yes, and that's what worries me," Dr. Pipt admitted. "It is only a very powerful magic worker that can change shapes so rapidly, and the fact that all the forms you saw were frightening may be our most concrete piece of evidence that this is an evil creature."

"Then how can we find out its true shape?" Tik-Tok asked.

"What we need is a Magic Truth Powder to cast on this creature and return it to its true shape. I used to make such a good one—always guaranteed to work," Dr. Pipt concluded with a sigh.

"Oh, if only you could still practice magic," Ojo wished.

"Have you tried to see if you still have an-y pow-er?" the practical Tik-Tok asked.

"He has," Margolotte answered for her husband. "For instance, that set of self-washing dishes he promised me."

"Several times I have tried to make them," he said, taking up the story. "I follow the magic recipe exactly, using only the best ingredients, but it never works."

"Then you have no magic to help us," Ojo said sadly.

Because his head had drooped in despair, Ojo did not notice the significant look that passed between Dr. Pipt and his wife, but Tik-Tok did.

Soon Ojo went to bed, for the trip and the worry had made him very tired. Tik-Tok sat with the Magician and his wife outside the cottage in the twilight. The three had little to say. Tik-Tok knew that something troubled the humans, and his brains were wound up and working very well so he was certain that he should let them work things out for themselves. Soon they, too, went to bed. Tik-Tok sat out under the stars until morning, carefully wiping away any of the dew that settled on his highly polished, copper body and listening to strange and beautiful music that came faintly from the depths of the forest near the house.

The next morning at breakfast, Ojo wondered why Dr. Pipt and Margolotte were so silent, but then, he did not feel very talkative himself. Finally, after they had cleared the table, Dr. Pipt began, "Ojo—Tik-Tok. There may be no danger to anyone from this presence in the Emerald City, but then again, it may be a great threat to Oz. Because of that possibility, we have decided that we must tell you a secret."

Margolotte reached out and took her husband's hand to reassure him. "It is true that the Wizard, at Ozma's direction, took my magical powers away from me. And he was right to do so; there was the possibility of further accidents like the one that befell your uncle and my dear Margolotte. And it is true that I can no longer make magic potions and powders. But Ozma, in her wisdom, did not take the power from those I had already made. If she had, Jack Pumpkinhead, the Sawhorse, Scraps, and the Glass Cat would have ceased to live."

Dr. Pipt paused, and Tik-Tok asked, "What are you try-ing to tell us?"

"Well, in the days when there was money in Oz, we made our living by selling or trading my magic. Old Mombi was one of my best customers—another reason my powers should have been taken away!"

"What he's trying to say," Margolotte cut in, "is that we still have a cupboard full of those potions—the stock we had built up to sell—and among them is one dose of the Powder of Truth."

"And do these potions still work?" Ojo asked excitedly.

"Yes," Dr. Pipt said. "I don't know if I am breaking the law by keeping them, but now I'm very glad that I did!"

Ojo and Tik-Tok had intended to start back for the Emerald City after breakfast, but now that they had a means to fight this magical being, their departure was put off until the next morning so that Dr. Pipt would have time to show Ojo how to use the magical powder.

"It must be thrown at the subject, just as you throw the ball when you and Button-Bright play baseball, and at the same time, you must say the words, 'hic, haec, hoc!'"

"But what if it turns out to be a horrible monster and comes after me?" Ojo asked fearfully. "I'm just a boy."

"That's all right," Dr. Pipt reassured him. "I'm adding a little of my Powder of Immobilization to the Truth Powder. That will freeze this thing in its true form for at least an hour."

They spent much of the morning getting everything ready and developing a plan of action. They decided that Ojo should wait until he could find the Wizard alone, possibly when he was in his private garden. At that time he would use the Powder of Truth and make the Wizard return to his true form. In the event that the true form tried to attack, Ojo would have time to summon help. On the other hand, if it turned out to be benevolent, the Wizard's secret would be safe. Because Ojo and Tik-Tok could not now get back to the Emerald City until the night before the Festival, Ojo did not see any way of approaching the Wizard until the festivities were over, but he felt certain that he could easily find an opportunity then.

Since they could not predict how close Ojo would be able to get to the Wizard, he spent most of the rest of the day practicing throwing handfuls of flour at targets until he got very good with his aim. The person casting the powder did not have to make a direct hit, but a substantial amount of the powder did have to reach the target for the spell to work.

Ojo and Tik-Tok started out the next morning before the sun was up, and although they traveled as fast as they could, they still did not arrive back at Unc Nunkie's until very late the night before the Grand Festival. Ojo was exhausted, but even so, he did not sleep well. He had nightmares in which he and his friends were being chased by some unseen horror. The dreams upset Ojo terribly, and once he was awake, he still could not shake the feeling that some great danger was coming closer and closer to them.

Therefore, while dressing in his best Munchkin outfit that morning, Ojo decided to confront the Wizard as soon as possible. He would do it that evening after the banquet. He would follow the Wizard to his suite and use the powder there. Grimly, Ojo finished getting ready. He then gave Tik-

Tok a quick polish, and they left for the palace. Unc Nunkie would be joining the crowd on its way to the meadow, but Ojo and Tik-Tok were expected to be in the procession.

When they reached the gates of the City, the little Guardian was overjoyed to see them. "Where in Oz have you been?" the little man asked excitedly. "What happened in the Wizard's rooms? We've been terribly worried!"

"I found out that it's a lot worse than we thought," Ojo said evasively, not wanting to mention his suspicions of the Wizard just yet. "But I've been to Dr. Pipt for help. Contact Jellia and Omby as soon as possible, and all of you meet me at the marble bench in the Private Gardens on the east side of the palace before the banquet tonight—Jellia will know which bench. I'll explain everything then. We're late now for the procession."

But just as they started through the gates, Ojo stopped, felt in his pocket, and said to Tik-Tok, "Wait here. I'll be right back."

He had left the packet of Magic Truth Powder back at the cottage, but now that he planned to use it that evening, he was not certain he would have a chance to get back to the cottage before the banquet. By the time he returned to the gates with it and they had made their way through the large happy crowds thronging the streets, Ojo and Tik-Tok were just in time to take their places. The band was playing and the procession had already begun moving out of the palace courtyard. Ojo felt his heart skip a beat when, running back to his place, his eyes encountered the Wizard's. The Wizard looked at him questioningly and then frowned.

CHAPTER VI
THE GRAND FESTIVAL

Most days are beautiful in the Emerald City of Oz, but there seemed to be something even more special about this particular one—the sun shone more golden, the emeralds sparkled more brightly, the breezes were softer and more refreshing, and the perfumes from the millions of flowers were more enchanting. It was as if the City itself were celebrating its birth. This excitement had also spread to its inhabitants, and by early morning the streets were already filled with laughing, happy people. All were dressed in their finest and adorned with colorful ribbons and glittering decorations. Bands played so merrily in all parts of the city that many people could not resist dancing. Colored balloons were popular with everyone, but especially with the children. These commemorated the Wizard's first arrival in Oz in his giant hot air circus balloon.

Inside the Royal Palace, things were just as festive, but also confused as everyone gathered in the great hall to form the procession. An army of palace servants scurried here and there to make certain that all found their assigned places. At last they were ready, and as the City clocks started to strike ten and the palace band began to play, Ozma raised her scepter as a signal to begin. The massive doors opened, and she led the procession down the grand staircase.

Leading the procession with her were the Wizard and Glinda the Good. The Cowardly Lion and the Hungry Tiger walked on each side of them, providing magnificent escorts. Next came the former Good Witch of the North, Queen Orin, and her husband, the Munchkin King, and a transformed Dorothy, looking every inch a princess for the occasion rather than the fun loving girl she was normally. She wore her coronet and, over her white satin dress, the Magic Belt she had captured from the Nome King. Toto, of course, trotted along close by her, Eureka not far behind. Dorothy's first companions, the Scarecrow, former ruler of the Emerald City, and the Tin Woodman, the Emperor of the Winkies, came next. Behind them were Professor H.M. Woggle-Bug T.E. and the Sawhorse. Jack Pumpkinhead and Billina the yellow hen were riding on the Sawhorse's back. Next were Omby Amby and General Jinjur, the girl who had once briefly ruled the Emerald City. Following them, amongst other famous personages and old friends of the Wizard, were Trot, Betsy Bobbin, Button-Bright, and the Patchwork Girl, carrying the Glass Cat.

Ojo was supposed to be in this group, and his friends were worried by his absence. The Wizard had already inquired about him when they were assembling, but none of the children had seen Ojo for days. Those in the next group— the Shaggy Man, Dorothy's Uncle Henry and Aunt Em, and Cap'n Bill—were also concerned about Tik-Tok, who was supposed to march with them. However, the beginning of the Festival could not be delayed, and the procession started without them. As the last of the celebrities marched out of the door, Jellia and the palace servants fell in behind them.

It was only as Ozma and her group were approaching the palace gates that Ojo and Tik-Tok finally appeared. They did not stop to explain but hurried to take their places, Ojo putting on extra speed when he saw the Wizard frown at him.

To the beat of the "Royal Wizard March," the procession made its jubilant way out of the palace grounds and onto the main avenue of the City. Cheering crowds lined the street, but as soon as the cortege passed them, the people joined in at the end of it. By the time those at the head of the procession reached the meadow and began mounting the steps of the green marble dais, almost the entire population of the Emerald City was marching behind them in a glittering, joyous parade.

While the people took seats in a gigantic semicircle, Ozma, the Wizard, Glinda, Dorothy, and the Good Witch of the North took their places on the dais. The Wizard stood in the center with Glinda and Ozma on his right facing the crowd and Dorothy and Orin on his left. The other celebrities and inhabitants of the palace arranged themselves on the six broad circular steps leading up to the platform. Ojo was on the left side of the Wizard on the second step down with Tik-Tok next to him. They spotted Jellia and Omby across from them and down two more steps, but Ojo could not see where the Guardian of the Gates was. He hoped his message about the meeting had been delivered.

When everyone was in place, Ozma raised her scepter and the massive crowd fell silent. "My loyal friends," she began, "We are gathered here today to celebrate our magnificent Emerald City. But may we never forget that to celebrate our City is also to celebrate its Founder, our Wonderful Wizard of Oz!"

The crowd broke into prolonged cheers. The Wizard bowed to acknowledge the crowd, but Ojo thought that he looked acutely uncomfortable. Ozma finally had to raise her scepter again to be heard. Then she continued, her clear voice easily carrying to the fringes of the crowd, "To honor the City and its Founder, we have planned a day of fun and merriment for all of us. We here on the dais have used our magical skills to provide wonders of entertainment and splendid treats of all kinds. But before we open that part of the Festival with a song composed by Professor Woggle-Bug and sung by some of the Wizard's own countrymen, I want you to greet our special guests, all of whom had some important association with the Wizard during his first years in Oz. We are very happy to welcome the greatest protector of Oz—Glinda the Good!"

This stately woman stepped forward and bowed to the crowd, and it was fully ten minutes before the cheering for her stopped.

Then Ozma looked around and smiled at those on the platform before saying to the crowd, "Of the four witches who were in power when the Wizard arrived in our magical land, we are very glad *not* to be welcoming the two Wicked ones!"

The crowd laughed at Ozma's humor, but some laughed a little nervously because they still remembered those evil times.

"Now, please greet these Oz heroes who were responsible for freeing us from the two Wicked Witches and also for revealing the Wizard's true self to his subjects. Here are Princess Dorothy, the Scarecrow, the Tin Woodman, the Cowardly Lion, and Toto!"

Dorothy, holding up Toto, curtseyed from the platform, while the other three bowed in all directions from their places on the first step down and to the right of Glinda and Ozma. The cheering was just as loud and prolonged for these equally loved figures. But Ojo was disturbed by the expression on the Wizard's face. *Had* Dorothy and the others revealed the Wizard's true self? The Wizard certainly did not look happy.

Then, as the noise began to die down, Professor Woggle-Bug, Trot, Betsy Bobbin, Button-Bright, and the Shaggy Man took their places on the first step in front of those on the dais. Ozma stepped forward and had just finished introducing the singers when her attention was caught by a frantic signal from the Guardian of the Gates at the back of the crowd. Suddenly a great smile lighted up her face, and she called out, "My friends! My friends! This is indeed an historic day—now *all* the great powers from the early days of the City are here to honor the Wizard.

"Look," she directed, pointing to a dignified figure making its way through the crowd, "the renowned King of the Winged Monkeys!"

This legendary figure made his way to the dais as the crowd welcomed him. On the platform, Dorothy could not resist clapping her hands with joy as her old friend climbed the steps and took his place between her and the former Good Witch. At that moment Professor Woggle-Bug gave the down-beat, the orchestra played a prelude that ended with a crash of cymbals and flourish of trumpets, and the song began. It was very good, even by the Professor's standards, and everyone in the audience was engrossed in the music—everyone, that is, except the two detectives on the second step.

Tik-Tok leaned over and said in Ojo's ear, "This is very bad."

Ojo nodded without taking his eyes off the Wizard, "I know. Now the most powerful Magic Workers in Oz are all assembled in one place. If that thing is the Wizard and he has something evil planned, there couldn't be a better time to carry it out!"

And even as Ojo was speaking, things began to happen. Afterwards, he could never sort out the exact order of the events because everything seemed to happen at once. He saw a look of anger contort the Wizard's face. He saw Glinda, with a look of horror, reach out to grab the Wizard's arm. He heard Dorothy scream even above the din of the music. He saw the King of the Winged Monkeys reach out to protect her. And he saw the Wizard clutch at the Magic Belt that Dorothy wore.

Maybe Ojo saw all these events at once as he stood there on the step, or maybe he saw some of them as he sprinted toward the edge of the dais. All he remembered later was pitching the Magic Powder of Truth with all his strength and shouting "hic, haec, hoc" just before he stumbled against the edge of the platform and fell.

As the orchestra and singers ceased in surprise and discord, there came a loud explosion and the entire platform and steps were hidden in a cloud of blue, green, and purple smoke. Where there had been only happy cheers before, there were now screams and sounds of panic. Then the crowd's confused roar turned to one voice of horror as the smoke cleared from the dais, and they saw what was revealed there.

It was like a scene out of a nightmare. There stood a creature whose grotesquely misshapen body was covered with coarse hair like a wolf, but whose brown scaly head was that of a venomous reptile. It was frozen with one claw-like hand extended. Even immobilized, there was such a malevolent look in its glittering eyes that it chilled the hearts of all who saw it.

Ozma clung to Glinda's hand, and the Sorceress herself seemed to be in shock. Orin was kneeling beside Dorothy, who had fallen or been flung down at the feet of this creature and was immobilized from fright and shock. She was no longer wearing the Magic Belt, but it lay on the marble near her.

Ojo saw all this from the edge of the platform where he had fallen. The Magic Powder of Truth had revealed more to him than he could stand. The creature that stood there was the most evil thing Ojo had ever seen. He felt as if his world had turned upside down.

But then it turned right side up again. He saw someone step forward and pick Dorothy up in his arms. It was the Wizard! Their own beloved Wizard! Ojo was so happy that he felt like crying. The Wizard put Dorothy down beside Ojo on the edge of the top step and whispered to the boy, "How long will this thing stay frozen?"

"An hour, I think," Ojo quavered. "But what is it?

"And where is the King of the Winged Monkeys?" Dorothy asked in bewilderment.

Their questions had to wait. Glinda and Ozma had regained their composure and were calming the crowd. Then after a quick consultation with them, the Wizard stepped forward and addressed the audience.

"My friends, I had a very long and probably very dry speech to deliver to you today. That would have been an unfair exchange for the great honor of this Festival, but now, thanks to Ojo, you won't have to hear it."

The crowd realized that the Wizard's light mood meant that the danger was over, and everyone relaxed and listened to what he had to say.

"I think Ojo has captured the palace ghost. We have sensed for quite a while that there was sometimes a presence in the palace that did not belong there. Here in Oz we live and let live, but recently I have been concerned because I also began to sense a desperation in this creature. Desperation can mean danger.

"You have noticed by now, I am certain, that the King of the Winged Monkeys is no longer on the dais. Well, my friends, I believe that the King was never here. I think that this thing took on his shape in order to join our group of magic workers. At the instant Ojo worked his magic, which I hope he will explain to us soon," the Wizard paused to wink at the boy, "I saw the King of the Winged Monkeys reach out to unclasp the Magic Belt. I seized it to pull Dorothy out of danger just as Glinda realized something was wrong and grabbed my arm. Then there was the explosion and the smoke, and this creature was revealed in its true shape."

"But what is the horrid thing?" shouted Scraps who had lost patience.

"Don't any of you recognize what it is?" asked the Wizard.

Several heads nodded, and the Scarecrow said, "It was before Scraps came to the Emerald City, but we once defeated a whole army of them. It is a Phanfasm!"

"Yes," the Wizard continued, "one of those shape shifting creatures recruited by the Nome King in his most dangerous attempt to conquer Oz. The Phanfasms were the most evil and feared of all his allies. I would guess that this one—maybe more greedy than the rest—did not drink from the Fountain of Oblivion like the others, but went immediately to loot and conquer. He may have seen what the water of the fountain did to his companions and hidden himself. He would have been stranded in Oz then because Ozma closed up the tunnel after the Nome King and his allies returned home. And very soon after that, Glinda cut Oz off from the outside world."

"What will you do with him?" the Shaggy Man asked.

The Wizard looked at Ozma, who answered, "Glinda will look into his thoughts to see if the Wizard is correct in his deductions, and then we will send the creature back to the Mountain Phantastico. He cannot harm us from there, and we have no right to destroy any living thing.

"Now," she continued, running to Ojo, taking his hand, and pulling him up to stand with her and the Wizard, "we have two reasons to celebrate. This Festival was to honor the Founder of the Emerald City, and now it is also to honor the new Hero of the City—Ojo the Lucky!"

How people who had already cheered themselves hoarse could produce an even greater volume of sound was something even the Wizard could not explain, but the noise was deafening as people shouted and the bands began to play. Ojo blushed and wished he were not the center of attention. He understood now why the Wizard had looked so uncomfortable. He wished even harder that he were somewhere else when the Wizard whispered to him, "You've got a lot of explaining to do, my boy!"

CHAPTER VII
THE MYSTERY SOLVED

The remainder of the Festival turned out to be as merry and magical as promised, but Ojo always remembered the banquet that night with mixed feelings. He was proud to be honored as a hero, but he was very embarrassed when he had to reveal that it was the Wizard he expected the Powder of Truth to transform.

"That's all right, Ojo," the Wizard laughed, perhaps a trifle grimly. "I don't blame you for your suspicions. Everyone knows that when I first lived in Oz, I was always trying to appear to be something I wasn't. It was actually a relief when

Dorothy and the others unmasked me. Even though not all your conclusions were correct, you've still proved yourself to be the best detective among us. Tell us the whole story and why you suspected me in the first place."

Ojo looked around the large table and realized that the scene was just like the ending of many classic detective stories—all the main characters gathered together to hear the great detective explain his methods and conclusions. He turned red at the thought of being the center of attention again, but he knew that he had to play out this game. He also knew that he was among friends, so the boy got up and went to stand at the head of the table where the Wizard sat on Ozma's left.

"I don't think I'm such a good detective because I still don't know the answers to a lot of things. But I'll tell my story, and Wizard, if you don't mind answering some questions, we might be able to get the whole story."

When the old man smiled his assent, Ojo began. He told them how the pretend mystery had turned into a real one and how his suspicion that something evil was in the palace was first aroused by what he heard from Jellia, Omby, and the Guardian of the Gates.

As Ojo got caught up in his story, he lost his shyness and began striding around, using broad gestures to illustrate his points. He was very like a real detective, and his hearers were on the edge of their seats. He next told about the plan to hide in the Wizard's suite while the Wizard was supposed to be unavailable.

"Where were you on those afternoons, Wizard?" Dorothy broke in, trusting that her old friend had nothing to hide.

"Well, my dear, I knew that I would be expected to make a speech at the festival, and since it was such an important honor for me, I wanted to make a good one. I went to my garden every day after lunch to work on it."

There was laughter when the Wizard added, "I'm afraid, though, that I did more napping in the hammock than working!"

Ojo then told them what had happened in the suite, concluding with a question, "And this thing—the Phanfasm—did come to your rooms. Did you find out why?"

Glinda, seated across from the Wizard, answered, "Yes, we did. We looked at the Phanfasm's thoughts before we used the Magic Belt to transport it back to its own land. It was rather sad, really. There is always so much activity in the palace that the poor creature could never find a place to rest. When it found that the Wizard was out of his rooms every afternoon, it began to seek refuge there. You probably scared it as badly as it scared you."

"It scared me bad enough! You mean it wasn't after the Wizard's magic?"

"I don't believe those creatures can practice magic such as Ozma, the Wizard and I practice," stated Glinda.

"And Ozma and I are diligent about locking up our magical implements," the Wizard added.

"Why was it haunting the palace, then?"

"It had been searching for a way to return to Mount Phantastico and to cause as much harm to us as possible. The Wizard was correct about what happened when the Phanfasms invaded Oz with the Nome King. This one fled from the City when it saw what happened to the others when they drank from the Fountain of Oblivion. Then it was trapped in Oz."

"Was it here in the palace all the time?" Button-Bright asked with a shiver.

"No," the Wizard answered. "It wandered all over Oz, and I think it got only more angry and frustrated when it found that the Deadly Desert blocked its way in all directions. It returned to the Emerald City periodically, hoping to find out how Ozma had transported the rest of its people over the desert. Finally, not too long ago, it overheard us talking in the garden about that famous episode in Oz history and how Ozma had used the Magic Belt. From that time on, it wanted only to obtain the Belt and get revenge. I won't tell you what its evil nature had in mind for us and the City."

"It would have gotten the Belt, too," Dorothy cried, "if Ojo hadn't used the Powder just then!"

Everyone began talking at once, and it was a few minutes before Ojo could go on with his story. He did not say anything about what he had found in the Wizard's closet because he thought it might be a secret and because it still caused him too much uneasiness. He did have to tell them about the trip to Dr. Pipt's and how the good doctor had helped them. He could not leave out that part of the story, even though he really wanted to.

"Oh, Ozma, I know that practicing magic is against the law, but you're not going to punish Dr. Pipt for helping us, are you? Punish me. I'm the one who used the Powder!"

Ozma smiled kindly at the boy. "Dr. Pipt did not practice magic, Ojo. I knew that he still had many completed potions and powders. We only took his ability to create new magic away from him. He is a good man, and today we have one more thing to thank him for since his Powder prevented an evil creature from causing untold harm."

Ojo, much relieved, rushed on to the end of his story. "Tik-Tok and I had planned to see the Wizard alone tonight and use the Powder, but then, when all the greatest Magicians in Oz were there together, and the Wizard suddenly grabbed Dorothy with that awful look on his face, I just acted without thinking!"

"And a good thing, too," the Wizard said kindly. "I had just realized that something was wrong, but all I thought of was to get Dorothy out of danger. I did not know that the creature had already unclasped her Magic Belt. He could still have used it before we realized that something should be done."

"Well," Ojo said, drawing a deep breath, "you were all there and know how the Powder worked. So I guess that's about all."

The Wizard reached out and drew the boy to him, asking, "But *is* that all, Ojo? Isn't there something you aren't telling us?"

"Oh, no—"

"What about what you found in my closet?"

"Oh, Wizard, I don't want to know."

"But Ojo, I think you should tell everyone."

Then Ojo, feeling completely miserable, told them about finding the disguise of the Wizard in his closet—the disguise that looked exactly like the Wizard looked to them at that moment. And the boy did not leave out anything, "So I figured that if the way we thought the Wizard looked was just another disguise, like the beast or the lady, then we didn't know his real shape!"

This news was such a surprise that there was silence at the table, and there was an audible gasp from many when Jellia, at a signal from the Wizard, brought the disguise out from behind a screen.

Some, however, had not been surprised. Glinda, Ozma, and Dorothy smiled fondly at their beloved friend.

"I think you had better explain to the others before they start getting strange ideas, too," Dorothy laughed.

The Wizard also laughed. "My friends, when I first secluded myself in this wonderful City, after the battles with the Witches, I knew that my only chance of survival was to appear as powerful as possible. Thus, I stopped letting my subjects see me, except those few times when I allowed myself to be glimpsed in one of my disguises. This fueled the rumors, and the stories about my power grew until all over Oz I was reputed to be the greatest Wizard in the land. When Dorothy first arrived at the Emerald City, the Soldier with the Green Whiskers told her that I gave orders from behind a screen and that no one ever saw me, but that was not strictly true. Can you guess what I mean, Ojo?"

The boy thought a moment and then his face lit up, "It's like that famous mystery story you told me about—there are some people who are invisible—that we don't see or consider—because we expect them to be there—the gardeners, the maids—those kinds of people!"

"Exactly," the Wizard said, "While I could stay hidden from most of my subjects, I couldn't stay hidden all the time from all those who worked in the palace. Those who brought my meals and kept my apartments tidy—there was always the chance that they would see me accidentally."

"I know. I know, now!" Ojo exclaimed, clapping his hands and jumping around with pleasure. "You made the disguise of yourself as you actually look because Jellia and those others might see the disguises when keeping your rooms in order. Then, if they saw you as you are, they would think your real man shape was just another disguise!"

"Exactly right! No one could say what the Great Oz *really* looked like, even though they could say he sometimes appeared as a beast, a lady, a great head, *or* a man. You've solved the mystery, my boy. You are a good detective!"

But while everyone at the table gave a cheer for Ojo, he shook his head at them. The cheers turned to laughter as Ojo earnestly exclaimed, "No! No! I'm tired of this game. It became *too* real. This mystery was 'Ojo's Last Case'!"

INTERLUDE I

"That was super-creepy," exclaimed Trot. "But good!"

"I enjoyed it too!" exclaimed Betsy. "Let's compare notes when we're done reading the stories we borrowed," suggested Betsy. "They might help with your project."

"Actually, since you mentioned it," proposed Dorothy. "If you two can write down some introductory notes about each story after you've read it, that would help me sort through them all later,"

"I was just going to suggest that!" replied Trot. "Besides, the librarian said we might be in some!"

"Then they're bound to be fun no matter what the subject is," smiled Dorothy. "Let's have a late dinner. Then we can share what we've found."

"That's a good idea," agreed Betsy.

"We'll need snacks," added Trot.

With that, Betsy and Trot went upstairs to check out their books. The librarian on duty carefully placed an invisible, magical mark on each one.

"I've seen you do that before, but what's it about?" Trot asked.

"It ensures that the book is automatically returned to the library on the due date in the event that the borrower forgets or is otherwise *engaged*," the librarian responded with emphasis on the latter word.

"He means 'on an adventure,'" Betsy clarified.

"That's a good system!" Trot exclaimed.

After this, the two girls bid each other happy reading and set off. Trot procured a plate of nuts and dried fruits and a mug of gooseberry tea and located a cushioned window in a high tower overlooking Lake Quad in the distance.

Betsy secured a bowl of lupini beans and a glass of cold Ozade, and met up with her mule-companion Hank. Together they found a quiet alcove near the gardens where the sweet scent of honeysuckle was wafting in. As Betsy knew Hank liked to read too, she'd procured an automatic book stand that adjusted to one's ideal reading height, and even turned pages for you.

Dorothy, meanwhile, stayed with her books and notes at her table in the Ancient History section. As Toto began snoring softly under her chair, she soon lost herself in reading...

THE WITCH'S MOTHER OF OZ

by Paul Dana

It took me a long time to understand Ozma's regard for Mombi. How could anyone care about a Wicked Witch, let alone one who had caused so much trouble? But Ozma never forgot that Mombi raised her for nine years, and while she was hardly affectionate, the truth is that she never beat, starved or otherwise mistreated Tip. Scared him a little, but he played tricks on her too! This story, which takes place during General Jinjur's conquest of the Emerald City, in The Marvelous Land of Oz, *gave me new insight into Mombi, and as odd as it sounds, helped me understand her better, even sympathize a bit. And that means I understand Ozma better too.*

Betsy Bobbin

When an army of young women marched through the green country on their way to the Emerald City, they left behind a buzz of astonishment and speculation. Local farm families and homesteaders had never seen anything like this before, and for hours after the army had moved on they leaned over their fences and gossiped about it.

Ramana Radget, however, merely picked up what news she could and then flew back to her treetop perch. These people and their goings-on meant little to her.

That night, fresh news emerged from the Emerald City. The Scarecrow King had been overthrown, Ramana heard the neighbors telling one another. He and his new friends had fled westward and abandoned the palace to their colorfully clad conquerors, whose long-term plans remained a mystery. Ramana shook her tufted head. She didn't care who ruled the great green city two or three miles to the south. Nor did she care, next day, when word got around that city women had dumped their housekeeping chores into the feckless hands of their husbands.

Ramana had no husband. She had no house to keep, either. She was a Yookoohoo enchantress who preferred to spend her days and nights in the form of a woodpecker, unsuspected by her neighbors and unperturbed by such mundane matters as gardening, window-washing, mending, or grocery shopping. Local trees provided her with all she needed by way of lodging, along with a lofty perch from which she could keep an eye on her little son, Kram.

Kram was always easy to find. Ramana had only to follow the latest trail of cracked and crumbled soil winding its way among Nobi Groon's zealously tended cabbages or Ma Garter's prized green chard. For, unlike his tree and leaf-loving mother, Kram chose to dwell underground in the form of a mole—an exceptionally single-minded mole that did nothing but dig, dig, dig. Neither son nor mother quite got the concept of kitchen gardens, let alone the work that went into them, and Kram's digging certainly would have upset the neighbors were it not for his Yookoohoo cousin, Jenta. Jenta had formed the habit of following in his wake and repairing his horticultural damage before anyone noticed.

In this way they had managed well enough for almost two-hundred years. What difference could any ruler in the Emerald City make to a trio of Yookoohoos hidden in plain sight?

Ramana and Kram were not native to these parts. They'd been born well to the north, amid the purple hues of the Gillikin Country. That's where they'd been living when Queen Lurline worked the spell that changed Oz forever, bringing immortality even to the powerful Yookoohoos.

But it wasn't Queen Lurline who had driven them from their purple home long ago. No, the blame for that fell on Ramana's own eldest child, a girl named Bina who had disgraced herself by taking the horrid form of an old witch she called Mombi and using that form to bully and intimidate her little brother Kram. This sad charade had gone on for years before Kram finally grew desperate enough to tell their mother. With Bina's perfidy unmasked, Ramana's judgment on her daughter had been implacable. She had gathered up the tearful Kram and bundled him right out of the Gillikin Country, leaving Bina to make her own way in the world. Kram had soon retreated into mole-ishness. As for Bina, she had disappeared out of their lives.

But had she disappeared altogether? Perhaps not. Since that time a witch known as Mombi had gotten herself talked of in the Land of Oz. She had seized power in the Gillikin Country, and lost it twice! She had done away with the royal family in Morrow. Oddest of all, she had conceived a passion for the Munchkin king and had flung herself at him, with predictable results that had long since passed into song and satire. Could this Mombi have been Ramana's lost daughter?

Ramana fervently hoped not. Yookoohoos minded their own business, as a rule. Few were known outside their own immediate neighborhoods and fewer still had ever meddled in affairs of state. For Bina to embark on such a mad career would have been almost unthinkable.

Almost. The coincidence of the two Mombis was too great to ignore. So were their bullying ways. Ramana kept her head down and tried not to know more than she had to.

This had become easier when the notorious Mombi seemingly retired and was not as frequently heard from. The Wizard had dropped down out of the sky and overseen the building of the Emerald City, only to fly away again decades later. After that it had been the Scarecrow King's turn.

Now came this young woman Jinjur, with her Army of Revolt and her new ideas about how people should live. Ramana followed the gossip with mild interest. There were funny stories about Emerald City men struggling to get their laundry done or put edible meals on their tables, monumental tasks for which they were in no way prepared. The Scarecrow returned with his friend the Tin Emperor of the Winkies, only to flee again straightaway on an outlandish flying contraption. To Ramana the whole situation quickly became a tired joke.

Soon, however, she overheard a conversation that shook her to the core.

"A witch?" cried Nobi Groon, throwing up her floury hands.

"That's right," confirmed Ma Garter, who always seemed to know everything. "A Gillikin witch, if you please. Folks saw her hobbling in from the north with a cane and a basket full of goodness knows what wickedness. They say it's old Mombi, back from whatever Gillikin hole she's been keeping herself in."

"Fancy that! But this Jinjur girl already has an army. What does she need with a witch?"

"Hard to tell. The Scarecrow must have some kind of magic, for he brought that strange flying thing to life. And some say he's got friends in high places, such as the Quadling sorceress Glinda. Maybe that's why Jinjur needs Mombi."

"How frightful!"

Frightful indeed—more frightful, perhaps, than Nobi Groon knew. Mombi was back! And she'd taken up residence in the Emerald City, mere miles away from Ramana's hideaway. What would come of it?

Rat-tat-tat-tat-tat! With her hard, sharp beak, Ramana drilled away at the tree she clung to. She loved being a woodpecker. The constant pecking, the vibrations that rattled her small skull, and the noise that filled her tiny ears, all helped to stifle the clamor of her own memories. Or at least, they had for the past two-hundred years. But not now. Mombi! The memories came roaring back. *Rat-tat-tat-tat-tat!* How could Ramana have abandoned her own daughter so heartlessly? Yes, Bina had done wrong. She had made a virtual slave of her brother, who still bore the scars of those dark days. Had that justified Bina's exile from the family? *Rat-tat-tat-tat-tat!* Oh, the rage and anguish on poor Bina's young face! The girl had been born with an anomaly, as Yookoohoos sometimes were. She could transform herself into any form she chose, including the witchy one she'd invented to keep Kram in a state of abject fear; but she could transform nothing else, not the tiniest twig. It had been her secret shame. It was also why she'd enslaved Kram.

Of course Ramana had to rescue her son. But she wished, oh how she wished that she'd found a way to do it without abandoning her only daughter. How much tragedy might have been avoided if she had? *Rat-tat-tat-tat-tat!*

Days went by. What was going on behind the closed gates of the Royal Palace? Rumors flew thick and fast, and Ramana made sure she heard them all. It was said that Mombi magicked up fabulous feasts and untold luxuries for Jinjur and her army. Moreover, Mombi saw from afar what her enemies were doing and sent terrifying illusions to confuse and bedevil them.

Could such things be possible? Bina, with her anomaly, hadn't been able to feed herself, let alone an army. As for scrying and sending apparitions, these were feats no Yookoohoo could accomplish. Had Bina acquired arts that made her a witch in fact as well as in feature? Was she using these powers now, rather than her maimed Yookoohoo birthright? Or were these rumors merely rumors—the addled imaginings of stupid people who had nothing better to do than repeat each other's lies?

The only way to find out would be to go to the Emerald City and meet Mombi.

This was something Ramana did not want to do. She dithered and delayed. City life repelled her, as it did most Yookoohoos. The busy streets, the multitudes of people, the soaring edifices, all made her head ache. And what if the whole thing was a big mistake? What if this Mombi really was someone else altogether? Or, even if she did turn out to be Bina, what could Ramana do about it? Would they have anything to say to one another after so many years? These were the questions Ramana pondered. And while she pondered them, more time went by.

Then a second army appeared outside the city gates.

It must have come by night. There it stood one morning, spread out before the walls like a glittering carpet of red and silver. Quadlings, obviously. Ramana flew out to investigate and realized at once that this army could crush Jinjur's in an afternoon. Its women were better trained and better armed, as well as far more numerous. Moreover, Ramana gleaned from their talk that the sorceress Glinda commanded them. And mighty Glinda wanted one thing above all: the surrender of the witch called Mombi.

That did it. Ramana flew over the city walls and straight to the palace.

Finding her quarry was not easy. She hadn't set foot (or wing) in a building of any kind for decades, and she'd never navigated one as large and complex as this. As a result, she quickly lost her bearings amid the long corridors and staircases. It also appeared that a woodpecker was an unwelcome visitor, so that Ramana constantly found herself shooed and flapped at by aprons, hats, knitting needles, and any other implements that came to hand. In the end she became a housefly—not her favorite form by any means—and buzzed along the ceilings.

It was almost by chance that she found General Jinjur at last, in the act of hearing an emissary's report.

"What does Glinda say?" Jinjur demanded. Though she had seen the army outside her walls and knew that her options were running out, she still meant to drive as hard a bargain as she could. The emissary delivered up Glinda's ultimatum. Mombi must be handed over. Jinjur immediately sent for the witch.

It all came down to this. Ramana's moment of truth could be put off no longer. She hid atop the door frame and waited.

Mombi was not long in coming—and with her came unmistakable certainty. Nature could not have made so perfect a copy of Bina's hideous brainchild, with her towering hat, her stooped form, and her haggard face. Somewhere inside this crone, this schemer who had long ago terrified a lonely little boy and afterward blighted untold lives, lurked the daughter Ramana had cast out. In more ways than one, Ramana realized, she was the mother of Mombi's wicked career. She forced herself to hear and see all.

Mombi began by bullying Jinjur's guards and threatening Jinjur herself, just as she'd bullied and threatened poor Kram. Yet these got off lightly compared to Jellia Jamb, the diminutive maid who was forced to endure a cruel rite of witchcraft with an even crueler outcome. Ramana shuddered at it. A transformation that she herself, or any Yookoohoo in full command of her powers, could have performed in an instant, took Mombi two hours and a great deal of hard work. Foul fumes filled the air, together with chants in some unknown language. Jinjur and her soldiers fled the scene. Jellia coughed and wept. Where had Bina learned this monstrousness?

At the end of it all, a terrified Jellia was led away in Mombi's form while Mombi remained behind in Jellia's form.

Lie upon lie. For almost one hundred and fifty years, Bina had worn a false shape of her own creation. Now she had forced that shape onto a servant who wanted no part of it, while her own malevolent eyes stared out from that same servant's fresh young face. And for this she had learned arts that would appall any honest Yookoohoo! Ramana had no doubt that the Quadling sorceress waiting outside the walls would see through these stratagems, the pathetic devices of an angry little girl. And then? What punishment awaited Bina? Was there anything Ramana could do about it?

If there was, now was the time to do it. The transformed Jellia had been removed. Everyone else had fled from the smoky, malodorous room. Mombi, wearing poor Jellia's form, opened a window, capped her powders and potions, boxed her mats and braziers, and wiped up her ashes and arcane markings.

Ramana buzzed down to the floor and resumed her own true form.

"Bina," she said.

At the sound of her voice, the servant's form seemed to flicker. A different form took her place, the form of a girl with narrow shoulders and a purple dress. She straightened slowly and turned around, revealing a pale, pinched face full of sudden doubt. Reflected in this girl's eyes Ramana saw her own self as she truly was—a wild woman with leaves in her hair, dirt on her face, and mossy streaks on her skirt. The girl and the woman stared at one another.

"Mother," the girl whispered.

This moment of vulnerability did not last. Bina vanished as quickly as she'd come. An incongruously defiant Jellia Jamb rose from the floor. "*Bina!*" she sneered. "That's a name I haven't heard in a good long while. Have you come to give me a spanking?"

"What?"

"We both know I deserve it. I've been bad, Mother. Oh, yes. I've been such a bad girl."

"You're in danger here!" whispered Ramana. "You must get away!"

"Get away? How apt! You know all about getting away, don't you? Disappearing without a trace is a talent of yours, isn't it? Not that I ever tried to find you after you took Kram and vanished. Why would I? There was so much to do, so much to learn."

"Such as this," said Ramana, gesturing at the paraphernalia that littered the room.

"All this and much more! I've gone on to bigger and better things, Mother. I forgot you and your backwoods shapeshifting long ago."

"Then remember it now! The sorceress is too strong for you, Bina. She'll take all you've got and leave you with nothing. Is that what you want? Remember your Yookoohoo birthright! Transform yourself. Give yourself wings. Fly out of here and never come back."

A thoughtful expression came over the maid's pretty face. She plopped into a chair and composed her hands in her lap. "I *could* fly away," she mused. "Yes, I could. This isn't really my fight, after all. Jinjur is nothing to me. I could leave her to clean up her own mess while I go back to my quiet little retirement. But that's what *you'd* do, isn't it? That's what any Yookoohoo would do in the unlikely event that they found themselves in this foolish position. Don't like your life? Poof! Turn into something else and start a brand new life! Don't like your daughter? Poof! Float away on the breeze and never look back. Easiest thing in the world for our kind."

"Not as easy as all that," said Ramana.

"Easy enough, it seems. Too easy! You see, Mother, I don't blame you for what you did. It was because of you that I left the easy ways behind. They don't suit me. What I like are the hard ways, the twisted ways, the ways that take time and tools and hard work. I've walked my feet into corns for the sake of my craft. I've begged, bartered and burgled every kind of magic in Oz from every magician I've ever heard of. I've studied and practiced 'til my eyes were crossed and my brain was numb. You set me on this path and I've never stepped off it since. Nor am I going to step off it now. Let Glinda look to her own safety, for I'll meet her head on with all my wits about me. Maybe I'll come out on top, too. Stranger things have happened. What I will *not* do is transform myself into some filthy animal or bird just to wiggle out of a tight spot. That may be the easy way, the Yookoohoo Way, but it's not my way."

"Your way will end in ruin!" cried Ramana. "*Your* ruin!"

The seeming maid gave an angry cry. She wasn't ready to go to her ruin just yet. She also wasn't ready to accept sympathy from Ramana Radget. "What's it to you?" she snarled.

"You're my daughter, Bina!"

"You think so? Guess again! There's no Bina anymore. I am Mombi, and I am my own creation. I owe nothing to you."

"No you don't," agreed Ramana, "and I don't want anything from you. You are your own woman now."

That gave Mombi pause. "Besides, I couldn't transform myself if I wanted to, not in the way you do."

"Why not?"

"I don't have my Yookoohoo talisman. I threw that old thing away eons ago."

"Then make a new one! You still have time before they find out what you've done. Just think what a talisman will do for you! You'll be able to transform yourself in the wink of an eye, under Glinda's very nose. You'll be able to take ten different shapes in ten seconds, each more baffling than the last. The sorceress won't know where to look for you. You know how it's done. Here, let me help you."

Before Mombi could answer, Ramana seized a small, woven mat and tore it in two. Then she tore it again. Again and again she tore it, slowly reducing it to a bundle of ragged fibers. These she thrust into the contemptuous maid's hands.

"You can't be serious," said Mombi. "There's nothing…"

At that moment, without any warning, the form of the maid melted into that of the witch.

They both knew what had happened. The masquerade had ended. Glinda had seen through the ruse, as expected, and was now entertaining a restored Jellia Jamb in her tent. Old Mombi nodded silently. Then she looked at the fibrous bundle in her hands. A bitter laugh escaped her withered lips.

"What kind of talisman can I make out of this?" she asked.

"Anything at all. A brooch. A bracelet. Just fill it with your power and it will work, no matter what it is."

Mombi shrugged. "All right, Mother," she said. "I'll do it—on one condition."

"What's that?"

"Leave here and never try to see me again."

Ramana closed her eyes. Was this what she'd come here for? She hadn't honestly expected a reconciliation, perhaps. How could she, after all that had happened? But neither had she expected to help a half-crazed villain who, if she prevailed today, might go forth and wreak fresh havoc on new victims. "Am I crazy?" she thought to herself. "Won't it be better for everyone if Mombi surrenders herself to Glinda?"

Ramana didn't know. She didn't know anything anymore.

No, that wasn't quite true. She did know that she couldn't send her daughter into danger without the one power that was truly hers, the Yookoohoo power she'd been born with.

Goodbye, my brave, benighted daughter! And good speed to you!

Ramana Radget said none of this. She merely said, "Very well, Bina. You have my word." Then she transformed herself into a woodpecker and flew away through the open window.

THE TRADE
A LANGWIDERE STORY

by Mike Conway

This story takes place shortly after the events of The Marvelous Land of Oz. *Because of what happened to me when I met Langwidere, I find it particularly interesting, but even if she'd never tried to make me trade my head for one of her old castoffs, I'd still be fascinated by her. I also think we can all learn something from poor Cari.*

Dorothy Gale

This newly discovered tale has piqued my curiosity about Princess Langwidere! How did she get like that? Why didn't she die when her head was chopped off? What happened to her original head? Who are the heads' original owners? It all sounds like the makings of a good mystery, and I'm going to have to talk Betsy into taking a trip to Ev with me. Whatever happens, I'll have this story to thank for it!

Trot Griffiths

The Trade: A Langwidere Story

Langwidere, wearing Head #5, turned the page of her book and reached for the glass of lemonade on the stand beside her. Head #5 had a lust for knowledge, which she indulged whenever she wore it.

She unconsciously rubbed the humidity on the glass with her fingers and brought it to her lips to take a sip. Then she lowered the glass, but held onto it as she continued reading.

Head #5 liked to talk out loud when it was engaged in heavy thinking. "So, let me get this straight," she said to the air, "according to this book, the Yith race not only have a history in Oz across the desert, but also an ancient history before the dawn of humans or even fairies." She took another sip. "Disturbing. If true, that could upset my entire hypothesis. On the other hand..."

The princess's train of thought was interrupted by Nanda entering. Langwidere's eyes widened as she snapped the book shut and quickly stuffed it under a pillow, then hastily picked up her mandolin.

"Your Highness..."

"Nanda," Langwidere interrupted, "Did I not tell you to ring before coming in?"

"Yes, Your Highness, but..."

"I installed that bell-pull outside my sitting room for a reason."

"I assure you, Princess," Nanda said, "I didn't see you feeding your intellect again. Your secret is safe with me."

"Very good, then." She sipped again. "Now what was it that brought you in here?"

"I have a young lady visitor here who is asking to see

you," the maid said. "She seems very distraught."

"Is that a fact?" Langwidere frowned a little. "Why do you suppose she is distraught? And why is she troubling *me*? Does she think I'm a psychologist?"

"I'm sure that I don't know," Nanda said. "I only know that she wanted to see you."

"I see." Langwidere considered the matter. She didn't particularly like the idea of seeing this visitor, but Head #5 was, among other things, extremely curious, and this won out in the end. "Very well, then. Go ahead and send her in."

Nanda nodded and left. Langwidere played on the instrument for a few minutes while she waited for the girl to enter, wondering if she had made a mistake. On the whole she preferred to keep her own company, and hardly saw anyone but a few servants, especially now that the royal family had returned and relieved her of the unwanted duty of ruling Ev. Yet, apart from being uncomfortable with visitors, especially strangers, she had a bad feeling about this.

Finally, the door opened again, and the woman entered. Langwidere put down the instrument and rose, taking another sip of her drink. The woman stood tall and had a confident, purposeful stride that impressed Langwidere in spite of herself. She looked down for a moment as she placed her glass on the table, and when she looked up next, the woman stood right before her. Her eyes widened at her appearance. *Oh, my...* she thought.

"Hello, Princess Langwidere," she said, bowing. "My name is Cari, and I have come to ask for your help."

"*My* help?" Langwidere asked. "I'm not normally the

one that someone approaches for help. There's not much I can do, and even less I will do. You'd be much better off asking the king for help."

"I know," Cari said, "but in this case, I think you're the only one who can help me."

Langwidere sighed. She obviously was not going to be able to get rid of this woman until she listened to her request. "Very well, tell me what you want, and I'll consider it."

"Your Highness," Cari replied, keeping her eyes lowered at the floor, "I want to end my life."

The princess took a step back and raised an eyebrow. "Fancy that. That seems to be a trend around here."

Cari looked up at her. "I beg your pardon?"

"Nothing," Langwidere replied. There was no point in talking about her abominable uncle, the lately deceased former king. "Tell me, Cari, why did you come to me about this? Do I look like the violent sort?"

"No, Your Highness," Cari said. "I came to you because of your beautiful collection of heads."

"I do have an outstanding collection of heads," Langwidere admitted, "but what does that have to do with anything? Speak!"

"Look at me, Your Highness," Cari said, gesturing to her face. "I am homely, which is the reason I want to die, but I feel that you might have use for my head after I am gone."

Langwidere was taken aback by this revelation. "You... you wish to donate your head to me."

"Yes, your highness."

At no point had Langwidere ever considered that

someone would *want* to donate her own head to her. In fact, the last time that she had tried to get a new head, the little girl had fought her on it. But here was another girl who wanted to freely give it away.

"Why do you believe you are homely?" asked Langwidere.

"Because it is the truth," Cari responded. "It has always been. Since I was a young girl, my father told me I'd never get a suitor because I was so hideous. My mother was equally as candid. In truth, I have always thought of myself as average, but since I've been unable to find a suitor—and those who've tried are repugnant to me—I have concluded that my parents were correct in their assessment."

"So if I am to understand you correctly," Langwidere said, starting to pace, "You wish to do away with yourself because of your homeliness, so you are going to end your life, and your method of suicide is to give me your head."

She stopped and looked at Cari, who replied, "Yes, that's correct."

"Now," Langwidere went on, "you know that all the heads in my collection are beautiful, but you think I should add your so-called homely face to it. Please explain."

"I have two reasons," Cari said. "Beauty has no meaning without something homely to compare it to, and my head would be perfect for that. Also, if you ever needed to go among the people of the kingdom, then you'd have an inconspicuous head to wear."

"I see," Langwidere said. "You have obviously given this a lot of thought."

"I have, your highness," Cari answered.

Langwidere thought for a moment. "Cari, I feel that there has been enough suffering in this kingdom, so I will not grant your request." Cari's head sagged in disappointment. Then she looked up in surprise, when Langwidere continued, "But I *will* make a trade"

"A trade?" Cari's mouth fell open. "Truly? But Your Highness…"

"A trade!" Langwidere confirmed. "There are a few heads that I will not part with. Pick out one that catches your eye, and I will tell you if it is available." Cari remained frozen in place. "Those are my terms, and they are not negotiable. Go on, take a look."

Cari gingerly stepped past the princess and walked along the row of cabinets containing the heads. She looked from case to case, examining each head, and comparing it to herself in the many mirrors adorning the chamber.

"Well?" Langwidere asked. "I only have thirty heads and I don't have all day to wait for you to make up your mind. Do you see one you find appealing or not?"

"I do," Cari finally said. She pointed. "That one. Number 23."

Langwidere's eyebrows both rose this time.

"Number 23, you say? Why did you choose that one?"

"I don't imagine you'll want to part with it, Your Highness, but it's the most beautiful one I see, and if I could wear any face, it would be that one."

"I see," Langwidere said. "All right then, just relax. This may sting a little."

Cari turned around to face Langwidere. "What? What do you inten..." She trailed off when she saw that the princess now held a bladed weapon of some sort in her hand. It fell upon her too quick to process anything further.

"This will only hurt for a second..." Langwidere said.

Cari screamed.

Langwidere sat examining her new Head #23. She turned it about in her hands, taking in every feature. Nanda entered and stood before Langwidere.

"I'm glad she finally calmed down," the princess said. "But at least she left happy." She looked up at Nanda. "Women... we are a variegated lot, are we not? It is why men—such as they can be—never understand us."

"Perhaps," Nanda responded. "But what makes you think on such matters?"

"Cari," Langwidere said, rising. "She came to me wanting to end it all because of her ugliness, and when I offered a trade, she took Head #23."

"Why is that a surprise?" Nanda asked.

"When she walked in, I thought her the most beautiful woman I'd ever seen, and yet, when I offered her the chance to switch, which most women will never have the chance to do, she chose the plainest head I have.

"Beauty," Langwidere concluded as she put the head away, "and even homeliness, really is in the eye of the beholder..."

OJO AND THE WOOZY

by J.L. Bell

This coming-of-age story about our friend Ojo is from the time shortly after he and his uncle moved from their lonely cottage and came to live just outside the Emerald City. You might remember that from the book, The Patchwork Girl of Oz. *We first met the Woozy in that story, and he's in this one too!*

The Woozy's one of my favorite magical creatures in all of Oz, and if you ask me, we don't get enough stories of the Woozy's adventures, so here's a good one!

Things get a little hairy, but if you know anything about our square friend's anatomy, you'll know everything turns out all right.

Trot Griffiths

THOK THOK THOK! Ojo heard someone knock squarely on the front door of the new cottage outside the Emerald City. The Munchkin boy stood on tiptoe to look out through the small panes of green glass at the top of the door. He could see nobody.

Back in the Munchkin forest, nobody had ever knocked at the little house where Ojo had lived with his Unc Nunkie. Now nobody seemed to be knocking on their door again, but more loudly. THOK THOK THOK!

Ojo cracked open the door. The Woozy was standing on the stoop, turned away so he could slap his tail against the green-painted wood. He looked cheerfully up over one square shoulder.

"Hello," said Ojo.

The beast set down the large green object he held in his square jaw. "Would you play fetch with me?"

"All right." Ojo grabbed his hat ringed with golden bells off the long peg behind the door. He had played by himself that morning, and all the previous day. He was feeling almost as solitary as if he had stayed in the Munchkin forest.

The boy picked up the object the Woozy had brought. It was a cube of hard, bouncy rubber, its edges and corners rounded.

"That's my ball," said the beast. "The Wizard made it for me because I missed my exercise chasing honeybees. Princess Ozma said I mustn't chase them anymore." He sighed slightly.

As the pair walked toward the meadows beyond an

asparagus field, Ojo asked, "How do you like Ozma's stable?"

"It's steady," the Woozy replied. "I was penned up for so long that it feels good to have company. How do *you* like living here?"

Ojo stared at the green grass beside his blue leather shoes. "Unc Nunkie's happy about being under Ozma's protection. Last week he even said, 'Safe.' Now he's off learning how to shop."

The Woozy trotted ahead into a clover patch. His bluish-gray hide stood out from the sunny green landscape like a mismatched button. He called back, "And what about *you*?"

"I like visiting Dorothy and Scraps and the Scarecrow in the palace," Ojo said carefully. "The Shaggy Man's gone away, you know." To change the subject, he planted his feet and threw the Woozy's ball ahead as hard as he could. It went about thirty feet. When it landed, it came down on one corner and bounced off in a new direction.

The Woozy dashed after the rubber cube, dodging left and right on his square paws. Before the fourth crazy bounce, he snatched his ball from the air with his mouth. He trotted back to Ojo, grinning, and laid it at the boy's feet.

Ojo threw the ball two more times for the Woozy to fetch. After the third throw, two boys came out of the nearest farmhouse. Instead of Ojo's ruff, lace cuffs, and gold buckles, these boys wore light green coveralls and caps that set off their orange hair. One called, "Hey, can we play?"

The Woozy trotted over to the boys and dropped his ball at their feet.

"Just my luck," Ojo muttered.

"What kind of animal are you?" asked one of the boys.

"I'm the Woozy," said the Woozy. "Who are you?"

"I'm Erry." That boy jerked his thumb at the other. "That's my brother Nary."

Erry grabbed the ball and flung it almost all the way to Ojo. The Woozy sprinted after it, snatched it on the second bounce, and dropped it at the Munchkin boy's feet.

"Do you know Erry and Nary?" the beast asked.

"Yeah," Ojo muttered. "I tried playing with them last week. They're the same age now, but I think Erry was born first."

Ojo threw the ball back. This time it flew twenty-five feet, about halfway to the brothers. The Woozy chased it down and carried it onward to Nary. The redhead tossed the ball back toward Ojo, just as far as his brother had.

Soon the Woozy delivered the ball to Ojo again. "Why couldn't you play with these boys?"

"What?"

"You said you 'tried playing' with them. What went wrong?"

"Well, back home—back in the forest—I made up my own games. But here they play baseball, cricket and quoits and other stuff I'm no good at." Ojo threw the Woozy's ball again. Again it traveled halfway to where the Emerald City boys were chatting.

The next time the Woozy came back, he asked, "Are these games hard to learn?"

"There are lots of rules. And I can't throw far enough."

"Could you learn the rules? Could you learn to throw farther?"

Ojo felt his face grow hot. "If you don't want to play fetch with me, I'll go back home!" He hurled the ball back, further this time, but still not nearly all the way to the other boys.

"I do want you to play," the Woozy said straightforwardly before dashing off.

When the Woozy trotted back again, he said, "Nary and Erry throw with their right hands."

"Well, I'm left-handed," Ojo snapped as he took the ball.

The Woozy watched Ojo throw, then ran to catch up with the ball while it was rolling. He eyed Erry just as carefully as the boy tossed it back. "Erry steps forward with his left foot when he throws," the beast reported.

Ojo considered that news. If a step like that really made a difference, he should put his *right* foot forward. He looked down. He went through the tentative motions of throwing normally. Then he pretended to step forward at the same time.

"Come on!" called one brother.

"Throw it!" yelled the other.

Blushing, Ojo pulled back his left arm, half-heartedly extended his right foot, and threw. The ball went about the same distance as before, but with less effort. Hey, I *can* throw farther, Ojo thought.

He could barely wait for the Woozy to return with the ball again. This time Ojo leaned back, kicked out his right foot, and put his whole body behind the toss. The ball soared fifty feet, over the brothers' heads to the edge of the meadow.

"Wow!" said Nary as the Woozy sped past.

"Aw, I can throw that far," Erry insisted. He grabbed the ball from the Woozy's mouth, bent all the way back, and threw so hard that he nearly fell over.

The ball soared on a wild diagonal toward a green-leafed oak tree. It bounced off a waxy mass in the crook of a branch and caromed to the ground. The Woozy leaped and snatched the ball from the air. Above him a swarm of insects buzzed out of their hive, a black and yellow cloud.

"Bees!" shouted Nary.

"Run!" shouted Erry. The brothers sprinted toward their family's haystack.

Ojo stared as the bees dove and swirled around the Woozy like a dust devil. "Leave him alone!" he shouted. He ran forward, swatting at the air with his hat. "It wasn't the Woozy's fault!"

Bees were settling like splotches of thick, dark syrup on the beast's blue hide. He let his ball fall from his mouth. The bees spread across his head and back. The Woozy stood stiff, eyes shut. "Get away from him!" Ojo yelled.

The next instant, a fuzzy insect the size of his thumb knuckle was hovering in front of his nose. Ojo saw a tiny circlet of gold behind her black eyes. She dove at his left ear and buzzed, "Ze killer beez do not ztand for zuch azzaultz!"

High-pitched whines rose from the mass of insects. One soldier flew up to the queen and complained, "Ze houze-wrecker'z zkin iz too zick!"

Another circled Ojo. "Ziz boy zeemz eazier to zting."

The queen bobbed in agreement. "Zen zwarm ze boy."

Ojo took a step back, swinging his hat so its bells tinkled wildly. "Stop! No one meant to hit your hive!"

"Run, Ojo!" the Woozy barked.

The boy turned to flee, but more hairy insects buzzed around his face, a perfect swarm of black and yellow. He could see nothing else. Bees flicked against his hair, ears, cheeks. He batted at the empty air. "I'm sorry!" he shrieked.

The queen was buzzing an inch from his left ear: "'Zorry' izn't zuffizhient! Zomeone muzt zuffer!"

Ojo clapped his hands to his face. Insects landed on his neck and scalp. He could feel their little legs scrabbling around his lace collar and cuffs, seeking an opening under his clothes. He curled up on the ground, sobbing.

"Zavor ze wrazz of ze killer beez!"

The Woozy announced, "I used to eat bees."

The queen hung in midair. "What zort of grizly beazt iz ziz?"

"I'm the Woozy. Honeybees are delicious. Do killer bees make honey?"

"Zubzhectz!" the queen exclaimed. "Deztroy ziz monzter!"

Ojo felt the fuzzy bees taking off from his head and shoulders in waves. The air filled again with their buzzing. He ventured to peek through his fingers.

"But your mazhezty," said the captain, "ze zquare beazt haz no zoft zpotz."

The Woozy agreed: "My only soft flesh is inside my mouth."

"Ztorm ze monzter's mouz!" the queen ordered. "Zave ze inzolent boy for afterwardz."

Ojo leaped to his feet and ran. Ahead he could see the little farm pond, its surface a bright green film. He paused at the edge, wondering how deep the water was. Just my luck, he thought, not knowing how to swim.

While the majority of killer bees followed their queen's command, a squad zipped past the boy's right ear and circled back. Ojo pinched his nose and flung himself into the pond.

Crouched on the muddy bottom, Ojo could hear only his heartbeat. He started counting seconds: 1...2...3... If these killer bees were different than honeybees, they might actually reach the Woozy's vulnerable flesh? 9...10...11... What good had he done for his friend, waving his stupid hat? 16...17... The loyal beast would probably sacrifice himself, running off to lead the bees far away. 23...24... But maybe the swarm would return, waiting for him to surface from the water. Ojo heard his heart speed up. 30...31...32...33...

Only I could be this unlucky, he thought. As soon as I learn to throw better, I get stuck in this pond. And I'll probably never see the Woozy again. 39...40... Ojo's lungs were straining. His chest ached. Could the bee stings possibly hurt worse? 44...45... On fifty, he told himself, I'll come out and take what happens. 49...50!

Ojo burst up from the water. He gulped a mouthful of fresh air. He pushed his wet hair off his face and gazed around.

The Woozy was sitting beside the pond, wagging his three-haired tail. His square ball lay on the ground beside him. There was not a single bee in sight.

Panting, Ojo waded ashore. Water dripped from ruffled sleeves. His lace collar slumped over his chest and shoulders like a soggy, undercooked pancake. "What happened?"

Before the Woozy could answer, Erry and Nary ran up. Wisps of straw clung to every crease of their suits. Nary had lost his cap. The brothers' red cheeks matched their tousled hair. Erry puffed, "I'm sorry I got the bees mad!"

"And I'm sorry we ran away," added Nary. "You were real brave to help the Woozy, Ojo."

Ojo blinked. I *did* try to help, he thought. That *was* brave. He tugged off his sodden collar and told the brothers, "Well, the Woozy and I went through a lot together, back in Munchkinland. Where did all the bees go?"

The Woozy licked his lips. "They won't bother anyone now."

Ojo looked down. "You didn't break Ozma's rule, did you?"

The sharp-edged beast blinked back. "No, I didn't chase a single bee. But I'm too full to play fetch now, Ojo."

"We'll get the rest of the fellows and play baseball," called Nary, running ahead. "I want Ojo on *my* team!"

THE OTHER SEARCHES FOR THE LOST PRINCESS

by Nathan M. DeHoff

Some of you might recall the time Princess Ozma was abducted by the wicked magician Ugu the Shoemaker, as Mr. Baum wrote of it in his book The Lost Princess of Oz. *As several magical items were also stolen, Glinda sent out four search parties to discover where she might be. Although the Royal Historian justifiably recorded only the adventures of the party that found her, in fact, the other three parties had some wild and fascinating adventures of their own, and at long last, those stories have been found and can be shared with all!*

It all began with the arrival of Glinda at the Emerald City, where she was met by a large party of concerned friends:

Dorothy: "Glinda, do you have any news yet?"

Betsy: "What sort of person would do such a thing?!"

Jack Pumpkinhead: "Does this mean I'm an orphan?"

Dorothy: "The Wizard an' I should just march 'cross the Desert and make the Nomes give us back Ozma, shouldn't we?"

Toto: "When you have a minute, Glinda, would you look for my growl?"

Trot: "Shall I go to the lake and call for Queen Aquareine?"

Dorothy: "What if I took the Cowardly Lion an' looked in the most dang'rous forests in the Gillikin Country?"

Cowardly Lion: "What if you don't?"

Betsy: "Would it be all right if I stayed home and looked around the palace one more time?"

Tik-tok: "Sor-cer-ess, are we both-er-ing you?"

Button-Bright: "Is it lunchtime yet?"

By the look on Glinda's face, I could tell she wasn't in the mood, and rather quickly established parties to head out. These are the three parties:

1) The Scarecrow and Tin Woodman,
2) The Shaggy Man, his brother Daniel, Tik-Tok, and Jack Pumpkinhead,
3) Ojo, Unc Nunkie, and Dr. Pipt.

Betsy Bobbin

MEETING THE MARSHMALLOW TWINS

THE SCARECROW AND TIN WOODMAN'S JOURNEY

O n the morning after the disappearance of Ozma was discovered, Glinda left the Emerald City and flew back to her castle, stopping along the way to instruct the Scarecrow and the Tin Woodman, who were at that time staying at the college of Professor H.M. Wogglebug, T.E., where they were taking a course of his Patent Educational Pills. On hearing of Ozma's loss they started at once for the Quadling Country to search for her. The college was located in the Munchkin Country not far from the Quadling border, so a short walk took them from a land where most of the flowers and houses were blue to one where they were red. As they walked, the Scarecrow recited, "Amo, amas, amat, amamus, ama—I can't recall the rest. I thought that Latin pill would enable me to learn the language. How is your mechanical engineering pill working, Nick?"

"It doesn't seem to be doing anything," the Tin Woodman replied. "At least, I don't feel as if I know any more about engineering than before. Perhaps I would have to be faced with an actual problem."

"That may be," said the Scarecrow. "Of course, the Professor did say it was an unproven hypothesis that grinding the pills into powder and inserting them into our heads would work the same as swallowing does for meat people, and that it might not work."

As the two progressed into Quadling territory, they stopped at every house and castle they passed to ask the inhabitants if they had seen Ozma. They even queried the paper people of Miss Cuttenclip's village, which was surrounded with a high wall to keep them from blowing away. They soon came to the main road to the south that they had used years before when they were taking Dorothy to Glinda's Palace the first time she was in Oz. After questioning a goat that had been asleep in the middle of the path if he'd seen anything unusual, the Tin Woodman asked the Scarecrow, "How many people live in the Quadling Country anyway?"

"The Professor once told me that about 500,000 people live in all of Oz," the Scarecrow answered, "and assuming for argument's sake that they're more or less evenly distributed, then I suppose around... 125,000. But I don't know if that counts the animals or magically constructed people like the ones in the China Country."

"I wonder if we'll have to search the China Country," the Tin Woodman said." I really would rather not. I'd be afraid of breaking somebody."

"I couldn't say," said the Scarecrow. "I suppose Ozma could have somehow ended up there: she's as likely to be there as anywhere else, as far as we know."

"I have to say that I'm not sure our method of searching is likely to be of much success. It will take quite a long time to ask every single person in the quadrant if they have seen Ozma, and even if we found that person who took her, I doubt that he would tell us the truth, anyway."

"True," said the Scarecrow, "and isn't it odd that the two of us, who are originally from the Munchkin Country, and are now living in the Winkie Country, are looking *here* in the Quadling Country?"

"I'm sure Glinda had her reasons, though I'm certain I don't know what they are. Well, it looks as if we've reached a fork in the road."

"Does that mean we're close to Utensia?" asked the Scarecrow.

"No, not the eating kind of fork, but the one that means multiple paths."

"Well, if I'm not mistaken," the Straw Man said, "this is around where we encountered the Fighting Trees."

"Then I would prefer to go around. I know we can get past them with my axe, but it pains my heart to have to injure even a cruel tree. Unless you think the trees might have stolen Ozma?"

"I wouldn't see how they could. They can't walk, at least as far as we know, and Ozma told us she made peace with them the last time she visited. That doesn't necessarily mean they wouldn't pose a danger to us, though."

So the two searchers took the road around the forest, which was marked with what appeared to be oyster shells. Alongside it were the cottages of several woodcutters, who happily greeted their compatriot Nick Chopper, but had heard nothing of what might have happened to Ozma. The rather flat land soon began to ascend gradually, and the friends noticed a range of mountains, some red and some pink, with one appearing to be as green as the Emerald City. Nearby were some foothills, and a passing sparrow advised them that there were people living on the closest hill. Climbing to the top, they saw a sign that read, "BUNKUM HILL."

"Welcome, illustrious strangers, to our humble hilltop community," said a man in a red uniform who stood nearby. "We are known for three things, the *Book of Bunkum*, the manufacture of bunk beds—which are excellent for saving space—and the manufacture of rumors, which are made in our rumor mill." With that, the man waved toward a large windmill in the center of town.

"Those are all interesting, I'm sure," said the Scarecrow, "but we're on something of a mission. Would you happen to have heard anything of a lost ruler?" asked the Scarecrow.

"Oh, most certainly!" the man answered. "Her disappearance has been quite a boon to our society. We've created so many juicy rumors about what happened to Queen Ozma."

"But just rumors?" asked the Scarecrow. "No facts?"

"Facts! We don't deal in such things here. They're far too dull. What *could* have happened is always more interesting than what has happened."

"I wouldn't say that's always true," argued the Tin Woodman.

The man was about to say something else, when a boy in a tattered brown hat and red shirt with a bucket of newspapers walked past yelling, "Extry! Extry! Princess Dorothy suspected in disappearance of the Queen of Oz!"

"Dorothy?" exclaimed the Scarecrow. "She'd never do anything to Ozma! They're the best of friends!"

"Don't talk to me, mister. I just deliver the papers, not write them. If you have a complaint, you'll have to take it up with the rumor miller." And with that, the boy ran off, yelling all the while.

"Ah, little Tommy Rot is one of our best."

"He seems to be losing his hair," observed the Scarecrow. "Isn't he a little young for that?"

"Well, that's a job hazard of being a balder-dasher," said the man. "It will grow back, given time, but in the meantime there are always False Hoods to wear."

"And those open shoes don't look very good for running," commented the Tin Woodman.

"No, but everybody in Bunkum Hill wears scandals." The Scarecrow and Tin Woodman looked at him with considerable skepticism, but he just ignored them, and said, "Speaking of Bunkum Hill, you should ask about in town and see what you find."

Reluctantly, the visitors took his advice and strolled into the center of town, passing people who were gossiping in small groups. Some were also listening to a grapevine, which was providing them with juicy new rumors. They came to a building which was identified by a large sign as "The Rumor

Mill." When they knocked on the door, an old man with a feather in his cap opened it, and said, "How may I help you, gentlemen?"

"Our beloved Ruler, Ozma of Oz, has disappeared," declared the Scarecrow, "and we are looking for her. Have you heard anything about what might have *really* happened to her?"

The man patted the doorframe, and said, "Can't say for sure, but ol' Millie has churned out plenty of ideas about it. Why, it's the biggest subject of rumors we've had around here since the death of the Witch of the West! Did you hear..."

"I'm sorry to interrupt, but we already know what happened to the Witch," objected Nick. "Dorothy melted her with a bucket of water. We're looking..."

"That's what *she* says happened," interrupted the old man. "Were you there?"

"Well, no," acknowledged the Scarecrow, "but she told us what happened immediately afterwards."

"And you believed her?" the man asked scornfully. "What are the chances that such a powerful witch could be killed so easily? And even if she could be melted by a bucket of water, how could a little mortal girl without any magic at all have discovered the Witch's weakness when no one else knew it? Isn't it more likely that Dorothy was trying to cover up what really happened?"

"Well, that's just silly," said Nick Chopper heatedly. "Why would she do that? Anyway, we know Dorothy, and she's as honest as the day is long!"

"You *would* say that, wouldn't you, considering how much you gained from the assassination of the Witch? From simple woodchopper to Emperor of the Winkies, so quickly! That's not something that happens every day, is it?"

Urging Nick not to blow his top, the Scarecrow stated calmly to the miller, "The fact that things don't happen often is no proof that they did not happen."

"I suppose not, but we thrive on doubt here. Ah, another set of fresh rumors!" And with that, the miller pulled a piece of paper from the chute below the turning millstones, which said on it, "King Rinkitink killed in goating accident."

"Oh no! King Rinkitink was a very fine fellow," said the Tin Woodman, close to tears.

"Between you and me," said the miller, "I doubt it actually happened."

"Then why get people worried about it?" asked the Scarecrow, starting to feel incensed as well.

"It keeps them interested."

"Yes, but that kind of thing could be harmful!" argued Nick, as he and the Scarecrow followed him inside the building. "I mean, one of your newsboys said that Dorothy was involved in Ozma's disappearance. Both of them are loved by everyone in Oz, and anyone who reads and believes it might take sides against one or the other."

The Scarecrow was examining the walls, which were lined with clippings from papers. Noticing one, he called out, "Scraps and I aren't married! We're just very good friends! And Eureka *didn't* actually eat Ozma's piglet!"

"If you were in my country," said the Tin Emperor, with a gleam in his eye and a hand on his axe, "I'd personally tear this place down!"

"You two skeptics are starting to get on my bad side," responded the Miller, but noticing the Tin Woodman's hand clench on his axe handle, he added more congenially, "Surely you know humbug is an old Ozian tradition. Look at your friend, Oscar Diggs. Why, he was the biggest humbug of all!"

"The Wizard? Well, yes, but as you said, he *was* a humbug," admitted the Scarecrow. "He's since reformed, and is now a real Wizard."

"And even when he was a humbug wizard, he was still able to give me the kindest heart in all of Oz," added the Tin Woodman, "for which you should be grateful!"

"Yes, and me my—" began the Scarecrow, but he was cut off by a loud clucking sound.

The noises were coming from a strange bird that had just appeared in the mill. It looked like a chicken, but had poppy flowers in place of feathers. Two large poppies on the sides of its head reminded the Scarecrow and Tin Woodman uncomfortably of Ozma, but they did not have much time to think about it. When it stopped clucking, the creature loudly proclaimed, "A little bird told me that the Queen is being held prisoner by the Nome King, who is seeking revenge."

"Ah! Very good!" chortled the Miller. "We can feed that into the mill. But what of the connection to Dorothy?"

"Well, obviously she's in league with the Nomes!" exclaimed the poppy-headed bird. "Any flapdoodle could have figured that one out, Codswallop."

"Excuse me, Mr.—" said Nick.

"Gibbet," responded the bird. "Flibber T. Gibbet. I'm a poppycock, in case you couldn't tell."

"Ah! I should have guessed," replied the Tin Woodman. "Mr. Gibbet, as I told your... partner here, spreading rumors can be dangerous! The Nomes are troublesome, and we don't want anyone disturbing them for no reason."

"And who are *you* to tell us how to run a rumor mill?" asked the poppycock, riled up.

"Who am I?" asked the Tin Woodman. "I'm the Emperor of the Winkies, and..."

"Then go back to your Winkie Country," the bird said flatly. "You don't rule us here!"

"These two have been causing me a lot of trouble," said the miller. "They've been wasting all my time criticizing us, and all the while production has fallen way off!

"Well, lock them up in the mill," Flibber T. Gibbet advised. "We can use the straw one for cattle fodder, and feed the metal one to the goats. Then we'll create some rumors about what happened to them. The Flutterbudgets will eat it up!"

"Don't you even think about..." the Scarecrow started to say.

"Good idea, Flibber!"

But just as the man was about to advance on the visitors with a rope, and the Tin Woodman raised his axe to stop him, a soft but hearty voice called out, "You'd better let them go!"

"What? What? What's this?" asked the poppycock, running around excitedly. Two people made of some soft white substance resembling clouds had entered the mill. One was dressed in what appeared to be a military uniform of hardened chocolate, while the other wore a dress of spun icing. The first one was holding a ball with a fuse at the top.

"Let them go, or we'll set off this truth bomb!" threatened the one in the dress.

"No! No! We'll be ruined!" squawked Flibber.

"How do we know they're not bluffing?" asked the miller.

"Do you really want to take the chance?" questioned the uniformed one.

"Fine!" the Miller said angrily. "Go!" he said to the Scarecrow and Tin Woodman. "But you'd best get out of town without bothering anybody else!"

The two newcomers led the Scarecrow and Tin Woodman out of the mill and out of the town. On the way they passed a place in the back where people were bathing pigs. When the Scarecrow asked about that, the woman in the dress said, "Where do you think hogwash comes from?"

On their way down the hill, the Scarecrow said, "Thank you for coming to our rescue, and theirs, as I fear what my friend here might have had to do to protect us. We haven't been introduced yet."

"Well, we know who *you* are!" said the uniformed man. "You're the famous Scarecrow, former ruler of Oz, and you are the Tin Woodman, Emperor of the Winkies!"

"I see our reputation precedes us," said Nick. "And who might you be?"

"We're the Marshmallow Twins," said the uniformed man. "I'm Marshal, and she's Marsha. We're from the Candy Country up north."

"Oh, yes, near Gayelette's palace," observed the Scarecrow. "So what are you doing in these parts?"

"Marshal has a sweetheart around here," said Marsha in a teasing voice.

"Yes, my sister is correct, although I suppose that technically my heart is sweeter than hers. She's Portia Lynn, Princess of the China Country," Marshal said

"A marshmallow and a china doll? Quite an *interesting* combination," the Scarecrow observed.

"Now, Scarecrow, you know we can't always choose whom we love," chided the Tin Woodman with a wink. "I had a sweetheart once."

"We met when she was in the area with Dorothy, back when the Jester was causing trouble," Marshal explained. "The problem is, when she leaves Chinatown, she can talk, but cannot move. We were on our way to ask Glinda if she could help us."

"Glinda can do many things," said the Scarecrow, "and perhaps she would be able to help you. We're currently occupied on a mission that Glinda herself sent us on. The Royal Ruler of Oz is missing!"

"That's terrible news!" exclaimed Marshall.

"Can't Glinda find her?" inquired Marsha.

"No, for her magic has been stolen as well," answered Nick. "We were looking for Ozma when we wandered into that strange town. By the way, while we're grateful for the help, I'm not certain that threatening people with explosives is a very kind act, as it could have hurt others who were innocent."

"It's all right. *This* bomb wouldn't have hurt anybody," said Marshal.

"Yes, it just would have dropped some truth on them!" added Marsha.

"Well, I have heard that the truth can hurt," said the Scarecrow.

"Indeed, and it sounds like a very frank bomb," nodded the Tin Man. "Those professional liars can certainly use some of that!"

"For certain, but where did you get such a thing?" asked the Scarecrow.

"From a band of friendly goblins who live near these parts," answered Marshal. "They said we might need it if we were going to be traveling these hills. Bunkum Hill is on the most direct route from Cinnamon City to Glinda's Palace."

"We should have just dropped the bomb," said Marsha. "Those rumor-mongers are trouble, besides which they wouldn't stop insisting that we were from the Gelatin Isles. We're marshmallow, not gelatin! And relatives of the King of the Candy Country, for that matter!"

"Maybe on our way back, sister," said Marshall. Then, directing his attention to the Ozian celebrities, "I realize you're not going to Glinda's, but as our roads converge, perhaps we can join you part of the way."

"Certainly," said the Scarecrow.

"That would be quite lovely," Nick Chopper agreed. "In fact, here is a sign that may point to our next destination."

"Club House," the Scarecrow read aloud. "The arrow points up to this mountain. If you don't mind a brief detour, I believe we should ask at the Club House if they've seen Ozma."

As the Club House could be seen from where they stood, the Marshmallow Twins agreed, and the four companions started up the nearby mountain, which had a steady slope toward the summit. About halfway to the top stood a large house, with a door and windows about twice the size of normal ones. A sign above it read "Club House" and just below that and above the lintel of the door, hung a large-sized club. The door had a button for the bell, but as the Scarecrow went to ring it, the Tin Woodman stopped him, and rapped on the door instead. The door opened to reveal a large man in clothing rather too small for him. One of his eyes was much smaller than the other and his hair was an uncombed tangle. "What is it you want?" growled the man. "If you're selling brushes, I don't need any."

"We are looking for the Ruler of Oz," said the Scarecrow, thinking that the man might actually need a brush or two. "Have you seen her, or heard anything about her recently?"

"The Ruler of Oz?" the man echoed. "I don't even know who that is! Is that Pastoria fellow still the King?"

"No, his daughter Ozma, is now the ruling Princess," replied Nick.

"Well, it's all the same to me," the man said. "I really don't care who's ruling. What I do care about is getting myself a sweet snack, and I think I smell one right now."

"You must be mistaken, sir. We don't eat, so we didn't bring any..." began Nick, then he stopped and exclaimed "...Oh, shears and snippers! You certainly don't mean our friends here, do you?"

"What, these huge delicious-looking marshmallows?" the man asked. "Of course, I do. They're perfect! I have a hot chocolate spring in the backyard, but no marshmallows."

"But, good sir, we're living beings!" insisted Marshal.

"So what if you are?" the man said. "I don't mind that so long as you don't squirm too much."

"What?! How can you say such things?" demanded the outraged Marsha. "What are you, an ogre?"

"Well since my parents were ogres, yes, I suppose am I am." With that, the ogre grabbed Marshal and Marsha before they could escape, and dragged them into the house. The

Scarecrow and Tin Woodman, whom he disregarded completely, had the door slammed in their faces.

"We must do something before our friends come to harm!" said the Scarecrow.

"I agree," and with that, Nick Chopper began chopping down the front door. Before too long, they were inside the house, where they noticed a complex system of gears and pulleys leading from the front door to the giant club they had thought was a decoration outside the front door.

"We only avoided that because you knocked instead of ringing," the Scarecrow exclaimed.

"I had a bad feeling," Nick said. "Stand next to the bell and be ready when I tell you," he whispered to him, just as the ogre bellowed at them to get out of his house.

Axe raised, the Tin Woodman walked over to the stunned ogre, who let go of his prisoners. "Outside," he said to the Marshmallow Twins, who ran. Nick followed. It didn't take long for the ogre to recover his wits, however, and in a rage he began to pursue them outside.

"Bring them back to me," threatened the ogre. "Or you'll live to regret it!"

Focused on the Tin Woodman and his prize, the ogre didn't notice that the Scarecrow had been standing next to the door lintel, and at a signal from his friend, the Scarecrow rang the doorbell. The club swung down hard to hit the ogre right in the forehead, causing him to collapse.

"Looks like that mechanical engineering pill might have worked after all," observed the Scarecrow.

"Now you've saved us," Marsha said with a smile.

"And not a moment too soon!" Marshall added. "That ogre was ready to eat!"

Looking down at the fallen ogre, the Tin Woodman said, "Well, I am sorry to have to have done that, but although I have the softest heart in all of Oz, I'm not about to let my friends be hurt by any carnivorous creature!"

"He'll live," the Scarecrow rejoined. "But we should remove the sign so he doesn't ensnare others."

"And once we save Ozma, she'll figure out what to do with him," Nick agreed.

After they had done all that, they followed another sign that pointed towards the south, and this led them up another, smaller mountain. This time they only came across a grazing yak whose hairs were braided into ribbons. The yak walked over to the travelers and greeted them in a deep, lowing voice. "Well met, strangers. No offense intended, but you are the most unusual group of travelers I have seen in a long time."

"No offense taken, friend yak," said the Scarecrow. "We pride ourselves in our uniqueness. Allow me to make introductions. This is my friend Nick Chopper, Emperor of the Winkies. These are Marshal and Marsha, the Marshmallow Twins from Cinnamon City," he added. Then, placing a gloved hand on his breast and bowing slightly, "and I am the Scarecrow of Oz, at your service."

"Twins, eh?" repeated the yak. "I knew some twins once. Twin ounces, they are, although they weighed more than two ounces combined. They were fraternal twins, not identical, even though both were female. One was much bigger than the other. What were their names again? Oh, yes. Dawa and Nyima. Very nice ladies, if you like cats, which I do. They used to live over on the next mountain, but they were talking about moving to the Gillikin Country. I don't know if they ever did. Anyway, what brings you here?"

"We're looking for a lost princess..." the Scarecrow began.

"A princess, you say?" the creature interrupted. "Princesses are quite the nuisance, aren't they: always getting lost. I recall the time a few years ago when the Princess of Prezumba went missing. There was such a to-do over it, but of course she was found again, even if we had to enlist aid from the Mystic Monks. I'll tell you, they have some amazing abilities! But where was I? Oh, yes. It turned out the Princess had fallen into a mud puddle that led to the underground kingdom of Schlepp, and the king there wanted to marry her. She told him she couldn't possibly, because it was the tradition in Prezumba they are not permitted to marry until the age of twenty-three, and she was only twenty-one. The King decided to keep her until she was old enough to marry him, but that just happened to be the day that they were invaded by an army of rabbits, the Lapine Legion, who were there to demand payment for the Golden Cabbage their chief, Cottontail the Conqueror, had lent to the King, with an additional two hundred years of interest and penalties. The total amount was so big that—"

"I don't mean to be rude, but that isn't the princess we're looking for," said the Tin Woodman. "*We're* looking for Princess—"

"Well, of course you aren't," the yak agreed. That's merely an example of how princesses are always losing themselves, like the buttons on an old shirt. Not that I personally wear shirts, of course, or use buttons at all, for that matter, but they do have a way of coming loose at the most inconvenient moments, and..."

Marsha, who had been listening to the yakking very carefully, interrupted. "Who are these Mystic Monks you mentioned?"

"The Mystic Monks?" repeated the yak. "You mean the ones who live on Mount Quarm, over to the west. Did I mention that they have some amazing abilities? Well, anyway, the Princess of Prezumba had a bad habit of losing her buttons, and once lost herself as well. It must have been back in '79, or was it '78? Oh, it was '78, the year of that storm of fish over on Big Enough. You see, the Princess was—"

"Enough, Yarkum!" squawked a new voice. Everyone turned to see the voice belonged to a giant red eagle who had landed unnoticed on a low branch of a nearby yenta tree. "You've bent the ears of these unfortunate strangers quite long enough."

"But Ebrin," the yak protested, "I was just telling them about the time when the Princess of Pezumba went missing."

"Did they ask you about her?" the Eagle wanted to know.

"Well," Yarku answered, "they asked me if I knew anything about a lost princess."

"I was trying to ask you about Princess Ozma, but I never got the chance," said the Scarecrow.

"Princess Ozma? The ruler of Oz?" asked Ebrin. "*She's missing?*"

"Ozma? You should have said so in the first place!" exclaimed the yak." Did you know Ozma used to be a boy? She was transformed by a wicked witch up in the north named Mombi. The way I heard the story, the Wizard of Oz..."

"Yes, we know that story well," The Scarecrow cut in, as Yarku seemed about to launch into another long speech.

"Well, then why did you come up here to ask me about it?" sniffed the yak, who then wandered off to find more grass.

"Yarkum isn't a bad fellow," explained Ebrin, "but sometimes it's difficult to get him to stop talking and listen, a fault of many yaks, from what I hear. Is there any way I can help you find Ozma?"

"We were just traveling around, asking everyone we meet if they know anything what happened to her or where she is," the Tin Woodman explained. "Perhaps we should consult these Mystic Monks over on Mount Quarm."

"Well, I have to be home in time for dinner," Ebrin said, "but I think I can take you over there, if you're not afraid of flying, that is."

"Sounds like fun to us," expressed the Marshmallow Twins. With that, the eagle lifted the Tin Woodman in one talon, with the Scarecrow holding onto him. With the other, he grabbed the Marshmallow Twins, and flew off west over the Quadling countryside.

A short time later, the great Eagle lowered his passengers gently to the ground. "Here you are!" he said. "Good luck! I hope you find the Princess soon," and flapped away before the winded travelers could regain their breath enough to thank him.

They looked around. They were on the flat top of a mountain covered in nut trees. There stood a large temple in the center, and a lake with a waterfall next to it. Coming from the temple was the sound of high-pitched, squeaky chanting. The four travelers approached the temple door, and knocked. When the door opened, they were confronted by a stack of chipmunks dressed in red robes, standing on each other's shoulders.

"Are you the Mystic Monks?" asked Marshal.

"No!" squeaked the one on top. "We are the Mystic *Munks*, as in chipmunks! I suppose you were expecting someone bigger."

"Not necessarily," said the Scarecrow. "But we weren't expecting rodents, either."

"No? Why not?" the topmost munk demanded. "Why do you think we're called chipmunks, anyway?"

"Then you make chips?" questioned Marshal.

"Oh, yes!" said the third chipmunk from the top. "Chocolate chips, potato chips, poker chips, you name it. That's how we spend our time when we aren't gathering nuts, meditating, or researching the nature of eternity."

"So what have you found out about eternity?" the Scarecrow asked.

"It's very long!" yelled the chipmunk on the bottom

"An accurate, if less than profound observation, Acolyte Chirmin," said a munk with patches of gray fur on the sides of his head, who crouched on a nearby table over a book. "He'll learn eventually. Let me introduce myself, since my acolytes have evidently forgotten their manners. I am Rukkit, Abbot of this monastery, and you must be the Scarecrow, the Emperor of the Winkies, and the Marshmallow Twins from the Candy Country."

"You seem very well-informed," observed the Scarecrow.

"Well, you're all part of the infinite, you know."

The Scarecrow and Tin Woodman didn't quite know, but as there was little time to find out, they let it pass.

"We've heard you have some skill at finding lost princesses," said Marsha.

"Oh, you must be referring to Brother Brikkuk," the Abbot answered. "Unfortunately, he isn't among us any longer. He achieved enlightenment back in '88, and floated away."

"Oh, no! Was he all right?" asked Nick.

"We've yet to hear from him, but I don't see why he wouldn't be. I've heard the sky is a fine place to live. We no longer have anyone here very good at locating lost people. We *do* have an acolyte who is particularly skilled at massage, which most travelers who've come to us are in dire need of." He turned and whistled sharply.

A new munk scurried into the room, took one look at the Woodman, and said, "Oh, acorns and walnuts! You look stiff as anything!"

"That's just the way I'm made," the Tin Woodman said. "There's nothing to be done about it."

"Nonsense! Let me see what I can do." And the chipmunk proceeded to run up and down Nick's body adjusting his joints. "Now try them," the acolyte said.

The Tin Woodman tested his limbs and exclaimed, "That's remarkable! My joints have never worked so smoothly."

"I have an idea," announced Marsha. "Do you think you'd be able to remove the stiffness from somebody made of porcelain? It's quite important to me."

"You mean like the people of the China Country?" the chipmunk asked.

"Oh, so you've heard of them," Marsha answered.

"But of course," the Abbot replied. "They're part of the infinite too. Besides, their realm is a relatively short distance away. Do you know where the China Country came from?"

"No," Marsha said. "But I've always wondered."

"It was made by the Wizard Wam, who used to have a kiln in Old Smokey, not far from here," stated the Abbot. "He made the country and brought its people to life, but they were unable to live outside its borders. This was back when he was still trying to perfect his animation magic."

"I've actually been pondering if I could do anything about their situation, but I've never had the occasion to go there before," announced the massaging munk. "Abbot, may I go there with them?"

"I feel it is the path you must take, Acolyte Haichek." And with that, the Abbot blew on a whistle, and an eagle even larger than the one who had brought the four travelers to the temple appeared.

"This had better be important. It's almost time for dinner!" said the eagle.

"It is only a short flight," the Abbot reassured him. "I would like you to take some passengers down to the China Country."

"Oh, all right," the eagle answered, a little less grumpily.

The Scarecrow and Tin Woodman decided they should return to the search for Ozma, so they bade goodbye to their new friends, who promised they would report to the Emerald City if they discovered that Ozma was hidden in the China

Country or anywhere else they might happen upon. After many hugs, thanks, and goodbyes, the eagle, who was father to Ebrin and ruler of the eagles in the area, took the Marshmallow Twins off to the east. The Abbot then gave Nick and the Straw Man a brief tour of his beautiful and well-maintained monastery, assuring them that Ozma was still part of the infinite, which the Scarecrow and Tin Woodman took to mean "was still among the living." They resumed their journey more heartened than before.

Being magically constructed so that they did not need to stop to sleep or eat, the two friends were able to search the Quadling Country by both day and night, and were therefore able to cover a very large area quickly. But no one they talked to could tell them anything about what might have happened to Ozma or the stolen magic.

After leaving the mountains, they walked almost as far as the Great Sandy Waste, just skirting the mountain of the Hammer-Heads that they both wished to avoid. They knew from a previous adventure Ozma had had with the Hammer-Heads that she wouldn't be there. After passing along a message by Postie, a kind of living mailbox, to Princess Cozytoes, who governed the southeastern quadrant of the Quadling Country, to keep an eye out for the lost princess, they passed along the eastern side of the great Quadling Forest, and eventually made their way back to where they started. The Scarecrow's straw was starting to become musty and moldy by this point, so after passing by Fuddlecumjig, they stopped at a farm to get fresh straw.

The Other Searches for the Lost Princess

It was not long after this that the other search party found Cayke the Cookie Cook's diamond-studded gold dishpan, and our friends learned from a donkey coming from the Emerald City that Ozma had been found. The Scarecrow and Tin Woodman rejoiced and immediately went to the Emerald City to share in the good fortune. Glinda had also returned to the Emerald City, bringing the Marshmallow Twins and the China Princess with her. Portia Lynn had been massaged by Acolyte Haichek, and was now able to move around quite easily. Haichek offered to do this for any other china person who might want to venture out. Most were terrified of the prospect, yet a few intrepid explorers took their chances, being sure to bring along plenty of glue just in case, but when the wedding of Marshal and Portia Lynn was announced, even more decided to do so. It was a celebratory time in Oz, and the entire Emerald City and many from the Quadling Country turned out for the wedding of Marshal and Portia Lynn, which everyone agreed was the social event of the season.

Ozma then turned her attention to the Rumor Mill in Bunkum, and decided that while freedom of expression was invaluable, so too was truth. In the end, she allowed the miller and poppycock to continue their operations, but only in the capacity of a fiction book publisher. No more could they publish falsehoods disguised as truths. They whinged and complained at first, but after Marshal threatened to drop truth bombs all over Bunkum Hill, they complied.

THE ENCHANTED PIGS OF OZ

THE ADVENTURES OF SHAGGY, DANIEL, TIK-TOK, AND JACK PUMPKINHEAD

As soon as Glinda had left the Emerald City, Tik-Tok, the Shaggy Man and Jack Pumpkinhead, who had been present at the conference concerning the search for Ozma, began their journey into the Gillikin Country. Shaggy's brother accompanied them as well, but the Royal Historian tended to forget about him. His given name was Ichabod Mann, and his brother used to call him Wiggy when they were kids, but as he wasn't fond of either, he asked that others call him Daniel. Shaggy had been the first to agree, provided Daniel not call him by his given name Shagrick.

As the four progressed north into the purple land along the Road of Yellow Brick, Daniel admonished Jack for stopping to search the branches of every tree. "I don't think Ozma is going to be found on a tree branch, Jack," he said.

"Well, you never know, do you?" replied the Pumpkinhead, who was temporarily stopping his search of the trees to look under a rock.

"Jack does have a point," said Tik-Tok, in his slow, mechanical fashion. "When you are deal-ing with mag-ic, just a-bout a-ny-thing is poss-i-ble."

"Then maybe we should go ahead and look under every brick in the road," said Daniel sarcastically.

"You know, I never even thought of that!" exclaimed Jack.

"I wasn't serious."

"Let's not argue," advised Shaggy. "We're more likely to find Ozma united than divided."

"I know, Shags. It's just that, when faced with something like this with no clues whatsoever, where do you even start looking? Who would be able to capture our Ruler?"

"Old Mombi held her prisoner for years," answered Jack.

"That is true," said Shaggy. "I don't suspect she would have kidnapped her again, do you?"

"It would be diff-i-cult, as Glin-da took away her mag-ic," stated Tik-Tok.

"Still, it's a good a place as any to start," Daniel reasoned. "Mombi lived around here, didn't she?"

Sure enough, Jack remembered the location just off the road where Mombi's old hut stood, not far from a small Gillikin village. He pointed out where Mombi had locked him up, allegedly for years.

"Wasn't it actually only a few hours, Jack?" inquired Shaggy.

"Maybe. I might have lost track of time."

The searchers saw that the hut itself looked abandoned, and the fields around it had not been cared for. Jack stopped a while to observe the birthplace of his original head, now an overgrown patch full of squashed and moldy pumpkins. Also missing were the animals Mombi had kept.

"I remember hearing that the four-horned cow was taken to another farm, but I see a pigpen here, and I don't know what happened with the pigs," observed the Shaggy Man.

The Other Searches for the Lost Princess

The travelers looked around the grounds for a little while, but were unable to find anything that might have been a clue as to what happened to Ozma, or Mombi for that matter. Jack did, however, find a strange item inside a tree. It appeared to be a pipe with a long wooden stem hung with feathers and a stone bowl, with a pouch of tobacco attached.

"Interesting," said Shaggy. "It looks like an Indian design from back in America."

"Sioux, most likely," added his brother. "I don't know how it would have gotten here in Oz, though. And did Mombi smoke pipes?"

"Not that I know of," replied Jack, "but there's a lot nobody knows about her."

Shaggy placed the pipe inside a bag he was carrying, and the searchers continued on to a house that looked much better kept, with children playing on the lawn. A boy and a girl were playing tag when they noticed the visitors and approached them.

"You must be Jack Pumpkinhead!" exclaimed the girl, who was wearing a purple frock and shoes decorated with cabbages. "You were brought to life by that nasty Mombi down the way."

"And that's the machine man from the Emerald City!" added the boy. "And the Shaggy Man!"

"And his brother," Daniel added, somewhat used to not being recognized. "You can call me Daniel."

"I'm Pectina Jamb, and this is my brother Boysenbarry."

"Any relation to Jellia Jamb in the Emerald City?" questioned Jack.

"Jellia? She's our cousin! How is she doing?"

"Oh, everybody does well in the city. Well, except for recently."

"Yes, Queen Oz-ma has gone miss-ing, and we are try-ing to find her," said Tik-Tok.

"That's terrible!" shouted Pectina. "You'd better come inside and talk to our folks."

The four travelers entered the house, where a large family was starting to gather for dinner. The head of the household was Jimb Jamb, who lived there with his wife Marmalada and brother Phigg, along with their children of many different ages. Some were almost adults, while the youngest was a toddler named Butteranne. All four sat down when invited, although Jack and Tik-Tok were unable to eat anything. The meal was a glazed ham with a fruit salad, and some tasty sherbet for dessert. During the meal, the visitors discussed their dilemma, as well as the latest news from the capital and Jimb and Marmalada's daughter Jellia. The Jambs could offer them no advice on where to look for Ozma or the missing magic, or what might have happened to Mombi, although Marmalada did mention that she thought she noticed Mombi's pigs making their way up toward the north. This caused Daniel to suddenly stop and stare down at his plate. He looked stricken. His brother only laughed.

"Oh no, silly!" said Marmalada, laughing as well. "We have a ham tree in the yard." Everyone now joined in the laughter as Daniel took a breath of relief. He'd only been living in Oz for a short time and was still getting used to life here. Overall, he liked it quite a bit.

Jimb advised consulting the Good Witch of the North, which Shaggy and the others agreed was a good idea. The two humans spent the night there, while Jack and Tik-Tok stayed up and talked until the mechanical man wound down. As Jack's fingers were not good at such tasks, he waited by himself until Shaggy woke up and was able to restore Tik-Tok's functions.

That morning, after a quick breakfast of oatmeal with apples and cinnamon, the party continued its trek to the north, heading down a road that they heard led toward the Good Witch's house. After a few hours, they came upon a pig lying in the middle of it, with another rooting around in the field nearby. Shaggy greeted the second pig, who turned out to be a sow, and she promptly woke the other one with her nose.

"What? What is it?" sleepily asked the pig in the road.

"I think these good people might want to get around you," said the sow.

"Oh, all right." And with that, the large pig slowly rose to his feet and said, "My apologies, but where else is a road hog going to sleep but in the middle of a road?"

"Oh, are you a road hog?" questioned Daniel.

"Most certainly. Roger's my name, and Sue here is a pig pen." Sue showed off her tail, which had an end that had been dipped in ink. Tearing a leaf from paper from a nearby tree with her mouth, she wrote on it, "Greetings and salutations!"

"That's wonderful," Daniel exclaimed.

"And what does a road hog do?" asked Jack.

"Good question, friend Pumpkin! I have an affinity for roads, and can usually tell where they go," answered the hog. "It's a magical ability, I suppose, as is Sue's writing."

"Do you practice magic, then?" questioned Shaggy.

"Not by choice, you understand. We used to live with Mombi, an old woman everyone said was a witch, although she wouldn't admit it herself. Anyway, she was kind to us. I suspect the scraps she fed us had magic in them, which gave us these abilities. They've been quite helpful, though it didn't work out so well for my sister and Sue's brother."

Wishing to avoid any lengthy stories that would keep them from their task, the Shaggy Man asked, "Might you happen to know the way to the home of the Good Witch of the North?"

"You're on the right path," announced the road hog. "Here, I'll be happy to guide you." And with that, the hog began sniffing the ground, leading the way along the road. It forked a few times, but the pig was always completely certain about which way to go. As they approached the Gillikin River, they noticed a familiar figure sitting on a rock and fishing.

"Why, it's Omby Amby!" called the Shaggy Man.

"Shaggy? What are you doing here?" asked the fisherman, who had a long green beard and was dressed in green civilian clothes, uncharacteristic for him, as he was usually in uniform, but appropriate for vacation.

"We're looking for Princess Ozma."

"Ozma? Why? Is she lost?"

"Yes," replied Jack Pumpkinhead. "Nobody knows what happened to her, so we were sent here to look for her."

"My stars!" shouted the Soldier, as he rose to his feet. "My Queen missing? I see I have been derelict in my duties!"

"There was no way for you to know," said Jack.

"Yes, but now it's my job, as the Royal Army, to find her! Besides, I've been fishing for nearly two months, and I haven't caught anything except a ball, a bug, and a cold," he added with a sneeze. "But I managed to trade some good jokes with the fish."

"What's this?" inquired the road hog, pointing to a large wheel.

"Oh yes, I'd forgotten about that," said Omby. "That's a wheel from a horse and carriage. They call them roadsters. Must have fallen off into the lake. I was going to properly dispose of it."

"May I? the road hog asked.

"I don't see why not," the Soldier with the Green Whiskers said. The hog promptly ran over to the wheel and gobbled it up.

"Tastes a little buggy," he said with a burp.

Sue laughed and introduced herself to Omby Amby. "Are you really Princess Ozma's entire Royal Army?" she asked.

"Well, mostly. There are some other officers, but they don't do much other than appear in parades and pageants. Not since our raid on the Nome Kingdom, anyway."

"And you're very busy, aren't you?" said Daniel.

"I do have my moments. In February, the Royal Gardener and I chased a groundhog out of the garden. He'd already seen his shadow, so I suspect he was snacking on the vegetation! I told him to go back home and come back next year. Anyway, where were you headed?"

"We were go-ing to con-sult the Good Witch of the North," replied Tik-Tok.

"Then I shall accompany you. For-ward march!" And with that the Soldier shouldered his gun, which had flowers in the barrel, and followed the hog across a bridge, with the others following closely.

After a time, they entered a purple forest, with soft mossy ground and purple flags planted near the trees. Taking a stop to rest, the pigs ate some mushrooms while the three humans feasted on huckleberry pie that grew wild in the forest and old-fashioned grape soda from a nearby stream. The party made steady progress through the woods until Jack Pumpkinhead noticed something off the side of the road.

"Oh, yes!" said Shaggy. "It looks like a stack of trinkets."

The Shaggy Man was correct about this, and a closer look revealed that it included trophies, party horns, tops, medals, and even some coins. From this stack emerged another pig, somewhat smaller than Sue. With a surprised look on her face, she called out, "Roger? Sue!"

"Sal!" exclaimed these two pigs together. Roger introduced his sister to their new friends, adding proudly, "Sally became a prize pig!"

"It's true," she replied. "I generate one prize a day. To be honest, though, I really don't know what to do with the prizes most of the time. I try to give as much as I can to people in the neighboring villages, and I did even get myself a little house, but most of the time it's a real burden."

"I'm certain the people who receive your prizes are grateful," said Shaggy.

"They try to be, but it would be better if I came out with useful things. Most of what I produce is just junk."

"Have you seen Fred?" asked Sue.

"It's awful," answered Sally.

"What happened?" cried Sue.

"Do you remember how all of us got our powers, except for him? Well, they finally manifested. Your brother's become a war hog! I pleaded with him not to go, to come with me to the Emerald City, or to see Goody North, but he insisted he had to be on his own, otherwise he might hurt me or someone else."

"I suppose it could've been worse. He could've become a war pig," mused Roger. "Then he'd *want* to hurt others!"

"He may not want to hurt anyone, but he's become like me," explained Sally. "He can't help it. Only instead of producing useless junk, he automatically generates weapons. I've never seen anything like it!"

"Oh, poor Fred!" Sue exclaimed, her eyes scrunched up in sorrow.

Roger agreed, "We'll find help for him, Sue. Maybe our new friends can help us."

"I don't see how a pig would be able to hurt much of anybody," said Jack.

"Oh, they can be pretty dangerous," stated Shaggy. "Especially if they have weapons. There's an old Greek myth about a wild pig that took multiple heroes to hunt down."

"That was a boar, not a domesticated pig," objected Daniel.

"Yes, but what is it that makes a pig domesticated?" asked Sue philosophically.

"We should probably move along," said the Shaggy Man. "We'd be happy to help Fred. We're on our way to see the Good Witch of the North."

"Oh, that's wonderful," exclaimed Sally. "Might I join you?"

"The more the merrier," said Daniel, who despite the pigs' predicament was enjoying his adventure.

"If she can help Fred," said Sally, "she might even be able to stop my prize generation."

"Is she a long way from here?" asked Sue.

"The Tah-Tipuu, who around here we call Goody North, lives in Ogoshen," said Roger, "which is not very far."

"Do you remember that boar that came sneaking around Mombi's house?" asked Sue. "According to Mombi, he stole some of her magic books. Maybe he was a war boar."

"I remember," said Sally. "That was before I got my gifts and left with Fred to distribute prizes. He was a different boar altogether."

As Roger led the way along the road, Sally had to stop at one point to produce her daily prize, which came out of her mouth. It was a red ribbon for the best pumpkin to which Jack took a bit of a fancy, so Shaggy pinned it to the Pumpkinhead's shirt. By this time, it was starting to get dark, but Roger announced, "There should be a town up ahead where we can spend the night."

The Other Searches for the Lost Princess

It was still a few hours before the party reached the town, which was made up of dome-shaped purple houses. According to a small, pretty sign on the gate, it was called Mulbury. Right outside the gate stood a small old woman dressed in white and holding a wand with a letter N on the end. Accompanying her was a dragon in rubber boots.

"Why, you're the Good Witch of the North!" exclaimed Shaggy. "We were just heading to your home in Ogoshen to find you."

"At your service," said the woman, with a curtsy. "You may call me Tattypoo, and this is Agnes, the Amiable Dragon."

"We can't *actually* be at your service right now, though," insisted Agnes. "We're here to prevent a war."

"A war?" chorused the travelers.

"Yes, Mulbury is at war with an invader," explained the Witch. "They asked me to bring my companion here to help fight them, but I much prefer not to use a violent solution if I can help it."

"I agree whole-heartedly!" said the Soldier.

"Who is this invader?" inquired Daniel.

"From what I've heard, it appears to be an armored pig. He arrived firing bullets from his snout, and when attacked, he just kept fighting back with more weapons."

"That *has* to be Fred!" cried Sally. "Oh, thank the Maker we've found him!"

"Who is this Fred?" asked the Good Witch.

"My brother," replied Sue. "He can't help producing weapons. We think he was magically turned into a war hog by eating Mombi's scraps."

"Sue and my brother Roger and I came here hoping you could find a way to calm him down," added Sally.

Tattypoo gave serious consideration to this. "In fact, I did once have an artifact that could stop warlike behavior," said the Witch, "but it was stolen some years ago. A peace pipe, to be exact. But try not to worry, I'm sure we'll find a solution."

"Hold on a minute!" started Shaggy. "Do you mean like this?" He went into Jack's bag and held before him the pipe they had earlier discovered.

"Yes, that's it! I'd love to know where you found it, but right now, it's vital we stop Fred before he hurts anyone."

"What must we do?" asked Jack.

"You have to get close to Fred," Tattypoo answered, "and light it. The smoke should eliminate any ability to wage violent conflict."

"I could probably do it," said Agnes, "but he might perceive me as a threat."

"I could go," volunteered Daniel.

"It is my duty as Army of Oz to fight against such conflicts," stated Omby Amby, "but it is also foolish to put myself in unnecessary danger. I propose that Tik-Tok, who cannot be injured by most weapons, find this war pig."

"War boar!" corrected Sally and Sue.

"Hap-py to be of ser-vice," the mechanical man said as he steadily marched into the city with the pipe and a box of matches provided by the Shaggy Man. Suddenly, a projectile weapon knocked Tik-Tok down just as entered the gates! Jack ran after him to pick him up. As Tik-Tok was unhurt, they proceeded into the war-torn town. All of the houses were boarded up, and not only were bullets flying through the air, but so were cannonballs and the occasional small missile. A few particularly brave citizens were approaching the center of town with swords, only to back away when attacked.

The pig turned out to be sitting in the middle of the town square on the steps beneath a large fountain of Lurline and her fairy band. As Tik-Tok and Jack approached, they could see he was covered in armor and firing bullets from his nose. "Hold your fire. We are here to help," said the mechanical man, but Fred just looked at them with an expression of utter terror on his face, and a bullet shot off, grazing Jack's head and breaking off a bit of the side of the shell. The Pumpkinhead fell to the ground, knocking the mechanical man over with him. Tik-Tok was basically helpless like this, but Jack managed to reach out to the pig and place the pipe in his mouth.

"Try not to move," Jack said. He was very unsure about lighting matches, being made of wood, but as it seemed the only choice in a desperate situation he struck one against Tik-Tok's body and threw it into the pipe bowl.

"Oh no!" Jack exclaimed. The match went out before it could light the bowl. Just then, Daniel arrived, took the matches from Jack's outstretched hand, lit one, and threw it into the bowl. This time it worked!

The change was instantaneous! The pig immediately ceased firing bullets, and breathed a deep sigh of relief, "Thank you!" Unfortunately, as soon as the residents discovered that there were no more weapons firing, a man with a sword came rushing in, shouting, "Have at you, pig!"

"No!" cried Daniel.

"Stop!" shouted Jack, and did the first thing he could think of: he threw his own head at the man before he could harm the pig. His aim proved true and knocked him over. Daniel promptly took the man's sword from him and flung it far away.

"I owe you my life, wooden man," said Fred, coughing a bit, "and you human man, and you, metal man. Because of you three, I don't think I could fire another shot."

"Don't mention it," responded Jack, in a rather crushed voice, as his battered head was now lying on top of the man who had fallen on the ground.

The Good Witch entered the area with the others, and after a brief conversation with Fred, Tik-Tok, and Jack, who told her everything that transpired, she instructed the Soldier to go to the armed citizens, and Daniel and Shaggy to go from door to door, telling everyone what had happened and why, and that it was now safe. They did as instructed, diffusing the explosive situation.

Due to the magic of the Peace Pipe, not only had the weapons stopped being produced, but the armor fell off Fred in scales, and he had a joyful and tearful reunion with his old companions. Sue thanked the Good Witch and asked her if she might also be able to stop her incessant prize-making.

The Tah-Tipuu said she would do whatever she could. Finally, Shaggy told her that Ozma and all of the most important magic in Oz had gone missing.

"This is quite disturbing. Let's return to my hut and see what we can do," advised the Good Witch. "I would like for you pigs to accompany us, if you can. It's not a long journey to the town where I live, and I have some herbal snacks that will restore your energy."

As promised, it was a short distance to Tattypoo's home in Ogoshen, and with the victuals she'd provided them, everyone was feeling much better. The Good Witch had feared that her magic would be gone too, but it appeared that it hadn't been stolen with that of Ozma, Glinda, and the Wizard's. Still, none of it was of any use in locating the lost Ozma or any of their magical items. The only hint came from her magic slate, which spelled out, "Seek out the castle of wicker and the single fruit in the center of the Great Orchard."

"What Great Orchard would this be?" inquired the Shaggy Man.

"I couldn't say," said Tattypoo. "There are numerous orchards in the Land of Oz. Come to think of it, there is a large land of orchards in the southern Munchkin Country, but I don't know if that's its official name."

"Ojo and Unc Nunkie are searching the Munchkin Country," stated Daniel, "so if it's there, they'll probably come across it. Are there any great orchards in the Gillikin Country we should try?"

"None that go by that name, and I suspect the slate used that term for that reason, so as to distinguish between all the other orchards around. I will continue to do what I can to find our beloved Ruler. Some of the magic here was originally Mombi's, and I still haven't figured out all of it. Still, you should probably keep searching, since you might find Ozma before I can."

The party spent the night at Tattypoo's hut, and the pigs decided to remain there too, as she offered them the many tasty vegetables that grew in her extensive garden. She was able to alter the spell on Sally so that she would only generate prizes when she chose to, and was careful to make sure all trace of violence had been removed from Fred.

After saying hearty goodbyes and promising to visit each other again, the others left the house and looked elsewhere in the country, searching through the Forest of Gugu and even parts of the Great Grey Gillikin Swamp. On their return to the Witch's hut, Tattypoo informed them that her slate now read, "The Lost Princess of Oz has been found!" and she sent them back to the Emerald City by magic. They soon learned what the slate's earlier advice had meant, and were glad to meet the Frogman, being very polite to him and making him feel quite at home. A grand celebration soon ensued, and it being one of Daniel's first really big parties in the Emerald City, he was overjoyed to hear his name mentioned amongst the heroes, who although not having taken part in finding Ozma, had helped stop a war and save a pig.

THE COOKYWITCH COVEN

THE ADVENTURES OF OJO, UNC NUNKIE, AND DR. PIPT

An hour after the Shaggy Man's party had left the Emerald City, Ojo and Unc Nunkie joined their old friend Dr. Pipt and together they traveled to the Munchkin Country along a blue highway that, by the time night fell, had reached Jinjur's ranch. The former General of the Army of Revolt had settled down to raise cows and grow crops, including cream-puffs, macaroons, and caramels. The searchers explained the situation to Jinjur during dinner, but she had no information about what might have happened to Ozma or the missing magic.

"It's not like Ozma has any enemies," stated Ojo.

"Well, that's not entirely true, young man," argued Jinjur. "Mombi held her prisoner for years, and she made a bad enemy of the Nome King as well. Of course, Mombi no longer has magic powers, and I hear old Ruggedo was driven out of his own kingdom."

"Betsy and the Shaggy Man told us about that," said Ojo. "I think he might still be living there, but he's no longer king, and doesn't have any magic."

"Someone who's lost their own magic might be inclined to stealing it?" suggested Dr. Pipt.

"Motive," said Unc Nunkie, who had been silent throughout the meal so far. He was generally so, though no one quite knew why.

"This is a good dinner, by the way," said Dr. Pipt.

"Thank you, Ozwald, but I can't take credit for it. My husband used to cook, but he ran off and hasn't come back. Oh, don't look at me like that. Except for the chores he did, it's for the best. Anyway, that's why I hired a cook." The farmer summoned a tall attractive woman into the room, an ex-colonel whom she introduced as Cardamom Cornflower.

"After Ozma took back the Emerald City, I fell back on my career as a cook," said Cardamom, telling her story. "I studied under a chef named Paella, who lives to the south."

"If only there had been some kind of magic that turned someone into a good cook, I'd have done it myself," stated Jinjur. "Still, it was nice to get reacquainted with the Colonel."

"There might be some sort of magic like that," Cardamom said. "Chef Paella mentioned that her order knew of an old talisman that could make its owner a good cook. She has never been able to find any further information, but she thinks it's part of their legacy."

"I wish my wife had access to that magic," said Dr. Pipt.

"You men are all alike," laughed Jinjur. "We have to cater to your needs in every way."

"Needs," said Nunkie.

Ojo explained, "Do you have a restroom my uncle could use?" Jinjur showed him where it was and went about cleaning the dishes.

"You mentioned an order before," Ozwald reminded Cardamom, who was clearing off the table.

"I did..." she hesitated. "I really shouldn't say anything. I tend to speak more than is appropriate. Jinjur tells me all the time that..."

"I'm a former magic worker," explained Dr. Pipt. "You probably heard of me, the Crooked Magician."

"I see," she said. "And you're looking to get back into..."

"No, no, you misunderstand," he corrected. "As you know we're searching for Ozma and the magical items that were stolen. Perhaps this order might have a better idea what happened to her. And I admit it would be nice if I could find more about this talisman. My wife is a wonderful woman, but she does not cook like you."

"They're an order of *cooks*, I suppose you might call them. They sometimes jokingly refer to themselves as the Dinner Order, but... uh, some of the things they've accomplished are, well... they're nothing short of wizardry."

"I think I might have heard of the order before. Do you think you could introduce us?"

"I don't know," she replied, "I'm not sure that's such a good idea, and besides, Chef Paella's place is some journey away, and I can't leave the General without food."

"That's all right," Jinjur said, having overheard enough of the conversation to understand the main thrust of it. "You've made enough to last me for a few more days. I'd come with you, but I have to harvest the macaroons. Look," she said to Cardamom. "Ozma comes first, right?"

"Right. Yes, of course. I'll take you in the morning."

"Where are we going in the morning?" asked Ojo returning to the dining area.

"Some people who might know where Ozma is," Dr. Pipt said.

The next morning, after a breakfast of scrambled eggs and toast, the party set out to the south, following a busy road along which farmers and animals were walking. By evening, they had come to an orange and brown village on the bank of the Munchkin River, in an area full of wildflowers of many colors. This was Herville, inhabited by former members of the Army of Revolt, and ruled by the former Brigadier General Tanjrine. They greeted Cardamom warmly, and asked news of their former commander. Ojo and Dr. Pipt then explained about the missing Ozma, they were all quite worried, and Tanjrine asked what they could do to help.

"Nothing!" said Unc Nunkie.

"What he *means*," explained Ojo, giving his uncle a sidewise glance, "is that there really isn't anything you can do, other than to keep an eye out for her, and let the Emerald City know if you discover anything."

Tanjrine promised to rally the former troops and begin a search.

"Thanks," Nunkie said.

Further walking brought the group into a blue forest, which seemed to be thankfully free of dangerous animals. At around noon, Ojo and Unc Nunkie searched for food, while Cardamom talked with Dr. Pipt.

"This Unc Nunkie is a rather quiet fellow, isn't he?" inquired the cook.

"Yes, he's been that way for years."

"Is there something *wrong* with him?" she asked delicately.

"Nothing physical, as far as I know," acknowledged Ozwald. "If I could still practice magic, I could find out, and maybe even heal him."

"I wonder..." said Cardamom pensively.

"What?" the former magician asked.

"Probably nothing," she replied with a smile, but after a moment she said, "Although the Army of Revolt was successful in taking the Emerald City, some of the women later experienced some form of trauma. I'm reluctant to tell you this because you're likely to assume that it's because women are weak..."

"On the contrary," Ozwald said. "Many men have come home from battle deeply scarred. I'm thankful we don't see war anymore, and aren't likely to with Ozma on the throne. So, you think this is the case with Stephen?"

"I don't know him well enough to say," she acknowledged. "He bears at least one of the symptoms. And that aside, he also seems a little nervous to be in this area."

"He hasn't told me much, *obviously*, but I do recall him mentioning an enemy living in the south. There's a lot about Stephen I don't know, and nobody else seems to either. If I were to hazard a guess, I'd say he's related to the Southern House of Seebania, and might even have ruled himself had it not been for that business with Froom."

"Oh, right. Froom the Fraud," the cook recalled, "who convinced everyone he was the rightful king. The Munchkins didn't want a king after he was exposed, North or South. I question what really happened to the old rulers."

"Impossible to say," Dr. Pipt reflected. "Do you remember a High King Obediah ruling the Northern House from Munchkenny back before it was destroyed?" When she said yes, he added, "Then, there was the awful King Knotso ruling over most of the small countries in the south. He disappeared, as well."

"After the Blue Emperor..."

"Ozroar," Pipt filled in. "He ruled all of Oz at one time."

"Yeah, after Ozroar..."

"Disappeared too," they said at the same time.

"Are you sensing a pattern?" Cardamom asked.

"You think they're all connected," Pipt said, considering it. "The Wicked Witch of the East ruled during most of those disappearances, though other players are rumored to have been involved. Mooj, for example, took over the southern house before vanishing when Ozma came to the throne."

"But the Wicked Witch is gone now," the cook said thoughtfully. "And what would Mooj gain?" she asked. "He's barely present, from what I've heard."

"You've got a point," Pipt admitted. "It would have to be someone who would benefit from Ozma's abduction..."

"The Wicked Witch's daughter," suggested Ozwald. "What's her name?"

"Vaneeda," Cardamom considered. "She's wanted power in the East for a long time. She's actually a friend of the woman we're going to meet. I suppose we could ask."

"How close a friend is she to her?" Pipt asked.

"No, she wouldn't be involved in anything like that," Cardamom defended. "I know her well."

"You're probably right. We're probably on the wrong track altogether," Pipt acknowledged. "For all we know Nunkie's enemy, this Mooj, could have been the one who captured Ozma and stole her magic for reasons we don't know."

"Certainly, but—Oh, they're coming back!"

Ojo and his uncle returned with their arms full of fruit and nuts, which Cardamom expertly made into a tasty dish. Then, after resting for a little while, the four companions resumed their journey. The cook had some trouble finding her way in the woods, but a friendly deer guided them to a building with teacup turrets and a pie on top.

"I have to caution you all," said Cardamom. "Don't be too quick to judge things by appearances. What you see is not always what it really is." Nunkie narrowed his eyes, but said nothing, and Cardamom wondered if it was a mistake bringing them here.

The sign on the café door said, "Closed for Meeting," but Cardamom knocked anyway. It was answered by a tall woman in an apron who had bright red hair.

"Why, Cardamom!" exclaimed the woman. "And I see you've brought some customers. I'm glad but I'm afraid we're closed for the next few hours."

"It's good to see you too, Paella!" answered Cardamom. "But these aren't customers. My friend here, Dr. Ozwald Pipt, is a former magician. He had some questions for the order. I know it's unusual…"

"It is," Paella said. "Not everybody… *understands.*"

"I know, but these are good people," Cardamom stressed, explaining how they were looking for the missing Ozma.

"All right," Paella conceded. "In that case, it should be fine. Besides, Dr. Pipt's reputation precedes him. Follow me." After welcoming them, she led the way past the dining area into a deeper part of the building, where several women were sitting around an ornately-carved oval table. Ojo was immediately taken aback by an enormous woman holding a giant fork and spoon. There was also an old lady wearing a peaked hat, with a long nose and chin, and another woman with auburn hair and glasses wearing a Victorian-style red dress. There had been a fourth person there as well, but as soon as she saw the guests she dashed out of the room so quickly no one could recall what she looked like.

"*That* was an abrupt exit," observed Paella.

"She had important business elsewhere, Ella," rasped the giant lady. "Who are these interlopers you've brought us? Culinary tasters?"

"I told you, Mother, I prefer Paella."

"That sounds too foreign," Ella's mother said, shaking her spoon in her daughter's direction.

"Answer the question, *Paella*," said the woman in the peaked hat. "Who are these strangers and what are they doing here?"

"I think you already know my student, Cardamom Cornflower."

"And I'm Dr. Ozwald Pipt..."

"Oh, we know *you*, Crooked Magician," chirped the giant woman. "Come to bring us some Powder of Life?"

"Witches," said Unk Nunkie.

"Oh no!" cried Ojo.

"Settle down," said Cardamom. "It's not like that."

"You are correct," said Dr. Pipt. "I am the *former* Crooked Magician."

"What name you going by these days?" teased the giant woman. "Pipt? Nikidik? Or are you stealing someone else's name now?"

"No, just Dr. Pipt," he chuckled. "And he stole *my* name."

"Shrewd magicians," she laughed.

"And these are Unc Nunkie and his nephew Ojo," he added.

"Nobodies," said the old woman, the witchiest-looking of the three.

"Maybe, maybe not," said the giant one.

"And these women," began Paella, "are Sugarene from Overhill in the Gillikin Country..."

"Pleased to make your acquaintance, I'm sure!" she said sarcastically. She was the old one with the peaked hat.

"Floss Confection from Cinnamon City in the Quadling Country," Paella went on, indicating the red head in the red dress. She simply nodded uncertainly. "And my mother, who you've already heard from," Paella sighed, "Squalma, *the Imperial Squawmos*, who rules from Preservatory."

"I've *earned* that title!" chortled Squalma. "I have my own town! What have you accomplished?"

"A town where you keep people in cans and jars is *not* my idea of an accomplishment."

"Well, how else are they going to keep from spoiling?"

"But I thought no one died or became seriously ill in Oz," objected Ojo.

"You're too young to understand such things. What might be the case *now*, little one, might not be the case tomorrow! Fairy spells cannot always to be relied upon, nor can fairies, for that matter! I prefer good old cookywitchery."

"Cookywitchery? I believe I've heard of that," said Dr. Pipt. "That derives from the old cook-witches. They say they're next in wizardry to sorceresses."

"Illegal!" Unc Nunkie said, wagging a finger at the women.

"*That* is none of your business, old man," retorted Sugarene, "and it's not *really* magic, not in the illegal sense."

"You're a familiar face," said Squalma. "What did you say his name was? Nunkie... *None who*, it means, right? One who is nothing, or no one... Clever, old man. What's your real name, I wonder."

"His real name is Stephen!" exclaimed Ojo. "And he's my uncle and a good man."

The witch's eyebrows raised, not at Ojo's outburst, but at the name Stephen. "Crown," she smirked, but said no more.

"You'll find many foodstuffs in Oz have natural magical properties," Floss interjected. Pipt found her auburn hair striking. "All we do is bring that out. The woman that you scared off was just telling me her idea about a baking powder that could make anything rise."

"Who was she, anyway?" asked Cardamom. "She looked familiar."

"She's not a full-fledged cookywitch," said Squalma with a barely concealed grin, "just someone who occasionally dabbles. I think her name is Bina or something."

Dr. Pipt looked at her curiously, but neither said anything further.

"Now that you know about us, it's your turn!" said Sugarene testily. "You certainly didn't come to learn about our culinary skills. So what really brings you here?"

"Our ruler, Princess Ozma, has been captured by some unknown person, who seems to have also stolen all the important magic in the land," explained Ojo.

"*That* sounds like an opportunity!" snorted Squalma.

"Mother!" warned Paella.

"We were wondering if you knew anything or had any way to locate her," added Dr. Pipt.

"So, you think *we* had something to do with it," scowled Sugarene.

"No," reassured Cardamom. "It's nothing like that. I just thought you could help."

"I had heard that maybe Vaneeda…" started Dr. Pipt.

"Every time something goes wrong in the Munchkin Country, Vaneeda gets the blame," chided Paella. "It wasn't her."

"Perhaps not, but it must have been a powerful sorcerer," suggested Sugarene. "Or witch!"

"Someone who lusts for power," rasped Squalma, "but is careful enough to conceal it. Maybe someone who had power and lost it," the giant witch added, looking around the room. "Could be anyone, really, a former master… a former crooked sorcerer… even you, nameless one," she leered at Nunkie.

"I can't speak to anyone else here," said Floss, breaking the tension, "but in my town, we swear by tea leaves."

"Oh, I hate that!" said Sugarene. "I never know where to start reading."

"It's said that the scryers of old would obtain information from the entrails of animals," stated Paella. "I know that was terribly cruel," she added when Ojo made a retching sound, "but perhaps the fruit of sausage trees would work as a substitute?"

The cookywitches found that intriguing, and after Paella invited her guests to relax, they tried it along with several other methods. Unfortunately, none of them revealed anything. Finally, after over an hour had passed, Squalma cried out, "Enough of this weak witchery. If you really want our help to find your Ozma, we'll have to engage in demonology!"

"Demonology?" exclaimed Dr. Pipt.

"That doesn't sound like a good idea," worried Ojo.

"Dangerous," said Nunkie.

"I have to admit, I think they're right," Floss cautioned. "That does sound dangerous."

"Oh, don't be such cowards!" cackled Sugarene. "It's just another form of cooking. Miss Confection here has access to dough and an oven from Bunbury, and it would be a simple matter to make a Devil's Food Cake."

"Oh, I see," said Floss. "Well, I suppose that's fine then."

"If you don't mind my asking," inquired Dr. Pipt. "How did you acquire these?"

"Oh, Jacob Bunn and I are old friends," explained Floss. "Still, I'm not sure I like the idea."

"If Mother's behind it, I'm sure I don't either," said Paella.

But Squalma just cackled, "Desperate times call for desperate measuring cups!" and she began preparations.

"I always wondered how the inhabitants of Bunbury could be alive," mused Dr. Pipt. "When I invented my Powder of Life, I thought it was something unique."

"Invented?" laughed Sugarene. "I think Wam would have something to say about that!"

"I suppose that's true," he acknowledged. "He *did* make a very similar powder. I adapted it to replace some ingredients that are much harder to acquire these days, and made it rather more potent. Some of Wam's creations could only live under very specific conditions."

"Yes, the china people can only move around in their own country," said Floss. "Bunbury was something like that as well. After Wam disappeared, Glinda obtained a few bits of life-giving magic from his supplies, including the dough recipe and the living paper that Miss Cuttenclip uses to make her dolls."

After some further debate on the dangers of Squalma's plan, the cookywitches finally decided to try it, mixing the ingredients together and baking the result in a special oven. When it was finally ready, they opened the oven door, and out jumped a devil's food cake, complete with arms, legs, and a horned head. Ojo and the others grew alarmed, but on seeing this, the devil's food cake put on a sweet smile, which somewhat disarmed them.

"Ah, thank you, my dear ladies, for bringing me to life," said the cake in a dark, rich voice. "I feel I have great power, but I have not yet had the opportunity to test it."

"Oh, Devils Food, we beseech your help in finding Ozma, the lost Royal Ruler of Oz," exhorted Sugarene.

"Ozma?" he said with a rude sound. "Why would I want to help you find *her*?"

"Why, because she's the rightful ruler of Oz!" exclaimed Ojo.

"Rightful by *whose* standards? My great and fiendish mind has decided that it would be best for me to join forces with another who currently stands on the brink of conquering the Land of Oz. I shall offer my services to Ugu!"

"Who-gu?" asked Floss. "Is he a blowfish?"

"No, sweet lady, he is a great magician, the descendant of the most powerful wizard and sorcerer who ever lived. Alas, I must bid you all adieu!" After giving them a devilish grin and the sign of the horns, the Devils Food attempted to run out of the room and jump out a window.

"Not so fast, spawn of Satan" said Paella, who uttered a short spell. "The windows are magically sealed. You're not going anywhere!"

"What are we going to do with the little devil?" asked Sugarene.

They could hear him running around the other rooms trying to get out.

"Well, he can't stay here!" argued Paella. That was followed by the sound of crashing. "He'll tear the place apart!"

"We should get him back in the oven and cook him to a crisp!" suggested Squalma.

"That wouldn't be right," admonished Cardamom. "He's still a living creature. It's not his fault he's as diabolical as he is."

"Ozma!" admonished Unc Nunkie.

"I think Unc is right," said Ojo. "Helping Princess Ozma should be our first priority. Once she's back, I'm sure she could deal with the problem."

"You are a foolish thing," chided Squalma. "We'd be lucky to get away with our memories intact! And the rest of you had better not say anything either, or you'll answer to me!"

"That's not necessary, mother," corrected Paella. "But I do suppose it would be best for me to handle matters."

"The way I see it," said Cardomom, "this is your mess, Squalma. I think you should fix it."

"Don't get spicy with me, Cornflower!" the giant witch spat back. "You all agreed to try."

"Let's not argue," reasoned Floss. "Let's just figure what we're going to do."

"How does one fight a devil's food cake?" asked Paella.

"With an angel food cake?" suggested Ojo.

"Why, you might just make an apprentice yet!" exclaimed Sugarene. "We'll get to work right away!"

It didn't take long for the women to bake a light, airy angel's food cake, which after a short time floated out of the oven bearing small wings, a halo and a cherubic face. Looking around at each of the faces, he finally said, "You have summoned me to combat my counterpart, Devil's Food."

"Do you think you can you stop him?" questioned Paella.

"I have faith that I can!"

The people in the café rushed behind him, as the cake levitated them into the air and flew to the other room where Devil's Food was making a mess. Angels Food settled down and confronted Devil's Food.

"Do you really think you can stop me, goody-two-shoes?" demanded the chocolate cake.

"Actually, I wasn't baked with shoes, but yes."

"Bah! You and all your powers of goodness can't destroy me."

"You're right. I have no intention of destroying you. I merely want to bring some sweetness and light into your baked heart." Angel Food then shined a light at Devil's Food, shooting out glittery sprinkles upon him. When hit with them, the chocolate cake tried resisting, but then stopped. Suddenly, a real smile formed on his face.

"I didn't think it was possible," he said, "but I believe you've shown me the light. Well met, brother, I shall now recant of my wicked desires, and perform good works."

The vanilla and chocolate angels then turned their attention to the party that had assembled them.

"Can either of you tell us where to find Princess Ozma?" inquired Ojo.

"I don't think my powers extend quite that far," said the Angel Food.

"Nor mine, but I'll do my best," said the former Devil's Food.

Both cakes agreed to help the cookywitches to attempt to find the missing princess.

"Go," said Nunkie.

"Uncle's right," Ojo said. "It's time for us to depart. While you're working on a magical solution here, we could be looking elsewhere."

While everyone was busy making their farewells, Cardamom, who'd decided to stay, took Dr. Pipt aside. "This has been an unexpected adventure," she said.

"Indeed it has," he agreed.

"And you still aren't any closer to that talisman I spoke of to help make your wife cook better."

"That's true," he acknowledged. "But I can always come back. Besides, I've made new friends and discovered a lovely café."

"You're a wiser man than you let on, and I think you've seen things today that are not always what they appear to be."

"Things never are!" The two hugged and parted.

Finally, after promising not to say anything to their friends in the Emerald City, the travelers left the café to continue their search. If the boy and the former magician noticed that Nunkie was leading them mostly to places in the northern Munchkin Country, they said nothing about it. After growing weary, they decided to return to the Emerald City to freshen up and get proper rest, and there they learned that Ozma had been found. Ugu was the one who had kidnapped her, and had since been rendered harmless. "Devils Food had been on the right track after all," said Ozwald.

When recounting their adventures, Ojo and Dr. Pipt made good on their promises and said little of the cookywitches. They were pretty sure that their magic was not limited to the natural sort, but at the same time they were grateful for their help and not eager to report them to the authorities. Dr. Pipt also swore that the woman he had seen sneaking out of the café was Mombi, but Ozma assured him that the witch had been turned back into a child several years earlier. Sometime later he discovered that Mombi had regained her former age, and was once again living in her old house.

As for the two cakes, Angel Food decided to explore the sky, while Devil's Food relocated to the town of Bunbury. Whether he kept his promise to only do good was debatable, but he did perform his magic in the service of King Hun Bun.

Dr. Pipt approached Nunkie while Ojo was running around with Button-Bright and out of earshot. "You know, Stephen, you can always talk me if you want to."

"No," he said.

"I'm not trying to pry, just offering help. Sometimes we just need a friend to let a little light into our lives."

"No," Nunkie said again with more finality.

Dr. Pipt just looked at him, then, nodding, said in a low tone: "Secrets," mimicking Nunkie's speech pattern.

Stephen Nunkie just smiled and walked away. Dr. Pipt shook his head and began the long journey home. Whatever demons that man was dealing with he'd have to deal with alone.

CHOP

by Eric Shanower

There are some who are under the impression that Oz is all sunshine and rainbows. I'm not sure where they got that idea, but it's definitely not true. Oz may have more happy endings than most, but as this story shows, it also has its share of things that go bump in the night.

They say experience is the best teacher, and it's really what happened in this dark encounter that woke up a certain reckless boy who thought it was fun to be irresponsible. In it we also discover what happened to another two characters from Oz history.

Don't read this one before going to bed!

Betsy Bobbin

An hour ago the boy had been lost.

Now he stood on a bare bluff overlooking a vast desert under a darkening sky. He knew where he was. He'd seen this desert before—dune after dune rolling to the horizon. One touch of those burning sands turned living flesh instantly to dust.

A draft rising from the desert carried the smoky odor of burning bone. Twilight hadn't yet hidden little bits of pale rubbish lining the foot of the bluff. It took him a moment to realize what these were—skeletons of small animals who had tumbled over the edge.

He stepped back. Venturing into the desert meant crossing the border, leaving the enchantment of this land where no one ever died. He didn't want to end up as one more skeleton lying on the deadly sand below.

At the top of the bluff, safe inside the enchantment, death couldn't reach him. But the hot breeze off the desert could. It grew stronger, wrapping him in a stink of sulphur. Putrid. He gagged. Stomach acid seared his throat. He doubled over, retching up half-digested chunks of pear plucked from trees he'd passed hours ago. When the heaving stopped, he spit several times and swiped away goo from his chin. Breathing through his mouth, he turned away from the desert toward the west where the sun was setting. He started back over the dusty plain—toward home.

Ahead, black against the golden-red sky, sat a lone cottage. It was small and domed, with two tall thin chimneys, one on each side, the typical style. A cottage this close to the desert? How could anyone stand the stink? But maybe whoever lived there would let him spend the night.

As the sun sank behind the horizon, a warm glow rose in one window. Someone was home. He was within a stone's throw of the cottage when his foot struck something hard and his nose and forehead bashed into something. But there was nothing there to see. He raised a hand to his smarting face. No blood. But there'd probably be bruising.

He reached forward. His hands met a hard surface, smooth and solid, but invisible. He felt to both sides, upward, and downward. The surface continued in all directions. He felt it down to the ground where the dry, stiff grass stopped in a line, leaving bare earth beyond. On the other side of the bare patch, about a foot across, grass began again, fresh and green in the lingering light.

A shadow fell across the grass. He looked up. The silhouette of a man loomed, shoulders angled awkwardly against the twilight sky.

The man spoke. "You're a long way from home."

"Hoping for a place to sleep the night," said the boy. "But there's an invisible wall in front of your cottage."

"What brings you to this lonely spot?"

"My feet. They start walking and I follow."

"A wanderer, hey?"

"I like to just go. Always have. Travel here and there. See new things."

The man grunted and shifted his weight. He seemed assembled from mismatched parts—a normal right arm and a left one so thin the sleeve hung loosely—one leg longer than the other. "What's your name?"

"Everyone calls me Button-Bright."

"You're out here all alone, Button-Bright. So far from anything. Won't your folks worry?"

"They got used to my ways long ago."

The man grunted again. He raised his hands chest high. His fingers made quick little movements. The left hand seemed jerky, as if something might be wrong with it. But it had grown too dark to see clearly.

"I'm removing the wall around my cottage to let you in. I'll give you a meal and you can stay the night. You can step across now."

The boy stepped over the bare strip of ground. The grass on this side was soft and springy.

The man's hands made little movements again. The boy reached back. There was the wall, solid, smooth, and as invisible as before.

"Keeps out the stink." The man walked toward the cottage, tottering from long leg to short and back again. "This way."

The boy followed, taking in a deep breath of fresh air. The aroma of something cooking inside the cottage made him hungry.

The front door creaked open at one push of the man's thin left arm. The boy stepped inside. In the fireplace a pot steamed on a hook above glowing, orange coals.

The man touched a taper to the coals and raised it to light fat candles in a rough chandelier near the domed ceiling. His sleeve drew back. In the candlelight his thin arm gleamed dully. It looked like metal. The wrist and fingers were jointed, thin and tubular. The man stuck the taper into a wax-caked holder on the table. The tiny flame shed feeble light.

The man ladled some of the pot's contents into a bowl. He set the bowl and a tarnished silver spoon onto the table, then slapped the seat of a wooden stool. "Sit down and eat, Button-Bright."

The meaty chunks were a little tough, but the dark, spicy broth flowed silkily down his throat.

The man waited by the fire, watching, hip cocked, resting on his short leg, the other leg relaxed and bent at the knee. "How's the stew?"

"Fine. Aren't you having any?"

"I'll eat later."

The boy shrugged and kept eating.

"You haven't asked my name," said the man as he filled the bowl with a second helping.

"You're Chopfyt," said the boy. "I saw your arm. Recognized you from descriptions."

"Did you notice the line around my neck, too?" The man raised a metallic finger and drew it across his throat.

"Too dark," said the boy.

"Look closer." The man leaned over, hovering. He pulled his collar down, exposing skin glistening with a thin film of perspiration. He twisted his head to the side. A thin dark line circled his neck. Below it the flesh bulged. Above it his neck was thinner, like a pillar sitting on a slightly larger base.

The man smiled. "That's where the magic glue joined my head to my shoulders. Old Ku-klip put me together from spare body parts. Only he didn't have any spare left arms, so he made me one out of tin." The man flexed his jointed metal fingers in front of the boy's face.

The second helping of stew was gone. The boy let the spoon clatter into the empty bowl.

"Had enough?" asked the man.

The boy nodded.

"Old Ku-klip was a tinsmith," said the man. "He liked to make things—put smaller parts together into something big." He crossed to a window and stared out into the darkness. "I like to take things apart. Chopping them down into smaller parts to find what makes them do the things they do. So now I just call myself Chop. No more Chopfyt."

"Fine," said the boy. "Chop."

The man lumbered on his mismatched legs back to the table and stared at the boy. "What do you like—putting things together or taking them apart?"

"Don't know." He yawned. He was tired. He'd noticed the end of a bed sticking out from behind a large wooden screen standing on the far side of the room.

The man grunted. "Got a workshop down in the cellar. That's where I chop things apart. Sit here. I want to bring up something I bet you've never seen before."

"All right," said the boy. He liked seeing new things. One of the joys of travel.

The man pulled a metal ring in the wooden floor. A door creaked up from the floor, leaving a long narrow hole of empty darkness. He took the candle from the table, stepped into the hole, and disappeared below floor level, wood creaking at each step. The light coming from the hole grew stronger. The man must have been lighting more candles down there. He reappeared from the hole, carrying something in both hands. A clump of blue fur. He set it on the floor. It gave a weak hop.

"Is that—a rabbit?" asked the boy.

"Rabbit skin."

The clump of fur gave several more hops. It was navy blue along the back and at the tips of the ears, shading to lighter blue on the sides. The eye holes were empty. The ends of the legs splayed out flat. It was humped up into the shape of a rabbit, but there was clearly nothing inside.

"What happened to it?"

"What do you think was in your stew?"

The boy's glance darted to his empty bowl. It felt as though a fist had clenched his stomach lining.

"You can pet it if you want."

The boy reached out and stroked the pitiful fur shell. It was soft and cool to the touch. The head of the skin nuzzled his hand. "Poor thing."

"It wants you to pick it up," said the man.

The boy cradled the rabbit skin against his chest. "Where's his tail?"

"I have a whole collection of their tails in a big jar in the workshop."

"What? How many rabbits have you done this to?"

"Don't be so indignant," said the man. "Food doesn't grow on trees here."

"How many?"

The man sighed. "Plenty. Bring that skin to put back

in its pen and you can come down and see."

The man tottered back down into the hole. The boy supported the skin in one hand and clutched the rail of the steep, rickety staircase with the other as he followed down into a large, crowded workshop. Bright candlelight shone on wooden cupboards. Dusty jars and bottles filled wooden shelves. Stacks of wooden boxes and slatted wooden pens formed narrow aisles.

"The pen is over here," said the man. The boy followed him past a rack on the wall where tools of all sizes hung. They ranged from a large silver axe down to tiny tweezers, all clean and gleaming.

The man slid back the slatted top of a crate. Rabbit skins of various shades of blue hopped around in the bottom. "Drop it in."

The boy set the rabbit skin gently down inside and paused to pet the others. Movement in the next crate drew his attention. His breath caught. The crate was full of little skeletons, hopping around just like the skins. He had to breathe again to speak. "Are—are those their skeletons?"

"Yes, they're fun to take apart piece by piece. The rabbit tails are over here."

Shelves lined with glass jars rose above a wide, empty worktable. The man lifted a large glass jar with a top held on by metal brackets. Short strips of light blue fluff whirled inside.

"And here are their eyes." The man pointed to a jar containing several dozen soft brown eyeballs floating in liquid. "And their claws." Inside a smaller jar, curved chip-like bits made soft tinking sounds, hitting the glass as if trying to escape. Another jar was half filled with what looked like tiny yellow-brown pebbles, forming a mosaic against the glass. "This holds their teeth. But teeth don't move, so it's not very interesting. Everything else goes into the stew—including their tongues. Rabbit tongue is surprisingly sweet."

The man tapped his nails against a jar full of tiny fluttering bits. "The wings of flies, mosquitoes, and bees. I used to keep their legs in a jar, too, but all their kicking shoved the jar off the shelf. It was a lot of trouble to recapture every last one of those insect legs. Now I lock them in a heavy wooden box."

The boy was staring at a small jar. Inside floated a single pair of eyeballs, the irises a piercing blue. Their gaze bored steadily back, bare and unblinking, begging him not to turn away. So intent. So full of—what? Fear? Rage? Alarm? Warning?

"Ahhhh." The man's sigh was full of satisfaction. "You've noticed my masterpiece. Part of it, anyway. Would you like to see the rest?" The man leaned toward the boy a little, eyebrows raised, lips slightly parted in an eager half-smile. His flesh fingers and his tin fingers were interlaced in front of his chest. The thumbs patted rapidly against each other.

"Well," said the boy. "All right." He had to get away from all these chopped up rabbits and insects and things. "Then I'll be on my way."

The man's half-smile stretched to reveal snaggle teeth as yellow-brown as the rabbit teeth in the jar. He stepped toward a tall cupboard. He ran his flesh fingers quickly through his hair. Then he unlatched the cupboard doors and opened them wide. He stepped back.

At the top hung a row of body parts, arms, legs, pieces of torso. All clean and pink. All pieces of someone. A woman. Lower down, a peg-board held smaller body parts—nose, ears, fingers. Was that a belly-button?

"My masterpiece. What do you think?"

The boy's mind raced. Could he make it back through the cellar and up the stairs without the man catching him? If he could get upstairs, shut the trap door, pile something heavy on top—

He pointed to one of the arms hanging in the cupboard. "Uh… there's a left arm you could use—to replace the tin one." He needed time to think, to plan.

The man reached up into the cupboard. "I couldn't use this arm." He lifted the hanging arm off its hook. It flexed and pumped in the man's grip, so that he had to hold it tight with both his hands. Its three remaining fingers curled into claws. "See that? Terrible temper. I've tried to find her temper to chop it out, but so far I can't locate it."

The invisible wall surrounding the cottage—how high was it? Low enough to climb over?

The man hung the struggling arm back on its hook. "Nimmie Amee was the first I ever chopped. I liked it. So I've been chopping ever since."

If he could make a ladder. Plenty of wood here in the cellar. And tools.

The man patted one of the legs affectionately. "My wife, of course. She'd give me such tongue-lashings. So cross."

The boy thought about how he was always wandering across the countryside, never telling anyone where he was going, never with a fixed destination. No one would miss him for a long, long time.

"At first I only planned to chop her tongue out. But taking away her tongue wouldn't have made her sweeter. She'd have found other ways to make me miserable. Such a shrew. Here, listen."

The man reached toward an object on the pegboard inside the cupboard. It looked like a thick rubber band stretched square around a series of four pegs. The man plucked out the two lower pegs. The rubber band sprang together, then undulated open and closed.

"Run, boy!" The voice from the rubber band was high, wispy, without force. "Run for help! Quick! He's insane!"

The man sighed. He grabbed the squirming, worm-like thing with his tin hand. "You heard it from her own lips."

The boy sprang away. Away from the man and the horror hanging in the cupboard. He ran. The staircase was just past the end of this aisle, past the pens of rabbit skins, past the wall of gleaming tools. He tugged at a pile of boxes as he dashed by, heard them clatter behind him, hoped they blocked the way.

His foot hit the bottom stair. He took the next three steps in one bound. He reached up for the sides of the trap doorway— and felt metal fingers close around one ankle. He smacked down onto the staircase and the edges of the steps cut into him.

But the gleaming axe, swinging high as he tried to roll away, would cut deeper.

"They say mixed marriages can be a challenge," the Wizard said trying to lighten the mood after Button-Bright told him and Ozma the terrifying story. If you've ever asked yourself why there weren't more stories of Button-Bright during this time period, it's because he wisely chose to stay closer to home. In time, his wanderlust got the better of him again, and that led to an adventure where he learned why he was always getting lost.

They immediately immobilized Chopfyt and contacted Glinda, who agreed the problem had to be dealt with immediately. Chopfyt's "experiments" were brought to the Royal Palace, and his hut and tools destroyed. It took time, but with the assistance of Ku-Klip, his special glue, and Herby the Medicine Man, all the animals and insects were restored to their former selves (and they certainly had a few choice words for Chopfyt)!

It's not known how his mind had gotten so damaged, though his mixed-up nature, proximity to the Deadly Desert, less-than-ideal marriage, or all of those combined, were suggested. After full immersion in the Fountain of Oblivion, his sanity seems to have been restored. Nimmie Aimee took longer to heal, but after a bit of time she returned to her old self and surprised everyone by announcing that she'd forgiven Chopfyte and intended to try again.

"It seems nothing will get in the way of true love!" the Wizard exclaimed when he found out, but Glinda was considerably graver and tried to talk Nimmie out of it, saying they'd had a mutually abusive relationship. In the end, it was decided she might benefit from some private time with Tollydiggle, the Emerald City's resident therapist (when she wasn't also serving as jailor), before making her final decision.

After a week, Nimmie's decision remained unchanged, though she acknowledged that she'd learned a lot and would be a better wife as a result. Only time will tell.

As it turns out, Trot and I found the following fragment amongst all the other "lost histories" that pertains to Nimmie Aimee's past, which seems appropriate to share. I can sense a mystery here, and will keep an eye out for the rest of the story.

IN FLESH OF BURNISHED TIN
a prolusio in dolor

by Jeffrey Rester

The taste of copper stung in Nimmie Amee's mouth as her ears rang with the force of the blow the old hag had dealt her. The helpless Munchkin girl looked up from her collapsed position on the floor to see the Wicked Witch of the East looming large over her. The glint of one of the Witch's Silver Shoes was besmirched with a trickle of crimson blood.

"Not so defiant now, are you?" asked the Witch as her tongue flickered across her parched lips with sadistic glee.

Nimmie's blue eyes blurred with tears, but whether from physical pain or heartache she could not tell. The two had become intertwined long ago and the poor girl did not know where one began and the other ended. Such was her lot in life, and she had stopped questioning it for the sake of what little sanity she had left.

"Come on, you little wretch! Where's your bark and bite now? Show me!" The Wicked Witch of the East leaned in threateningly close. Nimmie felt the bile rise in her throat as the smell of rot took her breath away.

"Bah! What a waste! You're not worth the two sheep and cow that I traded for you."

Nimmie, anger flaring, found her voice again. "Who asked you to barter for me anyway? I was fine where I was!"

The Witch snarled at the girl as she drew up to her full stature. "You insufferable ingrate! Believe me, if it wasn't for the blood debt owed, you could twist in the wind for all I care."

"There you go again with your hints and innuendos! What *blood debt* do you speak of? Why did you seek me out?"

"Never you mind, dearie. I have made recompense. You have food in your belly and a roof over your head. It is far more than you deserve. I daresay the scales are well-balanced."

"You act as if you do all this out of the kindness. Please! Every scrap of stale bread you throw at me and what little sleep I get, I have earned by the sweat of my brow."

The Witch's expression curdled like sour milk as she lifted her skeletal hand in fury. The blow struck Nimmie across her face, jarring her teeth together so hard that she bit her tongue. The Witch, trembling with rage, lifted her Silver Shoe and kicked the girl with all the dreadful force she could muster...

DIPLOMATIC IMMUNITY

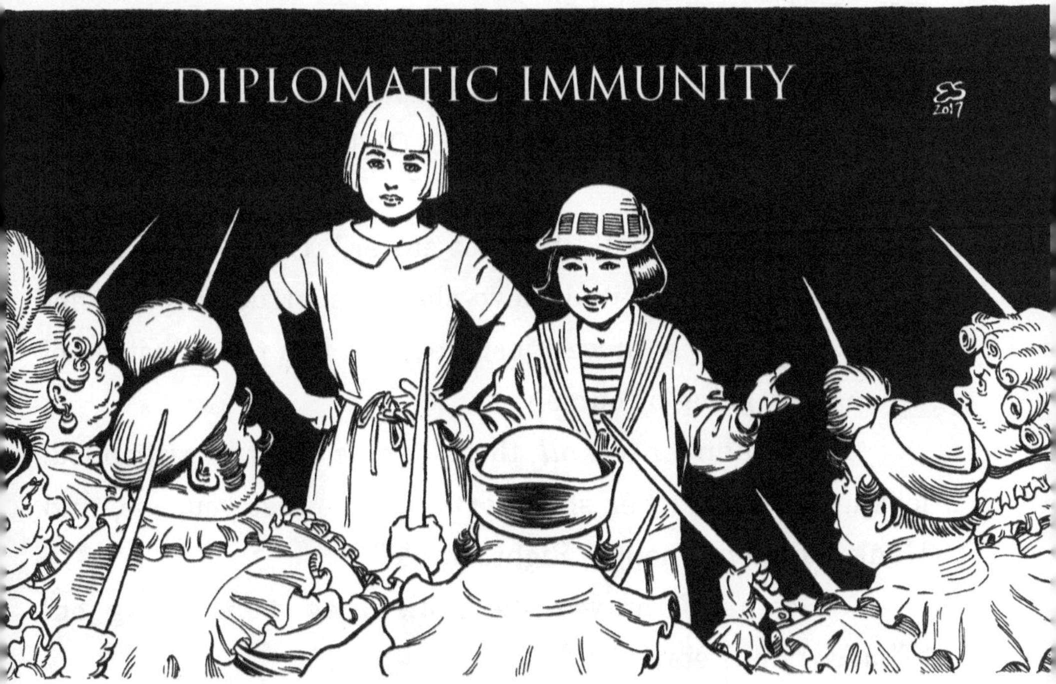

by David Tai

"This is a story of Betsy and I…" Trot began.
"You mean 'Betsy and me,'" Betsy corrected.
"That's what I said, you and me," Trot retorted.
"No, you said 'Betsy and I,' and that's incorrect. You wouldn't say 'This is a story of I…'"
"Unless it was about an eye."
Betsy stared at her.
"Ok, ok," Trot conceded. "Let me start again: This is a story of me and Betsy…"
"No, it's 'Betsy and me,'"
"Oh, I get it now," Trot said. "You just want to be first."
"No," Betsy cried. "That has nothing to do with it!"
"Of course it does. You wouldn't say 'This is a story of me.'"
"Yes, I would actually…"
"See?" Trot said. "Told you so!"
"Wha… Oh, forget it. I can't."
"This is a story of us! Hope you enjoy it!"

Trot Griffiths & Betsy Bobbin

CHAPTER 1
AMBASSADORS OF OZ

"Things would be a lot easier," Trot said in a tone that showed how she was struggling to not whine, "if we'd just travelled in a party instead of going by ourselves."

"We didn't need *all* those people," Betsy responded, looking back over her shoulder at Trot. "Just you, me, and Hank should be enough. Right, Hank?"

"Hee-haw!" brayed the mule they were riding on. "That's right, Betsy!"

Betsy and Trot were riding Hank through the purple countryside leisurely. It was mostly a pleasant trip, thanks to Hank's steady pace and the fact that they kept to the main roads, reflected Betsy. Trot seemed more determined, however, to have a running commentary rather than enjoying the scenery.

"He's siding with you because he's *your* companion," Trot said. "If Cap'n Bill were here, he'd say different."

"Of course he would, he's *your* companion," Betsy responded.

"I think you're just trying to show you can do things as well as Ozma or Dorothy can, despite not being a princess," said Trot grumpily.

Betsy stiffened, something that both Hank and Trot picked up on immediately. "Don't be silly, Trot," Betsy said sweetly. "We're just diplomats on behalf of Ozma. That's all."

"So the three of us are going to go greet the new visitors to Oz and ask them to please stop using magic?" Trot said skeptically.

Betsy took a deep breath before answering, "No. The *two* of us are going to go greet them and ask them to please stop using magic in Oz. Hank is going to be our backup, and will go get the Hungry Tiger and the Cowardly Lion if we run into trouble."

"Why didn't we just bring them along in the first place?" Trot sighed.

"Because if they get scared, they might use the very magic we're asking them to stop using in the first place," Betsy patiently replied. "That's diplomacy. You have to talk to people to get people to agree on something. Anyway, we're just about there, and... what?"

Hank came to a stop. Trot had to peer around Betsy to see what both the mule and his mistress were looking down at.

A large chunk of land had somehow gotten wedged tightly between two hills, blocking the valley. It had a large fog hovering over the middle of it, forming a partition that split the land into two distinctive colors, blue and pink.

Betsy sighed. "Well, that explains why this area suddenly started using magic. Hank, be a dear, and let us off here. If we're not back by tomorrow, you know what to do."

"Hee-haw! Get the Cowardly Lion and the Hungry Tiger!" Hank replied, as Betsy and Trot climbed off his back.

He nuzzled Betsy with great enthusiasm. "Be careful, Betsy," he said.

"Hey, what about me?" Trot demanded.

"Betsy'll take care of you," Hank responded. "She just needs to be careful herself."

"Well, *I* can take care of her too," Trot responded indignantly.

"Hee-haw!" Hank whinnied, in a suspiciously snickering tone, before trotting off to eat grass.

"Never mind Hank," Betsy said with a smile. "I'll go first. You can follow me. Just step where I step; the terrain's unsteady..."

CHAPTER 2
PINK AND BLUE

"The water's for drinking, Trot," Betsy noted, as she watched Trot walk around clutching her canteen of water, ready to splash it around.

"You never know. If there are magic users here, there might be witches too," Trot replied, her eyes darting every which way.

"We're here as *diplomats*, Trot," Betsy noted dryly. "I know diplomatic immunity means people can't punish you for trying to be diplomats, but I don't think it applies to melting people, even if they *are* witches. And if they happen to be good, they might not be so willing to talk after you go around splashing them. It's rude, you know. Put it away."

Trot pouted, but did as Betsy suggested. "Well, if they *are* witches practicing illegal magic, do you really think they're going to care about our diplomatic immunity?"

"Probably not," Betsy admitted. "Our immunity only applies if the leader of the other party recognizes it. But it's our job to try anyway."

"This looks familiar," Trot said at length, peering around for landmarks as they stood on the pink section of the land, having carefully moved from the side of the valley onto the wedged-in land. "I think I've been here before."

"Oh come on," Betsy said. "Unless you've been on an island before that's split in two colors, I hardly think you'd have been—"

"But I have!" Trot exclaimed. "I'm Queen of Sky Island!"

"Yes, I know," Betsy said rolling her eyes, "You seem to forget that I visited there, as well."

"Exactly!" exclaimed Trot. "You were just visiting! You didn't have the adventure I had!" Betsy knew Trot was speaking of the time before she came to Oz when she first met Button-Bright, and Polychrome. "And... oh, it was fun! I had to stop the Pinkies and the Blues from fighting, and..." Trot blathered on, waving her arms animatedly as she reminisced.

"Hold on a second," Betsy interrupted, arching an inquiring eyebrow and looking pointedly at the pink ground. "Did you say Pinkies and the Blues?"

Trot continued on, oblivious to Betsy's reaction. "Yeah, you know the story! There are people who called themselves the Pinkies, and others who call themselves the Blues, and they're kept apart by the fog bank..."

"Just like the fog cloud we saw?" Betsy looked thoughtful.

"Yeah, like that!" Trot babbled. "Remember the Boolooroo who was a tyrant? And the Pinkies had a good witch, and Cap'n Bill got a parrot and..."

"Trot," Betsy said softly.

"... they needed a good ruler, so I..." Trot continued to prattle.

"TROT," Betsy repeated firmly.

Now Trot paid attention. "What?"

One of Betsy's eyebrows arched in a questioning manner. "Pinkies, Blues, fog cloud?"

"What about it?" Trot asked obliviously.

Betsy merely waited, tapping a foot.

"... OH!" Trot slapped her forehead. "Oh, pink *and* blue. We *are* on Sky Island! Oh my gosh, we're on Sky Island! But it was flying along high and a long way from here, so what's it doing here? It's been *ages* since I've been here; the first time was when Button-Bright's umbrella was taking us from..."

"All right. We'll figure out what happened later. Now we'd better find out what's setting off the Wizard's magic alarms," Betsy interrupted impatiently. "I don't want Hank worrying about us, and getting the Hungry Tiger and the

Cowardly Lion and scaring these poor people. I see a path. Time to live up to your name, Trot."

"You know," Trot mused, after a few minutes of walking. "I've been back a few times, so I really should remember where things are. If we go this way, we should be at the Pinkies' City. Come on!" And she marched down the path.

"Wait, Trot. It could be dangerous to..." Betsy exclaimed as she brought her hand to her forehead in exasperation. With a loud sigh she shook her head and trailed behind at a slower pace than the increasingly excitable march Trot was setting.

It wasn't long before Trot gave a great triumphant shout, and Betsy picked up the pace, making her way through the pink streets, closing ground to see what had her friend so excited. She arrived to see Trot, with a triumphant look on her face and her hands on her hips, standing in front of a statue. "See!" Trot exclaimed proudly.

Betsy looked up. "I-It's a statue of *you*."

"Of course it is!" Trot said proudly, gesturing around. "They put it up for respect to all the Pinkies' rulers, like all the others... see?"

"Yes," Betsy said, noticing all the other statues of men and women arrayed in two rows, mounted on pink marble pedestals. "Still, you'd think we'd have seen *someone* by now."

As if on cue, the two girls found themselves surrounded by short rotund jolly pink people, popping seemingly out of nowhere and wielding sharp-pointed rosewood sticks. "Halt!"

"I have to stop tempting fate," Betsy lamented.

Trot, however, seemed exceedingly excited. "It's the Pinkies!" she exclaimed, clapping her hands. "Do you remember me? It's Trot!"

"Trot!" exclaimed one of the Pinkies. "Of course we remember you! Oh, Rosalie will be happy to see you! Follow us, follow us!"

"Rosalie?" Betsy asked, as the girls were escorted by the Pinkies.

"Don't you remember? She's Queen of the Pinkies," Trot replied with a wide smile.

Betsy furrowed her eyebrows closely together. "I thought *you* were," she said.

"I was the Boss of the Blues, and Queen of the Pinkies, so that made me Queen of Sky Island. They have their own rulers again, but I'm still Queen over them."

"I'm glad for you," Betsy said, her expression unreadable.

"I'm so thrilled to be back on Sky Island; I really should visit more often... hey, are you being sarcastic?" Trot frowned.

"Perish the thought," Betsy said, deadpan. "But aren't they magic users?"

"Well, Rosalie is. She's a good witch, though. Hey, maybe..." Trot mused.

"Maybe she's the one using magic, in which case everything will be nice and easy," Betsy observed.

Trot clasped her hands together. "Oh, I hope so! Do you think they're using magic to get Sky Island afloat?"

"Unless they plan to call it Ground Island, I think so," Betsy remarked, as they arrived at a simple house, no better or worse than any of the others.

"The queen is ready to see you," said the rotund Pinkie. "Go right in."

Trot entered, and after a moment of regarding the house curiously, Betsy followed.

Inside, Trot was hugging a beautiful tall slender woman, and Betsy looked on with surprise, for Rosalie was unlike any of her people.

Betsy greeted her with a smile and a curtsey, and Rosalie returned the favor, waving it off. "We don't stand on ceremony here, dear," the Pinkie Queen said.

"In that case, what happened?" Trot blurted out, as Betsy started to respond.

"Sky Island has gradually been descending from the sky for a while. From what we can tell in our research, we believe it requires a renewal of its magic," Rosalie calmly explained.

"We?" Betsy asked, her brows furrowing.

Rosalie pursed her lips. "The Blues and the Pinkies together. We were trying to revive the magic to get Sky Island afloat."

"But no one's supposed to use magic in Oz, except for people specially permitted," Trot said anxiously.

"We're simply trying to move on along," Rosalie said with a frown. "Once the island is afloat, we'll be gone, and your laws won't apply at all."

"I'm afraid we have to ask you to stop," Betsy stubbornly said. "It's Ozma's decree."

Rosalie shook her head. "We will not. We have no interest in staying here. The Boolooroo and I are in complete agreement."

Betsy turned to the younger girl. "Trot, you're their queen, tell them to stop."

"As our queen, you need to think what's best for your people," Rosalie rejoined. "And for us, we want to remain in the sky, not ground-bound."

"I-I..." Trot stammered.

"Trot," Betsy said calmly.

"Your Majesty," Rosalie said, just as calmly.

"Leave me alone!" Trot shouted, covering her ears. "I can't hear myself think!"

"I'm afraid we can't do that, your Majesty," Rosalie said gently. "We need to resolve this. We are not interested in serving your Ozma, and her rules are not ours."

Betsy crossed her arms. "We're at an impasse, then. Trot, we should head back to Ozma and let her know what we can."

"You may not," Rosalie replied. "We can't have our Queen subjected to Oz's rules."

"But we're *diplomats*! We shouldn't be held bound by your rules either," Betsy argued.

"And Trot is a queen first," Rosalie replied, dismissing Betsy's concern with a wave of her hand. "Of Sky Island."

Betsy sighed. "Well, then, Trot, resign and move on."

"She should not," Rosalie replied. "The Boolooroo and I have discussed this, but have not yet settled on a particular plan. Respect for *you*, Your Majesty, is what keeps us working together."

"Do we really need to stand on ceremony here, Trot?" Betsy asked.

"No, we don't." Now Trot looked confident, stepping ahead of Betsy. "I thought about it, and the best thing for Sky Island is to get it off the ground."

"But Trot..." began Betsy.

"I'm the Queen of Sky Island," Trot said flatly. "That means I need to make the best decision for my people. And as they said, the best thing to do is to get it off Oz, and then they can be free to do as they will."

Betsy weighted her options. "Your Majesty," she said resignedly. "What magic are you using?"

Trot blinked and looked immediately towards Rosalie. "Levitation magic. We're trying to get the island afloat again," the Good Witch said. "But we require a locus for the magic."

"A *locus*?" asked Trot with a blank stare.

"A central place." Rosalie frowned as she continued. "Our difficulty is that we don't have access."

"Why not?" asked Betsy.

"The center of the island belongs to the Frog People," Rosalie replied.

"Oh dear," Trot replied glumly, hanging her head.

Betsy gave her friend a quizzical look. "So, why can't we just ask them?"

Rosalie frowned at Betsy. "It's not that simple. They're still upset about the first time Trot arrived here," said the Good Witch. "They considered it a grave insult."

"But it wasn't intentional!" Trot protested.

Betsy only folded her arms across her chest and frowned.

"Don't look at me like that, I didn't do anything. It was just that the Frog King didn't like the umbrella Button-Bright was carrying. He said it was an insult to his country. Then Button-Bright's umbrella came alive, and became an elephant, and stomped through so we could get back to the Pinkie country!"

"I seem to recall all that," Betsy sighed. "So because Button Bright insulted them, they won't let you in."

"Then there was the *other* time..."

"The point is they don't want to hear from you."

Rosalie turned to nod solemnly at Betsy. "That's correct. They won't accept any attempts to talk with them, so we're left with very little alternative."

Trot's eyes widened. "What are you planning?"

Rosalie turned back to Trot with a grim look on her face. "We'll have to capture them and hold them until we can get the island afloat."

CHAPTER 3
DIFFICULT DECISIONS

"Do you really think this is the best thing to do, Trot?" Betsy inquired, standing across the table from Trot, inside Rosalie's home. Rosalie and the other Pinkies had left the two girls alone to talk.

Pushing up her hat, Trot wrinkled her nose. "Why not? If they don't want to help, they should get out of the way."

"But after that, what happens then? The frogs'll be even madder than a nest of hornets about being locked up," Betsy pointed out, folding her arms across her chest. "You'll have to find a way to keep them wet so they don't dry out. And you're supposed to be Queen of *all* Sky Island, not just the pink and blue territories, so you should make sure what they want, too."

"Not them," Trot sulked. "They wouldn't listen, even when I tried to tell them it was an accident."

"Well, then *find* someone who can talk to them!" Betsy exclaimed.

"Who?" Trot asked, holding her hands up in frustration. "You heard what Rosalie said. They wouldn't talk to her, or the Boolooroo, or anyone else."

Betsy lowered her head, thinking. Trot waited for a few minutes, before throwing up her hands. "Okay, Betsy, what are you thinking?" the younger girl asked resignedly.

"I was just thinking maybe *I* should go talk to them," Betsy replied distractedly.

"I don't think so!" Trot exploded. "You've seen them. They're *huge*! And we would have a hard time finding you in the fog if things went wrong!"

"Nothing will go wrong. Besides, you can't stop me," Betsy pointed out, folding her arms across her chest. "I'm a diplomat."

"And *I'm* the Queen," Trot retorted. "I can just keep you locked up."

"You can't do that!" Betsy shouted in outrage.

"You told me before diplomatic immunity only applies if the leader recognizes it," Trot said, a stubborn pout marring her face. "Well, I don't!"

"Y-y-you brat!" Betsy sputtered. She spun around, and stormed out the house.

Trot followed her out. "Stop her!" she commanded. "Don't let her go!"

Immediately, Pinkies surrounded Betsy.

Betsy frowned. "Trot..." she said warningly.

Trot stood her ground, shaking her head. "I don't want to lose you to these frogs if things go wrong," she said.

"They won't," Betsy's harsh stare softened, and she took a step towards Trot.

The younger girl stepped back. "I can't let you go."

"It's my decision to make," Betsy said softly. "I'm not a Queen, nor a princess. I don't have the responsibilities you have. I have to try."

Trot flared up. "Well, I say you can't! I'm the Queen of Sky Island. You're not! And I say you're not leaving!"

Betsy glanced about, and pursed her lips. "So am I going to be under house arrest?" she said coolly.

"I... yes!" Trot motioned to the Pinkies. "Put her under house arrest, and don't let her leave 'til I say so!"

"Yes, your Majesty," a few of the Pinkies said, approaching Betsy.

Betsy smiled. "All right, Trot. As you say, you're the Queen."

And as Betsy went with the Pinkies, Trot frowned, feeling very much like she was being humored.

CHAPTER 4
QUICK THINKING

"Betsy?" Trot asked nervously as she entered the house where the older girl was being kept under house arrest. "Are you mad at me? I brought dinner, and I've been thinking. Maybe..."

There was no answer. Trot's eyes swept across the inside of the house, as she placed the dinner on the dining table. The fireplace was full of ashes, the bed unslept in, the kitchen unused. No signs of Betsy.

Panicking, Trot frantically ran around, peeking under tables and opening cabinets, before running outside. "Did you let her out?" she asked.

"No one has entered, or left," one of the Pinkie guards answered.

"Find her, quick!" Trot exclaimed, as she ran for Rosalie's house.

The guards did as she commanded.

Inside the house, Betsy coughed as she dropped down from the fireplace where she'd squared herself in. Glancing quickly at the open door, she quickly ran to wash the soot off, scrubbing herself vigorously until she was as pink as the Pinkies. She snatched a pink overcoat, put it on, and then checked quickly for Trot and the Guards before walking out the door and blending into the village as quickly as she could.

"You still can't find me at Hide-and-Seek, Trot," Betsy murmured as she left the village, a small smile playing on her lips as she walked towards the Fog Bank.

"She tricked me!" Trot fumed, glowering at the pink mist that Rosalie had conjured between them showing them Betsy's final few steps into the Fog Bank.

"That she did," Rosalie said, her lips quivering as though to smother a laugh. "But I would recommend leaving her be."

"What for?" Trot wrinkled her nose.

"I don't think the Frogs truly mean to harm anyone, just keep us out of their territory," Rosalie said as she lowered her hands, letting the pink mist dissipate. "They will quite likely escort Betsy out promptly."

Trot pondered. "So if they won't hurt Betsy, I shouldn't worry about her?"

Rosalie nodded. "Quite likely, if we don't find her with the Frogs, we'll find her on the way in or out."

Trot accepted that with a nod, then had another thought. "So we just have to get the Frogs out of the way, get the magic to Sky Island working again, then you won't be using magic in Oz anymore...?"

"Because we'll be gone, yes," Rosalie finished Trot's thought.

"Good. I suppose it won't hurt if we can use magic to get you out of Oz. Especially since you're supposed to be a whole other country when you're not in Oz," Trot reasoned. "But what do you need to get the island floating again?"

"Besides the locus we need an item to invoke the levitation magic." Rosalie frowned. "Unfortunately, neither the Boolooroo nor I know where it is."

"How do you communicate with the Boolooroo, anyway?" asked Trot.

Rosalie smiled. "Through an old friend of yours," she replied. "Surely you remember your friend, the parrot?"

Trot widened her eyes. "The parrot! I haven't seen him since I left him with you. Gosh, it's been ages! How is he?"

"Doing quite well. He's carrying messages back and forth. The Frogs have left him unbothered, for the most part, since he's neither a Pinkie nor a Blue," Rosalie smiled. "Although he did tell me that the Frog King doesn't appreciate the intrusions and would be keeping the Blues and the Pinkies out. He was quite adamant about that."

"That's unfortunate. So what do we do now?" Trot asked with a pout.

"The Boolooroo has been working on ways to round up the Frogs. We will be helping the Blues shortly with our magic," Rosalie said. "Our main issue is where to keep them."

"I think we should keep them right there in their own home," said Trot. "Otherwise, they'll dry out. We don't want to harm them."

"Hmmm," Rosalie pondered. "We could do it if we kept enough guards. We'd need a lot of cooperation. I believe I can find enough people who will be willing to do this if we can get the Boolooroo's people to help too."

Trot nodded. "Okay. I hope Betsy comes back soon, then. I don't want her caught up in the mess."

CHAPTER 5
INTO THE FOG BANK

"You're not planning on letting me go anytime soon, are you?" Betsy sighed, as she bobbled up and down. "This is disgusting. And smelly."

The large frog holding her prisoner did not answer as it kept leaping, its powerful legs propelling him forward with great force. It couldn't speak, as its tongue was wrapped tightly around Betsy, carrying her in his mouth in such a way that only her head, shoulders and feet were exposed.

Betsy closed her eyes, trying to calm her thoughts as best she could. Clearly, if the frog wasn't intent on eating her, as she'd first feared, she was being taken somewhere.

Quite likely to the Frog King that Trot had mentioned earlier. So this was all working out in her favor... sort of.

If only it wasn't so revolting.

Eventually the leaping stopped, and Betsy opened her eyes just in time to drop to the ground in an undignified position as the frog released her.

She gathered herself, raising her head, and quickly assessing that she was in front of the largest frog she had ever seen in her life. It made the frog who'd captured her seem positively small by comparison. She managed to raise herself to her feet and nod at the largest frog, only to discover herself tongue-tied at the most inopportune moment.

Fortunately, at least, the large frog spoke. "What have we here? A spy for the Pinkies?"

Betsy shook her head, managing to ask, "No, I am not. Are you the Frog King?"

"I am," the large frog acknowledged. "Why are you wearing Pinkies clothing, then?"

Betsy curtseyed, and then quickly removed the overcoat, and daintily put it aside. "Long story, your Majesty," she said. "But my name is Betsy Bobbin, and I'm here as a representative of Princess Ozma of Oz. Oz is where this island landed when it stopped floating. I happened to cross the Pinkies land first." She pursed her lips. "I'm here to offer to help *everyone* on Sky Island." Best not to get into too much detail, or diplomacy would be very hard.

"You're very polite. I like that," the Frog King approved. "Proper respect for royalty. And how do you propose to get this island afloat?"

Betsy quirked her lips. "I was going to request your assistance with that, actually. Would you allow the Pinkies to enter your land and get the island afloat?"

"And why would I do that?" the Frog King asked. "They have dealt me a grievous insult."

"And how did they do that, your Majesty?" Betsy asked, though she knew the answer already.

"They unleashed a large... large *creature* through my land after I made a perfectly reasonable request that they respect my rules!"

"Rules about an umbrella, Your Majesty?" Betsy said without thinking, before she quickly stifled herself, hoping the Frog King didn't think to ask how she knew.

"Yes! That's an insult to our beloved foggy country," replied the Frog King with a harrumph. "It prevents the moisture from getting to our skin."

Betsy tilted her head to think. It was a silly rule, since fog surrounded them, but it might not have been so silly when it was raining. "Where did this rule come from?" she asked.

"It has ever been so. The same way the Pinkies have their rules that allow no Blues to come to their land, and the Blues have their Boolooroo resign after serving no more than three hundred years," the Frog King proclaimed.

Betsy frowned. They were just blindly following rules rather than thinking about the intent for having laws? It made no sense to her. Rather than offend the Frog King further, however, she nodded. "Putting that aside for the moment, Your Majesty," she said. "We need your help. It's very important."

"How so?" the Frog King said, puffing up at the thought of being of importance.

"The Pinkies need to be able to enter the center of the Island to get it afloat. Would you find it in the kindness of your heart to let them in?" Betsy asked, clasping her hands together in supplication.

"Perhaps, perhaps," the Frog King mused. "But what proof do I have that they're doing this to get the Island afloat and not to do something nefarious?"

Betsy thought for a moment before replying, "You don't, your Majesty. It just would be much better for everyone," she spread her hands apart widely, "to help each other right now."

"I don't generally care for Oz people, but I like you, human girl," the Frog King chuckled. "I have no reason to trust you, and you know that, so you tell me so. Very well, I'll give you a reason."

"Oh?" Betsy was intrigued. How would that work?

The Frog King drew in breath, puffing his chest out in a large bubble, before croaking loudly. A moment later, a smaller frog hopped in, squatting next to the Frog King. "You called me, father?" the smaller frog asked.

"My son," the Frog King introduced.

The Frog Prince bowed his head against the ground.

"Your Highness," Betsy curtsied.

"Marry him, and I will do what you ask," the Frog King proclaimed.

"*What?!*" Betsy and the Frog Prince exclaimed at the same time.

Without even pausing to consider it, Betsy locked eyes with the Frog King, and shook her head, making her refusal known.

"Surely you aren't turning down a chance to be a princess," the Frog King harrumphed, puffing his chest up threateningly.

"Your Majesty, I have no interest in being married off to someone I only just met a minute ago," Betsy responded, lifting her chin up in defiance.

"Then I have no reason to trust your sincerity," said the Frog King. "A political alliance must first be formally cemented."

"But Father..." the Frog Prince began, before being harrumphed to silence by the King.

"Be that as it may, Your Majesty, I must still refuse," Betsy said, crossing her arms.

"Harrumph! Well then, away with you! Guards!" the Frog King ordered.

Betsy squinched up her face immediately, bringing her arms up close against her chest. "Oh, ugh!" she squeaked, as once more a tongue wrapped around her and yanked her back into a guard's mouth.

"House arrest twice in a day. How Trot would laugh," Betsy muttered to herself, lifting her nose as far away as possible from the tongue wrapped around her while the guard hopped away.

CHAPTER 6
WINGED MESSENGER

"The parrot!" Trot laughed as she seized upon her old friend and hugged hard, ignoring the loud squawk of protest and ruffled feathers fluttering about.

Rosalie smiled, waiting for the young girl to release her friend, before gently suggesting, "Trot, dear, Cy can't breathe."

"Cy?" Trot asked as she released the parrot.

The blue parrot fluttered unsteadily onto Rosalie's shoulders, settling down and regarding Trot with a mixture of pleasure and annoyance, grooming his feathers back in place, before declaring, "Cyan's the name, flying's the game! Delivering messages to and fro, soaring and gliding, always on the go!"

"Oh, you have a name!" Trot exclaimed.

"We couldn't very well keep calling him 'the parrot', after all," Rosalie said with a laugh. "You wouldn't very well like being called 'the girl' all the time."

"No, I suppose I wouldn't," said Trot. "Oh! Are you here to share news?"

"Ready Set Go, rounding up our foe! They will soon fall, waiting on your call!" exclaimed the parrot.

"Excellent!" Rosalie said, highly pleased. "It looks like they completed the Roundup Machine!"

"*Roundup machine?* To catch the Frogs, I suppose you mean," Trot reasoned uneasily.

"Finished and ready, now get going already!" exclaimed the parrot.

"Yes. I suppose we should let the Boolooroo know what we need." said Rosalie. "Cy, we have to find a large metal cudgel, which is needed for the spell. So we'll have to have troops searching, but also enough to keep the Frogs at home, at least until everything is over. Please let the Boolooroo know."

"Oh. *Oh!*" Trot exclaimed. "Cy, can you find Betsy for me when you're done telling the Boolooroo what's going on? She's a human girl like me, not blue or pink."

"Find a girl, I'll give it a twirl! But first comes the Blues, I'll share the clues!" squawked the blue parrot, as he flew off Rosalie's shoulder, around the two Queens, and then out the window.

Trot watched the bird fly off, before turning to Rosalie. "A cudgel?" asked Trot. "For a spell?"

"Placed at the right spot, it will be the focus, yes," Rosalie said as she walked over to pick up a scroll and tap it meaningfully. "But you must be tired. Come rest for a while."

Trot slumped her shoulders, now noticing how tired she was. "I just hope Betsy's doing okay with the frog people."

CHAPTER 7
THE FROG PRINCE

Betsy drew her knees up to her chin and sighed. It might not have been so bad sitting around on a large lilypad, if it wasn't for the large frog-eyes staring at her from the water, making sure she wasn't going to run off. As if! She certainly wasn't going swimming in *this* dress. She considered it at first, but realized it would be too heavy, and she certainly had no intentions of going about undressed! Even if she could disregard her dignity, the foggy conditions would mean she'd be sick quickly. She wished she hadn't discarded the pink overcoat she had worn earlier.

She looked around and considered her options. She would have to distract the frogs with something and then try and paddle to shore... if she could get the lilypad to move, but how would she cut the stem? Maybe she could jump from pad to pad until she was close to shore, but that would require the frogs to be really distracted, and she wasn't sure she could manage it anyway. She contemplated the lotus flower sharing her lilypad. The blossom was bigger than her. She *could* use it as a boat, but she'd still needed to think of a distraction.

Before she pondered any further, a large frog hopped onto the lilypad. Startled, Betsy drew back.

"Greetings, girl," the Frog Prince croaked. Then, turning towards the eyes in the water, he commanded, "You may go. I wish to discuss my father's proposal privately."

The frog eyes in the large pond blinked, and then sank underwater. As the frog prince turned towards Betsy, she lifted her chin. "The answer is still no," she said.

"That wasn't the question I was going to ask," the Frog Prince chuckled, his chest puffing with laughter. "Who are you, and what brought you here?"

"My name is Betsy Bobbin, and I'm here because I was hoping to convince your father to help the others get this island afloat." Betsy settled herself to a more comfortable seated position, arranging her dress about her and attempting to look as presentable as she could.

"The Pinkies and the Blues," the Frog Prince croaked. "I quite agree, but as you can tell, my father has tremendous pride. So we shall have to work around him."

"You're willing to risk treason?" Betsy asked, incredulously.

"Work *around* him, I said, not against him," the Frog Prince frowned. "We don't actually have to help you. You just have to do the hard work yourself."

"I think they just want you out of the way," she revealed.

"Of course they do," the Frog Prince said, puffing his chest up. "But they have to catch us first!"

Boys and their games, Betsy thought dourly.

"But that's not what we were going to discuss. Since they need the island afloat, I think I have something that might help, though I am uncertain how," the Frog Prince croaked.

"Oh?" Betsy arched an eyebrow.

"There's been a treasure long held by our people that would help keep our island afloat, but it's been lost since the attack of the Outsider Queen who sent a large *thing* through our kingdom." A note of distaste crept into the Frog Prince's voice at the mention of the stranger who had caused such an uproar. "You'll have to find it and get it back in its proper position."

"I see," Betsy said softly, keeping quiet about Trot. "The King knows about it?"

The Frog Prince looked intently at Betsy. "Of course he does. It was his job to keep the rod straight and the Pinkies and Blues from destroying it. He has been quite upset ever since."

"So how—how do I find it?" Betsy asked, irritated at the scratchiness in her throat that interrupted her question.

The Frog Prince tilted his body sideways. "I have no idea. I just know that it's somewhere in our land."

"Do you even know what it looks like?" said Betsy, wondering to herself how she was going to accomplish this.

"It's a metal rod," said the Prince. "I can get you off the lilypad, but I can't help you find it."

Betsy eyed the Frog Prince suspiciously. "You're not going to put me in your mouth, are you?"

Again the Frog Prince chuckled, his chest puffing up in a big balloon. "Would you rather ride on my back?"

Betsy's eyes widened with joyful desperation. "Oh yes, *please!*"

CHAPTER 8

NEEDLE IN A HAYSTACK

Betsy sneezed, as she trudged along in the middle of an overgrowth. She had no idea how long she'd been searching. It felt like forever.

The Frog Prince had been apologetic, but there was nothing to keep Betsy covered and warm, nor did the frogs have anything to dry her off with, naturally. The best he could do was point her toward the wild overgrowth that had marked the remnants of the elephant's path. As it had been explained to her, while the rod had not been directly in the path of the elephant, it had been dislodged, and over the years, fallen and been overtaken by wild growth.

Of course, it would help much more if she just went back to Trot and a warm house, but if she did that, Betsy was certain the younger girl would never let her go again. She wiped her nose and shivered against the cold. The temperature seemed to be going down. She needed to concentrate, but she was ever so tired. Still, she wouldn't give up.

So! First things first.

If only her eyes would stop blurring... she could have sworn she just saw something blue flitter before her eyes.

A... parrot?

"After a twirl, I've found a girl," said the blue parrot. "Is it a Betsy, all wetsy?"

".... Trot sent you, didn't she?" Betsy tried to focus on the bird, but exhaustion finally overtook her. She reached out towards the parrot, only to fall flat on her face. Looking up just a bit, she spied a glint, and then reached out for it. Could it be?

It was a small iron rod. For a moment, she felt disappointed at the size of it, but then she reveled in her luck and clung tightly to it, like a staff.

"Betsy follow the bird, it's the word," said the parrot.

Betsy staggered to her feet. "N-no time," she said. "Tell Trot... tell her tomorrow..." And then she toppled over.

"Where is the girl?" bellowed the Frog King, glaring in turn at each of his guards.

The frog guards looked at each other, then guiltily toward the Frog Prince. The Frog Prince said nothing, and the King harrumphed, his chest puffing out grandly. "No matter, we have search parties looking for her and..." He shifted. "Did you hear something?"

A slow steady hum echoed through the air, and the next moment a gigantic blue whirling machine came bursting in out of the fog, whipping about blue lassos. Faster than a wink of an eye, several of the frogs were entangled in blue cords, forcing them to the ground with heavy thuds.

Chaos ensued.

The frogs croaked loudly in protest. The King barely had enough presence of mind to bound off, which he did in a hurry, diving into the pond with a splash. The Prince and the rest of the frogs of the court scattered in different directions, but more Round-Up Machines poured out of the overgrowth and rumbled after them.

"Surround the water! Don't let them out!" exclaimed Ghip-Ghisizzle, the Boolooroo, standing firm and holding out a blue staff.

Two troops of Blues and Pinkies marched forward in rows of five and quickly formed ranks encircling the area as they had practiced. The execution was perfect but for the great pains they took to maintain a distance from each other and the glares of distaste shooting across the circle. They stood tall, bearing their weapons of blue lassos and sharp pink sticks, ready to attack.

As soon as the pond was surrounded, Trot and Rosalie made their appearance, walking carefully so to keep the hems of their skirts dry.

"We did it!" Trot exclaimed as she looked around and shot a fist of victory into the air.

"Not quite," Rosalie said, smiling at Trot's reaction. She looked towards the water where baleful eyes glared at her. Her voice was firm but kind. "We're sorry, but you weren't listening, so we had to go ahead. Now, where is the iron cudgel?"

Menacing bubbles burst from the water, as the Frog King exclaimed unintelligible things at her.

Rosalie was unfazed. She turned to Trot and Ghip-Ghisizzle. "Well, we'll have to hurry and find it... If the magic has worn off enough that we're on the ground, we may never get the island up again."

"Sky Island forever ground-bound?" the Boolooroo said in dismay. "That *would* be tragic."

"All right, we have these Frogs contained," said Trot with positive determination to the leaders of the Pinkies and Blues. "Now you need to concentrate on getting the island afloat, and find Betsy!"

Rosalie lifted an eyebrow and turned toward the pond again to address the Frog King, asking in a mild voice. "I don't suppose you've seen another young girl like Queen Trot, have you, Your Majesty?"

But the Frog King had dived back down underwater.

"Can't really blame him," Ghip-Ghisizzle muttered. "Anyway, we need to get our island afloat quickly. Find your locus and get going as quickly as possible while we try and find your item."

Pulling out a scroll, Rosalie nodded. "Things might have shifted around here since the last time."

"I should go look for Betsy," stated Trot anxiously. "It's partly my fault she's out here by herself."

"We *will* find her," said the Boolooroo. "We can do that while we search."

"AWK!" shrieked a voice. "I've found one that looks like you; she is not pink, she is not blue!"

"Cy!" exclaimed Trot, as the blue parrot swooped in, and landed on Rosalie's shoulder. "You're a life saver! Where is she?"

"Tomorrow she said, before she hung her head. Out did she pass, none of her sass," the parrot responded, fluffing his wings. "Ere I departed, the frogs were charted; that way they sway..."

"We can't delay!" Trot exclaimed, not intending to rhyme. "If she's gotten sick, tomorrow might be too late!"

"Then we need to get her quickly," said Ghip-Ghisizzle.

"Sir," the Boolooroo's second-in-command interjected. "We don't have the troops to spare. If we're to keep these frogs where they are and hunt for the item and the girl, we will have problems stopping the frogs we haven't yet ensnared."

"Why would Betsy say tomorrow?" Rosalie mused. "Our plans were set for today."

"Tomorrow... *Oh!*" Trot exclaimed. "Cy, quick! I need you to..."

CHAPTER 9
THE IRON ROD

"What have we here?" croaked a frog. He poked a webbed forefoot at Betsy. Another prod and the frog harrumphed.

"Take her to the king," he said to his companion, unaware that their king was currently bound.

Betsy groaned, stirring, causing the frogs to jump. It took them a few short hops to reorient themselves, by which time Betsy had pulled herself to her feet and held the iron staff out in front of her.

"Leave me alone," she said, trying her best to ignore the pounding headache and focus on what looked like a thousand frogs before her eyes.

One frog stuck its tongue out, wrapping it around the staff, the other hopping around to try and wrap its tongue around her waist. Betsy clung to the staff stubbornly, bringing her arms in to wrap them around the staff tightly, causing a little bit of trouble for the frogs as they tried to figure out how to carry her and the staff off.

"Release her," a new voice commanded, as the Frog Prince hopped into view.

"Hnghhhgh" said one of the frogs. The other was wise enough to release his hold on Betsy, and greet the Prince with a "Your Highness!"

"Betsy, are you all right?" said the Frog Prince, before doing a double-take. "By the skin of my great uncle, I think you've found it!"

"Have I?" Betsy mumbled, twisting the staff so she could lean against it, but also trapping the tongue of the frog trying to disengage. She did feel only slightly stronger after the rest, and still sickly.

"Hnnnghhhh!" went the frog, while the Frog Prince spoke. "It's the iron rod that kept the island afloat," he said. "Er, could you let him go?"

Betsy sneezed, adjusted her grip on the staff to let the frog go, and sniffled, trying to not wipe her nose. It was so undignified to do that! "Oh. I thought it'd be bigger," she said, just before breaking into a coughing fit.

"The magic wore off when the rod was separated from the spell," the Frog Prince said as he observed Betsy. "What's the matter with you?"

"Sick," she muttered. "Take me back to the Pinkies, please."

"They're here," said the Frog Prince, now looking quite unhappy. "They've taken my people and my father prisoner."

"I'll explain," said Betsy in a scratchy voice, as she stumbled over.

All at once, there were twin roars, a bray and a squawk, as a blue parrot swooped in from the fog, followed by a donkey, a very large lion, and an equally giant tiger.

Startled, the frogs leapt a long way, all except the Frog Prince. Roaring, the Cowardly Lion leapt for the Frog Prince...

...Only to be met by an iron staff rapping his nose sharply.

"Stop!" cried Betsy, staggering. "He's my fr—" She slumped against the Frog Prince, and was out like a light, as sickness and exhaustion caught up to her again.

CHAPTER 10
A PRINCESS IN ALL BUT NAME

When Betsy opened her eyes again, she found herself staring at a pink ceiling. A quick glance indicated she was lying in bed.

She sniffled, ran a hand quickly under her nose, and then decided to get out of bed, only to be admonished.

"You're still sick, Betsy," Trot said, her hands on her hips as she glowered at her friend. "Lie back down,"

"The staff, it has to..." said Betsy, legs dangling over the side as she started to get out of bed anyway.

Trot shoved her back down. "If you try and get up again," she said with a threatening scowl, "I'll have Hank sit on you."

Betsy regarded Trot for a moment, then pulled her legs back and wrapped herself in the blanket. "All right," she said. "But you have to tell me what happened."

"Oh, you reminded me that tomorrow was when Hank was supposed to get the Hungry Tiger and the Cowardly Lion. So we sent Cy... he's the parrot who found you... anyway, he found Hank, Hank got the Lion and the Tiger, and they found you." Trot looked at Betsy reproachfully. "You didn't have to hit the Lion on the nose to save the Frog Prince."

"I didn't mean to," said Betsy as she leaned back, coughing.

"It's okay, he forgives you. Anyway, Rosalie and the Boolooroo, they got the rod set up, made it bigger, and recharged it with magic. Even the Frogs helped, thanks to the Prince. All of them—the Blues, the Pinkies, and the Frogs—they actually made it work," Trot said, as she walked over to a table and poured something hot into a cup. "It took a little while, but the island should be floating in a few days again."

"Oh good," Betsy said, as Trot came back and handed her a cup of tea.

As Betsy sipped her tea, Trot continued, "So everything's all set. Once the island's afloat, we're done with our mission." She sighed. "I rather liked being Queen. I'm going to miss it when we leave." She tilted her head at Betsy. "They did say they wanted to give you an award before we left."

Betsy shook her head 'no.'

Trot leaned forward, eyebrows arched. "Not even if you were being awarded a title?" Trot's eyes twinkled as a wide smile spread on her face. "You sure you don't want to be called Princess Betsy?"

"Whatever would make you think I wanted to?" Betsy asked suspiciously.

Now Trot giggled. "The Frog Prince told us the whole story about his father and what he offered you, you know. Betsy and the Frog Prince sitting in a tree... K-I-"

The teacup shattered on the floor as Betsy hurled a pillow at Trot.

"I don't need titles or anything like that. I know who I am," Betsy said, turning her head to smile the largest smile that Trot had ever seen on her. "I'm Betsy Bobbin."

THE SCRAP BAG CIRCUS OF OZ

by Deciduous Equine (as told to M.A. Berg)

She may be mischievous, loud, and apt to get into trouble, but Scraps is probably the most fun citizen in all Oz, and what she lacks in decorum she makes up for in enthusiasm! Scraps is also loyal, honest and kindhearted, the traits that make for a solid friend, even it is a cotton-stuffed one that likes nothing better than singing silly verses and doing cartwheels around the Emerald City!

Scraps was constructed by Dr. Pipt for his wife, Margolotte, who wanted a maid, but it was Ojo who gave her her brains and personality. No one's slave, Scraps has been a constant presence at the palace ever since. Little did she know she wasn't the only one brought to life that day!

Trot Griffiths

The Sawhorse went on a trot-about whenever the ceremonies and duties of a palace legend became overwhelming. He took off on hoof to explore yet another of the many unpaved back roads that branched from the great Yellow Brick Road. He usually went alone, but this time he invited Scraps to accompany him. The Patchwork Girl was going through a creative block in her verse, the result of a Green Moon. A Green Moon had an adverse effect on her rhymes; her poems came out as modern blank verse. For example, upon hearing the Sawhorse's invitation, she said: "I am honored to be invited upon your planned trip to seek the calm back roads of Oz," causing the Sawhorse to realize that if Scraps was uttering dignified speech there wasn't a moment to lose.

As neither ever tired, it made little difference what time they left the city, so they departed the palace that evening after a fond farewell to friends. Scraps held a large Japanese lantern on a bamboo fishing pole in front of the Sawhorse's nose to light their way, and they left the sparkling towers of the Emerald City behind. The Green Moon had risen large and bright, and the Sawhorse suggested she avoid the poetic form well into the dark of the moon.

Though made of seasoned wood, he always felt his sap rising when he went into the wild, and each mile left the Sawhorse feeling like a green sprout again. The next day found the pair well off the Yellow Brick Road and in the Munchkin countryside. They went on down an unpaved country road at a good trot, waving to a farmer or woodcutter. Suddenly the road was filled with yellow dust, and a great cloud curtained the road ahead.

"Slow down Sawhorse," said Scraps. "There's no telling what's in front of that cloud. By the size of the billows, whatever it is must be as big as a house."

"We'll go around, hang on," said the Sawhorse as he took to the shoulder of the lane. The dust cleared, and the Sawhorse found himself trotting alongside a very small blue-spotted pony, pulling an equally small gypsy caravan, gaily decorated with painted circus clowns, elephants, and aerialists.

The blue-spotted pony rolled his blue eyes to look at the Sawhorse, and neighed a greeting.

"Didn't know there were any horses in these parts," said the Sawhorse. "You part of a circus?" Sawhorse had heard about the cruel shows from the Wizard, the camel Humpty, and some clowns who had all been in one.

"We're the oldest traveling show in all Oz," said the Blue-Spotted Pony, for that was his name. "We're headed for camp just around the next bend... in May Apple Meadow. Trot along and see the show." He tossed his mane, and then made a hard right into a meadow surrounded by blueberry bushes and plum trees.

"Now why would we do that?" said Scraps angrily. "We have a good mind to report you to Ozma!"

"Whatever do you mean?"

"Don't you know that animals are terribly abused and exploited in circuses?"

"Not ours!" the pony shot back. "We only employ stuffed animals, and they're all volunteers like me."

"Oh!" said Scraps, "I guess that's okay then."

"So, you'll come see our performance?"

"Sure, sounds like fun!"

As the Sawhorse began following the blue-spotted pony, Scraps hung over the Sawhorse's neck and whispered in his ear, "That's not a real horse. He's stuffed... blue polka dots on white percale. His mane is blue yarn, and his eyes are blue dress buttons."

"So what?" said the Sawhorse. "And I'm made of wood, and you're stuffed too."

"It's not that. It's just... there is something familiar about his hide. I've got a piece just like it..." she said as she fell off the Sawhorse, trying to see the back of her patchwork dress. She rolled, petticoats and drawers gathering dust, to a stop in May Apple Meadow in a clump of May Apple plants. There should have been no May Apples in May Apple Meadow because it was the wrong season of the year, for they grew and were picked on one day, May Day. But the meadow was filled with the bluest of flowers, blue bells, delphiniums, and bachelor buttons. Blue-Spotted Pony circled the meadow, and where the wagon's wheels bent the grass, tent poles sprang up. They opened up into multicolored circles of canvas, like clustered umbrellas. The pony stopped. Out of the back of the caravan scrambled one, two, three, four, five, six, seven, eight, nine, ten, twenty clowns, stuffed calico and gingham dogs, tigers, bears, and five chintz elephants. Each of them was no larger than a child's toy.

The clowns set up camp and unhitched the pony. The elephants tightened and pulled up guy ropes for the trapezes and high wire. When all was shipshape, they gathered around Scraps, who towered above them. The Blue-Spotted Pony trotted up with the Ring Master, a clown in a scarlet coat, black boots, and a top hat.

"Ladies and Gentlemen, Moms and Dads, and children of all ages," he shouted in a voice much larger than his size. A pink chintz elephant gave him a nudge with his trunk. "Sorry," he said in a smaller voice, "habit. We're off season now, getting some new acts together, and headed back to our winter quarters."

"Where's that?" said Scraps. There was a sense of having known or seen this troupe that she could not quite put her finger on.

"We're from the Munchkin Country, near Dr. Pipt's," said the Ring Master.

"Pipt!" exclaimed Scraps. "Mrs. Pipt, Margolotte, stitched me up, and Dr. Pipt's magic formula gave me life and smarts!" She didn't mention that Ojo had given her more smarts than the Pipts had wanted in a maid, and that she had run away, feeling herself above housework.

"Is that so!" exclaimed the Ring Master. "Mrs. Pipt made us all."

"We're from the same scrap bag," said the Spotted Pony. "Scraps must be from the same scrap bag too," he neighed to all the clowns and stuffed animals. They crowded around Scraps and the Sawhorse. Scraps was surrounded by a pointing, pushing crowd.

"There's my pink chintz," said one. "There's my yellow-and-red-strip," said another. "There's my plaid," "my checks," "my polka dots," they said as they reached over to point to the matching patches on Scraps. Scraps quite enjoyed all the attention she was getting from the admiring crowd.

"When did she make you?" said Scraps. "The material is familiar, but I don't remember your faces."

"It was after you left that Mrs. Pipt began to make clowns and stuffed animals for the neighbors' children. She made us one at a time from scraps of material from her scrap bag. All children like a stuffed animal for a playmate," said the Blue-Spotted Pony.

"The magic powder that brought you to your present fun-loving, independent condition had inadvertently been sprinkled among our stuffing, unbeknownst to Mrs. Pipt. You can see what happened. Unfortunately for us, the mothers wanted passive toys for their children to hold during naps," said the Ring Master with a sigh.

"We were too lively," said a cheerful green plaid clown as he executed a back flip.

"We were too sassy," said a yellow-and-brown striped cat with wonderful horsehair whiskers.

"The mothers said we got the children into trouble with our mischievous ways," said a red-and-yellow striped flannel monkey. Scraps recalled that material. It was from an old bathrobe of Dr. Pipt's and there was a similar piece on her right elbow.

"We thought our tricks would do well in a circus, and that we could entertain children all over Oz. We borrowed the gypsy van Dr. Pipt had made for camping; it's small for storage, but remarkably expandable. We practiced our acts, then took to the open road... the back open roads. We're an old fashion one-ring circus," explained the Blue Spotted Pony. "Animal-free, unless you've got stuffing inside of you instead of meat."

"We're perfecting new variations on our performances," said the Ring Master. "If you'll just sit down outside the tent, you can see very well. Reserved seats under the little tops are for children... and here are some now." Indeed, a woodcutter's five children had come to the meadow and were looking wide eyed at the colorful tent clusters. A red-and-yellow flannel monkey led them inside, where they sat on the grass, their heads almost touching the top of the canvas.

"Ladies and Gentlemen, Moms and Dads, Children of All Ages, and Honored Guests," shouted the Ring Master. "The Scrap Bag Circus is about to begin." A hearty tune was struck up by clowns playing kudzus and a pink calico elephant banging on a drum with his trunk. The circus parade circled the inner ring.

It was a marvelous show. The stuffed animal acts were well done; the performers donned spangled ruffles around their necks, which made Scraps laugh as they reminded her of Ojo and the silly ruff he wore when she first met him. The clowns did their 'twenty clowns from a small van' trick, and the children shouted with delight as more and more clowns tumbled out of the small wagon. There was a remarkable aerialist act. Though the clown Jingles missed his double, triple and quarter flips, no harm was done. He fell and was immediately pummeled back into shape by two rose chintz elephants.

"That was fun," said Scraps waving good-bye to the wood cutter's children, who waved their cotton candy, as their hands were filled with the sticky sweet treat.

"Excellent show," said the Sawhorse. "We'll have to be trotting along now. Perhaps we'll meet again along the road. I stick to the back roads when I want to be incognito. Did you say you were headed toward your winter quarters?"

"If you are, say hello to Margolotte for me," said Scraps.

"We will! We will! We will!" said the circus troupe in unison as they waved good-bye to Scraps and Mr. Incognito (a natural mistake on their part.) "We'll tell them we met the biggest Scrap in the whole scrap bag." The clowns laughed heartily and back-flipped, somersaulted, cartwheeled, and stood on their hands.

For his part, the Sawhorse was glad to move on down the road. One Scraps was enough for him! A circus of small Scraps, though they were clowns and stuffed animals doing undignified tricks, was too much of a good thing. All right for children, he supposed.

They were well down the road with only a moderate amount of yellow dust following behind, when Scraps spoke. "Imagine," said Scraps, "a whole circus made from the same scraps as me! We're practically siblings! How proud Margolotte must be of her handiwork. She has clever fingers. Why, just look at me!"

"You didn't listen too carefully, Scraps. Mrs. Pipt made them, but it was Dr. Pipt's Powder of Life that brought them to life, and they had to run away, or else were let go, in order to join the circus... or make up a circus to join, which wasn't what she had intended for them."

"You think so?" said Scraps.

"Yep," said Sawhorse, who was no block head, despite his knots. "Remember, they said the mothers disapproved because they got the children too excited and mischievous? The mothers wanted quiet toys for nap time. These toys left home rather than settling down."

"Just like me," said Scraps proudly. "We're all scraps from the same scrap bag! Hurray for us!"

Same rag bag, the Sawhorse thought to himself, but said, "Exactly," aloud. *What a hurry scurry bunch they were!* Not everyone could be made of such solid oak as he, the dignified and official mount of a royal ruler. "Now let's go and see what's behind the next bend in the road."

THE WIZARD IN NEW YORK

by Sam Sackett

Due to the famous American movie, many people know of the Wizard, but very few actually know the kind of man he really is. I was just a young girl when I first met him, and, if I'm perfectly frank, I didn't think he was such a good man for sending me and my friends to kill the Wicked Witch of the West.

When the Wizard and I returned to Oz a few years later, I came to see him in a different light, and I now know him to be one of the kindest, most supportive and optimistic people I've ever met; smart as a whip too!

In this tale, I learned a lot about the world we both came from, and about the Wizard as a person, as Oscar Diggs, not just as the wonderful Wizard of Oz. It turns out he's every bit as wonderful as the title claims.

Dorothy Gale

CHAPTER I
THE WIZARD TAKES A VACATION

As you may be aware, the Wizard of Oz came from the outside world and tries stays in touch with it by means of radio. He didn't often have the luxury of time to do so, but he'd just then been listening to reports of the World's Fair in the city of New York. Apparently, representatives of all the nations on Earth would be appearing there, and he was terribly curious about the new inventions that would be featured there.

Oscar loved to tinker and spent much of his time creating new inventions. As there weren't too many who still invented (or were allowed to since the practice of magic was restricted to just him, Ozma and Glinda), it would be interesting to see what other inventors were up to. Sure, they didn't have real magic, but he'd likely get some good ideas that he could implement for the benefit of Oz.

"Besides, I should take a vacation," he thought. His assistant was doing just that, and everyone else seemed to be busy enjoying life and work. Usually his own work kept him occupied and content, as well, but the failure of his last big invention had soured him somewhat.

Oscar approached Ozma, who had just finished up her duties for the day. The ruler of Oz, with her customary perceptivity, remarked, "You have that look in your eye. What are you thinking?"

"There's a World's Fair in New York right now that I'd

like to go to."

"Homesick?" Ozma teased.

"Oh, no," the Wizard replied. "It's more like professional curiosity. There are so many new things happening in the civilized world, and I think if I went to the World's Fair I could learn more about what they are. Some of the new inventions may have uses for us here."

"That sounds like fun," Ozma replied. "I'm sure you're also curious to see how your former countrymen are faring?"

"I'm hopeful we'll have learned the lessons of the past and are moving into a new golden age."

"I hope so too," Ozma said, though she chose not to add that she didn't have as much confidence in that as Oscar had. "Well, if you want to go to this World's Fair, that's simple enough."

"Would you like to accompany me?"

Ozma thought about it for a moment. "It *is* a tempting offer, but I have too much on my schedule. I'm still searching for better ways of protecting Oz from external threats without excluding our surrounding neighbors, especially since we've expanded our realm beyond our borders. Perhaps Glinda or some of your old friends would like to go?"

"I've already asked Galden, my old major domo, but his wife won't let him go. Notta and Bob Up came from the outside world, but they're touring with their circus, and Clakku, who I worked with in *my* old circus days, isn't interested in going back. Probably afraid he'll run into someone he owes money to!"

"Well, it *can* be a dangerous place," Ozma reasoned, "especially for those who've gotten used to life in Oz."

"True, but Oz still its share of dangers," Oscar reminded her.

"Try telling that to Dorothy and the girls," Ozma laughed. "Right now, they're off joyriding in their Scalawagons!"

"They didn't turn out the way I'd hoped," Oscar lamented. "They're more of a nuisance."

"No, they're just... idiosyncratic." Ozma thought they were a nuisance too, but she didn't want to hurt his feelings. "And they're certainly *entertaining*. I think we just need to build more roads. That's going to be another council discussion. Speaking of transportation, have you ever flown an ork before?"

The orks were large and unusual creatures, somewhat resembling ostriches, but featherless, flying by means of a propeller tail. An ork named Orville had helped the Scarecrow back when Trot and Cap'n Bill first came to Oz.

"I've flown by many means, from balloons to Ozoplanes, but never by ork!"

"Well," Ozma said, "Orville's been visiting with us, and is ready to return to Orkland. I'm sure he'd love to fly you to the Quadling Country. You can ask Glinda if she'd like to accompany you to the World's Fair. Either way, it'll be more fun than just sending you with a Wishing Pill or the Magic Belt."

"A good idea!" the Wizard said. "The expo's going to run six months, so there's plenty of time."

That night, as the Wizard donned his green silk pajamas, a thought suddenly struck him. He'd need money for lodging, and surely there was an admission charge to the fair, and the exhibits might require a separate fee. Oscar went to the chest of drawers in his room and opened the drawer to look for the cash he'd had in his pocket when he had returned to Oz for what had become his final stay. He soon found it and counted it carefully: eighty-seven dollars. This would likely not be enough. He'd have to magic more.

Then, after his morning breakfast and grooming ritual, Oscar realized that his usual black Victorian-era suit would be quite out of place in modern-day New York, so he chose a three-piece tan gabardine suit in the current style that he'd acquired from Pastoria and Snip's tailor shop. It seemed a bit... *casual* for his tastes, but he knew his preferences were merely an artifact of the era in which he grew up. "Thanks to having lived in Oz for so many years, I'm still agile and energetic, not quite as spry as I once was, but old only by the standards of the very young." He packed his valise, considering for a moment his black bag, which held some of his useful magical implements, but deciding against it. Most magic wouldn't work in the outside world, though there were exceptions, such as the magic that brought John Dough, the Gingerbread Man to life. In this case, however, it would be unwise to risk losing the bag. Best to bring mundane things only.

Then he went to the throne room to say goodbye to Ozma and a few others he ran into. An elevator brought him to ground floor, and he left the palace by a side door. The Royal Zoological Gardens, where Orville awaited him, was a brisk walk. When he reached it, he saw a teacher herding his class of young students through the various paths, pointing out to them the plant-grown animals on display.

It did not take the Wizard long to locate Orville. From the claws on his feet to the crest on his head, he stood a full eight feet tall. His four large wings were proportionately round and broad; and, as he walked around the enclosure, examining the strange creatures that lived there, he'd exercise his propeller and lift himself into the air. When he saw the Wizard, the Ork walked over to the edge of the enclosure. "Ah, there you are," he said, bending his long neck and dipping his head. "How are you, Wiz?"

"I'm quite well, thank you!"

"I hear you'd like to travel via something other than those impudent rolling contraptions you call Scalawagons."

"It sounds like you've met one or two," the Wizard said.

"The Emerald City's never been so jammed up! Sorry Wiz, I don't think that was your best invention."

"No offense taken. They're not for everybody. But I think with a little time to settle in, things will work out."

"If you say so. Well, where would you like to go?"

"Are you up for a trip south to see Glinda the Good?"

"Certainly! You ever ride one of us before?"

"Can't say I have."

"Then you're in for a treat! We're the best flyers in the three seas. Climb on board and let's fly!"

CHAPTER II
THE WIZARD FLIES SOUTH

As soon as the Wizard was comfortably situated, Orville stood, started up his propeller, and lifted off the ground. Oscar looked down and saw the zoological gardens growing smaller below. The ride was very smooth. Soon the palace diminished below them and the city disappeared. All told it was a far more comfortable flight than he'd anticipated, although at the speed Orville was flying, the wind blew a bit too much in his face. "Slow down!" the Wizard called out, uncertain whether the ork could hear him.

The ork slowed, and when the Wizard looked down again, he saw fields of grain. "So, why don't you go by Flipper if that's the name your father gave you?" the Wizard asked as he settled in.

"If you want this ride to continue smoothly, you won't use that name."

"Fair enough," the Wizard said agreeably. "I don't go by my full name either."

"That's because it's as long as a book!"

Oscar laughed, "My father had some sense of humor."

"Mine too. Don't you just hate that?"

"Indeed! That's why I left when I was ten years old to join the circus."

"That must have been upsetting for your parents. I understand human hatchlings tend to spend considerably longer in their nests."

"Generally, but my father was in jail at the time, and my mother had either died or left. I could never get a clear story out of him."

"I suspect you'd make a better sire than he was. Why have you not had offspring yet?" asked Orville. "Gather a few females, or just one, as you humans seem more inclined to do, and make babies."

"It was never my calling," Oscar said with a smile. "I believe one should be selfless to have children. I'm too interested in my work, in magic, in protecting the realm and all that. Besides, I have Dorothy, Trot, Betsy, Button-Bright and others around all the time. They're like my own."

The ork laughed good-naturedly. "You know I have the deepest respect for you all, but we orks find it a bit odd that you, Ozma and Glinda chose to remain single."

"Ozma's just a little girl," exclaimed the Wizard.

Orville laughed. "It's cute that you think so! But I'm pretty certain you're all well aware she's anything but. She's what you're people would call a teenager at least."

"Well, she's not quite old enough to take a suitor."

"In *most* cultures she is, besides which, she could age a few more years if she wanted to."

"Well, that's *her* business. For my part, I'm certain it seems odd, as you say, but I have no shame in admitting I'm a misfit. I sometimes think that's what the Land of Oz is really for; it belongs to the misfits."

"Yes, loveable misfits we all are."

After a time, the fields gave way to trees, and he knew

that a range of mountains lay to the north of Glinda's palace.

The air grew colder over the mountains. Even though the ork chose a path that avoided the highest peaks, the Wizard found himself shivering and wished he'd worn an overcoat. Once past, Orville descended to a lower level where the air was more temperate. It wasn't long before they could make out some details of the palace and surrounding wall.

"Land over by the entrance," the Wizard instructed, pointing to an open archway that passed through the wall. "I appreciate the ride, Orville. It was really quite pleasant. I hope you'll come to visit us again soon."

"Sure thing, Wiz! Just don't ask me to fly you to the Outside World!"

"Nothing doing," Oscar assured him. "While you're here, you should visit with the swans and storks."

Orville settled to the ground, and they could see two pretty handmaidens emerging. "Perhaps I will. What are they like?"

"The swans are a little snooty until you get to know them," Oscar recalled. "Fiercely loyal creatures! The storks are too, but they're wilder! You should hear the stories they tell!"

Orville chuckled. "Do the storks and swans get along?"

"Not at first! Glinda had to have a stern word with them. Now, they're fine. They gossip about each other, of course. Mostly they're happy because they have a lot more free time now. And the handmaidens help too."

"Whatever do you mean?" asked the ork.

"Glinda has special handmaidens who are trained as

aerial acrobats. If both groups of birds are away, which is rare, she transforms her handmaidens into storks!"

"I'm speechless," said the ork.

"True story."

"Why not just get another group of birds to help out? I'm sure the orks would love to send volunteers..."

"I'm not sure either group would appreciate that."

"I see your point. Tell Glinda the offer stands if she's ever interested."

"I most certainly will!"

The handmaidens arrived. One was Glinda's personal maid, Cherri Jelli. The other introduced herself as Maxine. Orville asked her if he could visit with the birds.

Cherri Jelli, meanwhile, led the Wizard through a beautiful garden-lawn to the Ruby Palace, not as large as Ozma's emerald one but still impressive, conducting him to an ornate foyer where she departed to inform Glinda. A short time later, he was led to Glinda's ruby throne room and announced.

Glinda smiled and asked her, "Did you know the Wizard was once my student?"

"Oh yes," Cherri said. "I've studied the history books."

"I'm handsomer than usually depicted," Oscar said with a wink.

Glinda smiled. "How was your first ork flight?"

"Surprisingly comfortable... when he's not speeding at a hundred miles an hour!"

"I've been tempted to try it out myself," Glinda said.

"My Ozoplanes still fly," the Wizard laughed, referring

to another of his recent inventions that had met with some mishap.

"I'd best stick with chariots!" she laughed good-naturedly. "So I hear you're off to the New York's World Fair."

"Yes, I was hoping you might want to join me."

"I'd love to, but I'd just as soon not leave Oz in case..."

"In case something bad happens, you mean," the Wizard added.

Glinda looked quizzically at the Wizard. "Most of the time we have long stretches of peace and quiet."

"I know," Oscar said with a smile.

"Tell me, why do you *really* want to go to this World's Fair?" Glinda asked.

Oscar sighed, "My last few inventions were something of a bust," he admitted. "And I suppose I could use some inspiration from fellow inventors..."

"There are still wizards and inventors in any number of the magical countries and islands in the Nonestic."

"It would probably be safer too. But I'm curious about the outside world. I'm hoping they've learned their lesson and are on the road to a better future..."

"Ever the optimist," Glinda said brightly. "Do you miss the world outside?"

"No," he answered flatly. "It was a hard place..."

"Did you know I lived for a time in the Great Outside World, long, long ago?"

"I don't think I knew that," said the Wizard, intrigued.

"I don't often talk about it," she said. "There's really

not much to tell. I was part of the Royal Household of Queen Elizabeth..."

"The Elizabethan Court?" the Wizard said, incredulously. "I'd say there was much to tell!"

Glinda smiled. "There *was* a bit of intrigue! But it never felt like home. It never felt like I belonged... *You* belong here, but I don't want you to feel so overwhelmed by your responsibilities that you don't take time for yourself."

"I appreciate that, Glinda. There's no better life I could ask for. But, I suppose I could use a diversion."

"You've certainly earned it," reassured Glinda.

"So have you. Are you sure you don't want to *see* what the modern world has to offer? It's not quite the same as reading about it."

"I don't disagree," she laughed. "And I'm sure you'll tell me all about it. You know, as much as I support the ban on magic, it's times like these that I wish we had another official magic worker in the land. It would be reckless for both of us to leave Oz at the same time."

"We've done it before," the Wizard reminded her. "Besides, Ozma's quite proficient now."

"True, but she's in the Emerald City. Oz is a vast land. There's Gloma in the West, but I'm still not reconciled to her former behavior enough to trust her."

"We *could* use a Good Witch in the North again..."

"We'd have had one had Mombi not broken the line of the Tah-Tipuu in the North."

"Perhaps Locasta would want to step back into her old

shoes," he suggested.

"Only if she had to," Glinda informed him. "She runs a music hall now, and is quite happy there."

"You and Ozma could appoint someone new to serve in that role. There's still plenty practicing magic on the sly."

"That's too dangerous," Glinda said flatly.

"That's why *you* should be training apprentices again."

"Same idea applies," Glinda said. "Not every wicked witch or wizard starts out wicked. Sometimes it just takes a taste of power." The Wizard surmised she was thinking of some unpleasant recollection from her past.

"Everything comes with a risk," he said. "You did a pretty good job with Jinnicky and me!"

Glinda smiled. "Thank you for saying so, but that's because Jinnicky and you are the least power-hungry people I know. When it comes down to it, power, greed, and apathy are three primary reasons we had wicked witches, wizards and rulers over the years. Speaking of risks, are you fully prepared for your trip?"

"Mostly," he answered. "There *is* the issue of money."

"I thought that might be the case." She stretched out to him a hand containing a wallet. "This is a magic wallet. It will always contain enough to cover your expenses, but not enough to draw too much attention to you. Each time you take out that one bill, another will appear to take its place."

"I know a lot of people who'd hand over their firstborn for something like this."

"That's the problem with the outside world," Glinda

scowled. "Everything I've heard about New York indicates that most of the people are decent enough. There are robbers and thieves, of course, but most of those are in the government. As far as petty thieves are concerned, if the wallet's taken from you, it will simply reappear again."

"Quite handy!"

"Now, when you're ready to go, perform this charm. Stand on your left foot and say, 'Zimba.' Then stand on your right foot and say, 'Zumba.' Finally stand on both feet and say, 'Zow.' Immediately you will find yourself on the northwest corner of Broadway and Forty Second Street."

"How will I come back?" the Wizard asked.

"The same charm will take you back to your quarters in the Emerald City."

"Thank you, Glinda," the Wizard said.

"Good. Now that that's out of the way, do you remember how to play klobbyosh?"

"I remember how you always beat me," he answered.

"Good. After dinner we'll play a few hands. Then after breakfast tomorrow morning, you can leave."

Cherri led him to his quarters where the Wizard occupied himself by repeating the charm, but without using the prescribed footwork. Later, at the banquet hall, Glinda shared a dinner of tomato soup and a delicious vegetable casserole made memorable by a red sauce with a taste as intense as its color. Dessert was marionberry ice cream, which cooled his mouth after the red sauce. After dinner, in which Glinda made some light conversation about the

Sorcerer Soob and the Wizard's recent rediscovery of the Silence Stone, Oscar and Glinda repaired to a game room, where she trounced him in five games of klobbyosh.

"What was your father like?" Oscar asked after a time.

"Not terribly different from yours, I'm afraid." Oscar had years before told Glinda of his childhood as second-fiddle to a con-artist. "Mother just says he got lost and ended up in the outside world, but that's not quite true. He left of his own accord. He was a magician of sorts, but he wanted to make a name for himself, and so he did. I suspect that he missed court intrigue, or he wanted to get away from mother."

"I'm sorry to hear it, and I hope you don't think I'm prying. It's just that I've been thinking about my own father of late. Did I ever mention that he was imprisoned in New York?"

"No, I don't recall that," Glinda said.

"Trying to scam the city was not his smartest con."

"He left out an important step... become a politician first."

Oscar laughed. "I was ten years old at the time. I would've been sent to an overcrowded orphanage or, if lucky, auctioned off to the highest bidder and sent across country to some unknown family. I escaped jail thinking I'd join a street gang. There were lots of them back then. This was 1841 and the cities were overrun and riddled with disease and desperation. But then I saw the circus had come to town. The rest, as they say, is history. I'll be glad to see how much the world has improved in nearly a century!"

"I hope you won't be too disappointed if it's not."

"Well, it can't have gotten any worse!"

After a hearty breakfast the next day, Glinda wished him well. "Be safe, Oscar, and have fun!"

Standing on his left foot, Oscar waved goodbye and said, "Zimba." Then, standing on his right foot, he said, "Zumba." Finally, standing on both feet, he said, "Zow."

CHAPTER III
THE WIZARD SEES THE WIZARD

The first thing the Wizard became aware of was the incredible amount of noise. The sounds of automobile engines, horns honking, police whistles, newsboys hawking their wares, all blended together into an indecipherable hum. The automobiles captured his attention; they had existed when his balloon returned him to the Great Outside World after he'd ruled Oz for so nearly thirty years, but they didn't look like these, nor were there so many of them. Those older cars had been the inspiration for the Scalawagons, but their elegance had been replaced by slapdash expediency and fumes! "Could Oz become noisy and congested like this?" he wondered.

Then he became aware of someone shoving his shoulder and a rough male voice saying, "Outa the way, buddy. Ya wanna cross the street or doncha?"

Half walking, half being pressed onward by the throng, he found himself crossing Broadway. The immense crowds must have been due to the World's Fair, but there were terribly long lines at soup kitchens operating out of army trucks. He continued slowly eastward on Forty-Second Street, pausing to look in store windows. So many of the theaters were closed, along with the burlesque shows, that it looked more like a frontier town. He walked along the street looking for a hotel. A lot of them were shut down, as well. Then suddenly the words on a theater marquee stopped him cold:

THE WIZARD OF OZ

"That I've got to see!"

He first embarked on getting a hotel on the next block. He signed the register, received his room key, relinquished his valise, and rode the elevator to the fourth floor. A grinning bellboy showed him his room, stowed the valise on a low stand at the foot of the bed, and stood by the open door with his hand outstretched, palm upward. When he left with a scornful look. Oscar remembered too late that bellboys expected to be tipped, and made a note to tip him later.

He looked around his room to see whether there were any marvels that he could tell Ozites about when he returned. He spotted a large box, made out of some reddish wood that had been polished. On its front were two knobs, a kind of rectangular panel, and an area which had been cut into an ornamental, decorative shape; the panel seemed to be made out of glass, and the ornamental area had a kind of fabric in the front. "Ah, I think I know what you are," he said, going over to the box and fiddling with the knobs. When he turned the left one to the right, he heard a click, the glass panel lit up, and suddenly music sounded.

The Wizard's initial experience with radio had involved a magical microphone and earphones. He'd developed a different kind for the Magic Picture, but it didn't always function. So it was interesting to see what radio in the outside world had advanced into!

He moved the right knob, and as he did so he saw a vertical line on the glass panel move to the right. There was a kind of whistling noise, and then the Wizard heard a man's voice speaking: "...ultimatum to Poland, demanding that Poland withdraw from the Polish Corridor, so that the province of East Prussia will be reunited with Germany, and the Free City of Danzig will return to German control." Well! That certainly didn't sound good! The voice continued: "Of course, only five days ago Mussolini warned Hitler that if Germany attacked Poland, Italy would not honor the Pact of Steel." The Wizard shook his head in bewilderment. Mussolini? Hitler? Who were these people? And Italy was at the other end of Europe from Poland. Why was Italy involved in all this? Discouraged, the Wizard turned the knob again, and the vertical line moved horizontally; the Wizard noted that there was a horizontal line marked with numbers. When the vertical line reached the next number, he heard a voice say, "...Lombardo and his Royal Canadians." Then music started to play again, and after an orchestral introduction, a nasal voice began to sing: "South of the border, down Mexico way..." The Wizard knew that Canada and Mexico did not have a common border, so he reasoned this was the name of a band. He turned the dial again, and the music was gone.

After locating four other points on the horizontal line which gave him either music or voices, one of which announced that he was listening to the Blue Network of the National Broadcasting Company, Oscar used the left knob to turn the radio off. He sat down, his head spinning. The civilized world had certainly changed since he'd left it. Perhaps it was just growing pains from the Great War and the Treaty of Versailles that followed. Oscar had been living in Oz when those events occurred, but even in the realm of Faerie, the Great War, and the countless lives it took, was news. But that was long ago. Surely the world would never repeat such a grotesquely grievous mistake again! In any case, he determined he'd have fun at the World's Fair.

Time for lunch, then back to the theater to watch *The Wizard of Oz*. That should prove interesting!

He went into the hotel dining room, sat down and looked at the menu. Since life in Oz had wholly destroyed his old appetite for meat, he ordered an eggplant dish with a side salad, and chose a piece of cherry pie for dessert.

Once the Wizard paid for the meal and got change, he summoned the bellboy from earlier and handed him a generous tip. Smiling at the young man's effusive gratitude, the two entered into a pleasant conversation, and Oscar learned that he was a Broadway actor, currently in-between shows, but he'd managed to land the lead in several, including a popular one the year before called *Dame Nature*.

Oscar left the hotel an hour or so later to see *The Wizard of Oz*, which the bellboy assured him was fantastic.

In the old days he'd seen live shows on the stage, but the moving pictures had consisted of slapstick comedies, documentaries, and westerns. Theaters had been smaller then and not as ornate, especially when compared to this movie palace, which amazed him in its opulence. A statue of a goddess that would've made Lurline blush stood at either side of the screen. Hanging from a cathedral ceiling was a giant crystal chandelier, illuminating the plushly carpeted stairs and marble floors. Also the screen was much larger than screens had been back at the turn of the century.

Many of the seats were taken, most by couples who were talking and eating popcorn. A smartly-dressed usher walked him to one on the aisle, half way between the entrance and the screen. Music was playing, he presumed in order to occupy the attention of those who had come early to the showing of the film. He ended up sitting next to a mother and her excited daughter.

At length the lights went out, the screen lit up, and the Wizard was puzzled to see not *The Wizard of Oz*, but an animated drawing which told a story about a mouse. What was even more remarkable was that the story was in color and the animals talked; when the Wizard had seen movies in the old days, they were always entirely in black and white, and they were silent; the dialogue was flashed on the screen after the characters' lips moved.

The cartoon was followed by something called

"Movietone News." This was a black and white newsreel. The narrator explained that he was seeing Vyacheslav Molotov, the foreign minister of the Soviet Union, and Joachim von Ribbentrop, the German foreign minister, signing a non-aggression pact. The newsreel went on to show Wendell Willkie announcing that he was seeking the Republican nomination for President in the 1940 election, and denouncing the Tennessee Valley Authority. This was followed by a film of President Roosevelt praising the Hatch Act, which prohibited federal employees from participating in political campaigns.

All well and good, he thought, but when would he finally get to see *The Wizard of Oz*? Not yet, apparently, as several advertisement reels for upcoming movies followed, what he later learned were called trailers. They were entertaining enough, but finally, the opening credits for the movie he wanted to see flashed on the screen, and the theater was filled with the sound of music. Next the cast of characters was displayed and the story began. The Wizard wasn't sure what to expect. He'd hoped it would be a faithful adaptation of the L. Frank Baum book based on Dorothy's first adventure in Oz, but most likely it would be a film version of the popular stage-play from 1902, which he'd managed to catch before returning to Oz. Of course, it could be neither, but given that he was a significant part of that story, and both the book and movie were named after his well-known title, he could barely contain his excitement.

It began in Kansas. Oscar was impressed by the

advancement in cinematic technique, but as the story of Almira Gulch and Professor Marvel unfolded, he made a mental note to ask Dorothy about them. He thought that the girl who played Dorothy was very pretty, but far older and taller than the real Dorothy. Still, she sang the song about going over the rainbow beautifully. Polychrome would certainly enjoy it! The tornado effect impressed him, and when the screen suddenly blossomed into color, he gasped along with the rest of the audience.

The Munchkins amused him; they were not very much like Boq or any other Munchkins he knew, and Oscar was surprised that the Witch's shoes that Dorothy put on were red; he knew very well they were silver. Yet, the Wizard became engrossed in the movie as it went on. He had met Dorothy, the Scarecrow, the Tin Woodman, and the Cowardly Lion only after they reached the Emerald City, and although he knew the tale of their journey, it was a joy to see it unfold before him, even if their representations were quite different. He particularly liked Ray Bolger's performance as the Scarecrow, both in the expressiveness of his face and the limberness of his legs. He wondered how the moviemakers would deal with the Cowardly Lion, and when he saw that it was only a man in a lion suit he was initially disappointed, but Bert Lahr's portrayal made him laugh, and he realized the filmmakers couldn't very well employ an actual lion for the role. He also liked the catchy songs everyone sang.

But the scene in the throne room set him back. He had not appeared to all four of them together as a giant talking head; he had seen them one at a time, in a different guise each time, though indeed the talking head had been one of the forms. Obviously the moviemakers had wanted to speed up the story and had combined the four appearances into one in order to do so.

He again knew how the Wicked Witch of the West had been killed, but seeing it happen on the big screen was fascinating, though with that was mixed considerable guilt for having sent Dorothy on such a task in the first place. The world must think him as a coward and terrible man. Perhaps he had been. Before he could fall into a despondent mood, Dorothy and her three friends returned to the palace, and the Wizard puzzled at the reasons for the departure from what had really happened. He focused his attention, of course, on the actor who played him. He had to admit that Frank Morgan was an interesting choice; but his hair was white instead of black, and more luxuriant. Then came the bestowal of the magic gifts: brains for the Scarecrow, a heart for the Woodman, and courage for the Lion. While the movie made in general the right point—that the three already had the qualities they were seeking—what the movie Wizard gave them was considerably inferior to what he had given them in actuality. And the Wizard snorted as Morgan stumbled over the word "philanthropists." He would never have had difficulty with that word! The laughter of the audience, however, informed him that Morgan's mispronunciation had been done for comic effect, but still he felt mis-portrayed.

Then came the scene of his departure in the balloon, leaving Dorothy behind. That was, he judged, fairly accurate, though he cringed when Morgan cried out, "I dunno how it works!" Oscar was an expert balloonist who knew exactly how his balloon worked. But the wind had been against him.

Dorothy had told him how she got back to Kansas, and the Wizard was surprised at the way the movie telescoped what had actually been a long and arduous journey to Glinda's palace. But the film's sentimental ending, with its return to black and white and its assumption that Dorothy's Oz experience had been merely a hallucinatory dream, outraged him. So much for Hollywood!

"So what did you think of the film?" he asked the mother and daughter as the credits rolled.

"I've never seen anything like it!" the mother effused. "It was truly a marvel!"

"And what about you?"

"It was good," the little girl started, "the Munchkins were funny and I liked the Scarecrow, Tin Man and Lion... but the books are better! It wasn't a dream. Dorothy really did go to Oz. I don't know why they had to change that part!"

"She's quite the critic," her mother chimed in. "I haven't read the book since I was a young girl myself, but I do recall that Dorothy went back to Oz."

"She did," the girl elaborated, "it was in the sixth book *The Emerald City of Oz*. She brought Aunt Em and Uncle Henry with her."

Oscar could only smile and agree.

CHAPTER IV
THE WIZARD MEETS ALI

The Wizard emerged from the theater content and walked back to his hotel. It was after five o'clock, and he decided to walk for a bit. When he came to an alley, he paused to see whether any vehicles were coming down it, when suddenly he felt a pressure against his right ankle. Looking down, he observed a small cat covered with black stripes on gray fur, rubbing himself against him. Accustomed to the cats in Oz, he leaned down and picked the animal up, cradling him and supporting his legs. The cat squirmed in his grasp at first, but when he began to stroke his face and neck, he soon stopped squirming and began to purr. Oscar estimated that he was just outgrowing kittenhood but had not yet reached full maturity. He clearly wasn't feral, but neither did he have a collar or any mark of having a guardian. Plus, he was skinnier than he should've been.

"Hello there. What are you doing out here all by your lonesome?" Impulsively, he started walking. As he neared his hotel, he stopped, deciding what to do next. Should he let the cat down? He had removed him from its habitat, as filthy and ill-suited as it, and wasn't about to turn him loose in a strange environment. The poor creature might come to harm. But if he took it with him into the hotel, he might be stopped; he didn't know the hotel policy on animals, but he knew some in the outside world weren't always as enamored of animals as those in Oz were. But what would he do with his new friend? That was a puzzle. Should he take the cat with him back to Oz? Pets were hardly unknown in Oz; Dorothy, after all, had both Toto and Eureka. Even Scraps had a pet stuffed bear once named Grumpy, at least until Grumpy became enamored of an actual bear named Snufferbux.

The cat looked up at him and nestled more deeply into his arm, purring more loudly. Oscar's heart was won. He had impetuously gotten a pet in New York. What would become of the little creature in Oz? Time would tell, but he'd certainly be better off there than here. Holding the cat so that it would be as inconspicuous as possible, he marched into the hotel and went directly to the elevators. The bellboy spotted him instantly and started to say something when he caught Oscar put his finger up to his lips in the universal sign of secrecy. Oscar's imploring look must have won him over because the bellboy just smiled and inclined his head upwards, as if to say "Get him up there and quick before we both get in trouble." Oscar smiled in thanks and took the elevator, which was thankfully empty. The cat squirmed and meowed as it felt the cage rise, but since the two of them were alone no harm was done; and Oscar's gentle stroking soon mollified the poor creature.

Oscar entered his room, placed the cat on the bed and removed his coat. The cat looked up at him and meowed.

"Hungry, my little chickadee?" he asked, recalling the phrase from the trailer of an upcoming W.C. Fields motion picture. "Well, so am I. What shall I call you? You're a tabby by your markings, but 'tabby' is short for Tabitha, which is a girl's name. I've been assuming you're a boy, but let's find out for sure." He reached down and turned the cat on its back; the cat meowed and tried to scratch him, but the Wizard began massaging its belly where the fur was paler and longer than elsewhere, and the cat gave up struggling and enjoyed the attention. "No, you're definitely a boy," the Wizard said. "So Tabitha's out. Let me see." He pondered for a few moments and then said, "I have it! I found you in an alley, you were an alley cat, so I'll call you Ali. That would be more appropriate to a Persian, I suppose, but at least it's better than Tabitha."

After a quick look at the room service menu, Oscar picked up the telephone and ordered halibut for Ali, coffee and salad for himself, and ice cream for both. Ali hid himself under the bed when a waiter arrived with the food. Smart boy. After the waiter left, Oscar took his coffee cup off the saucer and poured some of the cream into it. He set the saucer on the floor and in a few minutes, Ali emerged from beneath the bed and began lapping it up vigorously. While the cat was busy, Oscar cut several pieces of halibut; as soon as Ali had licked up all the cream, he dumped the bits of fish into the saucer. "Don't get used to it. The fish in Oz talk. But don't worry, you'll find plenty of good things to eat there!" The dessert was one scoop of vanilla ice cream in a small bowl; the Wizard was ready to begin when Ali had finished his halibut, so he sliced off one teaspoonful of it and added it to Ali's dish.

When both were finished, the Wizard seated himself in

the room's easy chair, and Ali leaped up into his lap and began to purr. "Well, my little chickadee," the Wizard said, "I have read that the typical life of a cat living in the wild is two or three years, while house cats may live for fifteen or more. In Oz, however, you can expect a far longer life, and I hope a happy one."

For reply Ali used his claws, not fully extended, to crawl up the Wizard's chest; when there, he spread out his arms. The Wizard understood this as an attempt to hug him, and he hugged softly back. "Would that I could rescue all of you," he said wistfully, "but not even Oz has magic enough for that."

CHAPTER V
THE WIZARD AT THE WORLD'S FAIR

"How do I get to the World's Fair?" Oscar asked the desk clerk.

"Oh," the clerk replied, "that's out in Flushing Meadows, on Long Island. The ISS has a special line that takes you right to the front gate."

"What's the ISS, and how do I get on its special line?"

"That's the Independent Subway System, which opened six years ago. Your best bet would be to go over to Eighth Avenue and get a train to Fifty-Third Street. You can transfer there to the train that goes under the East River to Queens. Then transfer to a train marked 'World's Fair.' When you get to the end of the line, you'll be in the

Amusement Area of the Fair; it'll cost you an extra nickel to get off the train."

"That sounds somewhat complicated. Is there an easier way?"

"You could take a taxi, but that's awfully expensive."

Oscar then left the hotel and stepped to the curb of Forty-Second Street. He imagined that motorized taxis responded to signals much as their predecessors did, and when he saw one coming, he raised his arm. The third one stopped. Getting in, he told the driver, "I'd like to go to the World's Fair."

"Sure thing," the cabbie replied, as he turned south on the first side street, then turned west again to follow Broadway south. The cabbie had his radio on, and the Wizard heard "South of the Border" again, followed by "You Are My Sunshine," "Day In, Day Out," "I Didn't Know What Time It Was," "This Can't Be Love," and more. The music had certainly improved since the records Victor Columbia Edison had played! Surely that was a good sign! The Wizard was interested in the buildings and the people as he saw Manhattan flash past the windows of his cab. At last, they went over the Triborough Bridge, with the East River below, and entered Queens.

"What part of the Fair do you want to go to?" the cabbie asked.

Oscar hadn't known that the Fair had "parts," but since the desk clerk had mentioned the Amusement Area, he answered with that.

When the cab pulled up at the Fair's entryway, the Wizard noted that a street sign said Horace Harding Blvd. He handed the driver a bill and left the cab, closing the door on the cabbie's fervently expressed gratitude. Looking around himself, he discovered the subway station, which was closer to him than a larger building marked "Long Island Railway." He noted that the subway emerged from the ground before reaching the Fair, separated from the Fair itself by a fence. He went into the subway station looking for information about the Fair. Not far away from where passengers were depositing fares in the turnstiles, he saw a kiosk selling pamphlets. He went over to the kiosk and saw that the pamphlets contained a map of the fairgrounds. It was laid out generally in the form of a circle, with what the map called the Theme Center—consisting of a tall white stylus labeled the Trylon and a white sphere called the Perisphere, evidently the Fair's symbols—in the center. The Amusement Area was on the east side.

Oscar exited the building and found himself in the Amusement Area. He felt immediately at home, since the merry-go-rounds, roller coasters, and Ferris wheels were much like those in the carnivals in which he'd plied his trade as a balloonist years before. But newer to him were the parachute jump, sponsored by Life Savers, and the miniature train ride, sponsored by Gimbels.

He briefly visited Frank Buck's Jungle Land, which showcased various birds, reptiles, and mammals, including a trained chimpanzee, performing elephants, a "monkey mountain," and camel rides, but he felt uncomfortable and knew Kabumpo and his other Oz friends would take a dim view to this exploitation; he knew all too well from his old days at the circus that the "training" of wild animals often involved painful and unethical methods.

Oscar passed by the Frozen Alive Girl, the Living Pictures, and Billy Rose's Aquacade without much interest. He was more attracted by Alexander Calder's huge orrery, which was a motorized model of the solar system, as well as the Bendix Lama Temple, which according to his brochure was a full-sized replica of the Potala Temple in Jehol, Manchuria, commissioned by William Bendix; yet, as he read further, he discovered that it was being used for a girlie show and rolled his eyes. His interest was also caught by the Dream of Venus Building, which the brochure told him was designed by Salvador Dali and contained living models posing as statues. Oscar found that Dali seemed to have touched upon the nature of dream and faerie quite well. The good artists could do that, he thought.

Oscar then walked toward the Theme Center and tried to decide which of the various pavilions he should explore first. There was so much going on, he decided to just explore.

From the Amusement Area it was easy to see the tip of the Trylon, and he walked in its direction. As he drew closer he could see the Perisphere, which had been obscured by some other buildings. The globe was entered by a moving stairway. Since his brochure told him that the Perisphere contained "a model City of Tomorrow," he joined the line of Fair visitors waiting to mount the stairway and soon found himself entering the globe itself. A walkway circled its interior wall; from it he looked down to see something that was really incomprehensible to him, since he had really no point of reference to a city of 1939 to compare it to.

The auditorium was said to be the size of Radio City Music Hall. Upon two moving balconies, crowds looked down on Democracity, a mammoth model of a city of wide streets, parks, and various large buildings. The crowd moved onward along the walkway, and the Wizard moved with it to the exit. It was as impressive a display as one could hope for, but given the current events he'd recently been hearing on the radio, he suddenly felt doubtful that such a thing would ever be realized. A curved walkway led to the ground, and the Wizard consulted his booklet to get an idea of where he should go next.

Since walking through the Amusement Area had stimulated his appetite, he decided to go to the Food Zone. Two buildings attracted his attention immediately: Borden's and Continental Baking. The brochure informed him that inside the Borden's were one hundred fifty pedigreed cows ("including the original Elsie," whose name sounded familiar; he'd have to inquire of Cowville back in Oz) all being milked mechanically. That seemed grotesque and unnatural. The Continental Baking building, on the other hand, was in the shape of a huge package of bread; the brochure said that it contained exhibits demonstrating the baking of bread and other products, all made from wheat grown in a field behind the building.

Perhaps it would have available some baked bread and other products to be consumed. He entered the building and found that his assumption was correct. There were loaves of bread, wrapped in some kind of shiny paper printed with the words "Wonder Bread"; and there were rolls and other products. Moreover, there were pretty young ladies, who Oscar thought looked like Glinda's girls, offering to make fresh sandwiches for hungry customers. A cheese sandwich took the edge off the Wizard's hunger, but it held no gastronomic appeal. "Is this what food is becoming: artificial, pre-packaged, nutritionless junk?"

From the Food Zone Oscar directed his steps to the Government Zone, where, his brochure told him, sixty governments had buildings. The entryway to the zone was the Court of Peace, a broad open area northwest of the Theme Center. That ought to be informative, he thought, as he wandered among the buildings, trying to decide which ones to enter. The Italian Pavilion attempted to recall the grandeur of the Roman Empire; it was one of the tallest buildings in the zone, and its facade was remarkable for a waterfall which cascaded down it. The brochure told him that there was an Italian restaurant inside it, but then he read that the French Pavilion also featured a restaurant, LePavillon, and he decided upon the latter.

The Lost Tales of Oz

Oscar entered the British Pavilion to look at the copy of the Magna Carta which was lent to the Fair by Lincoln Cathedral. Finding little else in that pavilion to attract his attention, he left and wandered on to contemplate the USSR Pavilion, which featured a gigantic statue in front. What in the world was the USSR? He went inside and asked one of the uniformed guides. The answer only added to his confusion. What did Soviet Socialist mean? The Wizard had, of course, heard of "socialism," which he knew was ridiculed by those who spoke of it in the pro-Capitalist U.S., but the words "Soviet Socialist" meant nothing to him until he remembered the Russian Revolution on the radio and talk of the Soviet Union in the newsreel.

He allowed the young man in the guide's uniform to show him the main feature of the pavilion, which was a life-sized replica of a subway station in Moscow. The Wizard seized on the word "Moscow." The guide went on to inform him that the subway station, designed by Alexey Dushkin, had received the Grand Prize for Design at the Fair. It was indeed a handsome building, but as Oz had thriving communities living underneath the surface, he knew a subway would hardly be welcome.

Oscar entered the Jewish Pavilion. This also puzzled him; he knew who the Jews were, of course, but knew they hadn't had a government since the destruction of over one million Jews and their temple by the Romans in 70 AD, and wondered why they were in the Government Zone. Once inside, he asked a guide for an explanation and was informed that the pavilion was looking forward to the creation of a modern Jewish state. "It would take a miracle for that to happen," he said to him not unkindly.

"And that is just what we are looking forward to," the guide said.

Oscar wished him well and went on to admire the pavilion's facade, which was decorated with a hammered copper bas relief called "The Scholar, the Laborer, and the Toiler of the Soil." That seemed appropriate to the Land of Oz.

The day was wearing on, and it was growing late for him to spend too much more time here. Although he'd left food for Ali and a "Do Not Disturb" sign on the door, he didn't want to spend too long away. He decided to go to one more pavilion; and, using a counting-out rhyme he learned as a boy, chose Poland. He found much to intrigue him, and wished that he had more time to examine the various exhibits, which included a dazzling collection of contemporary Polish paintings; a remarkable historical collection of ancient Polish weaponry and armor; a gallery of folk costumes; and a statue of Polish statesman Jozef Pilsudski.

By now it was time for dinner, and Oscar returned to the French Pavilion. It was crowded, but the headwaiter found him a table for one in a remote corner. Most of the items on the menu he could not read, since he only knew a smattering of French, but he inquired and soon ordered crêpes with blackberry sauce and orange-scented ricotta with a side of flageolet bean and lemony celery tartines. It was larger than he had expected, but he managed to eat it all. For dessert he simply pointed at something on the menu that looked promising, and was not disappointed; it turned out to be a deliciously fruity kind of custard.

By now it was growing late, and as the year slid down toward the autumn solstice the sky was darkening and the air was becoming chilly. There was much more to see, but Oscar was growing tired and decided to leave the rest for another day. He thought it might be interesting to try to return by subway.

While standing on the platform, waiting for his train, he struck up a conversation with the man standing next to him and learned about the complexities of the system, including how to get a transfer so that he would not have to pay another nickel when he changed trains. The Wizard had created a minor form of public transportation in Oz with the Footpath and Footbridge, and they were always free and clean.

The train filled rapidly, and Oscar discovered he would have to stand. He grabbed hold of a strap, as others did, and then the train was off, growling and swaying through the tunnels of the Independent Subway System. Once he forgot to get a transfer and had to put another nickel in the turnstile. And once he got on the wrong train, got off at the next stop, rode four blocks back to the station, and had to wait for the right one. But eventually he got out at Seventh Avenue and 51st Street, the nearest stop to his hotel, and began walking down Seventh Avenue, exhausted from all the confusion, but interested in the various buildings he was passing by.

CHAPTER VI
THE WIZARD IN THE WORLD

As Oscar walked between 47th and 46th streets, a man staggered out of the shadows toward him and lurched into him. "Whyncha watch where ya goin'?" the man demanded before stumbling on. When the Wizard returned to his hotel room and took off his coat, he discovered that the magic wallet was missing; his pocket had been picked. The man who bumped into him had only been pretending to be drunk. Glinda's incantation brought the wallet back in an instant, of course, and the Wizard smiled to think of the pickpocket's consternation.

Ali jumped on his lap as soon as he sat down and at once began to purr. Oscar turned on the radio. Suddenly there was music, and male voices were singing, "... hear Tanner when he whistles in a manner that is quite unique?" This was followed by some whistling that fell short of his interest, and he twisted the dial to hear a voice identify himself as Robert Trout: "Poland has not yet responded to Germany's ultimatum yesterday concerning the Polish Corridor and the Free City of Danzig. Our correspondent in Germany reports that German troops are massing on the Polish frontier. In the event that Poland does not agree to give Hitler what he wants, it seems likely that there will be war."

Poland. Oscar thought back on his experience in the Polish Pavilion at the Fair. He had no idea what the Polish Corridor was, where the Free City of Danzig was, or even what 1939 military equipment was like, but he felt drawn to Poland because of his experiences in its pavilion, and had a bad feeling as to where it would all lead. Again there was the name Hitler in the news report; the Wizard wondered what this leader was like, but the reporter had already gone on to talk about a certain Senator Taft who was considering running for president. He switched off the radio, ensured that Ali got to eat, and prepared for bed.

He awoke the next morning with some stiffness; that wouldn't have happened in Oz, but then again he had done more walking than usual the day before. Resolving to take his time this morning, he ordered breakfast. Ali was asleep on the chair, but awoke and hid himself when the food arrived, only to reemerge when the waiter departed. Oscar gave him all of the food, as he wasn't quite hungry, and he knew he'd be gone again for some hours. Promising Ali he'd return before long, he dressed and went in search of the friendly bellboy from the other day, but he wasn't on duty. So, as he had nothing else to do, he went for a walk around the city where he discovered just how good a New York bagel could be. Feeling considerably cheered, he looked forward to spending another day at the Fair. But he had had enough of the subway and decided to take another taxi. As he emerged from the hotel, he was approached by a man whose clothes gave him the appearance of one who'd seen better days and whose facial stubble suggested that he'd not used a razor in some time. The man held out his hat and said, "Brother, can you spare a dime?"

Oscar had some coins in his pocket, but he also had some bills which he had received as change from breakfast. He fished out one of the bills and dropped it into the man's hat. The man's eyes widened, and he exclaimed, "Oh, brother, thank you thank you thank you! Let me shake your hand!"

Oscar extended his hand and allowed it to be pumped vigorously. The man shoved the bill into his pocket and strode off jauntily towards a disturbingly large group of individuals lined up in front of a soup kitchen.

Ozma would never tolerate this in Oz. There had been panhandlers like this in the United States in the old days, such as the Shaggy Man had once been before he found his way into Oz, but the problem in the outside world had clearly worsened.

A man in an expensive suit strode over to him. "You shouldn't bother. They're all drunkards or else lazy."

"I'm sure that's not the case," Oscar responded. "And if so, it means they *really* do need our help."

The man made a haughty sound of disbelief and walked away.

"How did New York get this bad?" Oscar asked to no one in particular.

"Eh, don't listen to him, he's a bank man!" someone replied. It was the bellboy from the other day. "We've been in a depression since the Stock Market crash, but Roosevelt's fixing things. The New Deal's already making things better; it just takes time."

"Good to hear an optimistic view," Oscar exclaimed. "But I'm concerned about what I've been hearing on the news."

"A lot of people are," the bellboy said.

Oscar proceeded to ask his thoughts about the potential for war, as well as what constituted modern warfare. What he heard left him greatly disturbed.

"Are you heading back to work now?"

"I am," the bellboy said. "By the way, how is your *little friend*?"

"Oh Ali! He's quite good. Thank you for helping out."

"Well, you were lucky. Had the management been there, there'd have been nothing either of us could do. I guess you're keeping him then."

"Yes, I'll be bringing him back home with me."

"Then he's lucky too, then. See you back at the hotel."

The bellboy waved over a taxi, and Oscar stepped to the curb as one pulled over. How different autos were now from the steam cars which were just being introduced at the time of his first trip to Oz! Once more he thought of his Scalawagons and smiled ruefully. The Scalawagons had minds of their own, and even though the ork had been right—they were causing some congestion in the Emerald City—it was nothing like this; plus, they were non-polluting. He could easily make non-sentient automobiles for Oz, but even without an internal combustion engine, he didn't like where that could lead.

"Where to?" the cabbie asked.

"The Fair," the Wizard replied.

At last the cab pulled up at the Long Island Railway Station, where Oscar noticed a taxi stand at which he could get transportation back to Manhattan. He paid the driver, gave a generous tip and got out. He decided that today he would visit the Transportation Zone.

Since he'd been interested in the development of the automobile since the days when he had previously lived in the United States, he entered the General Motors Building. He was seated in a kind of chair which took off into a gigantic area that his brochure called the Futurama. He circled over another model of an American city of the future, which, according to his brochure, had been designed by Norman Bel Geddes and contained half a million individually designed houses, fifty thousand vehicles, and a million trees. His chair circled lower until the houses, cars, and trees became life-sized.

The ride ended when the Wizard's chair took him into another enormous area which had been constructed to replicate a city intersection, with multistory buildings, some of which contained stores. The Wizard passed by an appliance store which advertised Frigidaire refrigerators—"What is a refrigerator?" he wondered—and soon found out. Next, he entered a General Motors automobile dealership, where he could examine the latest models of cars. In addition to the 1940 model Chevrolets, Buicks, and Cadillacs, a number of "cars of the future" were on display.

Oscar passed on to the Ford Pavilion. There he was attracted to a sound of automobile engines coming from the roof. He got into an elevator and was lifted to the roof, where he found stadium-style seating. He sat in one of the seats to see what was making the noise and discovered that race cars were being driven on a figure-8 track. The cars all had the rounded look he had noticed in the streets and GM Pavilion. They went around and around the track, never stopping, except when one of them pulled off for refueling.

Nearby he saw the Chrysler Pavilion and found himself in a large auditorium, like the theater in which he had seen *The Wizard of Oz,* and startlingly cool. A sign told him that the next showing of the film would be at 10 AM, 15 minutes away. At exactly ten, the screen lit up, and the motion picture began. Unlike *The Wizard of Oz*, which had been flat on the screen, this film showed the assembling of a Plymouth automobile in three dimensions.

The internal combustion engine was a marvel, but his misgivings arose again. Although the film didn't show it, he knew gasoline and crude oil were filthy, both in terms of their use, and in terms of their extraction. He'd read of the electric car in one of the pamphlets and knew that it would have been a far better choice.

It was now nearly lunch time, and Oscar wandered around the city intersection in which all the pavilions were located, seeking a restaurant. After lunch, he went on to the Transportation Zone, starting off with what was labeled on a large metal sign the Railroad Conference. He spent some time watching "Railroads on Parade," a live drama telling the story of how railroads began and were developed. He knew a little about this subject, as well, and wasn't surprised to discover that all of the seedier, illegal, and immoral elements were left out. He wandered to an exhibit of early locomotives, some real and some reconstructed; one of the real ones was the original Tom Thumb engine. A steady noise attracted his attention, and he walked over to see the Pennsylvania Railroad had mounted its S1 engine on rollers and was running it continuously at sixty miles per hour.

Oscar strolled through the rest of the Railroad Conference, which was laid out over a broad expanse of territory, for the rest of the afternoon. Among other exhibits, he saw trains from the London Midland and Scottish Railway and the Italian state railway. The latter was powered by electricity, like the hybrid diesel-electric locomotives displayed by the Electro-Motive Division of General Motors. As evening fell, the Fair became lit by dozens of electric lights. The Wizard remembered when the only source of illumination in cities was gaslight. Oz itself got electricity nearly a decade after he'd arrived there.

The part of the Fair he had not yet seen which held the greatest interest for him was the Communications and Business Systems Zone. This attracted him because of his interest in radio. In the Masterpieces of Art Building the Wizard was overwhelmed with three hundred paintings and sculptures which had been borrowed from European museums and galleries for the two-year duration of the fair. He would have loved to spend more time regarding each masterpiece, but contented himself with appreciating only a few as he walked through the thirty-five galleries into which the building was divided.

Fortunately the Firestone Tires Pavilion did not

require much of his time; its only notable feature was a pygmy hippopotamus named Billy, which according to a sign on its enclosure had been a pet of President Calvin Coolidge. His real worth, however, was as a breeding stud. The Wizard was tempted to try and take Billy back to Oz when he returned home, but he knew he'd be pushing his luck.

The IBM Pavilion was more demanding. In addition to its display of electric typewriters and its demonstration of something called an electric calculator, which could achieve fantastically rapid answers to questions put to it on punchcards, IBM had mounted an art gallery with hundreds of paintings borrowed from some seventy nations.

He visited the AT&T Pavilion in the Communications & Business Zone, where he was impressed with the Voder, a machine which spoke to fair visitors with a mechanical voice. It was getting toward dinner time, and the Wizard decided he could visit only one more pavilion before taking on some food. He chose the RCA Pavilion. There was a line, and he found himself behind a boy, probably ten or twelve years old, and his mother. He could not help hearing the boy barraging his mother with questions, none of which she could answer. When the boy asked how the Voder worked, Oscar could not help communicating his guess: "It's probably powered by electricity.

The boy's mother confronted Oscar: "Did you work on the Voder?"

"No," he admitted, taken aback at having been so rudely challenged.

"Then I thank you not to offer your opinion!"

Oscar was speechless. Fortunately, just then the line began to move.

Within the RCA Pavilion was at last something possibly worthy of Oz: television. Standing in front of a little box about five inches high, the Wizard saw brown images of human beings moving and heard them speaking; then, turning his head, he saw and heard the human beings whose images were on the box. Next the Wizard was invited to take his place among the actors, and as he looked at the box he could see himself moving, as if he had been reduced to a being less than five inches high. Early movies had been photographed on celluloid tape, which was later run through a machine which cast the photographed images on a screen. But television did away with the celluloid. More significantly, it did away with the delay between making the photograph and running the film through the projector; television was instantaneous. It was wireless photography. It wasn't much—truth be told—and it was certainly no Magic Picture, but it was a start.

There were other displays in the RCA Pavilion, but after walking around for a time, Oscar grew hungry again and found a restaurant where he could sit and eat and think. Where should he go from here? He took the brochure out of his pocket, unfolded it, and looked through the other zones. Finally, he decided he'd had enough for the day and would head back.

Riding along, he looked out the window. He had not really seen much of New York, but there was too much of it to see and as he neared his hotel he observed a theater which advertised "Classic Comedies!" Realizing he would enjoy a few laughs, he rapped on the glass panel that separated him from the driver and said, "Stop here and let me off, please."

The young woman in the box office told him that the show was continuous; the theater was playing six motion pictures, four from the silent era and two with sound, over and over again; you could go in at any time, stay as long as you wanted to, and leave at any time. That suited him just fine; he bought a ticket, entered the theater, stood in the back for a while to let his eyes adjust to the darkness, found a seat, and began enjoying Chaplin, Lloyd, and Keaton, as well as Fields, in the film *Poppy,* and Laurel and Hardy in *The Music Box.*

The Wizard laughed especially heartily at *The Music Box.* This was the first time he had seen this duo, and he found the interplay between them delightful. 'They are so Ozzy!' he told himself, and in his imagination, he began to spin methods of transporting them to the Land of Oz, focusing at the outset on where they would fit in best. Eventually, he thought of Oogaboo, whose queen, Ann Soforth, was so bored so much of the time she got permission from Ozma to move her entire community from the Winkie Country to the Gillikin Country just so they could all have a vacation! Oogaboo could stand some amusement. In the end, however, he scolded himself for his impracticality: this Laurel or Hardy probably had lives and families here, besides which, they were entertaining a world that clearly needed it. Oz was not a refuge for mortals, after all. That had been an ancient decree from on high, and few exceptions to that rule were allowed. He'd been one of them, after all. No, he couldn't very well start bringing people from the outside world to live in Oz. Then again, Dorothy had been allowed to bring her family. She wasn't the only one. Betsy's parents had come to live in Oz, as had Trot's mother, though she'd opted not to stay. He didn't have any family, but perhaps he *could* bring a friend or two. Yet, even if he did, shouldn't it be someone who really needed it? But there were so many, including the throngs of homeless that he'd seen.

Safety Last was just beginning on the theater's screen; the Wizard had already seen and enjoyed it once, so he realized that the series of six classic comedies was beginning its sequence again. He rose and made his way out of the theater.

CHAPTER VII
THE WIZARD AND THE WISE CUSTODIAN

On his third day at the Fair, Oscar visited the Hall of Nations and its Court of Peace, which seemed ironic in light of the disturbing current events he kept hearing on the radio. Nearby was a Production and Distribution Zone, dedicated to "industries whose task it was to transform natural resources into commodities." This sounded ominous, a feeling that was confirmed when he met a member of the recently formed Wilderness Society and learned that the legacy of the Industrial Revolution was wreaking havoc with native flora, fauna and indigenous peoples. If the world wouldn't blow itself up in wars, it was determined to kill itself in other ways.

As these thoughts depressed him, he moved on to some of the quirkier attractions, such as the seven-foot tall "talking" robot Elektro. The robot couldn't hold a candle to Tik-Tok, but was entertaining, particularly when he chided passersby. There was a display of color slides shown in Kodak's Hall of Color and another of air conditioning inside a giant igloo marked Carrier Heating and Air Conditioning.

When all was said and done, Oscar had to admit to himself that the New York's World Fair had proved anticlimactic. He'd come to be inspired by the new inventions and world's progress, but inspiration seemed to be in short supply. Yes, there were some small leaps towards making the lives of people easier, but overall, he saw a world headed towards large-scale violence, crass consumerism, and the destruction of nature. As he walked towards the exit, lost in his own dark thoughts, he bumped headlong into a dark-skinned man sweeping the floor.

"I'm so sorry," Oscar apologized. "I wasn't paying attention."

"Happens a lot," the janitor said. "Least you had the courtesy to apologize."

"Where I come from, most people treat each other with love and respect, and when that fails, our leader has those traits in abundance."

"Then you must come from a special place," the janitor replied. "Here, in the rest of the world, people jus' want more power…"

"… and money," Oscar finished for him.

"Sign of the times," the janitor replied. "So, did you have a good time?"

Oscar almost said yes, but the man had such an open and honest expression that he reassessed his response. "If I'm to be perfectly honest, as magnificent as this all is—and I certainly enjoy new inventions, being an inventor myself—I can't help but feel that it's all… well, futile."

"Well, that's certainly a different response than any I heard since workin' here. If you got a spare moment, I'd be interested to hear why you think that way. And don't mind me sweeping. If they don't see me workin' every single moment, they're liable to let me go and hire someone else."

"I don't mind," replied the Wizard. "I'm Oscar, by the way." He extended his hand to shake the other man's.

"Pleasure to meet you, Oscar. Call me Stanley."

"Pleasure to meet you, as well."

"So," Stanley started conspiratorially, "What do you mean when you say it's all futile?"

"You've no doubt been hearing the news reports?" Oscar asked.

"Certainly."

"It seems to me like there's trouble on the horizon."

"Isn't there always?"

"I don't know," said Oscar. "To be honest, where I come

from things are peaceful most of the time. I guess I don't much pay attention to what's going on in the larger world. I suppose I assumed the governments of the world had learned their lesson from the Great War."

"Nothin' doin'," said Stanley. "The world's been the mess it is since the beginnin' of civilization and it's gonna stay that way 'til the end. And d'you know why?"

"Can't say as I do."

"Them rich folks who run the countries and companies, they're not stupid. They just don't care about doin' right by us. Sure, they put on a big show of it. But it's like this here World's Fair. Put on a big enough show and the people will think you really got their backs when all you're doin' is foolin' them so they won't notice all the bad things you're really doin' and the good things you ain't. When war breaks out, and it will, keep an eye out. War's boom time for them rich folk and their pals in the White House."

"So, that's it then," Oscar sighed. "The world's doomed."

"Always was... but what does that matter?"

"I don't think I follow," Oscar said, surprised.

"You and me ain't in charge of the world," Stanley clarified. "Never have been. You're in charge of you and yours. I'm in charge of me and mine. That's it. What the world does, well, that's their business; the Lord will deal with them in His own good time. My job is do the best I can while I'm here; and that's plenty work enough if y'know what I mean. Besides, it ain't all bad. Still plenty of good people out there trying to do the right thing."

The Wizard pondered a moment on what the man said before finally shaking his head. "You know, I came here looking for inspiration and hope, but until now I didn't find it."

"Why, that's a nice thing for you to say, Oscar. But it's just plain ol' common sense."

"Tell me," Oscar started, trying to suss him out, "if you could live where I live, a place of peace, kindness and comfort, would you want to?"

Stanley looked at him keenly. "You know, there was a time when I would have said 'absolutely' and packed my bags," he laughed, "but I've made do in this crazy world and now I've got kids and grandkids to think about. Sure, I could use more money, but that's most everybody. Besides, what would happen to New York if all the good people just picked up and left?"

"That's another good point," the Wizard smiled. "Well, it was truly a pleasure meeting you." With that, Oscar shook his hand. "Now, I have a gift for you," and with that he handed him a stack of large bills.

"You don't gotta be doin' that," Stanley said, surprised and a little put off. "I don't need a handout."

"It's not," assured Oscar. "Consider it an investment in your family's future from an old man who's got more than he knows what to do with."

"You ain't that old," Stanley pointed out. "I dunno."

"If I told you how old I really was, you wouldn't believe me. I just like to help good people. Besides what else am I going to do with it?"

Still shocked, Stanley thanked him, as Oscar walked off to return to the taxi stand by the Long Island Railway building, where he took a cab.

The sky was growing dark, and his stomach was announcing that it was time for dinner. He went to the corner and saw that he was on 41st Street, only a block south of the street where his hotel was situated, so he began walking north. He looked to see if the bellboy was at work.

He was. After greeting him, Oscar asked him "If you could live anywhere, where would it be?"

"Why, right here!" the bellboy said without missing a beat. "New York may not be perfect, but it's the best place in the world. There's always something to do, interesting people from all over—like yourself—and plenty of work for an actor. Believe me, I came from the Midwest, and it wasn't for me."

"What about all the noise and crime and pollution?" Oscar pressed. "Wouldn't an unspoilt paradise be more enjoyable, if it had good people, of course?"

"If such a place existed, I suppose it would be nice… But I'm happy here. Besides I just landed another part!"

"Congratulations!" exclaimed Oscar.

"Where do you live, by the way? I never got around to asking. Your accent is familiar."

"I was born and raised in Omaha," Oscar replied.

"Why, that's where I'm from!" the bellboy cried.

"No kidding! You don't have much of an accent left."

"Theater training; you have to sound like the

bourgeoisie to succeed in this business. What about you? Have you been back there?"

"Not for a long time. I joined the circus, traveled for a bit. And then I found my unspoilt paradise," Oscar added with a wink.

"I'm happy for you, Oscar. I think we both found the places we were meant to be."

Later in his room, after Ali ate and settled on the bed, Oscar turned on the radio. Immediately he heard the voice he identified as Robert Trout's: "... waiting for a response to its ultimatum, Germany has attacked Poland. Luftwaffe airplanes have bombed targets within Poland, and soldiers of Hitler's Wehrmacht have crossed the border into the country, meeting with only token opposition from the Polish army."

Oscar shook his head. Poor Poland, he thought. Poor everyone. War was a terrible business, and now with even more terrible weapons at each country's disposal... Again he heard the name Hitler. He switched the dial and heard an announcer's voice: "...Whiteman and his orchestra playing George Gershwin's 'Rhapsody in Blue.' This was followed by a long clarinet wail that immediately captured Oscar's attention, and he settled back to listen.

At the conclusion of the music, he turned the dial again and heard a man's voice: "... analysis of today's news by H.V. Kaltenborn." A reedy voice began speaking: "Well! Now we know what von Ribbentrop and Molotov were hatching at their meeting the other day. They were planning to carve up poor Poland between them." Oscar continued to listen for a few minutes, but what the speaker developed at greater length began to depress him.

What man might accomplish if they would but put all their energies towards helping the human race instead of destroying it, he wondered, musing on what things might be like if men were governed by love instead of that mad lust for greed and power that seemed to grip them. In the old days it was called gold sickness, referring to the belief that riches came with a curse, and that man was particularly vulnerable to it. Perhaps that's why Oz and the various fairylands were never truly stable until they were governed by the benevolent supernatural beings who were meant to govern them.

He turned the dial again and heard the beeping of a telegraph key, over which a man's breathless voice said, "Good evening, Mr. and Mrs. America and all the ships at sea, let's go to press. Flash!" But the disheartening news was not up to the man's excited delivery of it, and the Wizard switched off the radio and went outside for a walk.

The sky was darkening, but the city itself was becoming illuminated; in addition to the incandescent street lamps, every store along the streets shone out with an illuminated sign. "So many lonely and abandoned people..."

After getting far enough from his hotel that he thought he had better go back before he got lost, a flashily dressed woman walked up to him and said, "Hey, Big Boy, you lookin' for a good time?" He did not reply but turned his steps quickly in the direction of his hotel.

CHAPTER VIII

THE WIZARD OF THE EMERALD CITY

After breakfast the next morning, Oscar reached over and turned on the radio. He spun the dial until he found music to listen to. He heard a raspy voice singing, "...Ink a dinka do, a dinka dee, a dinka doo, it's got the whole world..." and turned the dial again until he found a baritone voice crooning, "Where the blue of the night meets the gold of the day..." This suited him better. "A lot has changed since last I lived here," he said to Ali, still licking his plate, "thankfully not all for the worse."

Eventually he began to yawn. "Ali," he addressed the cat, "I came here expecting to see the progress my former country was making, feel refreshed and maybe find ideas for new inventions. Sadly, I didn't find any of that. But I made some new friends, and that includes you." He removed the empty bowl, then showered, shaved and dressed. "Are you ready to go to Oz?" Ali looked up at him and meowed.

With the letter opener he found on the desk in his room, he punched holes in the fabric of his valise. Ali paid close attention, and Oscar told him, "You probably won't like having to ride in this, but consider it a necessary evil."

Oscar set his valise on the bed and began packing it. Ali hopped up on to watch. When he had everything else in it, he picked up Ali, popped him into the valise, and snapped the valise shut. Ali emitted loud meows of complaint at first, but after some coaxing on Oscar's part, eventually he got quiet;

the holes he had made were sufficient to allow Ali to breathe, so he wasn't concerned. "You won't be in there for long, just enough to get you to your new home."

Oscar considered leaving from the hotel room directly. He'd certainly have more privacy that way, but he didn't want to alarm anyone by just disappearing into thin air. Picking up the valise, Oscar made his way to the elevator and descended to the lobby. There, the bellboy caught sight of him and smiled broadly, walking over to vigorously shake his hand and bid him goodbye. Oscar then handed him a considerable tip. "Don't spend it all in one place, Monty," he joked. Astounded, the bellboy hugged him hard and departed.

The Wizard was touched. "I might not be able to bring everyone to Oz," he thought, "but at least I helped a few while I was here. And I can help a few more before I go."

With this in mind, he paid his hotel bill and then hurried to the soup kitchen that had caught his attention on his first day. There, to the astonishment of all, he created a stir by handing out cash to everyone in line. Some of his beneficiaries winked at one another, evidently concluding that he was some eccentric madman. Nevertheless, he enjoyed helping people who needed it and soon found himself playing to the appreciative crowd. Should he finish his act with a spectacular exit?

"I should just walk away," he thought. But no. These people could stand to believe in something besides what they saw and heard. Warming to the idea, he began, "I am the Wonderful Wizard of Oz." The crowd laughed, and he went on: "You might have heard of me from the famous book Mr. Baum wrote about me. I came to visit your lovely city, but now I must return to my home country! I have a message for you from Oz. Are you listening?"

When the crowd shouted and giggled, he went on: "As a visitor from afar, I must say that while your technology's improved a bit since the last time I was here, I'm rather disappointed in the direction your world is going. Though you may not be able to change that, you can change your own small piece of the world, and do you know how?" After waiting a second for the crowd to absorb the question, he went on. "Love each other, no matter where another person comes from or what they look like or how different they seem from you. Do you think you can do that? Say yes, and I'll show you a feat of magic!" The crowd yelled "Yes!" and he proceeded to move his feet. He saw in the near distance a policeman in a blue uniform coming closer and calling out, "Here, now! What's all this?"

He had not a moment to lose. "Remember what I said, love each another!" he cried. Then he performed Glinda's spell. Left foot: "Zimba!" Right foot: "Zumba!" Both feet: "Zow!"

And he was suddenly in his room in Ozma's palace.

He could only imagine the looks on everyone's faces! He put his valise on his bed and unsnapped it. Out jumped the cat, who looked around at his new surroundings, stretched, and began licking himself. "Welcome to your new home, Ali!"

ALI CAT IN OZ

by Sam Sackett & Joe Bongiorno

Did you know that Oz is one of the most cat-friendly fairylands in the world? Most people know of Dorothy's pink kitten Eureka and Bungle the Glass Cat, but there's also Fraidy Cat of Ogodown, Pimpken of the Quadling Country, the Crotched Cat, who visits every so often, and the Patchwork Cat Bitsy, made from the scraps of Scraps! In just the Emerald City alone, there are numerous cats, who like to be paraded on leashes during special events. Oz also boasts several cat communities. Catty Corners has cats as large as boys! There are the two-headed Fraid Cats of Scare City, the mysterious cats of Caterpill, the cats and cat-people of Nekoosa, and the Cat Café, where cats eat, nap and chase magical yarn!

Even in the lands outside of Oz, there are cats aplenty. You've probably heard of the baffling Cheshire Cat of Wonderland (not to mention Dinah and her kittens), but there's also an entire Valley of Cats in Merryland, and the flying cats of Jelly Bean Island. Finally, it's said that if you venture into the Kingdom of Dreams (which is dangerous and I don't recommend), you may just find the Dreamlands, whereupon one can meet the Cats of Ulthar. But beware the Mooncats, who are not friendly at all!

Ali Cat is one of the sweetest cats you'll meet. The Wizard brought him here from New York back in 1939. This is his first recorded adventure in Oz, and I hope not his last!

Betsy Bobbin

CHAPTER I

THE PRINCESS AND THE GHOST CAT

Having just gotten back from a trip to New York in the Great Outside World, where he visited the World's Fair and caught a showing of the film *The Wizard of Oz*, Oscar Diggs, the real Wizard of Oz, placed his valise on his bed in the Palace and opened it. Out popped a grey-furred, black striped cat. The Wizard had met the young cat a block from his hotel, on 41st street. Ali, for that's what he named him when he decided to rescue the friendly tabby, looked around to take in his surroundings. The room seemed very much like the New York hotel room they had just come from.

"Well, my little chickadee," said the Wizard, who had recently viewed a W.C. Fields motion picture, "this is your new home, and you're going to love it! Oz is a veritable paradise compared to where you used to live."

Ali jumped down off the bed and began to explore. There were four doors; three were closed. Ali sniffed at them without learning anything about what lay on the other side, then moved on to the open door. It led into a large room with a sofa and two easy chairs. Through an open archway he saw another room with a table, four wooden chairs, and some things he could not identify along the wall. Ali returned to the room with the sofa and easy chairs and explored it without finding anything interesting. He did find another closed door on the far side of the room, but another olfactory examination yielded nothing.

Returning to the bedroom, Ali noticed a window. By standing on his back paws with his front paws on the sill, he could look out. He saw an expanse of grass, intersected with what his New York-trained eyes identified as sidewalks; the paths were bordered with flowers on both sides. As a cat, Ali was colorblind, but now it was as if he could identify the floral hues. This initially startled him, but he grew accustomed to it.

And then he saw scampering across the lawn, – was it? – could it be? – Yes, it surely was – a mouse! Ali's feline instincts launched him into the air to leap on this prey, and he slammed into the glass then fell back on the floor. As an alley cat, he was not unfamiliar with such features of buildings as windows, but he had never before seen a window that clean!

"Well, little Ali," the Wizard said. "We're going to have to make arrangements so that you'll be more comfortable looking out." There was a telephone on the nightstand beside the bed; the Wizard picked it up and spoke into it briefly. A few minutes later there was a knock on the door. Uncertain what to expect, Ali hid himself under the bed.

He heard the Wizard's voice say, "Thank you, Galden. Come on in."

Then there were sounds of a door opening and closing, footsteps, and some other sounds Ali could not identify.

And then a man's voice greeted Oscar, expressing his gladness to have him back. After some conversation, he said "That should do it, Oscar. Can I get you anything else?"

"No, thank you, old friend," the Wizard replied. "I'll be working most of the day. Why don't you take the time to relax."

They conversed for a little longer until finally the door opened and closed again. Cautiously Ali emerged from under the bed. There, below the window, stood a footstool; it was almost as tall as the bottom of the window frame. And sitting on the footstool was a pillow.

"Now, kitty," the Wizard said, "you can look out the window all you want and be more comfortable. You'll see lots of green in the Emerald City, which is quite unlike the grays of New York City, where you come from."

Ali hopped up onto the pillow and meowed his thanks.

"Now, if you were to head north, you'll find that the Gillikin people enjoy purple, and many of the flowers and buildings there reflect that color. In the east, the Munchkins like shades of blue, and again the plants and homes reflect that; in the west the Winkies prefer the brighter yellow colors; and in the south, where Glinda the Good lives, they prefer reddish hues. Perhaps most importantly, the animals talk here, as you'll soon find out when you discover your own voice. Also, there are various magical creatures about which you've never seen in the world we came from. Don't be alarmed by them. Most are friendly."

The tabby marveled at this. It all sounded so exotic and strange. He determined he'd stay as close as possible to the palace, at least until he had a better idea of things.

"Ali," the Wizard said, "we ate breakfast this morning in New York, so you shouldn't be too hungry. I'm going to go down to the Throne Room to see Ozma. I know that cats are curious and like to explore, so when I go I'm going to leave the door open a crack so that you can get out. I'll have Galden bring some food for you up here this evening, so I hope you'll be back for that. You'll find most of the smells are pretty strange as there are a variety of creatures who live in the Royal Palace and beyond. Ah, and you should also be aware that there are two other cats living here, the Glass Cat of Oz, who is smart, but very vain, and Eureka, the Pink Kitten, who is sweet, but can be irascible at times. I leave it up to you to make friends with them if you'd like."

And then the Wizard left.

Ali settled down on his pillow for a while, looking out the window, hoping to see the mouse again, and thinking that he'd not much like meeting these strange cats, not at least until he'd staked out his territory and left more of his scent around. Cats being nocturnal animals, and the time being in the daylight, Ali found himself becoming a little drowsy; but the excitement of being in a new situation, very different from any he had previously experienced, kept him awake. After a few minutes he decided to take advantage of the Wizard's arrangement and go exploring.

As the Wizard had said, the door was left open just enough that Ali could get through it. He found himself in a long hallway, with many doors on each side. Not far away down the hallway to his right, was an opening; at the end of the hallway, to his left, were stairs going down. He paused, deciding what to do next.

One of the doors across the hallway to his right opened, and a small dark dog emerged. His toes clicked on the hallway floor as he came over to Ali. "My name is Toto," the dog announced. "I'm a dog, and dogs chase cats."

"Dogs don't usually explain themselves first," Ali said. He wasn't frightened. As a New York alley cat, he had dealt with more impressive attackers before.

"Yes, well my mistress doesn't like it when I bark or bother Eureka, so I'm giving you fair warning."

Ali didn't know who his mistress was, but suspected she'd not like his current behavior either. Unwilling to wait to find out if this Toto meant business or not, Ali arched his back and bristled, his hairs erecting themselves so that he seemed bulkier than he really was. He bared his teeth and hissed. Then, without further warning, he slapped the dog's nose with a lightning-fast lunge.

Toto yelped with surprise and pain. "Ouch! What'd you do that for?" Then he turned and scampered back through the door he had come out of.

Ali would have shaken his head if he could. He'd never understand dogs, not even talking ones, apparently. Then he turned and headed toward the stairs, intending to explore whatever lay beneath the floor he was on. Tail erect, he climbed down the stairs and found himself in a large room containing rows of shelving. He went to the nearest row and sniffed. He did not recognize the smell. He stood on his hind legs and supported himself with his front paws grasping the shelf above. Again the smell was unrecognizable.

Then suddenly a movement to his left caught his eye. It was a mouse! He dropped to the floor and sprang. The mouse screamed with pain and fear as Ali's claws gripped it. "Ouch!" the mouse said. "That hurts!"

Ali paused, blinking. This was the second time he had been spoken to by an animal that had never spoken in New York. He was amazed to find himself saying, "I didn't know you could talk too."

"Of course I can talk," the mouse said. "In Oz all the animals can talk. You're talking too. Now kindly remove your claws from my back. They're sharp."

Ali relaxed his grip, but not enough to let the mouse escape. His mind was confounded by this new information. "I forgot. The Wizard said I could talk," he said.

"How did you grow up to the size you are without ever finding out you could talk?" the mouse demanded.

"I grew up in New York, and none of the animals there can talk."

"New York!" The mouse sniffed. "Never heard of it, but it must be a poor place if the animals can't talk. Please take those claws out of my back. You're hurting me."

Ali complied. His stomach was really full from the breakfast in New York, and talking mice didn't seem so appetizing. On the other hand, they might still be fun to play with. He was about to ask as much when the mouse scampered away out of sight. So much for playing with him; Ali performed the feline equivalent of a shrug.

Ali spent the next few minutes roaming around the large room and not finding anything of interest. Giving another mental shrug, he climbed back up the stairs and found himself in the hallway again. Halfway down was an opening that he had not noticed before. He went to it and looked in. At the end were large double doors with soldiers seated on chairs in front of them. Ali guessed that this was an entryway and the soldiers were there to let people in and out; since they paid no attention to him, he turned to look at the side walls. On the right was a door much like the other doors he had seen in the hallway; on the left were double doors smaller than those guarded by the soldiers.

Tail erect, Ali went to the smaller double doors and found no obvious way that he could open them. He emitted a

"Meow," hoping that someone on the other side of the doors would open them and let him in.

It worked. There were footsteps on the other side of the doors, and the right one opened. To Ali's surprise, it was opened by his friend the Wizard.

For a moment Ali paused, taking in the contents of the room. At the far end was a large, elaborate chair, occupied by a girl – Ali had no standards of human beauty, but other humans would have called her lovely – with two large poppies in her hair, one above each ear. The girl was dressed in a loose white gown.

"Your Highness," the Wizard said, "allow me to present to you my friend, Ali the cat. Ali, this charming lady is Princess Ozma of Oz."

The girl smiled. "Ali, I'm pleased to make your acquaintance. Come here and let me get to know you better."

Ali padded across the floor and leaped into the Princess' lap. She stroked him gently and he began to purr.

"I'm glad you took him with you!" Ozma beamed.

"It was meant to be," the Wizard said with a wink.

"Are you a boy or a girl cat?"

"A boy cat, Your Highness."

"You seem very sweet. I'm sure you'll be a lovely addition to the kingdom."

Not knowing what else to say, Ali just purred louder.

"Now," Ozma said, "I'm curious about this Laurel and Hardy you mentioned. I'd like to see them for myself. Let's pull up one of their films on the Magic Picture."

"Certainly."

They turned to look at a picture on the wall which suddenly showed Laurel and Hardy driving through a town in an old car, selling fish. Laurel was blowing a battered trumpet to attract attention. The film continued for the better part of an hour, and Ali fell asleep as Ozma continued to pet him. He roused occasionally as the princess laughed at various scenes in the picture.

As the motion picture concluded, Ali awoke and Ozma said, "I see what you mean. You were right: they are very funny. The slapstick is a bit violent, though."

"The trend in modern entertainment, I'm afraid."

"Symptom of a greater ill, I believe. Nevertheless, these two would certainly cheer up anyone in need of it."

The Wizard pondered for a minute and said, "There aren't too many places in Oz that are in need cheering, but I can think of one where the residents seem somewhat *restless*."

Ozma laughed, as she'd guessed his thoughts. "Oogaboo!"

"Queen Ann and her subjects could use the diversion. Still, I'm not sure these men would be amenable to the idea. They probably have families and lives of their own."

"Perhaps," pondered Ozma, "but you were right about Sherlock Holmes, and I hear he's settling quite comfortably in Oz, even enjoying some light detective work."

"It was different for him. Watson was married, and Sherlock was looking to retire. Also, we knew each other from when I lived in the outside world, so he trusted me.

"True, most mortals would be shocked if we were to just whisk them here out of the blue. Perhaps Glinda might have an idea. Oogaboo could use some healthy distractions."

"I'll let you know what she says."

"Changing the subject; we have a problem that I need to consult with you about."

"What is it?"

"You know the Outside World frequently has trouble with tornadoes."

"Of course," the Wizard agreed. "That's how Dorothy came here."

"This time it brought a flock of gryphons."

"Oh, really? Our friend Snif the Iffin will be pleased! In all his time here, he's yet to meet another like him."

"I wish that were the case," sighed Ozma, "But these aren't griffins. They're *gryphons*. They look similar, but their dispositions are quite different: fierce and violent."

"I've heard about them, but have never seen one. We certainly don't have them in America. I suspect they come from another fairy-world..."

"That happens from time to time. Right now, there's a group causing problems in the Winkie Country. Take a look."

The Magic Picture now displayed an orchard. Among the trees could be seen animals that looked like small winged lions, ripping slabs of roast beef from the trees and gulping them down. A farmer clad in yellow overalls was trying, and failing, to reason with them. The meat from the trees was bountiful and free, but intended for all animals. The gryphons growled and raised their talons menacingly at the farmer, who astutely backed away.

The Wizard commented, "He's clearly not happy. And once they've stripped the beef trees…"

"… they might start going after animals or people," Ozma concluded. "They can't stay in Oz. Even the Kalidah tribes have become peaceable, most of them anways, but it's impossible to reason with these gryphons. Pleasure and domination are their only interests."

"They'd fit in well in the Outside World," the Wizard muttered. "But why not just use the Magic Belt to send them back where they came from?"

"If I ask it to send the gryphons back, there's a chance it will also send Snif and any other griffins in Oz along with them. No, in order for this to work, I'll need to send all the gryphons together, and right now they're not all in one place. Before you came in, I saw one in the Gillikin Country and one here in the Emerald City."

The Wizard pursed his lips thoughtfully. "Perhaps you could transport the outliers back to the main group one at a time. Then, when you have them all together, you could send the whole bunch of them home at once."

"Good idea!" Ozma agreed. "I'll try that"

Ali was fascinated by the conversation, but there was yet much he wanted to accomplish before he settled for a nap. He yawned, and jumped down from Ozma's lap. Tail erect, he marched to the double doors and sat, looking at one of them.

The Wizard laughed. "I think my little friend is hinting that he wants to go out." He went to the door and opened it. "The Emerald City is mostly safe, but if you leave it, just read the signs and avoid anything or anyone that might seem dangerous."

Ali thanked him and left the room, tail erect. He headed toward a set of double doors, guarded by seated men in uniforms. One had a long green beard; the other was clean-shaven and dressed differently altogether. It would take time to learn who everyone was, and whether they were as friendly to cats as the Wizard and Ozma were. Ali approached them, and said, "I'd like to go out please."

The older man rose and opened the door, letting in a burst of bright sunlight, and petting Ali as he marched out.

Ali found himself on a broad ledge from which several steps led downward to a wide sidewalk flanked by spacious lawns bordered by neatly trimmed hedges and lined with rows of flowers on both sides. How pretty!

As Ali descended the steps, he saw a mouse again! He wasn't certain if it was the same one he saw before or another, but he suddenly felt the urge to play!

The mouse scurried across grass towards the hedge. Ali leapt down after him, and in two bounds, rushed through the flowers and scampered across the lawn in pursuit.

Suddenly a bizarre creature stepped in his path. It was shaped like a cat, but completely transparent. He could see its brain in its head and what appeared to be a stylized heart in its chest. And the terrifying creature had no scent. This must be what they called ghosts!

"What exactly do you think you're doing?" said the ghost-cat.

"Ch-ch-chasing a mouse," Ali answered more bravely then he felt. "Does it belong to you, Ghost Cat?"

"*Ghost* cat?" the creature responded scornfully. "I'll have you know that I am the famous *Glass* Cat of Oz, and one of Ozma's most trusted advisors! I'm magically-constructed, but a cat no less. And you would be wise to remember that cats in Oz don't chase mice if they know what's good for them. At a guess, I'd say you're too small for one of those truant cats from Catty Corners. Why Ozma doesn't disband them I'll never understand."

"I've never heard of that place," said Ali, embarrassed and still a little frightened. "I'm not from here. I was brought from New York by the Wizard."

"I see," said the Glass Cat. "That explains it then. Now look at me. Can you see my pink brains?"

"I wish I couldn't, but yes!" Ali exclaimed. "They even move!" he added, horrified.

"That's right!" retorted the Glass Cat. "The Wizard restored these brains for a reason. They are very good, superior even to human brains. So, when I give you advice, you would be wise to follow it. I suggest that if you plan to stay in Oz very long, you'd better learn the rules here. That was lesson Number One. Good day!"

Then, in a flash, the Glass Cat had fled through the bushes and trees and could no longer be seen. What kind of place had the Wizard brought him to! New York was strange enough, but this place was unfathomable.

Ali began looking around to see where he should go next, when suddenly he felt talons grasp him on his shoulders and hips, as he was being lifted into the air. At first he struggled and growled; but as he rose higher, he realized that if he did get loose, he would fall such a great distance that even the fabled feline ability to land on one's feet would not save him, so he allowed his captor to take him without any further struggles.

CHAPTER II
GRYPHONS AND FARMERS

They flew rapidly over the palace grounds, streets, pastures and woods surrounding the city until there were only grain fields and orchards below.

At last his abductor settled upon one of the orchards, where he was greeted by several beings that looked like winged lions the size of large dogs. Ali recognized them as the gryphons he'd seen in the Magic Picture.

Several gryphons crowded around Ali's captor. "What do you have there, Adhémar?" one of them asked.

"I don't know, Maalot," Adhémar replied. "It was the only thing I saw that I could carry."

"It is called a cat," one of the other gryphons said.

"Is it good to eat?" another asked. "I want something fresh after that roast beef."

Ali shivered.

The one called Maalot said, "It can be eaten, but it's small and bony."

Ali looked around. From many of the tree branches dangled large slabs of beef in varying degrees of doneness. One of the gryphons was aloft, slowly circling. Apparently he had been posted as a lookout, for he flew lower and said, "Here comes that irritating farmer again, and he's carrying something. It may be a weapon."

A gryphon named Anzu growled, "We should tear him limb from limb! There's no meat fresher or sweeter than human!"

"Wait!" said another. "There are others behind him, and Ural isn't back yet!"

The lookout flew higher and circled for a few minutes. "I see him!" he called out. "Here he comes now!"

"As soon as he arrives," directed Maalot, "we'll find another food source. We have seen firsthand what the guns of man can do."

"It would be a shame to leave all this meat behind," said Adhémar.

"We'll return at night for it," Anzu barked. "Maybe get the farmer too!"

"Aye!" Maalot called out. "Let us see what Ural has found, then we will return at night and kill any who oppose us."

Suddenly, all the gryphons vanished into thin air!

Ali was surprised until he remembered what Ozma had planned. Relieved, he looked around to see where to return to the Emerald City. Before he could reach a decision, a man wearing overalls walked out from the orchard. Now that Ali was no longer colorblind, he could see they were yellow. The man was carrying a long stick with a metal rectangle on the end of it; if Ali had been raised in Kansas, he would have recognized it as a hoe.

"Well, I'd be dagnabbed," the man said. "Where'd them dadblamed critters go?"

Ali would have enlightened him about Ozma, but before he could find the words the man spied him.

"Well, I'll be dagnabbed twice," he said. "They left me a kittycat."

Ali held his peace. He had been called worse.

The man bent over and picked up the cat by the nape of his neck. Ali emitted a squeak of surprise; he hadn't been carried by the nape of his neck since he was a kitten. Walking with long strides with Ali swaying from his fist, but at least cradling his legs, the farmer took him to a farmhouse past other men also wielding hoes, spays and pitchforks. "Them beasts are gone," he told them before going around to the back of the house. Stomping up stairs, he opened a squeaking door, and entered a room occupied by a woman.

"Watcha got there, Philip?"

"Them nasty varmints left me a kittycat." He dropped Ali to the floor.

The woman stooped and examined Ali. "She's cute," the woman pronounced. "And I'll bet she's hungry."

Ali decided not to correct her gender mistake since apparently food was in the offing.

With smooth, quick actions the woman retrieved a saucer from a cupboard and a bottle of milk from an icebox, poured milk into the saucer, and set the saucer on the floor.

Ali wasn't a kitten and didn't drink milk any longer, but he lapped it up to be amiable. It had a funny taste, not at all like his mother's milk.

"We've got some mice out in the barn," Philip said, "and I thought I'd put 'er in there and let 'er catch 'em."

"Just don't hurt 'em," the woman said. "Our princess wouldn't like that."

She heard the man harrumph audibly. "Lotta good she is, lettin' them beasts fly about eatin' everythin' in sight!"

"I don't know anything about that," she said. "But the law's the law." Then to Ali, she said, "Just scare 'em away."

"And if you gets hungry," the farmer added, "I'm sure Ozmer won't miss one or two o'them. Heck, they even got their own village not a few miles south of here! Don't know why they don't stay with their own kind instead comin' into my barn!"

Catching mice was among Ali's talents, but this sounded both wrong and enticing at the same time. He didn't like this man very much, particularly what he was insinuating about Ozma. Ali determined to tell her. He also didn't like the idea of being shut up in a barn.

As if he could read his mind, Philip scooped him up by the scruff of his neck again and carried him the barn the man had referred to, and closed the door behind him.

It was dark after bright sunlight. Although cats see very well at night, it was a little while before his vision adjusted to his surroundings and he could see his surroundings. Not far to his left there was a crack in the wall. He went over to investigate whether it was large enough to escape through. It might be, but before he could attempt it, a brown mouse ran across his path, startling him.

"Let me guess," the mouse said. "The farmer convinced you to evict us."

"That's about right," Ali admitted, "though he's not too particular how I do it."

"He's a fossil, that one. He still acts like it's the old days. Can you believe cats used to hunt and kill mice?"

"Where I come from, they still do."

"And where would that be?" said the mouse, suddenly suspicious.

"A place called New York."

"Doesn't sound like such a nice place. Probably outside Oz."

"That's what I heard," said Ali. "The farmer said your people have a village nearby. If that's true, why are you risking your life here?"

"I enjoy the privacy," he replied. "Not everyone likes big cities and lots of neighbors. I prefer the country."

"Well, you'd better find another place besides here!"

"I suppose. Why, are you thinking about eating me?"

"Not really, but if the farmer and his wife decide not to feed me, I don't know if I'll have much choice."

"In that case, I'd better go. The farmer's a nasty piece of work anyway. He'd fit well in your New York."

"I thought Oz was all kittens and catnip."

"Believe me, it's the best place in all the worlds, but there are still a few rotten apples out there. The farmer's one of those who liked the Wicked Witch ruling over us, if you can believe it. Sadists, the whole lot of them!"

After the mouse gathered up his wife and belongings, he said goodbye and left through the crack in the wall. Having done his job as best he know how, Ali aimed to follow suit. Just then he heard the farmer approaching! It was going to be a tight squeeze, but he wasn't going to wait to see what else the farmer had in store.

Once outside again, he scampered, avoiding the place where he'd seen the other men. For all he knew they were just like Philip. His goal now was to rejoin the Wizard and Ozma. He hadn't known them long, but he liked what he knew; and he would feel far safer associated with him than with this disgruntled farmer and his wife.

"Pretty clever for an alley-cat," said a voice from the bushes. Ali could smell that it was another cat. But what greeted him was a surprise. It was an older male kitten. They were trouble at that age, but there was something else, something off about him. His color! Back in New York, he likely wouldn't have noticed.

"Let me guess," said Ali. "You're the Pink Kitten of Oz, Eureka."

"That's right, and I'm Princess Dorothy's cat. You'd do well to remember that."

"So I've heard," Ali said, restraining himself from sounding too sarcastic. "What is it *you* want?"

"Nothing, except to say you handled yourself well in there. I didn't think you'd pass up on a chance to kill and eat a mouse."

"I've learned a thing or two since I've gotten here."

"You had it easy. I had to learn the hard way. I even deluded myself into thinking there were talking mice and birds that were off-limits and non-talking ones I could kill and eat."

"I guess there aren't."

"No, but I've come to realize that's a good thing."

"Why's that?"

"Because if there were some who couldn't speak up for themselves like we can, things would be like your New York, where the strong constantly prey on the weak."

"But that's the natural order of things, isn't it?"

"That's why I used to think too. Except there's lots of creatures stronger than cats."

"Not many," said Ali, thinking back to his time in the streets. "Dogs, maybe, but most of them are on leashes. Besides, I've driven off my share, and I'm faster than them."

"Not what I meant," said Eureka. "But you get the idea..."

With that, Eureka stalked off into the woods and shrubs, just as the Glass Cat before him had done, and was soon nowhere to be found.

Ali pondered on what he'd said as he explored his surroundings. The farmer was bigger and he'd preyed on him in a way. In New York, there were dangerous groups of boys he'd learned to avoid. Ali didn't like dwelling on the bad things that sometimes happened to his kind, but he'd heard things and even seen a few. He remembered one woman screaming and throwing things at a colony, and others acting in ways that frightened him. It hadn't happened to him directly, thankfully, but he knew of cats that were deathly afraid of humans. And all of a sudden he remembered why, and remembered those who didn't make it. It was a wonder he let Oscar even touch him. Then, there were dangers like hunger and disease. Maybe Eureka was right. Maybe the natural order wasn't so natural after all.

It was a long day. He headed south, avoiding communities and farms. The day was nearly over before he discovered a brick road, which he now identified as yellow. It was nice to see colors, but how did he know their names, he wondered. His experience suggested that roads were intended to be traveled on; and maybe this one would take him to Oscar.

The day was nearly over and the sun was in decline. Ali recalled that the gryphon had carried him away from the direction in which the sun rose. Thus, he began walking southeast, in the opposite direction of the setting sun.

CHAPTER III
GLINDA'S GOOD PLAN

After he left Ozma, the Wizard used a side door of the palace to go to the Royal Zoological Gardens. He waited until a class of school children and their teacher passed by, and walked over to Orville, the ork on which he had flown to Glinda's palace before his trip to New York.

"Hello, Oscar. Are we taking another trip together?"

"If you're willing," the Wizard replied.

"And ready," said Orville. "Where to this time?"

"Back to Glinda's palace."

"Good. I like the way they take care of their guests. The food and company are good too, and I think there's a stork who has a shine on me!"

"You're a married ork!" the Wizard mocked.

"Happily, I might add. Still, it's nice to know one's still desirable!"

Oscar laughed and they chatted amiably as before. When they reached their destination, they were met as before by two of Glinda's girl soldiers. One of them took charge of Orville, and the other led the Wizard to Glinda's drawing room.

Glinda was seated before a large golden table, clad in a ruby-red gown, looking at her Great Book of Records, mounted on the table before her. When the Wizard entered, she smiled and said, "So what's this about Laurel and Hardy?"

Although not surprised by the foreknowledge, he couldn't help but chuckle. "Just a passing thought," he replied. I don't even know why I mentioned it to Ozma. I know the laws of Oz as well as anyone, as well as the improbability of anyone wanting to leave behind their lives to start anew. It was just a feeling, I suppose, that they would fit in well here."

"Interesting," Glinda said. "It's true we have to be very cautious about who we allow to settle in Oz. Exceptions are, of course, allowed, but we can't be a refuge for mortals. If we could, there are so many who are suffering who would benefit by what we have."

"I understand," Oscar said. "Ozma thought you might have another distraction for Oogaboo. It seems Queen Ann's growing restless again."

"I might," she said. "But tell me, why you're so enamored with these particular comedians?"

"They simply make me laugh."

Glinda smiled. "That's no small thing. Stan Laurel is forty-nine this year, and Oliver Hardy is forty-seven. While they likely don't have very long careers ahead of them, they are far from being ready to be yanked away from doing what they love, which is also what they do best. Yet I agree that they are by nature very Ozzy, to use your term."

The Wizard was puzzled. "I don't understand," he said.

"Have you heard the theory that everyone has a doppelganger?"

"I have," the Wizard stated. "It's not true, is it?"

"Well, not usually. In this case, however, your gut has proven unusually on target."

"Whatever do you mean?" Oscar asked.

"The Great Book of Records has revealed that in the Outside World, there happens to be two old friends who bear an uncanny resemblance to this Laurel and Hardy."

"Most curious."

"In fact, they put that resemblance to good use when they visit children's hospitals and read to them... Can you guess what they read to them?"

"Oz books?"

"Exactly. Now, the dealings of the outside world don't normally come to my attention, but in this case one of my girls came across an entry about the two friends, and found it amusing that they read the children Oz books. That's how I found it."

"That's an amazing example of synchronicity!"

"It gets better. When I examined further, I discovered that one of them has cancer and is soon going to die."

"But that's terrible!"

"It is," Glinda said more soberly. "And it will be a double-tragedy, as they are the only family either one has. Of course, if I bring them here..."

"... he'll be healed," Oscar concluded.

"And they can continue making people happy in Oogaboo. You and Ozma were right. Queen Ann is depressed. Although she successfully found her parents, and more people are moving into her realm, Jo Files and Ozga have been busy with their children, her sister has a new beau, and Ann's young companions are assissting Jodie with the Friendly Forest. Oddly, her people seem to share her ups and downs, and there's been talk of conquering somewhere just to stave off the boredom!"

"A few funny celebrities, even imitation ones, might breathe some new life into Oogaboo society."

"Now that that's been settled," she said with a smile, "it is time for lunch and another opportunity to defeat me at klobyosh! Besides, I'd like to hear all about Ali, the one refugee you did bring from New York!"

"That sounds like a grand idea!" the Wizard said.

Ali was very much on Oscar's mind; he wondered how his little feline friend had fared during his absence and hoped to find him in his apartment when he returned to the palace.

CHAPTER IV
FISH AND FLUTTERBUDGETS

Tail erect, Ali set off, following the brick road eastward. Being a nocturnal animal, he was not accustomed to being awake and active all day, but he was anxious to get home, and so he plodded onward.

When he heard the sound of dogs barking, howling and laughing in the distant east, he decided to veer off the brick road. One dog he could fend off. A pack would mean the death of him. The sounds of dogs diminished and he soon came to a strange, giant corncob tower. Whatever bizarre manner of being would live in such a place he didn't want to know. Thus far, this "paradise" that the Wizard called Oz resembled more of a dream he once had after eating bad food. He came to a river, and as he was hungry, decided to fish.

He sat upon the bank patiently. This was a lackadaisical river that had plenty of fish swimming in it. This would be easy! One iridescent blue fish passed by, a discus, as it turned out, and he swiped! Success! The fish was gasping on the ground beside him. Just as he prepared to bite down, it shrieked, and then seven others of the same kind popped their heads out of the water. "Just what exactly do you think you're doing?" asked the first one.

"Put him back in the water this instant!" said another.

"Why, I haven't seen a cat so foolish in ages!"

"Not since our great, great, great, great, great, great, great grandparents' day!"

Taking a deep sigh, Ali said, "So, you all speak too." It wasn't a question.

"Well, of course we speak!" they said.

"Will you please escort our schoolmate back in the water," said another discus. "It's quite uncomfortable being on land."

"I'd say!" said Ali. "Death seems pretty uncomfortable."

"Death!" said the first fish, looking at the others, who also looked befuddled. "What an odd thing to say. Nobody dies in Oz."

"Must... be... from... Kansas..." said the fish who Ali had scooped out of the water.

"More like New York," said Ali, finally gathering the fish in his mouth and dragging him back into the water.

"Thank you," said the grateful fish. "Much better!"

"Well, I'm sorry for taking you out of the water," apologized the tabby. "I'm still getting used to this place."

"You'll love it," said one fish, encouragingly, and the others agreed.

"You wouldn't happen to know where I might cross this river?" he asked.

"There's a bridge not a few fathoms east of here," offered the fish he'd rescued.

After saying goodbye, he followed the river east, and not too far a distance came upon a bridge, which he crossed.

Continuing south, he began to notice the hue of the landscape change to an almost Autumnal palette. What was it the Wizard had said about the different countries in Oz? The Winkies preferred shades of yellow, while the Quadlings liked red? Seeing all the orange before him, he figured he was likely passing from one to the other. He'd gone too far south and would have to begin moving northeast again if he was going to get to the Emerald Palace.

Just then he came to a side road with a sign that said:

This way to Fussbudget Municipality,
Just Outside Flutterbudget Center

"That doesn't sound too dangerous," he said, as his stomach growled. He hadn't eaten all day since the farmer's wife had given him milk. He didn't care for the name of Flutterbudget, as it made him think of wounded birds, which was now an unpleasant association, but he figured that perhaps he was being fanciful. Still, he'd try Fussbudget instead and hopefully someone there might feed him.

He turned east unto a well-worn path and followed the signs to a valley in which the path wound to a large circular space with six reddish houses symmetrically spaced on its far side. Each of the houses was in a different style, but all were neat with recently mowed grass yards and trimmed hedges. The lawn of one was bordered with evenly spaced flowers, which Ali's vision recognized as the same hue as Eureka.

As the sun was descending, the sky was growing dark, and in one house after the other the lights went on. No house looked to Ali more likely than another to feed him, so he decided at random to approach one on the far right, and approached the back of the house where he might more easily escape if the occupants proved unfriendly.

With more hope than confidence, Ali went up the steps and stationed himself by the side of the door that had a knob, since that was the side more likely to open. He meowed to announce his presence. There was no response.

He waited for a while and was about to meow again when he heard a woman's voice from inside the house: "Harold, it's time for you to take out the trash."

A man's voice—presumably Harold's—answered: "Yes, dear."

"Don't forget to put on your gloves before you handle the trash."

"Yes, dear."

"Don't forget to wash your hands first. We don't want the germs on your hands to go inside of the gloves."

"Yes, dear."

There was a short pause, and then Ali heard footsteps approaching. The door opened and Ali scurried inside.

He found himself confronting a woman wearing an apron over her dress. From her voice he identified her as Loretta: "Well! Look what we have here. It's a kitty. Come inside." She picked up a damp cloth and knelt beside Ali. "I'll bet those paws of yours are dirty," she said as she raised his paws one by one and wiped them with the cloth. "And I'm sure you're in need of a bath. But first things first. One thing I know about cats is that they shed. If I let you loose in here I'll be picking up cat hair from dawn to dusk. I know what to do about that." She rose. "Just you stay right where you are while I go fetch a razor. We'll get rid of all that hair, and then you won't shed." She walked out of the room.

As a cat, Ali had an intense dislike for baths, but being shaved was even worse! He looked at the door he had just entered by. The knob was much too high for him to reach.

Then he heard footsteps. Harold was returning from taking out the trash. As Harold opened the door, Ali whisked outside and didn't stop running until he was in the bushes.

Ali's New York experience had taught him that food was often to be found within garbage pails. His intention was to raid the one Harold had just brought, but he knew to wait until Harold and Loretta had gone to bed. Eventually the lights in the house went out, and he felt safe to approach.

The pail proved to be too high, and the sides did not afford any place for his claws to grip, and it had a lid which would be difficult to pry off. Still, he'd solved similar problems in New York. Standing on his hind legs, he pushed the pail to make it rock back and forth. Finally it fell over on its side, and the lid popped off.

Fearful that the crash might awaken Harold and Loretta, Ali hid among the bushes until he was certain that it was safe. At length he felt it was safe to come out and explore the pail's contents. Much of what he found was inedible, but he managed to sniff out table scraps to mitigate his hunger.

Satiated enough, he left Fussbudget Municipality. The sooner he was free of a place where they shaved cats, the better. He reasoned that he'd gone too far south, and wanting to make up for lost time traveled nearly all night, growing more and more tired as time went on. At last the lightening of the color of the road told him that day was breaking, and he began to think where he might spend the day. He came to a place where some broad-leaved weeds were growing at the side of the road. He was glad to see they were yellow. These, he thought, would make a good hiding place. He did not know of anything in particular that he should hide from, but he was a firm adherent of the proverb, "Better safe than sorry." He crawled in among the weeds, feeling safer for being hidden.

CHAPTER V

LAUREL AND HARDY IN OOGABOO

When the Wizard finally returned to the Emerald Palace, he looked through his apartment, hoping that Ali would have returned. He even checked under the bed. But the cat was nowhere to be found.

Oscar's personal servent Galden brought the Wizard his breakfast and a copy of the daily *Ozmapolitan*. After he had eaten and glanced through the newspaper, he decided to see Ozma and ask her to search for Ali in the Magic Picture.

"How was the trip?" she asked.

Oscar told her about Glinda's plans to bring the doppelgangers to Oz.

"Does she need me to use the Magic Belt?"

"They should be here already. Let's ask the Magic Picture to show us our new pseudo-Laurel and Hardy, and at the same time find Ali. I'm admittedly worried about him."

To the Wizard's disappointment, all the Picture showed was a patch of the Yellow Brick Road and some broad-leaved weeds beside it.

"Is there something wrong with it?" he asked.

"I don't think so," Ozma replied. "Let me try something else." She instructed the picture to show the Scarecrow, and immediately, there he was, ambling through his corncob castle. "No," she said, "there's nothing wrong with the picture. Let's try Ali again."

And again the Magic Picture showed the same patch of the Yellow Brick Road and the broad-leaved weeds beside it.

"The leaves have a yellow tint to them," Oscar observed, "so somewhere in the Winkie Country."

"We'll check again. Show us our new Laurel and Hardy," Ozma commanded. And at once the Magic Picture showed a room in a house. Through a window could be seen a daffodil field with buttery blossoms; in the far distance was a row of yellow columbine hills. And seated at a table were the men who resembled Laurel and Hardy.

"I still can't believe we're in Oz," Laurel said "It was awful nice of Queen Ann Soforth to give us this farm."

"I suppose," Hardy said, still in shock over the whole thing, "but what are we going to do with a farm full of tickseeds?"

"I don't know, but the Queen sure found it funny. Maybe if we looked through the house we could find something to tell us what tickseed farmers do. Let's look!"

"Go ahead," Hardy said.

Laurel rose and disappeared into the next room. In a short time strange noises could be heard: crashes and clankings and shattering glass. Through it all Hardy sat impassive, fanning himself with his derby.

Eventually Laurel emerged from the room, lugging a strange contraption. The body of it seemed to be a five-gallon can. Near the bottom was a spigot; on top was a rod scored with threads that led to a cross-shaped handle. On one side were large letters: WINE PRESS. Laurel placed it on the table.

Hardy stopped fanning himself. "What in the world is that?" he demanded.

Laurel smiled proudly. "It's a wine press. You use it to make tickseed wine."

"Who ever heard of tickseed wine?"

"Well, there's dandelion wine, so I suppose there must be tickseed wine."

"We have tickseeds, so let's try it!"

"I'll go get some." Laurel disappeared into another room, from which came another assortment of crashes, clankings and shattering glass. Hardy went back to fanning himself with his derby.

When Laurel reappeared, he was carrying an empty burlap sack. He left the room and could be seen through the window going up a row of tickseed plants, picking the flowers; about as many ended up on the ground as placed in the sack. Hardy continued fanning himself.

After a little while Laurel returned with the sack. He removed the top of the wine press, set it on the table, and poured in the tickseed flowers.

"Glasses," Hardy said.

"No, I don't need glasses. I can see fine."

"Not seeing glasses, you idiot; drinking glasses. If you want us to sample the wine, we'll need glasses to drink out of."

Laurel disappeared into still another room, which emitted more crashes, clankings, and shattering glass. He emerged holding a wine glass in each hand. Placing the glasses on the table, Laurel put the top back on the wine press and began turning the crank. After a few minutes the handle was level with the top of the press. Laurel took one of the glasses, held it beneath the spigot, and filled the glass half full; then he did the same with the other glass. Handing one of the glasses to Hardy he said, "Here's looking at you."

Hardy looked at Laurel and lifted the glass to his lips. He took a drink and immediately sprayed it out of his mouth, staining Laurel's shirt. "Ooh!" he exclaimed. "That was terrible! Are you trying to poison me?"

Laurel looked at the glass he held without drinking from it.

"Well," Hardy said, "here's another fine mess you've gotten us into."

Laurel screwed up his face and began to mock-cry.

Ozma laughed as she turned the Magic Picture to another scene. "Well, we know the Picture's functioning. Let's see if we can find Ali."

Again the Magic Picture showed a patch of the Yellow Brick Road bordered by broad-leaved weeds, but this time there was a tabby cat moving amongst it.

The Wizard asked, "Oh good! He must be sleeping in the field. He's probably scared, though. He's never been in the country before, and Oz can be startling to newcomers. Could you use the Magic Belt to bring him here?"

Ozma said, "I *could*, but I'd prefer not to."

The Wizard was surprised. "I hadn't expected that," he admitted. "May I ask why not?"

"Of course you may. One of the greatest pleasures in life is overcoming difficulties. As far as we can tell, Ali has so far overcome every difficulty he might have encountered. To bring him here now would rob him of the pleasure of overcoming whatever challenges lie ahead. If he's going to live in Oz, and not just in the palace, he's going to have to learn to overcome obstacles."

"But what if he encounters an obstacle that he can't overcome?"

Ozma said, "Of course I would use the Magic Belt if he gets into a situation where his life is in danger, or if it involves suffering of any kind, but at some point he won't have our eyes on him. We can't watch him every moment. Remember what almost happened to Button-Bright all those years ago? I nearly sent him back to the outside world after that! That's when I realized that for better or worse, if I don't give my subjects the opportunity to solve their problems by themselves, they'll always depend on us as baby-sitters."

"Those are good points," the Wizard admitted. "Nobody wants to babysit an entire kingdom."

"Now you understand why I didn't use the Belt in various circumstances in the past."

"I knew you had your reasons."

"And now you more fully understand how I feel about my subjects. Oz is a peaceful realm, but it yet has dangers."

"It that sense, we're not that different from the outside world," he reasoned. "But I'd still rather be here."

"Me too!"

CHAPTER VI
THE CATS OF KITTY CITY

Ali awoke and peered out from under the leaves which had concealed him. Judging by the length of the shadows, the sun was getting ready to set. Judging by the condition of his stomach, he was hungry again.

He emerged from concealment and proceeded north over a bridge fording the river he'd crossed the other day. This should bring him back to the yellow road, but further east than those barking dogs that had him scramble so far. Clouds obscured the moon, but since cats have vision six times more capable than that of humans for seeing in the dark, he was not impeded by the lack of moonlight. His hunger, however, was becoming more urgent, and it was with relief that he saw a sign:

THIS WAY TO KITTY CITY

Kitty City! That sounded like a place where a cat could get something to eat. He hoped this wasn't the Catty Corners he'd heard about. That didn't sound like such a nice place, but then again what would a cat made of glass know about such things? And so he followed the dusty path until he came to a place like nothing he had ever seen before. It was a large, semi-circular, bare space. On the far side of the space was a big chair upholstered in a material that had pictures of flowers all over it. A pillow covered the seat upon which was sleeping a cat of some kind.

While the space in front of the chair was bare in the sense that there were no structures on it, it was filled with a number of cats, some lying and resting, but most prowling around, sometimes hissing or playing with each other.

One of the recumbent cats, a white Persian, was the first to notice Ali. It yowled for attention and then announced: "Brothers and sisters, a newcomer has come to join us."

One of the prowlers, a calico, approached Ali and said, "Who are you and what are you doing here?"

"My name is Ali. I came because I'm hungry and was hoping I could get something to eat before I continue to the Emerald City."

"A city cat, eh?" The calico gave what might have passed for a feline laugh. "I'm called Randolph, and we're waiting for food, too. But you better not get in my way!"

Ali was puzzled, "Why are you waiting?"

The calico explained, "Once a week, a man comes here and leave a pile of meat for us. I suppose he likes cats and thinks he's doing us a big favor. But as soon as he leaves, the Boss Cat comes down from his chair and takes charge of it. He pushes it under the chair. And then every night he scatters some of the food out here for us to fight over."

A human might have wondered why the cats did not join forces and control the meat themselves, but it was not in feline nature to join forces, and the idea did not occur to Ali. Instead, he asked, "Who is the Boss Cat?"

A voice from the seat of the chair said, "I am."

Ali looked up and saw the giant head of an orange tabby looking down at him. The orange tabby rose up, and Ali could now see that he was much larger than the others.

"My name is Roscoe and I'm the Boss Cat and ruler of Kitty City. I have fought all these other cats and won." The cat leapt down from the chair, landing in front of Ali. "And I can beat you, too."

At this challenge the other cats drew back and formed a loose circle around the combatants.

Another cat might well have been intimidated by this, and declined to fight, submitting to the rule of Boss Cat, but Ali had experienced enough cat fights in the allies of New York, so that neither Boss Cat's size nor his challenge unnerved him. The two cats circled each other for a while, hissing and batting at each other and baring their teeth, and then Ali took the initiative. He lunged at Roscoe and raked the orange cat's nose with his claws. Startled, Boss Cat growled and drew back, and Ali followed up his advantage by leaping on his adversary's back, digging in his claws. Boss Cat yowled in pain. Ali reversed himself and sank his teeth into Roscoe's right ear. Predictably, the cat screamed. Through clenched teeth Ali growled, "Give up!"

The Boss Cat growled, "Never!"

Ali bit the ear harder and growled, "Give up!"

The Boss Cat squealed with pain and yowled, "All right, you win."

Ali released the ear and climbed down off of the Boss Cat's back.

A small brown and white cat named Aria said, "The rule is that the cat that defeats the Boss Cat becomes the new Boss Cat. So, Ali, if that's your name, you are now the Boss Cat of Kitty City."

The former Boss Cat crawled off into the shadows to groom himself.

Ali said, "I can smell the pile of food under the chair."

Various cats hungrily growled agreement.

"Let's pull it out, and everybody can have some. Don't eat too much! We want it to last until the man brings the next pile."

Ali watched as several cats did as instructed, pulling out small slabs of meat that they flung in various directions. One of them said, "There are other piles in here that Boss Cat had hidden away."

Ali said, "That was wise on his part. Leave them there. You may need them if the man doesn't return." Then, seeing that the other cats were eating the food that had been dumped out, Ali called out, "Roscoe. Come and eat." The large orange tabby looked at him oddly before joining in. Finally, Ali put his head down to eat until his stomach was satisfied. Afterwards he leaped up to the seat of the chair and looked out over the other cats. Most were still busily eating. A few hissed and spat if another cat came to close, but by and large they were contented and purring.

As the evening wore on, Ali observed that some of the younger cats were looking at him. "Where did you all come from?" he asked.

One Russian Blue named Shadow said, "Some of us left houses and communities where the people weren't as nice as they should have been."

Another, a sweet Apple-headed Siamese named Snowblind said, "Some of us just roam the land like our ancestors did."

Still another, a handsome Abyssinian named Strider, said "The old Boss came from Catty Corners when he lost a fight with the Queen."

"It was a revolt!" corrected a big orange and white cat, who introduced himself as Starbucket. "Several cats joined Roscoe and that's how we established our colony here."

This was interesting information, but Ali was growing concerned by the dangerous looks of a very large Norwegian Forest Cat who was trading sideways glances with another big Savannah Cat. This suggested to him that they were meditating a challenge. Since he had no ambition to become Boss Cat, the idea of maintaining the position, especially since that meant constant fights, held no appeal.

He pondered this while the other cats settled in various places for their early evening nap. Suddenly, a pretty calico approached him, eyes lidded in a sign of deference. Introducing herself as Tiger, she asked, "Are you enjoying your new position?" she asked.

"Not particularly, but it's better than the alternative."

They sat in silence for a time before the calico said, "I might have a solution for you."

Later that evening, prior to the evening meal, Ali leapt upon the chair and said in a commanding meow: "Everyone gather 'round." The cats were quick to respond, and Ali at last understood how easy it would be to become addicted to power. "I am making a new law! From now on, every cat shares. No more hoarding! You seven, Shadow, Strider, Randolph, Snowblind, Starbuck and Aria. You too, Roscoe. I appoint each of you as my deputies during my absence. You're to enforce this law as if you were Boss Cats yourselves! Nor is there to be any further fighting for power. All cats are equal in the eyes of the law. If any cat doesn't like this law, he is free to leave Kitty City."

Roscoe squeaked happily at this news, while Randolph and Snowblind purred quietly. Aria and Strider looked intently at Ali and the other cats, who deferred to this decision. Even the Norwegian Forest Cat expressed approval, as he understood it correctly to mean that no one cat would get most of the food while the others got scraps.

After that, Ali had the food evenly distributed and all the cats happily ate and ran off to play and frolic. "Are you sure you don't want to be one of the deputies?" Ali asked Tiger. "After all, it was your idea."

"I'm content to leave that to younger cats. Besides, now that you've made things right, I'm leaving."

"Leaving! Where are you going?"

"There's a place across the Deadly Desert called Merryland," she replied wistfully, "wherein lies the Valley of Cats. There, one can find a path to the Rainbow Bridge which will take me to my kittens whom I haven't seen in many, many years. In fact, they're not even kittens any longer, but full grown felines, but still they're mine and I have longed to see them."

"The Wizard told me that no living creature can cross this desert."

"That is true, but there is a safe route through it that the Fairy Queen placed there long ago, and this secret has been revealed to me."

"Very well, safe travels then, friend Tiger, and thank you for your help."

"Safe travels to you, friend Ali." And with that she departed.

Ali didn't know why he felt sad, just that he did, and he wondered if some of his former feline friends from New York had taken paths to the Rainbow Bridge themselves, and if that was a journey he'd one day have to make himself.

Eventually the early dawn came, and the cats began settling down for their daytime snooze. Ali was himself inclined to take a nap, but he forced himself to stay awake. He looked around at the peacefully sleeping cats, content he'd made the right decision, and jumped down from the chair. On silent feet he retraced his steps back to his journey north.

He walked all that day. The sun had passed its meridian when he entered a forest; the cool shade was welcome after a morning of walking in hot sunshine. Ali was still in the forest when the stars came out, and he was becoming tired. But he felt he should continue until the next morning dawned, and so he forced himself to pad onward.

Finally morning was on its way at last. The sky was becoming grayer, and the birds began to vocalize in the trees. Just then he saw a woodcutter's hut in the forest, not far from the brick road. The ground on which it was built was uneven, and so the floor of the hut had some spaces underneath it. It seemed to Ali that under the floor of the hut would be an excellent place for him to sleep until night fell. And so he found a large enough space for him to wedge himself into.

And the following morning, when Ozma looked into her Magic Picture to see where Ali was, what was visible was a patch of the Yellow Brick Road and a woodcutter's hut not far from it.

CHAPTER VII
BROOCEE'S BUS

Ali was awakened by a loud thumping overhead. He immediately realized that the woodcutter had returned to his hut and was going to go to sleep. That meant that the night was coming on and it was time for him to renew his journey. He went to the edge of the hut and looked out. Yes, it was getting dark outside. He crawled out from under the hut and returned to his journey.

Again his stomach told him that it was time to eat, but there was no food in sight. There was nothing left for him to do but plod on, tail erect, hoping that he would encounter something edible. Passing by a giant pumpkin, which he avoided, he at last came back to the road of yellow brick and followed it east.

Then, just as the terrain turned green and he rejoiced that at last he was nearing his destination, suddenly he heard a noise behind him. He turned and looked to see a machine coming along the brick road behind him. Anxious to get out of its way, he moved out of the road to the green grassy area beside it.

But then the machine stopped beside him. Ali was familiar with automobiles; they had them, of course, in New York, and he had much experience dodging out of their way. This one was unlike any he'd ever seen. He realized it was similar in color to the brick road. It had windows along the side, and painted below the windows were the words, "BROOCEE'S BUS."

Before he could puzzle out how he knew how to read, let alone unfamiliar words, a door in the front opened, and the driver, a young man with a shock of red hair, called out, "Want a ride?"

It was not a question that Ali could have expected. But being from New York, and new to the Land of Oz, where money was not used, he immediately wondered if money was involved, so he asked, "How much do you charge?" It was an empty question anyway, because he had none.

The driver answered, "There's no charge. I just enjoy giving rides. Are you going to the Emerald City?"

"I am," he answered

"Then come aboard."

Ali hesistated for a moment, looked at the man, who seemed friendly and kind, and then at the bus to see if there were any escape routes he might in case the driver proved to be not what he seemed. Seeing that some of the windows were open, he jumped in and trotted toward the back of the bus where he spotted two rows of two benches each. On one of the benches was a turtle who drawled a greeting.

Ali greeted him in return and asked the driver, "Why is this called 'Broocee's Bus'?"

The driver said, "Because it's a bus, and my name is Broocee. Actually I spell my name B-R-U-C-I, but if I put that on the bus people will keep mispronouncing it."

"Are there many buses, or automobiles, in Oz?" asked the cat.

"The Emerald City's full of Scalawagons," Bruci said. "And they're a bit too reckless for most animals' tastes. You wouldn't know it, but I used to be rather reckless myself. I was one of the Noyzy Boyz from the Quadling Country. Ever since Ozma placed the Spell of Tranquility on us, I realized I wanted to grow up and become a bus-driver like Tante Jeanne, who had a Flying Bus. Now, I give rides to all the animals who want to travel the land."

The tabby had no reference for any of this history, but was grateful for it all the same and told Bruci this.

Bruci grinned as he stepped on a pedal, and the bus lurched forward. Ali made his way to the bench where the turtle sat and asked, "May I sit by you?"

"Certainly," the turtle replied. "I was getting lonely back here by myself."

Ali hopped up beside the turtle. "My name is Ali. What's yours?"

"Myrtle. Are you going to the Emerald City?"

"Yes. Are you?"

The turtle said, "No. At least I'm not stopping there. I'm going beyond to the Munchkin Country."

"Why are you going there?"

"It's a long story, but the short of it is that the other turtles used to laugh at me because I'm colored blue."

"What is so terrible about that? Aren't turtles supposed to be blue?"

Myrtle replied, "I was in the Winkie Country, where shell colors come in a variety of yellow. They made fun of me because mine didn't. But in the Munchkin Country they favor blue, so I'm going there. I imagine that all the turtles are blue there."

"I hope you're right," Ali said politely. "Either way, you'll fit in."

"That's the plan. So, why are you going to the Emerald City?"

"I am friends of the Wizard of Oz and Princess Ozma, and they live in the Emerald City. I've been on a long adventure and have learned a lot, but I'm ready to go home."

"There's always something more to learn in Oz," the turtle remarked. "But it's good that you have a home."

"You'll find yours too," Ali replied. "If not, you can be my friend and live with me in the Royal Palace. Ozma and Oscar are very loving people."

The turtle was moved by this gesture and didn't say anything for a moment before quietly thanking the cat and promising that if the Munchkin Country proved to be a bust, she'd come and see him.

This got Ali to think of why he had trusted Oscar. The Wizard had just picked him up off the streets and carried him to his hotel room. There he named him and fed him from his own dinner. Sharing food meant a lot to a cat. Then the Wizard brought him to this strange country, made a place for him to be comfortable, and arranged for food to be brought to him. Suddenly Ali found himself eager to get back to his room in the palace.

Looking out the window, as Bruci announced the various features of the Emerald City that they passed by, he saw the living cars that Bruci had called Scalawagons, and understood what the driver had meant. Still, there were far fewer of them than the cars in Manhattan, and for all their spirit he could see they were also much safer than those had been, cleaner and far less noisy too. He determined to tell Oscar about this observation, but sleepiness overcame him and he stretched out on the bench beside the turtle.

Suddenly, he was awakened by a loud sound.

CHAPTER VIII
ALI FINDS HIS WAY

When the bus reached the east gate of the Emerald City, Bruci announced his arrival and beeped the loud horn in excitment. The great, green gates swung open to reveal the Guardian of the Gates himself, bowing and hurrying to open the door of the bus.

Ali and Myrtle alighted. Ali asked the turtle, "How will you get to the Munchkin Country from here?"

"The bus will just keep going east, right through the Emerald City and out the east gate."

"Well," Ali said, "good luck to you. I hope we'll meet again."

"Good luck to you as well," Myrtle replied. "I'm certain we will."

Ali then made his goodbyes to Bruci.

"Well, are you coming in?" the Guardian of the Gates asked with a twinkle, "or would you rather spend all day out here talking?"

"I'm coming in, thank you," Ali said. And he entered the Emerald City. Once inside the gate, Ali readily identified the palace, and, tail erect, he walked through the busy streets, noticing various other cats as he passed, most of whom were friendly enough to say a greeting, as well as additional Scalawagons, though they drove slower in the city proper, and he went up to the palace doors and yowled as loud as he could to attract the attention of those inside.

One of the doors opened, and the Soldier with the Green Whiskers stood looking around. "That's funny," he said. "I thought I heard something."

Ali didn't bother informing him and just scampered inside, jumping over one of the Soldier's booted feet.

Identifying the double doors that he led to Princess Ozma's room, he raised his voice once more.

At first there was only silence, and then he heard slippered feet come padding toward the door. It was opened by Princess Ozma herself.

"Why," the princess said, "there you are Ali. Oscar will be very glad to know you've come back safe and sound. We've been looking for you in my Magic Picture you know. Just recently, I saw you riding in a bus with a blue turtle."

"It's a long story," Ali said.

"Well, I'll be anxious to hear all about it at dinner. Suffice to say for now that I'm glad to see that you overcame whatever obstacles you had to face. Oscar's probably just getting ready to eat his lunch," and she gave him directions to his quarters.

En route, he saw a girl walking down the corridor with a dog at her heels. He recognized the dog as the rude Toto, but as soon as the dog saw Ali he began whining. The girl picked up the dog, held him in her arms, and said, "What's the matter, Toto? It's only a cat." Then, to Ali, she said, "Hello, kitty."

Ali thought the girl might be able to help him. He said, "Hi, my name is Ali, and I'm looking for the Wizard."

"Aww, aren't you precious," said Dorothy sweetly, bending down to pet the tabby. "I'll be glad to show you where his apartment is."

Ali followed Dorothy, still carrying Toto, as she led him to a door which was slightly ajar.

"This is his room," Dorothy said.

Ali remembered Oscar telling him those many days ago that he would leave the door slightly open so that he could get in when he returned.

"Thank you," he told Dorothy as he slipped in.

Passing through the rooms, he came to where the Wizard was seated at a table. As Ozma had predicted, he was eating his lunch.

Oscar threw down his fork and said, "Ali, my little chickadee! I'm so happy to see you. I've been wondering what happened to you. Are you hungry?"

This reminded Ali that it had been a long time since he had eaten. "Very much," he answered.

"Why," the Wizard said, "that's the first time I've heard you speak. You'll have to tell me all your adventures. But first, let's get you some food. I threw out what was in your bowls, because I didn't think you'd want to eat old food. So I'll call Galden and have him bring up some new food for you. I'm eating the best roast beef grown in the Winkie Country, so I'll cut some up for you." This suited Ali well, and he soon began placing the meat on a dish which he put on the floor for him.

It was as delicious as he'd boasted, and perhaps it tasted even better because Ali was remembering the day Oscar first shared his food with him.

When both man and cat had finished eating, the Wizard said, "Now, my little chickadee, you must tell me all your adventures."

Since Ali was getting sleepy, he fulfilled the request with a short version. The Wizard listened with keen attention, and made him promise to tell it again to everyone at dinner, for Ozites loved nothing more than good stories.

When he was through, Oscar said, "Ali, I'm proud of you. You had many difficulties to overcome, and you solved all your problems very well. Now, my little chickadee, it is my habit to take a nap after lunch."

Ali knew what a nap was, and was ready for some good sleep himself. He followed the Wizard into his bedroom and saw the footstool and pillow that Oscar had arranged for him so that he could look out the window were still in place. He hopped up on the pillow and settled himself for a snooze.

But before closing his eyes, he watched as the Wizard stretched out on his bed and prepared for his nap.

Oscar drifted off into sleep but was roused by feeling a pressure on one arm. He woke briefly to see that Ali had snuggled up next to him. Resting his head and one paw on his arm, he was fast asleep.

LURLINE AND THE TALKING ANIMALS OF OZ

by Joe Bongiorno

One of the oldest stories in the batch of books and manuscripts that we borrowed from the Lost Histories section, it concerns the immediate effect of Lurline's enchantment on a community of farmers and animals in the Munchkin Country. There are additional stories that take place before and after this one, but I left them back in the library and will have to get them next time. As this time period is something of which we still know very little, I thought it best to bring it to the attention of the Wogglebug, who was visiting the Royal Palace.

Betsy Bobbin

The Lost Tales of Oz

Based on the author's journal entries, I have calibrated the dates and converted them to the Gregorian calendar, which Nonestica adopted along with the English language some centuries ago. Apart from this, and the necessary modernization of period pronouns and language for the sake of readability, the content remains as it was written.

This document reveals a crucial moment in the history of our land never before told. More important, it reveals just how fortunate we all are, and how grateful we should be to have this beloved and blessed Fairyland that we know today, for things were not always as they are now.

H.M. Professor Wogglebug, T.E., Year of Lurline 270, 111th Period, Reign of Ozma, 2013 Anno Domini

May 2nd, 1742

I don't sleep anymore. The small hours are filled with a nameless dread. Profound changes have occurred in the land that have put many of us on edge. I've decided to keep a record. Someone should... if nothing else so that whoever's reading this will know what happened, and in case things go bad, will know we were here.

I should begin at the beginning.

We live in the Munchkin Country, east of the Kalidah Woods, and north of the Road of Yellow Brick. The main part of the Southern Munchkin River runs up north just east of us. King Orison, who ruled from Sapphire City, began construction on the road in the 13th Century, starting at

Munchkenny, the then new capital of the Munchkin Country, and intending to go all the way to Ozmara, the high capital of Oz in the Green Country, but it would be the Wise Woman of the East in 1700, who would mostly complete it, and even her efforts were stalled when she disappeared. The road is still an asset to travelers. For us, it means we get to hear news sooner than those who moved to more remote areas to get away from royals and other kinds of difficult people.

Farmers' lives are busy ones, but not terribly interesting, consisting mainly of hard work. When a farmer does well, he gets to enjoy some of the fruits of that work, maybe even hire on local farmhands to ease the load a little. At worst, your children pick up the slack. Barring catastrophes, or very bad decisions, you generally don't go hungry or in want of the necessities of life. If you like consistency and aren't afraid of hard work, a farmer's life isn't a terrible one.

But change, as they say, comes to everyone, whether we want it or not. I admit to wanting it, and then not being ready for it when it did come. Isn't that how it always goes?

That brings us to the events of two days ago.

Wildflowers, bushes and trees have suddenly sprung up around the country where they weren't before, many of them containing a host of fruits and vegetables, honeyberry, blue corn, blue potatoes, bilberries and blueberries, amongst them. Before yesterday, these were only found where people cultivated them. Now, they run wild in the fields and forests.

And did you happen to notice what's common with all of them? That's right. The colors.

Blue has always been discernably prevalent in the land, for which reason the Munchkin Country was known as "The Land of Sky Blue Waters," but few who weren't poets or bards really noticed it. Now, even the most dim-witted can see shades of blue everywhere. It's rather stunning, if disconcerting. You might be picturing it as dreary, dull or distasteful, even repellent, as I would have if I hadn't seen it firsthand, but it doesn't feel that way. It's actually *invigorating*. In fact, everything feels more vibrant and alive in a way that I can't quite describe. But it is definitely odd, and clearly portends something...

Oh, and there's one other important thing. The animals are talking.

Yes, you read that right. The animals are talking.

Pets, beasts of burden, and wild animals! Even the birds can be heard chattering in the common tongue!

While the children are thrilled, the adults have had a very different reaction, particularly for ranchers, as their sole means of livelihood stormed out of their pens. In a single day, every ranch for miles around is bare. The most disturbing part wasn't the sheer strangeness of it, nor even the reproachful stares of the cows, sheep, horses and pigs as they stalked away (but that was unnerving!) The worst part was the look of worry on my husband's face. He knew before I did what it would mean.

He knew it would mean war.

After the shock, fear was the preeminent reaction, fear that some unknown supernatural event had occurred, perhaps presaging an imminent cataclysm, fear that the beasts would seek revenge for untold years of slaughter, fear that the ranchers would no longer be able to provide for their families. Jeb's brother was a rancher, and so was their father before them. Raising livestock was the only world many understood, the only thing they were good at. You can imagine then that the next reaction after fear was anger. "An accounting has to be made," is the new catchphrase. It's what the people say when they're scared and upset and think that a fight is the only way to solve their problems. In this case, it wasn't hard to blame them. They couldn't be expected to just sit around and let their families go hungry. I suppose they could learn to grow vegetables, fruit and grain, especially now that they were freely available for the picking, but I didn't hear anyone even suggest that. The way they figured it was if their livestock wouldn't come back on their own, well, they'd just have to make them.

Hard lives make for hard people. The men around here tend to talk more than they think, and they think as little as they can. Don't misunderstand. These aren't bad men. Not most anyway. It's just that they've been taught to believe certain things, such as the use of force as a necessary evil. The women may not like it, but in a society governed by men no one pays much attention to what we think.

I married Jeb because he isn't like most men in that regard; I'm not his slave or surrogate mother, but a partner and friend. He's not threatened by me or afraid to communicate, though he still tends to keep a lot in. There are things in his past he doesn't speak of, but haunt him in the still hours of the night, worries about the future that preoccupy his thoughts by day. We all carry these secret burdens that we don't share.

Mother was a worrier too. When I got engaged, she'd start talking about the three things that a wife and mother must never fail to do: "Protect your kids, especially your girls, but your boys too." "Keep your husband happy so he's not tempted to stray." And "Keep your house in order so the neighbors don't wag their tongues." She always said that in Oz we had it better than most women in the old country, that we lived in a charmed land. I didn't really believe that any longer, but I took her advice.

Father had come from the Winkie Country, and grew up in a community of artisans, craftsman and musicians. As a result I had something not everyone had, an education. "Education can help you to think better," he used to say, "and make better choices, and you have to be smart, or the world will devour you." When I came to live in the Munchkin country, I saw what he meant and learned to be wise to the dangers that lurked beyond home and hearth. The city and the country have different kinds of perils; the country was generally safer, but the world can be cruel to women and children no matter where you live.

Mother did the opposite of me; she started out on a farm and moved to the city after she got married. She'd come from money, but was terribly unhappy. I once had a dream that I saw my mother lying down with her chest open. There, in place of a heart, sat a white stone. She explained it and said that she and her sisters were hardened by their childhood, and that they would have done anything, married anyone, to get away from their father. Mother rarely talked about him, saying only that it was best left in the past. My father said he was a terribly cruel man, an *evil* man. Father wasn't wont to speak of anyone that way; he says most people are misunderstood or damaged. But her father was an exception to the rule and the main reason they left the Winkie Country to come to Munchkenny: "Evil men with influence or power are the most dangerous men in the world."

I have since learned that my grandfather was considered a warlock with blood ties to the wealthy Wichelen clan. If his wife, my grandmother, hadn't died in childbirth, she'd have taught her daughters the secrets of the art. He blamed the girls for her death, and often ridiculed and beat them. Deeming them of no use to him, he intended to marry each off to other wealthy, wicked men like him, until the one day they all ran away as he stood there, vowing to find them.

My parents were both killed when a raiding party from Rimmersden invaded Munchkenny, pillaging their way south to Mudge. The Munchkin Country is divided in the north and south by the Road of Yellow Brick. Once the Wise Woman disappeared, both houses reasserted their claims to dominion, and peace between them was always tenuous at best. When this happened, the Southern Ruling House of

Seebania accused the North Ruling House of Munchkenny of either instigating the attacks or allowing marauders free reign in their country. They denied it vehemently, and in truth, the northerners hated the blonde-headed Rimmers as much as anyone. They managed to catch a few Rimmers and discovered that they'd been hired out by a nameless patron from the Winkie Country, who wanted certain parties exterminated. This gave me cause for concern. Could it have been *him,* punishing his children for his perceived disloyalty to him? I would never know.

In any case, the Seebanians deemed their lands off-limits to northerners. This was practically a declaration of war. The Northern King responded by blaming the Mudgers for instigating the Rimmers due to grudges and grievances each had with the other years earlier, and so tensions mounted once again, and to this day there remains talk of war.

In the painful days that followed, it was Gilbert who raised my spirits. A special child, full of joy and wonder at life—as I imagine his father had been as a boy—Gil saved my heart from turning to stone.

This wasn't the life we planned for ourselves when we first married. We'd intended to move to Munchkenny, where my parents lived, or perhaps a community near the Ozure Isles. It was Jeb's brother Zachary who convinced him to stay, a decision Jeb came to rue. Zachary was always bitter that their father had left Jeb the house. Jeb and I thought this had abated when Zachary got married and had a daughter, but we were wrong. Truth be told, my sister-in-law

Ella and her daughter Ada *needed* our friendship. So you can imagine our irritation when Zachary moved further away to the next town.

When the wealthy ranchers hollered, everyone was quick to obey. A lot of them hold positions as nobles or magistrates, and they finance the constabulary, so no one wishes to get on their bad side. Whatever grudges and rivalries existed were put aside for the "good of the country," though they'd go back to calling each other cattle thieves and worse once this was over.

Gilbert asked his father, "Do they really expect the animals to come back, tails between their legs? Why would they?"

"That's a good point, son. I know I wouldn't. But the men don't care about such things. They're angry and scared and just want everything to go back to the way it was."

"What if that doesn't happen?" I asked, but there was no answer, only a look of worry.

By early afternoon, all the men in town had gathered whatever muskets, arquebuses, calivers, bayonets, or hunting knives they had for what they called "the big hunt." They were going to teach the beasts a lesson about "getting above their station."

Jeb knew I was upset when said he was going with them, but he also knew I understood why he felt he had to. In small towns, things change slowly, if at all. They'll allow for trivial quirks, but there are consequences for being too different. Jeb staying home would mean he disagreed with everyone else on an important issue. So even if it meant doing something he disagreed with, Jeb wouldn't allow us to become pariahs.

May 3d, 1742

Speaking with some of the neighbors earlier for news and just to keep us from going mad, I got an earful from Old Ed. Our first real friend in the area, Edric Aylewynus is known as the town gossip, though he trades more in tall tales than he does local scandals. No one worried about him going on the hunt as he was considered either too old or too touched to fight. That was just as well, he said, since it was "best to leave the talking beasts in peace."

"Why do you say that?" I asked.

"Things are changing and changing fast, and we had best change with them or be swept away."

When Ed gave cryptic answers it meant he didn't know anymore than anyone else. Alcohol wafted off of him, but that wasn't uncommon. "A lot of the others are thinking of moving to other parts," I said, "or even other countries."

"That's 'cause they think it's only happening here!"

"You don't know that it's not," I countered, though I had a feeling the *disturbances* weren't isolated to the Munchkin Country. Where would we go anyway?

"Do you want to know what's *really* going on?"

"That depends on how much you've been drinking today," I said skeptically.

"Hardly enough I'd say."

"You may be right at that," I smirked. "All right, come inside and tell me what's really going on."

Once he was situated and I'd handed him some cool water from the well, he started. "Long ago, as you've heard, the Land of Oz was enchanted to become one of the 'in-between lands,' places where fairies and mortals might dwell together like it was intended from the beginning."

"Ed, you know I care for you like a brother, but I thought you were going to tell me something substantial, not fairy tales."

"And so I am," he insisted. "All of Oz, and the countries outside it, like An or Burzee, once belonged to the outside world!!"

I refrained from rolling my eyes. I'd heard of Burzee, of course. Every child read stories of the ancient forested land of bears and barley inhabited by powerful fairies who prohibited mortals from entering. "What does that have to do with what's going on?" I asked patiently.

"Don't y'see? The Fairy Queen who first enchanted these realms has come back!"

Did I mention that Old Ed drinks?

In fairness, all of the men drank, and so did a few of the women too. Perhaps the years affected Ed more. His own past was the one thing he never talked about, save for his traveling stories, which he said people needed to hear. Many enjoyed his tall tales, and a few even believed them, but most said he had a cracked pot. Of course, Gilbert and the other children loved his stories and they would sit with him for hours listening to wild tales of uncanny things, creatures who walked the wilds... people who could change shape... terrible giants who ate people. The one that kept Gilbert up at night was the the Tale of the Stone Man who was looking for the wizard Wammeranian who brought him to life and ran away. "You couldn't blame Wam for running away," Ed would say. "The Stone Man had a hollow gaze full of who knows what kinda malice!"

"Fairy queens and magic," I started doubtfully. "I guess it's a good an explanation as any for what's been going on. Some are saying the Wise Woman's back and it's her doing."

"Lady Malvonia *is* back!" he exclaimed. "Lurline's spell awakened her from the enchantment."

"Ed, how do you come by this information?" I asked. "This all only started two days ago."

"Why, the birds told me, and they heard it from the Great Eagle himself, who flies the lands of faerie and in-between!"

I sighed. "Is there anything you don't believe?"

"You think I'm crazy, but that's all right. You'll see!"

"Well, if she is back she can fight it out with the current rulers," I quipped.

"They'll bend to knee to her just like they did in the past. She and her sister come from a large family and long bloodline that stretches throughout Oz. If Lady Malvonia wants this country back she'll get it."

The idea was an uncomfortable one that reminded me of the rumors about my grandfather. "She'd be a withered crone by now," I said.

May 4th, 1742

Good news! The "Big Hunt" turned into a rather small affair, as they couldn't find a single two-or-four legged critter to shoot or harass. After a day of trudging through fields and forests, whispers started that the birds and other smaller animals were acting as spies and some of the men got spooked, claiming they were being watched. So, now the ranchers are sending a party to Governor Münchausen to demand he do something about the problem. Hieronymus Münchausen is young and popular. He only recently arrived from a country in the outside world called Germany. Edric said that no one's able to get back to the old countries, even if they wanted to, because they'd have to cross the deserts or locate the secret gates that go back and forth, but the fairies have been sealing them. One of the more common myths that people believe is that the deserts that surround Oz will kill any living creature that touches them. They certainly can, but it's not magic, but heat and fumes. How else could our intrepid ancestors have arrived here? (Gil counters that the deserts weren't yet enchanted when our ancestors arrived).

Munchausen never said how he arrived, just joked about finding the governor's seat empty, and since his name was Münchausen, it seemed a natural fit. He was probably unaware of it at the time, but the previous governor had been executed, which is why the seat was empty in the first place, and why no one was rushing to take the position. The Mad King had him beheaded on the grounds of treason.

Münchausen's managed to keep his head, likely because he's been increasing trade along the yellow and blue brick roads (the latter runs from outside the Ozure Isles to Ozmara) and into the deeper parts of the land, even as far as the King's Crown in the northeast, what we call the Seven Blue Mountains. The ranchers like Münchausen because he knows about making money, which means that he makes money for *them* and turns a blind eye to their less savory activities. It takes a lot of land for cattle to graze, to grow feed for the cattle, and for waste disposal, which a few have complained is fouling up the rivers.

Jeb won't sell our property, which has made him no friend to Carruthers. The biggest rancher in the county and the Head Magistrate, he's been grabbing up public lands that were set aside for everyone, claiming it's necessary to keep predators at bay, though it's really about having more land for more cattle.

A year ago, Gil brought home a fox cub that had been shot by a hunter in the leg. We were able to nurse her back to health, but I didn't have the heart to tell Gil that her siblings and mother were likely all dead.

"How can anyone keep and kill an animal, especially now that they speak?"

"I thought you were sleeping!" I said and smiled. I almost told him to just go back to sleep, but then I thought, he's going to learn the harsh truths of the world soon enough. So, I said: "Gil, people have been enslaving and killing each other since almost the beginning of the world. Talking animals won't matter at all."

We didn't have a lot of animals, just a few for ourselves and immediate neighbors. The ranchers were the big operations looking to supply all of the Munchkin Country. They were the few who could afford the horses and oxen, which were used to transport goods long distances.

I never liked it, even before they could talk. I knew what I was getting into when I married a farmer, but it still bothered me. When you raise creatures from birth, you grow to love them. You see the trust they put in you, how glad they are to see you when you bring them food, or give them a little extra something just because. But I never petted or named them; I knew better than that. Gil used to name them, which made it harder on him. After a while, he avoided going near the pens at all. Jeb didn't force him, for which I was grateful. Others would have.

I think for Jeb it was just something that had to get done. That's how boys are raised. They're brutalized by being taught to kill at young ages so that they they their feelings get stunted, and after awhile they either lose whatever they have or bury it deep inside, probably because if they didn't, it would hurt too much. I'll never forget the first time I saw it, the look of confusion in their eyes when Jeb brought them out on the killing floor... and then... well, I don't want to write about that.

Killing of any kind is unnatural; it's why men who come back from wars try to drown out the memories with whiskey and opium. Stranger still that some seem to enjoy it, animals or people, doesn't really matter; they can get away with the former, so they do it and defend it. It's like something gets into them. Or maybe it's that they lose something that makes us human. Jeb says "something takes its place... something dark and foul."

Maybe it *would* be better if things didn't go back to normal...

May 5th, 1742

A lot of the men have left this morning on a day and a half journey to Governor Munchausen's. I invited Lester and Tol's wives to come and stay. Zachary used to call Lester and Tol dimwits, but they're decent men, a lot more decent than him, actually. Since Zachary's going, I sent word to my sister-in-law to come as well. We don't have a lot of room, but our house is larger than some others, and if everyone brings blankets and sheets, the kids won't much mind sleeping on the floor. It's important to be together at times like these. There's talk of large beasts tramping across the woods and plains, with smaller animals at their side. It's all still hard to believe. It reminds me a bit of what Minister Wilkens used to preach from the book of Isaiah. Jeb never much liked church, mostly because of all the gossiping hens and small-minded folk, so he decided that nature and the open spaces were as good a church as any. The minister, who accompanies him fishing every other week, says he's half right.

Jeb's trying hard not to worry me. Carruthers must have thought he was going to back out because he arrived an hour ago with Zachary, rambling about one's patriotic duty to help bring the beasts to heel. He mentioned creatures called Kalidahs, which had the bodies of bears and heads of tigers, attacking people outside of their woods. Everyone knew to avoid the woods due to the presence of wild animals, but this was absurd. It was one thing with Ed to spread tall tales and another to use them to frighten people. As if we weren't frightened enough.

Two of the neighborhood wives came to stay, Tol's wife Albena, and Lester's wife Sara, along with their kids. He'd been gored by a bull at work three years ago. His employer said he was drinking on the job, but Sara says he never drank at work. Didn't matter what she said. The rancher didn't have to pay her anything in compensation. His brother is a magistrate. Sara doesn't talk about what she does now to earn a living and feed her family, and no one asks.

Together with Gil, there are four kids in the house, and I'm glad to have them here, though I'm upset that Ella and Ada didn't come. I asked Zachary why he didn't bring them along when he came with Carruthers, but he says he won't let any wife or child of his sleep in the same house as a whore. His pride is more important than their safety. If something happens to them, I won't hold my tongue.

The night's going to be a long one. Albena said she can hear things creeping around outside, but she doesn't want to scare the kids. They hear it anyway. Everyone's nervous and tense, and I doubt there will be much sleeping.

May 6th, 1742

Gil went missing this morning. His friends came running in the house, shouting that a big cat was prowling the wood behind the tool shed, and that Gil went to talk to it. I ran out, blind, panicking, not thinking of anything except to protect him! He's just a kid; he doesn't know what he's doing. I should've made sure, I should've warned him better! So I ran and hollered, scanning the field, praying for a miracle.

And there he was. I didn't know what I said or asked or yelled, but he emerged from the wood, the picture of calm. "It's all right, Ma," he said. "His name's Felis. He's friendly. They're all friendly, and they don't hold a grudge for what we did. Well, most of 'em. Anyway, they're worried the men are gonna force them to fight."

I couldn't make heads or tails of what he was saying, but Gilbert just went on, calmly talking to the other kids and their nervous mothers. "Everything's gonna be fine. Jus' so long as our fathers don't do anything stupid," he said, and then ran off to do chores like nothing had happened.

May 7th, 1742

I still can't sleep, but the night is much quieter, thankfully, and even Albena says she doesn't hear anything. "I think they all just moved on from here," she said, and Gil agreed. I forbade him to leave the house, and everyone says he hasn't, but he still comes up with more and more stories, and I can't help but wonder if he's gonna end up like old Ed.

He says there's a large army gathering of all kinds of animals, all getting ready in case they have to fight. "The domestic ones are saying they won't be anyone's slave anymore, and won't let no one try to eat them neither, and the wild ones are saying they're gonna pledge the old oath from before the time of man. I told them, 'You're incorporated now, and have rights,' but I'm not sure they understood."

May 8th, 1742

Most of the men are back. The governor has disappeared to parts unknown and the capital has sent someone named Purvoy to take charge of the region. Carruthers and Zachary and a few others stayed behind to "talk some sense into him."

But there was worse news. There was an attack on Zachary's farm! Ella and Ada are now here, and they're shaken and pale. No one said much at mealtime, but afterwards they opened up. In the middle of the night, two creatures smashed into their house, big and dark as nightmares, with vaguely bearish bodies, the heads of tigers, and eyes of the devil. So, Kalidahs *are* real! It's like the world has turned upside down. Or was I just not seeing things the way they really were?

The girls wouldn't be alive now but for this. Ella and Ada hid in the bedroom, trembling, as the terrifying sounds of crashes and growls shook the house. Ella had a poker ready, but not much hope. Just as the creatures broke down the door to their bedroom, six or seven animals, big cats mainly, came up behind the Kalidahs and attacked them! One of the cats told them to run! Ella didn't wait to find out who won. They fled and came here. Jeb says he'll keep a vigil overnight.

May 9th, 1742

Zachary came storming into the house this morning, stinking of whiskey and unwashed sweat, and aggravating an already tense afternoon. His eyes had a wild and dangerous look. "I said I didn't want them in this house!"

"So you want me to turn away my sister-in-law and niece?" Jeb shot back. "After what they'd been through? What's the matter with you?"

"I'll tell you what the matter is! Munchausen, that coward, has crawled back to wherever hole he came from, and that weakling Purvoy's callin' the shots, and he's a traitor!"

"He's been appointed viceroy, Zach. You want what? To fight him too?"

"*He's a traitor!* Did you forget what he said? That the king's gotta consider *both* sides! I said, 'The king listens to you, right?' He said, 'That's why I'm here.' I told him 'Then, you gotta declare war. We need the king's army!' But you know what he says then? 'This is a *delicate* situation, and nobody wants blood.' He should be ashamed! Blood's exactly what we want! Or would he rather we all starve? He just stands there, talking about how they have to figure out what's right for everyone! Damned fool! You can't make peace with 'em! They're goddamned animals and will kill you just as soon as look at you!"

"Some of those animals just saved your family's life!" I pointed out.

He just looked at me with utter contempt. "Jeb, tell your wife to mind her place." Not soon enough, he stalked off, still furious, leaving everyone uneasy and tense.

This afternoon, the rancher Carruthers came back again. He's plainly disgusted at Jeb. I saw it in his face when he asked for Zachary. I asked him about Tol, Albena's husband, who was one of the men who stayed behind with him. He looked at me and shook his head, "I don't know, miss. He's missing, maybe deserted, we don't know. He wasn't the brightest, if you catch my drift."

Albena started to cry behind me, but he had no time for her and walked off in a huff after I told him Zachary was out back. I tried to give Albena some hope. Tol could still turn up.

There's a lot of work to do, and I was about to put Carruthers out of my head, but then Ella passed by with a look. "If anyone knows a man, it's his wife," she said. "They're brewing trouble."

As it was a warm spring day, the windows were naturally open and that made for easy eavesdropping. Most men, except when they want something from us, tend to look past women as if we're invisible. Carruthers was speaking quieter than usual, but not quiet enough.

"To convince Purvoy to do the right thing," he said, "we're gonna have to make sacrifices. Are you man enough to do what has to be done?"

That kind of speech boded ill. Carruthers turned to look back at the house as if to make a point, while Zachary just stood there stupidly, nodding his head.

May 10th, 1742

Hundreds of animal pelts have been uncovered in a warehouse, mostly of wolves, bears, foxes, beavers, and wildcats, stuffed birds too, mallards from Lake Beryl, along with heads of lions and deer and containers of horse meat. For years, the ranchers had been culling predators from the area, as well as wild horses which they say degrade rangeland and compete with livestock for forage.

"This is meant to provoke war," Jeb said.

"You think Carruthers and them exposed the warehouse?"

"The beasts might have done it," Jeb reasoned. "They might have smelt the remains…"

"Jeb, did you have anything to do with those culls?" I had to ask.

"No, Zach was always trying to get me to go… anyhow, it doesn't matter who was responsible; the animals will want retribution."

"So, that's it then. We're caught in the middle of someone else's war."

"You know I'd only fight to protect you and Gil, but it might not come to that. The day after tomorrow, Purvoy's making the trip to Ozmara to let King Oz know what the Munchkin Country's doing regarding the recent events. He's agreed to stop in town and speak to the ranchers, and let them have their say."

It was then that I told Jeb about what I'd heard Carruthers telling Zachary that morning. I had convinced myself it was nothing, and that there was no need to worry Jeb unnecessarily. But it turns out he was already worried. "I had a feeling," was all he said.

A few hours after everyone had gone to bed, there was a sharp knock at the door! Jeb jumped out of his chair, and grabbed his musket, which he now kept at his side at all times. I ran to see to the kids and tell them to stay put until they heard from us. Their mothers had awoken too, startled and concerned. It was then I noticed that Gil wasn't in his room or with the other children.

Not again!

Frantic, I ran from room to room until I heard his voice. He was already downstairs, opening the door! We all stood in silent horror as four large, shaggy beasts stood at the threshold! I froze. Jeb appeared at my side, gun loaded and ready.

"Greetings, young master," the bear said to Gil. (The *bear* said... Never in my life!) Each of the animals followed with a greeting. There was a jungle cat, a wolf, and some kind of ape. "We apologize for the lateness of the hour, but we are here on urgent business. I am called Orso; I think you've already met Felis; the wolf is called Isangrim, and the ape is known as Hanno."

"Back away from the boy and tell us what you want!" ordered Jeb, tightly, from behind his rifle.

"Don't be alarmed, Father," Gil said.

"We mean you and young Gil no harm," assured Orso, diplomatically. "We knew your son was a friend and so assumed his family was equally disposed. We came to inform you that we know who tore open the warehouse. It wasn't your people after all."

"Kalidahs," the wolf intoned. "Looking to start a war; they knew we'd be angry and call for retribution."

"Why aren't you?" Gil asked.

"Because we know who the hunters are," Orso said. "We remember them from the days before we could speak." I walked down the stairs, anxious to get Gil out of harm's way. "Oh, good evening, ma'am," said the bear in a gentle manner, followed by another round of greetings from the other animals.

"The Kalidah King is crafty," said the jungle cat Felis, "but we know who our predators are, and we don't judge your race by a few bad seeds. Make no mistake. There will be retribution. Isangrim, Orso and my people have suffered the worst at their hands. But others have too."

"And the rest of us?" Jeb asked.

"We would prefer peace," said Hanno in a husky voice. "That's the other reason we're here."

"From some of the birds and fast-runners," the bear said, "we've heard that other parts of Oz are having troubles too, but many are working things out. One of your leaders, a viceroy, I think, is coming to town the day after tomorrow. As we understand it, he represents the interests of the Munchkin King... King Phillipos, I believe his name was. We seek an audience with the Viceroy. Perhaps you can tell him this, and together we can convince him that peace is in everyone's best interest."

"We can do that," I said, still not quite over the fact that I was conversing with four-legged creatures, or that they were as polite as they were. "We'll speak to him."

"Very well! Good evening then." And after they all repeated their farewells, they left. Just like that.

May 11th, 1742

Gil woke me up. It was a warm late afternoon, and I'd overslept, exhausted from everything. "We have to go," he said, repeating it. I didn't come to my senses until his father walked in.

"I'm going to wake everyone else," Jeb said.

"They're coming, ma!" Gil said.

"Who's coming?" I asked, starting to get anxious. "The Kalidahs?"

"Not them."

Had the animals changed their minds? I jumped up and told Gilbert to make sure all the kids were together.

There was no time to sort anything out. Out the window I could see not beasts, but a dozen or so men emerging from the woods; in their hands they held sickles, pitchforks and machetes. Only one had a musket.

Jeb came to stand next to me. "*What is going on?*" I asked.

He was upset like I'd never seen before, and only shook his head. Were they coming here to force him to join their war? It was the only thing that made sense.

"Come on out, Jeb!" shouted one of the men outside. It was Zachary. The rest had spread out in front of the house. "You and your wife and boy. Ella and Ada too, come on out! You ain't part of this."

"Zachary," yelled Jeb, "What the hell are you doing? We've got women and kids here we're protectin'!"

"Not anymore," said Zachary. "The whore and the dimwit's wife gotta stay! You don't have to understand it. Just take your family and go."

What is he talking about?

"This ain't right, Zach!" shouted Jeb. "You don't have to do this."

"Yeah, I do!" he replied. "We all have to make sacrifices, and that damned viceroy's gotta see what them animals are capable of. He's gotta see it firsthand, and then he'll have no choice but to listen to us. If the king decides to make nice with 'em, we're all gonna lose everything. You want that? You want to see your woman and boy starve? Just get outta the way. It's already been decided. We're takin' care of this."

So this was the sacrifice Zachary had to be willing to make. At least if it came at the hands of the animals, it would make some kind of sense. Anyone could understand a slave uprising. But *this*? Our neighbors and friends? To prove something that wasn't even true?

"No!" Jeb said angrily. "This isn't the way, and this isn't you. Killing innocent women and children is just plain wrong! We can find another way."

"Stubborn like a goat. You always were. There *is* no other way!" Zach shouted. "And it don't matter now. Ella!" Zachary yelled again. "Ada! Come on out there! *Now!*"

Ada was resistant, struggling to comprehend the situation, but her mother knew, and grabbed her tight. together they walked out of the house. Ella turned to me with such a look, I nearly broke. Her face was etched in such grief and remorse. I nodded to her, reassuring, and then turned to see if Gil was nearby; he wasn't, but I knew he was in the house at least.

"Look Jeb, this is the last time I'm gonna say it," Zachary said a little more calmly now that his wife and daughter had joined his side. "You've been smart your whole life. Don't get stupid now. They ain't got kin, and no one'll miss 'em or ask questions. You want to see that beautiful wife of yours die? And Gil? 'Cause that's what's gonna happen if you force this. Now, get the hell away from the house! This is your last warning!"

But Jeb just stood silent, not in fear, but defiance, rifle raised and ready. The people under his roof, those grieving women and children... they *were* kin even if they weren't related, and he wouldn't leave them to be slaughtered by stupid, evil men who knew only how to follow orders. I was never more proud of Jeb.

The men drew closer, and I could see their eyes, eyes full of fear, grim determination, and murder, but most were just blank, like the hollow ruins that lie east of the Blue Forest. It took consideral effort not to run, but seeing how brave Jeb was, I stood my ground. They would have to go through us, and maybe that would buy time for Gil and the others to escape.

A shot rang out, and I thought that was it, but it wasn't from the men. Zachary fell to his knees cursing, and there was blood on his leg. I was confused at first, and so were the others who were looking around to see what had happened. Then out from the bushes came Old Ed, caliver in hand, running to stand with us.

"Ain't none of these women and children gonna die tonight!" Edric said, holding up his gun.

"Good to see you, Ed," Jeb said.

"Oh, I never miss a party."

The men continued shouting angry threats, and although the odds had improved, they still had us outnumbered 4 to 1. "Get in the house," Edric said to us, "get the women and children ready to run. I'll hold them off."

The man with the musket raised it to shoot, but another one said, "No, stupid! It's gotta look like the beasts did it!"

Jeb looked at me gravely. "Go on. We'll take care of this."

"No," I refused. "You stand a better chance inside, using the windows to peg them off."

"She's got a point," said Edric, as a shot rang out, nearly hitting him.

"She usually does," said Jeb, firing off a retort before following him inside.

More shells rang out, splintering a window and a few wood-frame panels. We never had a lot of furniture, but what he had we began moving to bar the doors and windows. Jeb remembered a chest and pushed it to block the main entrance. Albena and the terrified children didn't understand what was happening, but knew enough to know it was bad. But Sara, who looked intense and angry, knew. I instructed the mothers to take the children into the bedroom, use the bed to block the door, and keep away from the windows.

The men tried to get closer to the house, but Edric's a surprisingly good shot for someone who never shoots, and I realized that he had at least one story in his past that he never mentioned.

I lost track of time. It could have been minutes or hours. Jeb crouched at one window, Edric at another. Ammo was running low, and there were still too many killers out there. You could hear the yelling and cursing through the pounding, firing and breaking of glass, the sounds of madness and death.

Soon enough, our bullets were spent, and the men outside seemed to know it. They began trying to crash their way in. The sun had set, but they must have brought torches because I could see grim shadows and the shapes of weapons behind the windows. It may as well have been the infernal legions themselves coming to take us. The thought of them forcing their way in so they could stab and butcher us like they did their hogs and cattle is something that'll haunt me the rest of my days.

Then the door splintered and began to push in under the weight of several bodies, while other men, smashing the remaining glass shards out of the window frames, started climbing through. Edric bashed one on the head with the butt of his rifle. "Get upstairs," he ordered before he also followed.

"We ain't leaving you here!" yelled Jeb. "Let's go!" Edric hesistated, but deciding there was little he could do, joined us as we ran up the stairs and into the master bedroom, barricading the door. There there was nothing now left to do but wait and pray. We wouldn't be the first innocents massacred, and I doubted we'd be the last. Maybe one day people would stare wicked men like Carruthers in the face and defy evil, but I'd at least go down knowing that *we* did.

There was a terrible noise then, a kind of howling or moaning, the kind of sounds men make when they die in agony. Then, other strange sounds emerged, a kind of mixture of rattling and hissing. This was followed by more men screaming, a few shots, and then silence.

I heard Gil from his bedroom cry out joyfully, "They're here!"

A few moans and screams pierced through the stranger sounds. The atmosphere had changed. I don't know how to describe it. It just felt uncanny. I pushed at the dresser blocking our door and walked outside the bedroom. Jeb and Edric yelled about stray bullets, but I just couldn't sit there in that uncanny darkness. One lantern alone now lit up the darkened room downstairs. I told Gil to stay in his room, but I needed to see more, and slowly began walking down the stairs. I heard Jeb and Ed behind me.

Yellow eyes glowed in the darkness around bodies of men that lay crumpled on the ground. Then, just outside the single circle of light: snakes. Hundreds of snakes, all of varying lengths, colors and sizes!

Some were still attached to the dying men, their bodies bloating from poison, as the mass of serpents weaved and undulated in and around their limbs. Some were spitting in men's eyes, the poison burning and blinding their victims, others were striking at their necks and legs, fangs piercing cloth and flesh!

Despite his instructions to stay in his room, Gil descended behind us in silence to stand beside me. I should have run back up the stairs, but I was paralyzed. The whole thing was as a dream. Then, as if in accordance with the dark world of night, one of the larger snakes lifted up his head and body to face me. He had an intricate diamond-shaped pattern upon his coils as glided halfway up the stairs towards me. As I recoiled, the creature stopped, smiled eerily, and said: "You may want to see this. Have a look."

Edric whispered that it would be all right. With his jewel-shaped head, the large serpent gestured to the opened front door, where the snakes now parted to make room for us. They were patient as we collected what wits we had remaining and walked the rest of the way down the stairs and outside the house.

At least a hundred or more creatures moved about in the night. They had surrounded three men. Other men were isolated and weaponless. Beasts stood on guard around them... Out of the corner of my eye I spotted mice carrying ropes. Overhead, herons, vultures and eagles circled, while hyenas and other big cats stalked the perimeter.

I stammered, amazed.

"We often get blamed for that *earlier* incident from your past," said the giant serpent who'd followed us down. "Consider this atonement." Then, he actually winked and glided off with that eerie smile.

Carruthers and two men stood amongst the prisoners, their clothes torn, their faces filthy with grime and blood. The other two stood panting in defensive postures, one bearing a pitchfork, and the other a long curved blade.

Carruthers spotted us first. His gaze went back to the beasts surrounding him, but then looked back up, screwing his face at Gil, before he spat and said, "It was that damned boy that did this, that warned them! He's the reason this happened!" He actually grabbed the other man's pitchfork and started towards Gil, but he never got far. In an instant, a wolf and a bear flew out of the shadows at his throat and leg, dragging him away to where his screams wouldn't be as loudly heard.

May 12ᵗʰ, 1742

Morning

We were awoken by a starling, which trilled and said, "It's time to get up, brave humans. The mayor and his entourage are fast approaching, and they're not alone."

Viceroy Purvoy had arrived as promised, and along with him about a dozen aides. But as the bird had noted, others came too, including at least seventy or so people from the surrounding villages, towns and regions. Several ranchers arrived armed, and not a few farmers, hunters and workers with them. Many brought their dogs. That puzzled me.

From the mountain and hill tribes came those who rarely visited the "lowlands." I only learned later who they were. Some of the wealthier nobles had come, men from the Saxon house of Mount Aquamarine of the Seven Blue Mountains, even King Kryppetarius from as far away as Lostland. And from the Ozure Isles, young Prince Eliphaz! After a few hours, it seemed as if all of Northern Munchkin Country was represented. There were stranger-looking folk too, not just the halflings, but other beings that could have only come from the fairy tales I'd earlier disdained. I caught Edric, who smiled at me as if he'd won a game of Spoilt-Five. My attention then turned to some of a less than savory nature that I was later told were court magicians, sorcerers, or hedge witches. The former came with the wealthier folk, and were better dressed, while others looked like they crept out of dark caves and run-down shacks from corners of the world best left forgotten.

They say that it takes a disaster to really get to know your neighbors.

Poor Albena searched amongst the crowd in vain for Tol, but I realized then that he'd likely refused to go along with Carruther's scheme and was killed. We would mourn him later.

Ella came to me concerned there would be no way to feed all these people, who by now must be hungry, but the viceroy's assistant overheard her, and said they'd brought provisions, after which he turned to a white-bearded man dressed in a peaked hat and a blue cloak covered with stars and moons. He bowed and muttered something about an ancient tradition, and before long there was food and drink aplenty.

Gilbert and Ada, meanwhile, were running around with looks akin to awe, for the fields surrounding us were filled with beasts of all shapes and sizes, many more of which had gathered since the previous night. They pointed out the different kinds of birds on the trees and in the sky. Some they didn't know, like the beautiful Lyrebirds, Edric identified many for them, but even was stumped a few times. Then came the elephants, hippos, zebras, lions, panthers and leopards. There were flightless birds, like the ostrich, ibis, rhea, moa and emus, and numerous lizards and reptiles, big and small; even alligators, crocodiles, caiman, gharial and other large and fearsome creatures, many we didn't know the names of, for we had never seen their kinds before. There was an abundance of smaller animals, prairie dogs, beavers, moles and badgers, along with the domestic sheep, llamas, goats, pigs, cats, and wild dogs. Even moles and rats ran to and fro unharmed amongst the larger animals who would normally be trying to eat them.

I thought for a moment that we'd actually died and were now in paradise, but in the distance stood the Kalidahs, and their crowned king among them, larger and russet-furred, and brimming with anger and barely restrained violence—so I knew that wasn't the case.

Viceroy Purvoy looked understandably nervous, but at a signal from his assistant, Jeb and I brought him into the house. We had to bring him upstairs, as the downstairs was in considerable shambles from the night before, the circumstance of which we explained. We also mentioned the request that the animals had made two days prior. He had heard this request from others they'd spoken to, as well, and agreed to give them an audience. The ranchers only came near once, with their dogs, to untie the surviving would-be murderers from the night before. Zachary was amongst them. Jeb refused to even look at him. As far as he was concerned, he no longer had a brother.

I voiced my objection to untying the men, but the viceroy said that while he understood my concern, under the circumstances, he had to deal with the present crisis first. To add salt to the wound, the ranchers armed the ones that could still stand. I took comfort from the fact that not many could.

The animals, meanwhile, had formed a delegation of four from amongst them: an eagle, a lion, an ox, and an old man whom I didn't know. Powerful scents of anxiety, fear and resentment were mingled with exhaustion and mistrust, and too many men were standing around apprehensively fingering firearms. It wouldn't take much for things to turn ugly.

The assembly of ranchers, hunters and hired men managed to find a wooden box to use as a pedestal. People could sense a discussion was beginning and started to gather. Some big-shots from this and the neighboring towns were chosen to speak, and each of them bellowed long and loud about their God-given right to dominate the earth and all the creatures on it, with harangues that centered on patriotic duty and manly pride. They said that anyone who wouldn't fight was a coward and a traitorous "animal-lover" who hated his own kind.

Most of what was said was a blur of anger and bluster, how free animals would take the women and eat the children, how the economy would collapse without produce to sell, and how everyone would be out of work and starving. It reminded me of a political rally with all of its obnoxious swagger and scorn, and just like a rally, this kind of talk resounded with the assembled masses as men and women clapped and raised their voices in agreement. The animals didn't much like these speeches, and there were a few growls and catcalls. Finally, the last speaker concluded by saying it was nature's way for man to take what was his, and that if the beast didn't go back to the natural order, man would show them why they were at the top of the food chain.

When he went back to his ranks, the viceroy invited the animal-delegation to speak. The crowd of humans booed and hurled epithets. The first to speak was an enormous eagle who stood up on the antler of an even larger moose.

"I am Ellil, son of the Windlord, ancient of the Great Eagles and blessed of the Great Spirit, who long ago endowed my family with speech and reason."

The reaction from the crowd was that of terror, not just because of his powerful voice, but because few had actually heard an animal speak before then.

"We are but travelers in this consecrated land, but we have heard from an emissary, the Great Mo-Gull, that a new thing has come to pass, and with it a crisis. It is clear to us that the Great Spirit has seen fit to give to all the beasts and birds and fish of this land the power to speak in the tongue of man. Since it is the will of the Great Spirit to elevate his creation in this way, you who call yourselves his children would do well to observe this, and leave your nonhuman siblings in peace.

"Yet, I know you will not, for our kind can see far across the surface of the worlds and deep into the dark hearts of man. So hear this, you who think of violence on this day: the beast will triumph. Where you must rely on your crude tools, we have been given the claw, the tooth and the beak. On your weak legs, you will flee in terror, but we can fly higher, run swifter, swim faster, and dig deeper. We can smell your kind long before you know we are near. Every bird will watch for you. Every serpent will wait to strike. The bulls will trample you into dust. The sea creatures will drown you in their waters.

"There will be no escape for you or your kind, who will perish from the face of Oz until Man is no more than a myth, a legend of a once great evil that was long ago destroyed. Have you not taught us to be merciless? How to start wars for selfish gain? How to kill for pleasure? How to lie, steal and cheat? Change your ways, sons and daughters of Adam, now that you can, or pay for your many crimes!"

The lion stepped up next, and seeing as this brought even greater discord, he roared mightily to silence it. But it was his speech that demonstrated why he was king of the forest. "The son of the Windlord speaks true! The Beast has had the right to life even before we could speak the tongue of man. Yet, it is not unjust for those who *must* kill their prey for food to do so, and for their prey to defend themselves. That is the Ancient Law of the Jungle, for man as much as for any other beast. But to Man, I say this: you have long violated the Law of the Jungle, for you have a lust for blood that goes well beyond your needs. You have decorated your halls with our heads and horns, your floors and bodies with our skins; you have over-fattened your bellies with our flesh; for useless potions you grind up our bones and tusks. Entire races of our kind have been wiped from the earth because of your cruelty and greed.

"The time has now come. You must prove to be a reasoning creature... or if you are not, then you are a creature of evil, whom every good and wise beast will strive to crush and destroy. Choose wisely, or your time on this land will be short."

The bull was the third speaker, and surprisingly eloquent. "Have you noticed that not only do we speak the language of men, but we all speak a single language? This is something that has not occurred since the First Days, and can be no mere accident, but must have been brought about for a purpose. Together, man and beast can attain to our greatest potential, but only through the pursuit of mutual love and peace. The humans have spoken of their heroism in having died for a cause, that is indeed a brave and noble. Yet, they have also said they should kill for their cause, but that is a lie, for murder is the path of oppression, and the cause is often power, land, or coin. Here now is a cause greater than power or land or coin, for can there be any greater pursuit than peace? For the beast, this is a new path, but for man, it is an opportunity to start again. Cooperation will pave the way for a great society in which all living creatures will help one another to grow and thrive."

Sadly, many of the men seemed confused, and not a few ridiculed, joking that he wouldn't speak so haughtily if he was properly gelded, while others laughed and said he'd make for tough steaks.

The old man spoke last, and not a few hurled the words "traitor" at him. But with a regal air, he ignored them and began with a question: "Have you seen the growing things across the land? Fruits and vegetables that no hand has cultivated. Have you noticed the colors? Why is this so?

Is this food not for all? I have lived a long span of years, longer than you know, but I have never seen such a thing occur in Oz. You have heard the animals speak, and deep down in your hearts you know it is wrong to fight against them, against what is happening in our land. Where our ignorance may be forgiven in lieu of the hardships man has faced, if you choose to fight now, the bitter years of war will be counted against you, and we who are human cannot long prevail, for where the beast has united under a single banner, I have seen in my travels that we are hopelessly incapable of getting along for any length of time." Turning even graver, he added, "It has been said that man is the crown of creation. If so, then let us make peace. If we cannot, however, I have heard it said from one who knows that we will be supplanted, for the Supreme Maker will see us as the lowliest of creation, and on your bellies will we crawl as the role of steward will pass to others in this new Kingdom of the Talking Beast, and they will not abuse the privilege."

Midday

Hours had passed since the viceroy first arrived, and to his credit, he'd listened to each speaker in turn. When at last he stood up, the crowd grew silent, and not even the birds could be heard chattering.

His position was a difficult one, and I suddenly had a horrible feeling that things would not turn out well for him. "This is a new day for Oz," he started, and then, seeing that he couldn't be heard by all, he repeated himself in a louder tone. "Violence threatens to destroy all that we have long cherished. There are rumors of war from our neighbors in the South. We cannot also fight an enemy who lives all around us. If we are to survive and even thrive, we must put aside the past and embrace a new future. If the animals are willing to make peace, as they have demonstrated, then I have it on good authority that so too will the king, for he has..."

He didn't get to finish his statement, as a shot rang out. Purvoy landed on his back, dead. The viceroy had made an unpopular choice, and paid for it with his life. Roars and squawks and bellows and hisses of fury arose from the men and beasts on all sides. Even the King Lion, who roared a terrible roar, could not quiet the crowd down. But as I turned to see them, I noticed the Kalidah King smiled.

Peace talks had failed.

Then, there was another shot. Then another. And then an eruption of noise and fury.

Everything after fell into a tumult of bullets, blood, claws and teeth! The larger animals leapt into bands of human hunters, biting, goring, crushing and impaling. Fangs, hooves and horns met with pitchforks, bayonets and sickles. The wizards and witches cast spells. Prince Eliphaz and many of the nobles sought to protect the women and children, while others fled. Predatory birds dipped into the crowds and tore away at muscle and cartilage. Dogs protected their masters in terrible battles with foxes and wildcats. The smaller animals played their part too, climbing and tripping and jumping upon faces of those who'd fallen.

As the beasts had predicted, the men were not faring well. It was a horror beyond imagining, beyond words, and I turned away with Jeb to grab Gil and get away from the madness, but once again Gil was nowhere to be found and I cursed myself for my failing to learn from my mistakes! The nightmare of days before now returned, and my eyes blurred with tears as I envisioned the worst.

And the worst came to pass. Jeb was the first to spot Gil's small body unmoving upon the ground. I checked to see if he breathed. He did, but there was blood pooling on his small stomach where a bullet had pierced him. From this vicious hole, his life-force drained away before my eyes, leaving him, leaving us. His father crouched down, cradling his head. It was the only time I ever saw him weep aloud. Edric hollered to Sara who brought a towel to stop the blood. Ella must have spotted us too, for she was holding me as I cried and rocked him.

Then something *else* happened.

A bright light descended from above, as if the sun had burst into colors. With it, a magnificent cloud dropped down into the center of the madness, which suddenly ceased. Out of this cloud cover stepped what looked like a woman, but was not a woman. She was taller, far more elegant and beautiful, as one of the Elves or Fairies I'd seen from the old books. She shimmered with a radiant glow and had the bearing of an angel and a true queen, and when she spoke, her voice projected far and wide, and with great authority.

"There will be no more violence today!" And with that, all the animals stooped or bowed their heads, all save the Kalidah King. The men, however, stared up in terror, for all their muskets and weapons suddenly melted into ash. Some of the people then began to kneel in obeisance, but the fairies ordered them not to. "Some in Oz have managed to achieve peace, yet you have not. For this we have come. Would that it had been sooner."

Several beings arose from the center of the cloud, which was growing clearer, and within it floated a kind of chariot, but not like any I'd ever seen. Out of it came strange forms, some half-human, half beast, some winged creatures. Again, the men started in fear and consternation, but the animals were silent, and remained in postures of respect.

So, it was true! Those things we'd believed were fairy tales were real, while the things we'd believed were real were false. Gil had known. And now he lay dying, unable to see it...

The Fairy Queen looked about her, as if to connect to every living being present. "Raise yourselves erect, Heirs of the Earth, Air and Sea," she commanded in a voice that reached the furthest distances of the assemblage. "Take courage, Children of the Supreme Maker, for in this land you have been set free!" The fairies then dispersed amongst the crowd, healing wounds where they could, but leaving the bodies of the dead as they were.

From amongst them came a beautiful girl of about thirteen or so, with dark hair in ringlets falling to her shoulders. She bore an air of dignity and compassion that belied her age. "Your boy has been injured," she said approaching us. "Do not despair. I can heal him." She knelt down to delicately touch his wound, and within seconds it sealed up. Even the blood dried away to nothing. As she stood, another young girl, gentle and kind, strode up to her. "Your Highness," she said, "it is not safe for you to be here."

The girl looked at her, and gently said, "You know that the well-being of the people is more important than my own."

"I do, Princess, and I do not wish to seem pedantic, but there may be dangerous individuals in and amongst the crowd. You are the key to the future in this land. You cannot be allowed to come to harm."

"You're right, of course," the princess said; then speaking to Jeb and me, she added "Your boy is special. He has a loving and courageous heart. Bring him before Queen Lurline. I'm certain she'll want to meet him."

With considerable thanks, Jeb and I helped Gilbert to his feet and approached the Fairy Queen, as the beautiful young girl disappeared back into the chariot. When Lurline spotted Gil, she smiled and said, "You remind me of another."

"Hello," he said to the Fairy Queen, politely, as if speaking to his teacher. But then Gilbert remembered something, and said, "Wait, some of the animals have been hurt." Our son, near death but a moment ago, now leapt away as if he'd only scratched himself.

The Fairy Queen smiled broadly, and Gibert returned with a duck in his arms. "His name's Siffer. He used to tell me about everything going on with all the animals, but now he can't talk or move."

So, that's where Gil got all his information. The Fairy Queen rested her hands upon the mallard, and the bird arose as if from deep slumber.

"How do you feel, Siffer?" she asked him.

"Better," he replied, "thanks to you and young Gil here!" Testing his wings, he flew off.

"There are others suffering too," Gil said. "Can you give me something to help heal them?"

"I certainly can," and with that she called over the young girl who had earlier warned the princess to remain safe. "This is Onna Val. I have given her an elixir of healing. Take her to every man or beast you know is suffering."

"Thank you, Your Highness," Gil said and ran off, with Onna Val behind him.

The Fairy Queen laughed gently, "Your son is brave and wise. He will be the start of a new generation in Oz. When he is of age, send him to the King's castle at Ozmara, upon the Greenlands of Morrow on the borders of the Winkie country. Have him bring this scroll," and by magic Lurline produced a sealed scroll. "It says that I have use of him in the lands to the North. Your offspring and his offspring will prosper and do great good in this land."

Jeb and I thanked her, for we knew that a great honor had been bestowed on us.

Twilight

By the time the amber sun began to set, all who could be healed were, and the Fairy Queen Lurline rose up into the center of the congregated throngs of men, beasts and fairies. Two fairies stood at each side of her, each one holding a quill and a scroll. They proceeded to record everything she said; one wrote what was meant for the people of Oz to remember, the other for the fairies. "Have many of the animals of the region come?" she asked. A furry creature materialized before her. It looked like beaver wearing a small crown.

"Many," he replied. "But not all. Though they've taken the Oath, some still don't trust the predatory races to keep their former ways in check, and there are a few who have no intention of changing just because their former prey can now speak."

Addressing the crowds, Lurline said: "A new day has dawned in Oz, and all of you who are here will experience its blessings. Yet, I wonder if you can truly live in peace..."

"What are we to eat?" cried out a shrill female voice.

"You can't expect us to last long on grass and water!" shrieked another.

"From this point forward, both man and beast will find food in great abundance."

"By what right do you make these laws?" hollered one of the men who had formerly spoken to the crowd. "I swore no allegiance to you, witch, and yet you come here with arcane magic, making changes and demands!"

"Ungrateful human," spat Avia, a fairy mockingbird. "If you knew whom you addressed, you would tremble!"

"No, Avia," said Lurline, "He has a point. You do not know me, so I will tell you. I am neither witch nor goddess. The lands in the outside world are under your temporary stewardship. Ages ago, your forefathers left those lands and came to settle here in Oz, which is but one of the lands consecrated by our Maker to Faerie. I am one of the Fairy Queens. In Nonestica, I am known as Lurline. Most who reign here descend from fairy blood."

"Then you admit it!" another of the prior speakers shouted back. "What is a fairy, but a demon in the guise of an angel, dispersed in the earth to lead men to their doom! Your strange ideas will not seduce me, nor any who would be men!"

As they grumbled amongst themselves, the circle of fairies around Lurline began to speak amongst themselves.

"In this journey we've taken," Avia started, "never did I suspect there could be so many kinds of wicked beings in the world. The terrible things they do to one another, and to the poor beasts."

"We've all sung this song before," hissed Herpetium, the King of the Serpent-Fairies.

"And we'll no doubt sing it again," Luba, Queen of the Wolf-Fairies, retorted. "The enchanted realms should be for those who deserve them! If I could, I would turn the wicked into a mountain of dung and bury them in the deepest, darkest hole, never to be seen or heard again!"

"A land without humans *would* be an unspoiled paradise," Pescus said wistfully.

"I must admit that this sentiment warms the depths of my coils," replied Herpetium, the King of the Serpent-Fairies, "for there are none here who have not seen our people by the millions made to suffer and die at their hands."

"For this reason did the Knooks, save for a few, cease to serve as the guardians of beasts," said Pescus.

"They were not made to cope with such grief," said Lurline. "We must now focus on the few goodhearted ones we have seen this day. As for the rest, twisted of mind and black of heart have they become since first they fell."

The other fairies nodded in silent agreement. "There is little we can do about that," said Luba, "One who is greater than us will deal with them."

The old man who had earlier spoken on behalf of the animals now stepped forth, addressing the complainers in the crowd: "If you will not listen to she who enchanted this land long ago, and now again, then you will listen to your king!" This startled everyone except the fairies. "I am Prince Pastoria the Second, the son of King Oz, and I have returned to Oz to take my father's place and become your king! Understand this: You are welcome to remain and live in peace, but only if you abide by the laws of this land."

"Then we shall leave this land!" shouted the earlier speaker. With that angry retort, about fifty or so men and women rose up and followed after him.

Zachary limped after them. But this time, he went alone. Ella would not go with him or share his fate, nor Ada his daughter, for they knew him now for what he was, a man bereft of conscience and heart. "You will rue this day," their leader threatened those who stayed behind, which numbered into the hundreds, "for we will return in greater numbers to take back what is ours!"

The dogs followed their masters, but one of them, a Wolfhound turned to Lurline and said, "Our masters were not perfect, but they were at least kind to us, and in their own way loved us. We cannot but repay kindness with fealty, for that is our nature."

Lurline smiled, "And a good nature it is. Farewell, faithful hounds, and may good fortune smile upon you the rest of your days." After so saying, she waved her hand. A bright light engulfed the human dissidents and their dogs.

"Do not despair of their fate," Lurline said, "for they have been returned to the mortal lands."

Other dogs, however, began barking and howling pitiably, running back and forth frantically.

"Speak," scolded the King of the Dog-Fairies, "you are no longer dumb brutes."

"Mistress," replied an elegant-looking Tazi, "Our masters beat, starved and fought us to death. We are all that remain." Several dogs keened a low and mournful sound at the recent memory.

"I am sorry for your tribulation and for the loss of your companions," said Lurline softly, "but be assured that where they now are, they are happy and safe, for never again will they be allowed to suffer."

"We felt this was so, but it is a comfort to hear."

"What is your desire?"

"Most of us wish to establish a community of our own, far from the habitations of those who betrayed our loyalty and trust. But not all. Young Prince here wishes to seek a new human, but he's yet young."

At that Prince barked a "yep."

"A royal name for a royal pup," laughed Pastoria.

"And his sires, where are they?" inquired Lurline.

"Most likely dead, your highness. His mother was used as a breeder and outlived all of her pups, save Prince, who was too young yet to fight. His father was a champion who lost but a single competition when his master sold him, along with other losing canines, to a butcher on the Silver Island."

The King of the Dog-Fairies gave Lurline a hard look, and Lurline, almost imperceptibly, nodded her head. "It is not the first time I've heard of the cruelty of the People of the Stars. We will send an emissary; if they do not listen, the Silver and Golden Islands will be cut off from the rest of Nonestica. As to Prince, I have a home befitting his name. A kindly king from another shore will love him dearly. As to the rest of you, wherever you settle, call my name, and I will see to it that your community has everything it needs to be content. If you cannot find a place, there is an island in the Nonestic presided over by dog-fairies, who allow no humans to alight upon its shores. It is a strong and safe harbor, where you will find delicious dogberry trees and chugu nut bushes. Merely call its name, Kaynyn, which means Land of Dogs, three times, and you will appear there."

With the Tazi's thanks, Lurline turned her attention to a contingent of cats that strode forth in a procession before the Queen and her entourage. Tigers, leopards, jaguars, ocelots, and even domestic cats came forth, all led by the lion king who had earlier spoken, and by his side a lioness. Both bowed their heads, but it was the lioness who now spoke to Lurline, saying, "We are by nature eaters of flesh, without which we cannot long survive. Is it the will of the Supreme Maker that our people suffer and die?"

"Hear me o great race of cats, great and small," declared Lurline. "The magic I have unleashed has changed you and your offspring forever. Not only do you reason and speak as the children of men, but you are now free from the need to kill and eat flesh, as they are and have always been. But to satisfy your tastes, my chosen wise men are in the land planting bushes and trees that will grow *meats*."

"Wammerian Hadrakis, come forth," announced the King of the Wolf Fairies.

At that, the wizard dressed in the blue cloak, walked out from the crowd and address Lurline. "Yes, Your Majesty."

"You have long been an advisor to King Phillipos and other kings before him, and trace your mixed ancestry to a cloud fairy, mortals, and the famous Blue Wizard who graced these shores long ago. Tell us what supernatural feats you have accomplished in your travels that can aid the people?"

"Ages ago I was taught the secrets of the plant world, and have since learned to produce plants upon which grow meats which have never been living creatures, but which taste magnificent to man and beast! I have planted many in An, Mo, Ev and Oz, and will continue to do so throughout Nonestica with the help of others I have trained. Because of these, along with the bounty of fruits and vegetables that you have caused to grow freely throughout Oz, none will ever again grow hungry in the land."

"Thank you, Wammerian." Then more quietly, she added "I know there are other matters of which you wish to speak. When we have completed our tasks, seek me in Burzee."

"I will indeed, Your Majesty."

This knowledge seemed to mollify the cats, all save for one saucy Maltese named Shadow, who slinked out and asked "What about fish?"

"What about them?" snapped Pescus, Queen of the Fish Fairies.

"You may not like it, but we need to chase and hunt or we'll grow fat; and since you've forbidden us mice and birds..." This part was interrupted by squeaking and chirping protests, and the low circling of a few predatory avians, until Lurline raised her hands, allowing Shadow to continue. "Since you've forbidden us our former prey, can you not allow us at least fish?" Some of the humans in the vicinity voiced their agreement, but the Maltese only narrowed her eyes at them.

"The waters of Oz have been enchanted and the sentient lifeforms within it can now think and reason like you. It is not my will to undo that. However, I shall not leave your people to grow fat. You will find in all the waters a moving thing that looks and tastes like a fish; but it cannot think, feel, or speak. When you and your kind go fishing, you must be sure *only* to catch this kind of fish. If you meet with the other, he or she will tell you, and you must toss her back in the waters. Is this understood?"

"It is, Your Highness," said the cat. "We are ever grateful!"

These speeches were well met by most, but not all. A small contingent of lions grumbled that they did not care for these new rules and would head to the far southeastern lands, which was said to be independent from Oz, to do as they wished. A lion-fairy warned them that if they pursued this path they would eventually be dominated by the "Men of Mudge," but fearing no man, they turned away and left for a land they said they'd call Lion Country.

Some of the jaguars, wildcats, and wolves also whispered to one another that they would similarly do as they pleased, albeit in secret, as they did not wish to leave their homes. This did not pass unnoticed by the fairies, but apart from their warnings, they would not compel any against their will, for they were considering another plan that would ease the transition for all living creatures in Oz.

A group of finely-clad men with tall hats and ornate cloaks then strode forth. Based on their dress and manner-of-speech, it was clear they were among the high ranking noble class from all over Oz. It is said that they are the real rulers of Oz, as the various kings and queens paid them more mind than their own council. "Fair and just queen, I am Elster of House Alston, Chancellor of Rose Cross University in Munchkenny. We, your loyal servants, represent the merchants, scientists, barristers and magistrates from all over this fair land. We had gathered in Munchkenny to speak with the Lord of the Ozure Isles, King Phillipos, when this auspicious event occurred, and so we traveled with the former viceroy on his journey to Ozmara. Our esteemed Colonel Braveman of the House Weston, High Magistrate of Winkie City, known for his valiant leadership in the decisive third battle of the Blues and Reds, is regarded as a respected writer and orator. If you might lend him your gracious ear, he will elucidate our position..."

At Lurline's nod, Braveman stepped forward and said, "Good Queen, it is clear that you are of great beauty and wisdom, and that you must, therefore, recognize that it is the nature of humankind to wear the mantle of civility, honor and duty, but only so far as it prevents us from falling too deeply into chaos, or causing needless injury to our fellow creatures, what you would deem cruelty for the sake of jest or wanton sport. Nevertheless, you are sagacious enough to see that there is a danger in mankind straying too far down the other path, for in that case he would cease to be human, for science tells us that a barbarous nature is both natural, useful and just, preventing us from becoming overly soft and sentimental, and dare I say 'feminine' in our weakness, where, thereby, we would lose the necessary ability to defend ourselves from enemies, to strive for greater purpose, and to exult in the glory of victory over those who would do us harm. Are not certain manly activities, such as hawking, the hunting of foxes, which prey on our fowl, or the destruction of the rude beasts who would otherwise exterminate mankind if left unchecked, nothing if not *just* pursuits, essential for our survival, and healthy, both in keeping the body fit, and for the soul? For as the cat, by its nature, enjoys the thrill of the hunt, so we, as the superior race, engage in this naturally-inspired wrestling match, do so with the proper exhilaration of spirits, both in personal sporting matches and in public tournaments that cheer and elevate the hearts of men who would otherwise be sorrowed by a life of drudgery, monotony and idleness."

This speech went on for some time and in similar manner, when Lurline put up her hand for silence. "It is clear from your words that you are *civilized* men," she said, to which they all smiled and beamed. "Avia, Pescus, Luba, see here before you a sterling example of the kind of sophistry that dominates the Outside World, for these men believe that because of their breeding and erudition they are superior to most."

"Horrid creatures," said the fairy called Avia, who looked like a mockingbird. "They not only commit evil acts, but justify them with false knowledge, and so convince similar weak-minded ones to follow their example."

Imagining this to be a pet of the Queen's, the nobles ignored her and continued to smile and look proud.

"I agree with Avia in this," said the flying-catfish fairy called Pescus. "Ordinary mortals assume that because of their accolades and grandiloquent worlds that what they say must be just and true. They have corrupted weak kings and hold rulers in thrall to their wills. Is it any wonder their world is as it is if men such as these lead it?"

"Already, one of these men has encouraged wars over lands bordering the Quadling nation," added Luba, "and another is attempting to start one between the north and south of this very country. I know it is not our policy, but we cannot allow them to remain in Oz, for ones such as these have led mortals astray for millennia, and would reintroduce all of the worst horrors that mankind has visited upon themselves."

"That is because they are in league with the so-called Wise Women," added Herpetium, "and the snake societies that have perverted the image of my people."

The nobles remained impassive, ignoring anything the fairy animals were saying, assuming it was but the musical language of birds and beasts. "You have wondrous pets, Madame," one of them said. "If you could show us where they breed, we would like to collect some. They would be a wonder at court."

Luba and Pescus scowled, but Lurline laughed. "No doubt they would. Yet, these are not pets, but my trusted advisors. Your presumption has caused you to fail to hear their speech, though they are speaking quite clearly in the common tongue. I see that you are unwilling to hear any but yourselves." This seemed to make the nobles a little uncomfortable, though they took pains not to show it.

"What... what do they say?" Braveman asked uncertainly.

"That you are the greatest example of civilized men we have yet met," Avia said.

"Ah yes, I think I can hear them now!"

"But Oz is *not* a civilized nation," said Lurline. "Nor will it ever be. For you, and those like you, civilization equates to the domination of the many for the benefit of the few. It equates to the perpetuation of power amongst the wealthy, for which you conspire with those who would bring war, slavery, persecution and cruelty of every kind; it equates to the justification of such actions through your corruption of science and religion.

"From your rhetoric and rigmarole, the earth burns, the poor live in squalor, men, women and children are killed by the sword, or enslaved; indeed, entire races of man and beast have been wiped from the face of the earth while you have smiled and enjoyed the spoils of such 'victory,' claiming it was necessary for the good of the country."

At this, the men grew pale and long in the face, for Lurline's countenance had turned dark and stormy as she spoke these words, and the men began to sputter and attempt to explain. But Lurline had heard enough.

"I will not stoop to cause injury for injury. Were I to do so, you would certainly be put to death for all that your words and schemes have caused. Nor will I send you to the Outside World where you would join your secret brethren to cause further mischief. No, instead you will be given a place suitable for a society such as yours and from where you can no longer do harm. Pescus, what fitting name would you give such a place?"

"*Rigmarole* sounds about right," she said.

"So be it. In the town of Rigmarole, not far south of Morrow, shall you remain with others of your ilk. Should it be discovered that you have found a way outside the town, or attempt to spread your ideas beyond its walls, you will find no further mercy from me. Is that understood?"

"Of course, Your Majesty, but..."

"Very well," she said, and with that, they were gone.

The crowd gasped aloud and began to murmur. "Daughter," said Lurline, "it seems that our actions have caused some to become fearful of us. This was not my intent, though I am not surprised. Men cannot long abide our presence before they begin to feel apprehensive. Perhaps you can reassure them of our good intent?"

With that request, the young princess arose and spoke out in a loud and clear voice. "Citizens of Oz, I beg of you, do not tremble at us, for we have not come to punish you. It is for your benefit that we have come, for we bring you life, joy, and peace. Ruled by compassion, kindness and humor, you will thrive in this new Land of Oz, and serve as an example to the warring nations in the Outside World. And if they will not learn from what we achieve, then at least their children, and those who wish to see, will know that there is a better way. But for now, you need only choose *how* to live in peace to enjoy the blessings that are to be granted when I come to the throne, as has been designated by your king and our queen Lurline. For my part, I hope that you will cast aside pride and thoughtless cruelty, and learn instead to revere life..."

But the people for the most part were split into camps, some which complained, grumbled, and said that they wish things would return to the way they were.

Others, despite the instructions of the fairies, continued bowing, praying and prostrating themselves before Lurline and her fairy band as if they were gods. The princess just looked at Lurline with sadness and uncertainty. "I see now that we must employ the solution we earlier spoke of."

Lurline looked at the other fairies and said, "We cannot allow them to worship us, for then would we fall into the same darkness as our forefathers when the nations were put into their keeping. Nor will peace succeed if they continue to rail against the changes we've made."

"The new residents of Rigmarole will not stay there long," stated Herpetium. "Already, they are discussing using it as their new, secret headquarters. Nor can we stay here to monitor them."

"It must be done then, and not just in this country but throughout all of Oz."

Suddenly, a thin river broke forth from the southwest, traveling like a giant snake through the land and passing not some meters before us as it undulated forward to other cities, villages and towns.

May 13th, 1742

I slept soundly for the first time in a long time, for I finally felt something I'd not felt in recent days: hope.

Everything was quiet again this morning. All the animals have returned to their forests and homes, and all the people who had come to hear the poor viceroy's address returned to theirs. I'd have been tempted to think it had all been a dream were it not for the new river that now ran through the town and before our doors.

I can see from the window the neighbors coming out to look upon it and drink. The river was proof. So were the fish, some of whom popped their heads out for a minute to say hello as they travelled downstream.

There was much Jeb and I didn't grasp about what had transpired the day before. Gilbert remembered most of what the Fairy Queen had said and done.

"Should we drink of the waters?" Jeb asked.

"I don't see that we have much choice, but Gilbert is to be exempt," I said. "Before her band moved west to the Kalidah Woods, Lurline told us that some should remember what life was like before."

To Gilbert's surprise, I handed him what Lurline had called the Orb of Purity that she'd handed me before her departure. "This will continue to refill magically. For the next week, drink only from it, and your memory will be preserved."

I was tempted to do the same. She hadn't said I couldn't, but I wasn't going to presume, not after everything I'd seen. Besides, I saw now that the old ways had to go. We needed a fresh start, a new way of thinking that wasn't founded on the dark and twisted ways of the past.

And so I'm heading down to the river to drink.

Turns out it's the most delicious thing I've ever tasted...

September 21st, 1752

Gilbert found my diary some time ago and kept it safe. He wasn't sure I'd want to read it. Neither was I.

It felt odd reading the words I'd written, but couldn't remember having experienced. It's been ten years, and I didn't learn until today who I'd been before I drank the Waters of Oblivion.

It had been confusing in those early days after all the rivers and lakes of Oz were enchanted with the Waters of Forgetfulness, but not unpleasant. Of course, the spell had not caused us to forget how to live as human beings. We just didn't know where we'd come from, or what we normally did every day. Most knew that something had happened to make us forget, but the fairies, with the help of birds and beasts, posted a letter in each town and village throughout the land, explaining that we lived in Oz, a fairyland enchanted by

Lurline, currently under the rule of King Pastoria, who would one day hand over the kingdom to the fairy princess Ozma. We were to live in peace with all other creatures who abided by the law of love, and to be wary of the few who did not.

In time we figured out the important things: we were a family, a community, who called ourselves Munchkins, a people who lived in a land called Oz.

In the end, with the fear of enslavement and death removed from their lives, most of the farm animals came to live back on the farms, happy to offer the farmers work or produce in exchange for regular food and protection from the wild animals who refused to live by Lurline's law.

The irony doesn't escape me now that I know our past. Our new world was one of talking beasts, occasional magic, and unusual beings who happened to pass through. It was a clean start for all. There's no poverty in the land, and for most the days of ignorance, hate and greed are in the past.

Unfortunately, the so-called Wise Women have made inroads back to power, though it is difficult for them to consolidate their rule over the various semi-independent kingdoms in the land. Pastoria's strong central rule in Ozmara has also forced them to play by his rules for the time being, at least...

Some of the recalcitrant animals and Kalidahs who had not wanted to follow Lurline's path saw what happened when their fellows drank from the river, and refused, seeking out shallow pools untouched by the enchanted waters that flowed throughout Oz. When the enchanted rains came the next day, they refused to drink at all until another two days had passed when they could no longer resist, but by then the spell had lifted. The presence of dangerous creatures, in turn, gave cause for some to take up arms or spells against them.

Some of the larger kingdoms discovered their old wicked customs through written records, and, foolishly, brought back some of them. It's said this has been aided by the rise of the Wicked Witches.

The Seebanians renewed rivalries with the North, and began again threatening war. To forestall it, Pastoria II sent his grandfather, Oz's former King OzAndahan (known better as Ozroar) to rule again in the South. I wouldn't have believed it before, but he's possibly the oldest living man in Oz, half-fairy, appointed by Lurline as the first king of Oz.

King Phillipos in Munchkenny is less belligerent than in times past, and so far there's been no talk of taxes, save for stores of food in case of emergency and help when there's a building project.

It's been argued that the old records should be destroyed to forestall future problems, but very few have gone so far as to do that, and the old records were helpful in the beginning to give us names for peoples, place and things, allowing us to readily discern the difference, say, between a ham bush and a turkey tree.[1] They've also been helpful to

---

[1] Some of the pigs and turkeys objected at first, but most said they didn't mind so long as we didn't start looking at them as food. In truth, except for the very wicked, it never crossed anyone's minds to do so.

remind us of a history we need to learn from if we don't wish to return to it.

With the help of the bear Orso and his mate Cindel, as well as Hanno and Jamilla, and the other human and animal neighbors who pitched in, we constructed new homes for ourselves and our neighbors, cozy, two-storied, domed houses in cobalt blue, most of them based on an architectural design by the Wizard Wam. Jeb and Gil say they look like smiling faces. They do, actually! Sarah decided to move north to the Gillikin Country with Wam, who she's training under. She's now known as Maleema.

As for Edric, I had Gilbert share the orb of pure water with him. He agreed that although some of his memories were of sorrow and pain, many were of important events from the past. To these, he's now adding new memories.

It didn't take long for Ella to fall in love with him, and he with her. Ada finally has a father she can love, and who adores her. She, of course, has no memory of her birth father; neither does Jeb remember having a brother. But that was the choice Zachary made when he decided to become a killer.

A fountain of the Water of Oblivion stands in the palace gardens of Ozmara, where we have moved at the invitation of King Pastoria II, son of the former Mad King, who'd ruled Oz five hundred years earlier.

We're uncertain what's become of this Princess Ozma who was supposed to have become ruler of Oz, and the king has additionally asked us not to make inquiries into his infant "daughter," but to be patient. Meanwhile, a prophecy has arisen in the land that claims that before Ozma comes to the throne, the reign of the Wicked Witches will end.

King Pastoria II asked Jeb to become the Royal Gardener, while I have been tasked with gathering and organizing books and extant information from the past so that Oz can have "a proper library," as the king says. He also jokingly insists that instead of Anne Di Corinne, I should henceforth be known as Ann Tiquarian, Royal Librarian of Oz.

I suppose it'll do.

Gil has been tasked to become ruler of the north in Gilkenny! The former king Trickolas Om was deposed, fortunately for him as the Gillikins were getting ready to lynch him, and the witch he had aligned himself remains unknown. None know what became of the older Royal Family of Gilkenny, but it is one of the tasks that has been presented me. Gil has allied with the powerful sorceress Gayelette and the Tah-Tipuu in that region, and together they act as a bulwark against any hidden dark forces. It is not an enviable task, as dark magic-users seem to have sprouted everywhere since the enchantment, and other entities have crawled out of their hidden places in the shadows to gain a foothold in our magical realm.

I can't speak for anyone else, but what Lurline did... well, it was worth the loss of the old memories and habits, most of which were not so wonderful anyway. If you could seen Gil and Jeb playing and exploring like kids, you'd understand.

We haven't seen Lurline in some time. Some say she left and forgot us, but I don't think so. She accomplished her purpose, though I do admit to some curiosity as to the fairies in general. As Royal Librarian, I can make formal inquiries into areas that others might. We shall see what I uncover.

I am among the very few who know how things had been before, and I shudder to think how things might have turned out. If you're reading this, you know what I mean. As a people, humans aren't perfect, but we're capable of tremendous good. Our lives have changed for the better, and no, that's not fairy powers that did that. That's the magic of love, and there's nothing in all the worlds better than that.

TOMMY KWIKSTEP AND THE MAGPIE

by Jared Davis

Some tales are lost when they become old and forgotten, and some because they were hidden away for so long that they got thrown out. But some tales are lost for no good reason at all. As soon as I read this one, I knew it needed to be found.

You might remember Tommy from his appearance in The Tin Woodman of Oz, *in which he'd accidentally caused himself to have twenty legs and Polychrome restored him to his original two! You'll also meet Perry here. He's the son of Jinjur, the former General. His sister Winnie appears in the story "Vaneeda in Oz," which Betsy and I also uncovered.*

But that's not at all. You'll finally get to catch up with the original Good Witch of the North before Mombi played a nasty trick on her!

Trot Griffiths

"The Magpie Song" is a traditional rhyme

"The Moon Will Help You Out" lyrics by Glen MacDonough

Dedicated to Isabelle Melançon and Eric Shanower

"Just search the whole world over—
Sail the seas from coast to coast—
No other nation in creation queerer folks can boast..."
~The Patchwork Girl of Oz

"Where are you going, Tommy?" chirped Corina.

Tommy Kwikstep looked up at the colorful bird. Corina was a Magpie with a bright blue chest and tail, red wings and a dark red head. Her beak and legs were also red.

"I'm off to Amethyston," Tommy replied. "I have a letter to deliver to Lora's music hall."

"Will you be all right?" she asked.

"Well, I've never been to Amethyston before, so I'm keeping an eye out for the signs."

Corina crowed twice, then fluttered down and alighted on his shoulder.

"Two for joy!" she chirped. "I can show you the way."

"What does 'two for joy' mean?" Tommy asked Corina as they headed down an old road.

"I'm a magpie," was the reply, "and we have a code: one for sorrow, two for joy."

"I think I've heard that before," replied Tommy, "but I remember it being part of something longer."

"Oh yes," replied Corina. "Sometimes I get a funny feeling and just crow. It's a very old tradition for us. Here, I'll recite it for you."

She puffed up her chest and delivered a little rhyme:

"One for sorrow,
Two for joy,
Three for a girl,
Four for a boy,
Five for silver,
Six for gold,
Seven for a secret
Never to be told.
Eight for a wish,
Nine for a kiss
Ten for a bird
You must not miss "

"Do you crow seven times often?" asked the young man.

"Not really. There've been a few times throughout the years, however."

"Do you go to Amethyston often?" Tommy asked after walking in silence for a time.

"Oh yes, I often sing at Lora's," Corina chirped. "You can hear all sorts of music there. There's something for everyone."

"I'm sure your songs are lovely."

"So I've been told," the bird said, briefly hiding her smiling face behind her wing. Perhaps she was blushing, but her face was always red, so Tommy couldn't tell.

Tommy made good time on foot before night fell. He'd set out that morning from the village of Mauville, a Gillikin town in the northern country of Oz, near the border of Munchkinland, for Amethyston, a mining town near the center of the Gillikin Country, famed for its beautiful purple gems. There was little traffic between the two towns, so Tommy had traveled cross-country, past rivers through mostly uninhabited fields and forests, occasionally glimpsing an isolated homestead.

Traveling in Oz is usually safe, as long as one is wary of the stranger settlements. Shelter and provisions are usually available to travelers, often freely, and sometimes in return for some small assistance. Tommy would always try to help out when he could and was always welcome in most homes. But danger sometimes lurked in the most unexpected places, so Tommy had learned to be vigilant.

The next day, Tommy and Corina reached Amethyston and quickly found the Music Hall, located in the center of town. It was a big domed lavender building with a small vestibule in the front.

Entering the anteroom and walking down the entrance hall, Tommy and the magpie noticed a counter where a cheery faced old woman served refreshments to the visitors. Reaching for the letter, Tommy approached her.

"Hello," he said cautiously, "I'm looking for someone named Lora. I have a letter here for her."

"That's me," the woman replied, reaching for the letter. "That's what my old friends call me. I'm better known as Locasta."

She opened the envelope and scanned the letter .

"Why, it's from Mayor Lavender in Mauville!" exclaimed Locasta. "She wants advice on how to open a music hall in her town. Oh, what a dear! I'll have to write back to her right away. It'd be lovely if everyone in Oz could enjoy music whenever they wished."

"Did you say your name was Locasta?" asked Corina.

"That is correct," the woman replied, tucking the letter away in a drawer.

"Isn't that the name of the old Good Witch of the North?" Corina crowed.

"Correct again!" Locasta laughed. "But Ozma and the king of the Gillikins have matters well in hand, so I decided to stay here."

"I'm not sure I understand," Tommy commented.

"Well, perhaps I should explain. Here take this," Locasta said, handing him a glass of cherry-flavored lacasa, "and have a seat. You may have heard about how Mombi once tried to turn the Queen of the Munchkins into a Wicked Witch?"

"I heard something of the sort," crowed Corina," But I could never understand why."

"I've often wondered myself," Locasta mused. "Now, a

witch keeps her own counsel, so I can only speculate, but I believe she was looking for an ally against the Wicked Witches of the East and West. She may have feared they were beginning to suspect that her powers were greater than she let on. The Wicked Witches of the South had already been defeated by Glinda, and the old alliance was now slanted in their favor.

"Anyway, Mombi couldn't transform people on her own," Locasta explained, "so she swapped my form with a young woman named Orin, who was then serving as Queen of the Munchkins. That's a story unto itself. Anyway, Mombi was a master of the Switcheroo spell, and had cast it several times before and after, but in this case, it seems my powers and the Queen's own good nature were too much for Mombi to corrupt, so Orin became a lot like me, taking up my role as the Tah-Tipuu in these parts, who the rest of Oz knows as the Good Witch of the North. Did a fine job of it, too."

"But I thought she conquered Mombi?" Tommy asked.

"She did at that, just as I'd done long before."

"Why did Orin let Mombi go?"

Locasta shrugged and Corina crowed seven times.

"A secret never to be told," the magpie commented when she'd finished.

"Well, what happened to you?" Tommy asked, sipping his drink.

"Since Mombi had used her magic over a great distance, I forgot who I was. I managed to piece together bits of my own name and that of the Queen of the Munchkins, so that was how I came up with the name Lora. I found Amethyston, and it was a gloomy little mining town. So, I decided to open up this hall where people could enjoy music."

"And we see what a happy town it's become!" cheered Corina.

"And when the Queen of the Munchkins was restored, you resumed your form?" Tommy asked, trying to guess at the end of Locasta's story.

The cheerful woman nodded. "Indeed. I consulted with Ozma, and we decided it was all right for me to retire and keep running my music hall. I'm happy here."

"But what if Ozma needs your help?"

"Then she knows where to find me."

Tommy finished his lacasa and handed the glass back to Locasta. "Thank you for sharing that story. I've always enjoyed getting a larger picture of Oz history than the books tell."

"It's my pleasure! Well, I'd better write a letter back to Mayor Lavender. Feel free to stay a while," the kindly woman offered.

"Oh, yes!" crowed Corina. "You should hear me sing, Tommy!"

With that, the Magpie flew down the hall.

Looking around, Tommy saw that Locasta's refreshment counter was in the center of the hall which curved around to open on several large rooms. As he walked past each room, Tommy heard music being played or sung from each one. With all of these performers, there was big enough variety of music that anyone could find something they enjoyed.

"In here, Tommy!" called Corina, who flew into one of the rooms.

He followed after her. The room had many tables and seats. At present, a flock of sparrows were whistling a jaunty tune. Tommy found sat down to listen to the twittering melodies.

After a few moments, he felt a tap on his shoulder. He looked up. Behind him stood a handsome young man dressed mainly in blue. His clothes were dusty and travel-worn.

"Is it all right if I sit here?" the stranger asked.

"Go right ahead," replied Tommy.

"You come here often?" the stranger asked.

"No, this is my first time," Tommy replied.

"Mine too."

They two sat silently for a while, listening to the winged musicians. At first, it sounded like a cacophony of whistles, shrieks and squawks. But Tommy knew first impressions could be deceiving, and so let himself relax, giving the music time to soak in.

Before very long, he began to hear something else emerge, something hypnotic and delicate that was building to a transcendent crescendo. But before it could, a flurry of dark notes crept in, softly at first, whispering of secret things in the darkness, and then, with a crash it was gone, and the original melody returned, now sweeter and stronger than before, resonant, and driving to its finale and finishing in an aria of splendor. The sparrows finished their song and left the stage amid the boys' applause.

Tommy glanced at the newcomer. "My name's Tommy," he said, offering his hand. "Tommy Kwikstep."

"Hi, Tommy, I'm Perry," was the reply.

Before they could say more, Corina flew onto the stage and began singing a comic song.

"There is something in the glimmer of the moon,
That always puts two loving hearts in tune.
And the lad who fears to say,
That he loves you in the day,
In the moonlight is inclined to tell you soon.

"So together in the moonlight stroll about,
It will surely put his abash to rout,
'Ere the ramble you complete,
You will find him at your feet,
That is how I think the moon will help out!"

Perry and Tommy applauded Corina's little song and as the next act came to the stage, Corina flew to Tommy's table and alighted on the back of a chair.

"Did you like my song?" she asked.

"That was amazing! You sang very well," Tommy commented.

"And what about your friend?" Corina asked, looking at Perry.

"I thought it was lovely," was the reply.

"What a gentleman," she commented. Suddenly, she chirped twice.

"Two for joy?" asked Tommy.

"I didn't mean to crow just then," she retorted. Then, she crowed four more times.

"Is that two for joy and four for a boy, or six for gold?" Tommy asked.

"I don't know," she commented. "I just felt like crowing just then and couldn't stop myself. There won't be another show for an hour, but I feel I can use some water." She flew out of the room.

"Odd little bird there," remarked Perry.

"She's all right," Tommy said, explaining what each of her ten crows meant. "I've always liked birds. A bird once helped me out of a nasty situation... well, sort of. It turned out the bird was really a fairy who'd been transformed."

"That sounds like an interesting story," Perry replied, grinning and sitting back in his seat.

"I run errands," Tommy explained, "and one day, a woman gave me a wish as a reward. I accidentally wished that I had twenty legs, and quickly regretted it. Luckily, sometime later, I ran into the Scarecrow and Tin Woodman who were traveling with Polychrome, the Rainbow's Daughter. They'd just had a run-in with a witch who'd turned them into a straw-stuffed bear, a tin owl, and a canary. But Polychrome had enough magic to restore me to normal."

"I know the Scarecrow very well," Perry commented,

sitting back in his chair. "You see, my mother is Jinjur, who I'm sure you know is the one who led the Army of Revolt long ago?"

Tommy nodded. "I've heard of her, of course."

"My twin sister Winnie and I have always helped Mother out on her farm. We keep birds out of her cream-puff bushes," Perry continued

"You have a twin sister?" Tommy asked.

"You wouldn't know it to see us. Winnie stopped aging when we turned ten. She said it was a nice age, and mother said it was all right. I decided I wanted to grow up and learn more about the world."

"You could've learned about the world at the age of ten..." Tommy said.

"I suppose that's true," Perry laughed. "I suppose there were things I wanted to learn that kids don't get to."

"I think I understand," said Tommy. "So, what brought you to Amethyston?"

"I just had to get away," Perry admitted quietly. "At home, Mother runs a tight ship, and everyone must do their share of the work. All very fine; it's not that I'm against work, but I needed a change. I had read so much about Oz and wanted to go out and see it for myself," he answered. "I just happened to wander into town on my ramblings."

"I've rarely gone far from Mauville," replied Tommy. "In the summer, I get a stock of Oz cream from an Oz cream shop and give it to children in local towns to help them keep cool."

"We didn't have Oz cream often at the farm," Perry

commented. "Mother said we had plenty of other treats for ourselves without it. But we did get it a few times. I loved that it didn't melt until you ate it."

"That's what makes it Oz cream!" Tommy laughed. "Now in the winter, when it snows, I make sure everyone has enough mittens and scarves to keep warm while they play outside."

"You enjoy helping people I guess?" Perry asked.

"I suppose so. There's almost nothing better than knowing you helped someone else," Tommy answered.

"Do you have a family?" Perry inquired.

"Yes, but they live far away, and I haven't seen them since I left home, which was a long time ago," Tommy said "I've often thought about going back for a visit. I get awfully lonely sometimes."

Perry nodded his head, and said, "I know what you mean. I feel the same way myself, sometimes, traveling around on my own."

Tommy looked Perry over. "Do you have anywhere to go?" he asked.

"Not really," was the admission. "I could go back to Mother and Winnie, but I don't really want to. I still want to see more of Oz."

Tommy thought this over. He liked Perry, and he also had a desire to see more of the wonders of Oz. There were plenty of boys and girls back in Tommy's town who would be happy to take over his deliveries and he could wander around Oz with his new friend.

"I want to see Oz, too," Tommy said at last. "How would you like it if we traveled together? We could find new people to help, and neither of us would be as lonely."

"That sounds like fun," replied Perry.

Corina flew back into the room. "Well, I'm going to be on my way, Tommy," she chirped. "Just wanted to say goodbye. I'm glad to see you found a new friend."

"Thanks for accompanying me on the way to Amethyston, Corina," Tommy said, gently stroking the feathers on her head. "I hope we meet again soon."

"Me, too," she cawed. "I hope to see both of you again sometime."

Then she startled them when she suddenly crowed nine times. She then stared in surprise at the two young men. "Nine for a kiss?" asked Tommy.

"A kiss?" exclaimed Perry, so loudly it interrupted a singing crane that was onstage in another room. "What is that supposed to mean?"

"Are you sure that it wasn't that three girls are going to come in with gold?" Tommy asked Corina.

"I don't think so," Corina replied, quietly. "I would have had a break in between them."

The three looked away, at the floor, out the door, anywhere but at each other.

"Look," Perry said at last, getting up. "I think maybe traveling together isn't such a good idea right now. I mean, I've been away from Mother and Winnie for a few months now, and I should probably go home. I appreciate the offer, but... I'm going to have to decline."

Tommy watched sadly after him as he walked out of the room. Corina volunteered a single crow.

"I should probably head home too," he said at last.

"Do you want me to come along?"

He looked at the little bird.

"You don't have to," he said at last.

"No, I *want* to," she replied and perched on his shoulder.

Tommy walked out into the hallway.

"Oh, there you are!" Locasta called from her counter. "I wrote up a letter to Mayor Lavender. You won't mind taking it to her, will you?"

"No," Tommy quietly responded.

"Oh, dear," Locasta cooed. "Are you all right?"

"Yeah," Tommy said, feigning cheerfulness, "just tired from the day."

"Oh, poor boy. Well, don't feel like you have to leave right away. Have a drink, if you like."

"No thanks," Tommy replied. He walked down the hallway and turned to exit the door in the foyer, but then walked to a cushioned chair by the door, and sat down in it sideways, burying his face in his hands. Corina hopped off of his shoulder and flew down the hallway, explaining that she had something she forgot to tell Locasta.

After a few moments, Tommy resolved to get up and return home when he heard someone enter the room.

He felt a kiss on the forehead.

Assuming it was Locasta, Tommy looked up, but saw no one, which puzzled him. From the other room, he heard Corina whistle seven times.

Then Perry walked into the room.

"Is it all right if I sit here?" he asked, but didn't wait for a reply. "Sorry about leaving so abruptly. When I came here, I wasn't expecting to... make a friend."

"You wanted to find out more about Oz," Tommy replied.

"I think I found out something about myself," Perry replied. "Had to happen sooner or later, I suppose. I've been running from it for awhile. I think it's time to stop."

Watching from the counter, Corina crowed twice.

About a year later, hand in hand, Tommy and Perry arrived in the Emerald City. The Scarecrow and Tin Woodman happened to be visiting Ozma at the time and recognized him as an old acquaintance. Ozma welcomed the two to have dinner with them, after which they'd be escorted to a vacant apartment in the city they could use while they visited.

"It's nice to see my subjects being such good friends," commented Ozma over dinner. She was accompanied by Dorothy and the Wizard as well as the Scarecrow and Tin Woodman.

"Well, I'd say we're a bit more than friends," chuckled Tommy.

"I often feel the same way about the Tin Woodman," remarked the Scarecrow.

"You two certainly love each other," commented the Tin Woodman. "My heart knows."

"Indeed," agreed Perry, looking at Tommy. "I knew it the moment I saw him. I hope we see Corina again soon so I can tell her she can add 'love bird' to her list of achievements."

"I think that would require ten crows," commented Tommy.

"I don't mean to be rude," said Dorothy, who was a little confused about this exchange. "I guess it just seems unusual to me for two men to love each other, romantically, I mean."

"Why do you think that is?" asked Ozma. "Love is the most natural thing in the world, and should be the most encouraged. Do you think it should be limited because of the way some people see the world?"

"I didn't say *that*. I just said I think it's unusual," Dorothy commented. "We don't really see a lot of romance around the Palace... at least *I* don't!" she added.

"That may be," admitted Tommy. "But I do love Perry, so I don't really mind if it's unusual."

"Same here," said Perry.

"I'm happy for you both," said Ozma. "Relationships of all sorts are welcome in the Land of Oz. And if it's unusual, well, all the better. Look at my family!"

"Indeed," the Wizard commented, sipping his coffee. "You've certainly built one of the most unusual families in the history of Fairyland, and I've seen many unusual things both in the Land of Oz and back in America."

"Like what?" asked Dorothy, curious to see if the Wizard would finally tell her some of his grown-up stories.

As she saw the Wizard looking somewhat uncomfortable, Ozma replied for him: "Long ago, when I made you a princess, I adopted you, and by extension, your family, into what I see as my family, which includes Jellia, the Wizard, Trot, Betsy, the Scarecrow, Nick, Scraps, the Hungry Tiger, Cowardly Lion, Bungle…"

"We'll be here all day if you intend to list all those you've welcomed into your home and heart," the Scarecrow pointed out.

"Ok, I understand all that," said Dorothy. "But you said Oz has the most unusual family in Fairyland…"

"Ah, I see what you mean," started the Wizard. "In most fairy countries, the story ends with a prince or princess getting married. That's not been the case here. In fact, Ozma, Glinda, and I have chosen to remain single. Some of our closest friends are either nonsexual beings or those who've made similar choices. That makes Oz rather unusual, and probably the reason why you haven't seen much romance around the Palace."

"And so," Ozma added, "if two people fall in love and

decide to be together, be they male or female, who's to raise an objection? In the Land of Oz, we have all the time in the world, and it's even better if we can spend it with the people who make us happy."

Dorothy thought about this for a moment before reaching for her dish of Oz cream. "Yes," she said at last, "I think you're right."

OZMA AND THE ORANGE OGRES IN OZ

by Nathan M. DeHoff & Joe Bongiorno

Those who've followed our adventures over the years have often wondered why we've gotten invaded so many times. Those of us who live here wonder why it hasn't happened more often!

Oz is a land abundant in the natural resources so many in the outside world fight and kill for. It's also a land filled with natural magic, and that draws those who would use that power for evil. Oz is also beautiful beyond description, as are its people. As many years as I've lived here, I still marvel at how stunning, diverse, and wondrous it all is.

I think you'll find that the outcome of this story defines who we are as a nation, how we survive crises, and why our way of life is even more beautiful and important than the land upon which we live.

Dorothy Gale

Ozma and the Orange Ogres in Oz

I belong to those manifold Existences
Once known, or once suspected,
That exist no more for man.
Was it not well to flee
Into the boundless realms of legend
Lest man should bridle me?
Sometimes I am glimpsed by poets
Whose eyes have not been blinded
By the hell-bright lamps of cities,
Who have not sent their souls
To be devoured by robot minotaurs
In the infamous Labyrinths of steel and mortar.
I know the freedom of fantastic things,
Ranging in fantasy.
I leap and bound and run
Below another sun.
Was it not well to flee
Long, long ago, lest man should bridle me?
~Clark Ashton Smith

To the south of the Land of Oz, just east of the country of the Scoodlers, sits the quiet valley of Arancia. There, where the Arancine Cliffs overlook the great Orange River, is the home of the Orange Ogres, who dwell in the deepest caves and passageways that run for miles through the mountains. For many long centuries, the ogres kept to themselves, squabbling amongst their own tribes and avoiding the world outside, which they feared. For generation after generation their elders had warned them that, because they were the offspring of a wicked race who were defeated in the Old Wars, they must stay hidden, for should their enemies on the outside discover their existence, they would be hunted down and killed.

But it came to pass that ten years ago the old stories and traditions of the elders began to grow wearisome to the ears of an ogre named Citros, who desired to learn the truth about the world outside Arancia for himself. So he determined to explore the lands beyond. Citros was small for his people, but canny and stout. He knew the tribal infighting so prevalent in his culture was wasteful and born from their insular restlessness and monotony.

Despite the elders' warnings, Citros packed his bags and left. After adjusting to the bright light of the sun, he began to find this new world pleasant, especially compared to the dank caves he was used to. The air was fresh and clean, the grass soft under his feet, the trees pleasant to look upon and the water sweet on his tongue, particularly the waters from the great Orange River, which tasted akin to what we would call orange juice. He returned home to report what he had found to his people, and though most would not venture from their cavern homes, a large number of others, particularly those from the tribes with the lowest status among the ogres, joined him to settle in the sunny valley on the banks of the great river, and they quickly came enjoy it as much as Citros did. For shelter, they learned to build stone huts under the open sky, forsaking their dank, torch-lit homes in the caves for the light of the sun and moon.

For eight years, the ogres were content to cultivate the fruit and food trees in the valley outside the caves, even trading with their fellow ogres from their former cave homes. But the old legends of the elders never left the mind of Citros, who felt resentful that for so long his people had been shut up inside holes like worms while the world, which seemed to offer so much, thrived and moved on without them. The Elders said it was the consequence of their past, but even if this were true—which Citros doubted—what reason had they to suffer for the actions of their ancestors, he wondered.

Citros began to make expeditions beyond their new home to spy on nearby human villages, disappearing for days on end. Were these puny creatures the same as the ones in the stories that made elder ogres tremble like little cubs? Could they truly be so dangerous to ogres? Then one day, Citros came across one of them. "What kind of creature are you?" Citros asked, startling the man.

"I... I am a human," the creature said. "A man; Amigus is my name. And you are... an ogre, I presume?"

"I am Citros, of the... Orange Ogres," he said, christening his newfound tribe.

"Orange Ogres!" the man exclaimed, and then warily asked, "So the old stories are true. Are there many more of you?"

But Citros only smiled a terrible smile and said, "Yes, the old stories are true!"

Having seen the fear in the man's eyes, he knew that these humans were nothing to tremble at. They would make restitution for all the years they had forced his people to spend in the darkness, trembling at fairytales and stories.

As the man fled in terror, Citros only laughed.

It didn't take much to convince his tribe of what they needed to do. The Elders did not approve, but they had no power over those whom Citros had led out of the caves. So it came to be that every month, in the darkest time of the night, the ogres would depart their homes to raid nearby towns. They took all of the treasure from these villages, although they had no use for it save as trophies. Their strategy worked without fail. The mere appearance of the ogres in a village at night was sufficient to terrify the people. The villagers had time neither to escape, nor mount an organized defense, and the few who fought back were either beaten into submission or, in rare instances, killed. The ogres took no pleasure from violence, but neither would they tolerate resistance from the descendants of the people who had driven their ancestors into the caves for so many years. They kidnapped youthful men and women as slaves, leaving behind the old and weak to care for the children. The men were made to tend the orange groves that surrounded the river, while the females waited on the ogres and worked in the houses.

When the tribes still living in the cliffs discovered the success of their kinsman living on the outside, they at last joined them. The Elders, acknowledging at last the vision and wisdom of Citros, sought to make him the Ogre King, but he decided that the Orange Ogres would be ruled not by a King, but by a Council made up of ten of the most successful amongst them, one from each of the tribes. There would be no more in-fighting, and together, as one, they would make decisions, much of which had to do with determining which of the villages to pillage next.

One day, late in July, the Council came across a problem. All the towns within twenty miles had been raided so many times that there was no one and nothing remaining that was worth taking. By this time, the ogres had grown lazy from having slaves do most of their work, and they were reluctant to walk long distances in the hopes of finding new villages to plunder. The ogres demanded that the Council come up with a solution to their problem. The Council members were forced to think, something which does not come easily to most ogres. After three hours of pointless questions and foolish suggestions, Citros, the most intelligent member of the Council, came up with an idea. "If no one's willing to walk, then we'll float," he said. When he was met by puzzled stares, he added: "We have the river,"

"The river?" questioned Seads, an obese ogre with many of his teeth missing.

"Yes, the river," Citros answered. "Do you remember that village that was right along the river, the one where you got all that dried fish?" The others scratched their heads, and eventually nodded. "They went out into the water in those hollow wooden things they called 'boats.' We'll get our own boats, and float down the river in them until we find someplace worth raiding. That way, we won't have to walk."

"But we don't have any boats," objected Polp, a tall ogre with long ochre hair.

"We have plenty of slaves from that fishing village, and some of them must know how to build boats," Citros answered. "We'll order them to make boats, and we can use human slaves to row them, too. Then we ogres can just sit back and relax until we find a fat village to plunder."

"What happens if we don't?" asked Seads.

"Then we'll have had an adventure and gotten much needed exercise," Citros responded.

The rest of the Council roared in approval of this idea, and so popular was it that the entire tribe of Orange Ogres volunteered to go. A search was soon made for humans who could construct boats, and eventually, a dozen carpenters were found, and were put to work at once fashioning vessels and oars from the orange trees, which, in the ogres' territory, sometimes grew to enormous proportions. Eventually, a fleet of fifty boats, each large enough to carry four ogres and two humans, was ready, plus an additional twenty empty boats for treasure and any good stock of human chattel they came across. These were tied to the backs of the boats that had captains.

Eight days after completion, a group of two hundred and forty-seven Orange Ogres, adults and children, armed themselves with swords and spears, and directed a hundred human slaves to begin rowing down the Orange River. Some slaves were sent back to the village to serve the ogres who remained behind.

Luckily for the rowers, the current carried the boats most of the way, so the oars were largely unnecessary. After flowing to the north for a little while, the river split into a delta with many smaller channels. The one they followed led to a hidden and little known river that flowed underground through sparkling titian caverns.

The Orange Ogres cared less for the natural beauty of these caves than they did who or what might dwell there. They were a superstitious lot, and knew that caverns held strange and deadly creatures, perhaps even unknown tribes of their kind, and so they were anxious to get back aboveground where they could find a town to raid. To hasten the journey, they threatened their slaves that they would drown them if they didn't get them out safely and quickly. Still, two dark days passed before the river emerged back above ground near a small village known as Kermes, which lay in the southwestern Quadling Country of Oz, a few miles west of South Mountain. Although rivers flow quite differently in the outside world, in the magical lands in and around Oz, they are considerably more variable. Having never been on any river before, Citros wasn't aware of the difference, and was merely glad to find a diverting place to disembark and explore. He hadn't realized before now just how curious he was about the world around him.

"At last!" shouted an ogre in the lead boat. "But what kind of place is this? Everything is red!" This was true, since most of the buildings in the Quadling Country were either painted red or made of red brick. While the river remained orange, the flowers and trees that grew on either side were also tinted in various shades of red. The strangely colored landscape made the invaders uncomfortable, as they associated red with the colors of war and blood, and though they were fierce and strong, they were no longer the war-like race of the ancient days.

At the order of their masters, the humans steered the boats to shore. After everyone had gotten out of the vessels, the people pulled the boat up onto the banks. While a few ogres stayed behind to guard the slaves and boats, the others ran toward the village, brandishing their weapons. The villagers were taken by surprise at the sight of the ferocious creatures, and as they had long ago eschewed violence, the place soon fell to the marauding tribe. The ogres discovered a great deal of gold, silver, and jewels, which they found beautiful and with which they could make jewelry. Also, they knew such items had been valued as great treasure from the stories of old. But for Citros the most exciting discovery was made at a small library.

"Look at this green city," stated Citros, pointing to a large map on the wall. It depicted an image of the Emerald City, the famous capital of Oz. Although many ogres could not read, Citros had long ago learned to do so from the accumulation of stories the Elders had safeguarded over the many years. He picked up a nearby book that had the same image on its cover, and began to turn its pages. The illustrations inside gave him some idea of the beauty that this city contained.

"We must go to this Green City and capture it," said Citros. "We'll have more than we ever imagined! Is this place not fitting for beings such as us?"

If the ogres had known of the powerful magic that defends the Emerald City, or how many times enemies had tried and failed to conquer it, they might have been more reluctant to try for themselves. After all, Ozma, a powerful fairy, and the great Wizard of Oz both live in the Emerald City, and the Magic Belt and other magical tools and charms are stored there. However, the ogres had no knowledge of these facts, so they decided to travel to the "Green City."

Citros asked the librarian in what direction it lay from where they stood, and she replied that it was far to the northeast. Then she warned him "Many have tried to conquer the Emerald City before you, and none has yet succeeded. You will be defeated."

"Perhaps they were weak," Citros answered, "or foolish. It does not matter: we shall be the first."

The librarian only shook her head and gave him a disapproving look. Citros found this amusing and admired her courage. "Understand, old woman, that we are an ancient race that have long been oppressed by you humans. Our time has come, and it is right that we who are stronger take our place on top."

"If you say so," she answered.

"You are the guardian of these books?" he asked, picking up the one that held the picture of the Green City on the cover, and rifling through it.

"In a manner of speaking, yes."

Citros held up the book. "Tell me," he said, "In this book are pictures of strange creatures that I have never before seen. Who and what are they?" He pointed.

"Ah," the librarian said, "the one on the left is the Scarecrow, who is stuffed with straw, and the one on the right is Nick Chopper, the Tin Woodman. They are two of many magical creatures in Oz. They're both old friends of our Ruler. In fact, the Scarecrow once ruled the Emerald City, and the Tin Woodman yet rules the Winkie Country!"

"Are they… *dangerous*?" the ogre asked.

"Not unless you try to harm another living creature." she said. "Oz is a land of love. Do no harm and no harm will come to you."

"A land of love… How curious!" Citros replied. "Thank you again, old woman. We leave you in peace."

"Better than in pieces!" she said with a laugh before getting back to her work.

A very curious people, these Ozites. They seemed very unconcerned with the fact that their valuables had been taken. This woman also seemed curiously confident. Citros nearly changed his mind about conquering this Emerald City, as she called it. The existence of these magical creatures concerned him, and yet they did not look formidable. Perhaps it was merely their odd appearance that frightened off so many would-be conquerors.

Since the Orange Ogres knew that the Orange River flowed in a northeasterly direction, they returned to it. Now, the Orange River ends in an expansive lake located near the base of Big Top Mountain. There, the ogres disembarked by the shore. Curious about the mountain, Seads and Polp said they wished to row over and explore. As the remaining ogres were not averse to a break, Citros agreed, but warned them not to take too long. Seads and Polp would not have gone ahead had they known giants lived on the peak of this mountain, which they called Huge Mountain, and that it was their habit to descend in the mornings to drink from the lake. Thus it was that before long the boat carrying Seads and Polp was scooped up by one of the giants, who didn't see what he'd brought up from the lake.

"There's something big floating around in my juice," the Giant complained to his neighbor.

"It's probably just seeds, or pulp," said the other giant. Of course, the giant was partially correct.

"Why, it's a boat," stated the first giant, his mug up close to his right eye, "and there's living creatures in it."

"Really? Let me see!" shouted the second giant.

The giant who had discovered the boat tried to pass the vessel to his neighbor, but he accidentally dropped it back on the water. As they were forbidden by their monarch, King Orlando, to eat other living creatures, even ogres, they laughed and let them go. The ogres, of course, didn't know this. They were terrified and swam for their lives. They didn't stop until they reached the shore where their companions were, and wouldn't stop shaking until certain that the giants weren't chasing after them.

Once the ogres had left the mountain behind, they began to march northeast. It was then that the grumbling amongst them began. "Why do we have to risk life and limb against giants and who knows what else when we were perfectly content as we were?" "Who can say what terrors lurk in this Green City?" "We should make a vote to return home." This grumbling was heard only among a few ogres at first, but it soon spread to the others until it reached the ears of Citros, who began to resent how his fellow ogres were suddenly doubting him and questioning his decisions. In truth, he was questioning his own wisdom in having embarked upon this mission to conquer a magical city.

After a day of walking through pleasant crimson countryside, they reached a road of yellow brick. The ogres seized a Quadling farmer who was unfortunate enough to live along their route, and they learned from him that the road led to the Emerald City.

The southern gate of the Emerald City was open when they approached it, as the Guardian of the Gates was admitting a visiting group from a nearby village school. The ogres rushed through, shoving aside the Guardian who tried to ask what their business was in the city. They immediately headed for the Royal Palace, an obvious target, as it was the largest building in the city and was located in the geographical center. The Soldier with the Green Whiskers was marching back and forth in front of the castle doors, but he quickly tried to lock the doors when he saw the armed ogres advancing upon him. He was too late.

The invaders ordered the Soldier to lead them into the palace and through its halls. They finally came to the Throne Room, where Ozma was sitting, reading the daily *Ozmapolitan*, the Cowardly Lion and Hungry Tiger were napping by the sides of the royal throne, the Wizard was reading a newspaper from the outside world, Dorothy was reading a book and taking notes and the Patchwork Girl was singing to herself. Citros quietly entered the room with his strongest ogres, who threw nets over the slumbering beasts. Once he knew they were subdued, he yelled: "You must now surrender to the Orange Ogres! We intend you no harm, but you are now our slaves. Turn all of your treasures over to us!"

The Ozites in the room, except for the Soldier (who apologized to Ozma), were surprised, but they showed even less fear than the villagers in the last town they'd raided. They had been through so many unsuccessful overthrow attempts that the very idea of another seemed rather absurd, though they were forced to take it more seriously when a dozens of other ogres entered the chamber.

"Ogres, I believe?" asked the Wizard.

Citros was surprised by this reaction. "We are the Orange Ogres of Arancia. I am Citros."

"I see," said the Wizard. "You'll forgive me if I don't bid you 'welcome,' as I see you are here to conquer us. We don't see many ogres in Oz. Are you related to the Ogre of Oh-go-wan, or perhaps Ogodown? Or, I hope not, the Ogre-Too-Thake, or the cannibal Org?

"I have not heard of them and they are not of our tribe," said Citros. "We are not cannibals or murderers, though we will fight for what is rightfully ours!"

Ozma, meanwhile, had risen from her throne and walked purposefully to the wall safe (where she kept her most powerful magic items). Surmising that she was looking to escape, Citros called for an ogre to block her before she could.

Citros ordered the ogres to capture everyone in the room, but they were terrified by the magical creatures, such as the Scarecrow, Tik-Tok, and Scraps, so Citros himself had to personally oversee their capture. He had them placed in a rarely used gallery, along with the many talking animals who resided there. The non-meat beings would have put up a fight, but as Ozma commanded them to remain peaceable, they went along with only a few grumbles. Not failing to notice the utter beauty of the Palace, as well as the way his people were afraid of the non-meat creatures, Citros began to think things that were foreign to his normal way of thinking. He even took Jack Pumpkinhead as his personal servant, claiming that his orange head would serve as an effective reminder of their old home.

Billina and the Nine Tiny Piglets still had memories from their time in the Outside World, and knew that there were those who would view them as things to be killed and eaten, so they had made plans for emergencies such as this. Together with other small animals, like Toto, Bungle, and Eureka, they were able to escape the invaders. So, safely hidden away, they plotted with each other and with the mice who lived in the palace, and sent messengers to carry the news of the invasion to Glinda and her sister Belinda, who currently served as Good Witch of the North.

"Now that we have conquered this city, let us take its treasures and depart," said an ogre named Mandar who was one of the Council members. He was very reluctantly holding Omby Amby, whose the long green beard seemed weird and threatening to the ogre. "We have been too long away from our homes in the Arancine Valley, and the journey back will be precarious if the giants are yet awake."

Instead of answering, Citros mounted Ozma's emerald throne, and sat down on its soft cushions. He then announced, "Why go home at all, Mandar? This is a far better place than our old home. Do not great folk such as us deserve to live in this fine palace filled with all manner of good things? I say we should stay here!"

"Stay here?" Mandar echoed. "You may stay. *I* wish go home!" Two others, Polp and Seads, agreed, and although they could not quite articulate it, they did not like the idea of Citros on the throne. For his part, Citros felt strangely invigorated by the experience, but knew he must be cautious for the time being. He had not too many years earlier rejected being the Ogre King. Now, he felt that it was the only natural thing in the world. Besides, was he not already their king in all but name?

"Perhaps one of our new slaves will know of a way to get back," Citros suggested. "But I don't see why you'd want to return there. Here, we have more treasure and slaves than we ever imagined. Plus, I have seen in a book that there is magic here!"

"In the old legends, it was magic that got us into trouble!" said Mandar. "We were content without such things!"

"I never want to hear those old legends again!" Citros roared. "I have freed us... We have been freed us from such superstitions and lies!"

For his part, Mandar could not disagree, and although he did not fear Citros, he did not like this turn of events. "As you say..."

Citros settled back in his throne. Mandar and the others had been content in their old home back the Orange River Valley. But now that he had seen the Emerald City, he knew he would never want to leave, and he could never be happy again living in a simple stone hut in the middle of nowhere. So his former contentment evaporated like a puddle of water under a hot sun. He was wise enough to recognize that his thinking had greatly altered since arriving here and was disturbed by it, but his desire to remain in the beautiful city overcame any reservations he had.

So the conquerors remained in the City and made the members of the Royal Court work for them. As a lesson in humility, Dorothy and Betsy Bobbin were made servants to clean up after the ogres; Jellia Jamb proved intractable and was locked in with those they called grotesques, while Ozma was given Jellia's job. She would ensure that food and drink was served to the ogres whenever they wanted it, which was quite often. Trot and others had to polish the creatures' weapons, Pastoria and Pajuka were to outfit them with new clothes, while Snip's job was to iron them. The Wizard was made a footman, while Jack Pumpkinhead, when not attending Citros, was charged with combing the orange hair of those of the Council members who had hair, which was not an easy job for him, as he had none himself.

"We have to get these ogres out of the Palace!" said Jack to Dorothy and the Wizard. "Every time an ogre bumps into me, he shrieks and knocks my head off. I never thought of myself as frightening before!"

"They watch Ozma and me like hawks," she said. "I'm surprised Glinda hasn't arrived yet."

"She is in Ix right now, visiting the Queen," the Wizard said. "If I could just recover my black bag or get to the Magic Belt in the safe, I'd be able to get rid of them. The only problem is they seem to know I'm up to something and won't let me out of their sight for a moment. They won't allow me to go into my chambers, the Tower Room or the Throne Room."

They started at a sound, but it was only Betsy. She surreptitiously walked over and quietly said, "I think the animals have a plan," and then rushed away on her errands.

That evening, some of the ogres began to complain again. They kept encountering more of the uncanny magical beings who frightened them so much, and they were increasingly uncomfortable in the opulent halls of the Royal Palace which felt unnaturally large and complex for a dwelling place. Some claimed they had seen ghosts, while others complained of a skeleton in a closet, and yet others wouldn't go down certain corridors. So they began to individually and collectively murmur, and before long Citros grew angry.

He gathered the Council of Ten. "I have taken the Royal Palace as mine to rule as I see fit. We have conquered this place and it is ours! We need only to hold it. Anyone who is afraid of these harmless mixed-up, non-meat creatures, or still believes the foolish old stories told to young ogrelings, is free to return to your old huts and orange trees, but the slaves and treasure shall remain with me. Those who choose to stay will do so as my loyal subjects."

The other elders didn't like this speech, and said as much. "So, Citros," Mandar said, speaking for the others, "now you would make yourself our king!"

"I do not wish to lord it over you, my fellow ogres," Citros, answered. "But it is clear that as some of you are discontented here and others wish to stay, someone must decide what to do. I have led us here just as I have led this tribe from the beginning. You asked me long ago to be your King, and I refused because I was not then ready. Now I am ready, and I ask you to merely acknowledge my leadership by naming me King of the Orange Ogres."

Most of the Council kept their misgivings to themselves, and agreed that they would name him king, but Mandar objected. "I have known you since you were a small ogreling. Always, you hated the traditions and customs, the old ways of human kings and queens, sending armies to kill and be killed. Now that you have a city you wish to imitate them, to be a king of old? I will not stay here and watch this. You may not be content with our humble ways, but I am!"

With that speech, Citros stood silent for a moment, and the other ogres grew worried. Finally, he said, "I consent to allow you, Mandar, along with no more than thirty other ogres who are afraid of change, who are frightened of the residents of this land, to go. Take one slave from the palace, that unpleasant Jellia Jamb, to serve as a guide on the journey home."

With that, the former Council of Ten departed. Citros was glad to be rid of Mandar, who he saw as undermining his authority. In truth, he wasn't looking to dominate his people. Yet, now that he'd decided to stay he needed to be king in order to secure the support of the majority in the event that others from outside tried to overthrow them. He would have to remain vigilant until Mandar departed the next day. He would not sleep this night, and ordered ten loyal ogres to stand vigil in the Throne Room with him.

Peele, Seads and Polp were anxious to get away from the strange Green City with its terrifying living puppets, giant insects and vegetable-headed creatures. They approached Mandar to see what his plan was, but he was in a terribly foul mood and sent them away, saying only that they were ogres and would find a way. Having barely escaped the clutches of a giant once, they were understandably unwilling to take chances on repeating the experience and discussed amongst themselves a better solution than the one Mandar seemed to have. Having heard from Citros about the magic of this place, they next went to the Wizard, whom they recognized as a shaman, to ask him how they might return to their boats at the base of Huge Mountain without encountering giants or any other dangerous foes on the way.

"It occurs to me that you're not the first ones to ask me for a way home," he said, smiling at the memory. "As it happens, I could easily get you back to your cliffs and you can avoid all the giants and dragons."

"Dragons!" exclaimed Peele.

"How can you live in such a dangerous place?" asked Seads, astounded.

"Oh, we're all very brave here, you know," the Wizard said, for he knew as they did not, that the giants and dragons were quite peaceable and friendly.

"If you can send us home safely, we will help you," said Peele. "What must we do?"

The Wizard thought for a moment. Realizing that the most potent magic was in the safe, he said, "I need my magic. Get me into the Throne Room, and I'll be able to get what I need to send you home safe and sound. But we have to make sure Citros doesn't find out what we're doing."

"So long as Mandar is in the palace," Seads said. "Citros will feel threatened. For this reason he has summoned ten of our people to stand guard with him."

"Hmmm," mused the Wizard, "we must lure him out of that room. Give him a crown. That should help. Then tell him that a great feast is being prepared for him in the Banquet Hall. When he and his guards arrive there, have the Council pledge a formal treaty of peace with his new kingdom and yours. I don't need very long."

"It shall be done!" exclaimed Peele.

"Allow us three hours," added Seads.

Three hours later, night had fallen, and the electric and magical lights of the palace and Emerald City sprang to life. This only made the ogres even more anxious, for they had never seen artificial lights other than the torches and candles they used when they lived in caves. After notifying the Wizard that they were about to put the plan into effect, Polp, Seads, and Peele went to the Throne Room to offer Citros one of Dorothy's spare golden crowns that the Wizard had told them about, and said that the Council had gathered to declare him king and sign a treaty, establishing peace between his new kingdom and the ogre domain that they were returning to.

"Why then have they not come here to the Throne Room to do so?" Citros demanded.

"Your people are traditionalists," said Peele, "and would say goodbye to you properly, with a celebration that we have prepared for you. Even the Ozites have said that you would not truly be king if you were to be robbed of this honor."

"They are a very curious tribe, these Oz people, and not at all like the humans at home," Citros observed. "Be wary!"

Citros was secretly glad to be acknowledged as king and to be rid of the Council. He recalled that only a few days ago he had no desire to rule, and wondered again at what had changed his mind. He had never imagined such wealth and beauty and grandeur. Yet, even now that he sat on the throne, he longed only to immerse himself in the splendor of this land and never again leave it. Perhaps he had been placed under a spell. Still, he knew in his heart that this wasn't true. The things Mandar had said had struck a nerve. It was not a pleasant feeling, but perhaps he was merely becoming too sensitive, like the humans.

So it was that he followed his former fellow council members to the Banquet Room. Yet when he arrived there, instead of a party, he found all of the ogres crouching down in terror or attempting to flee.

The animals' plan had worked; they'd released their friends, who were now terrifying the ogres. The Hungry Tiger and Cowardly Lion were roaring and leaping on the panicked ogres. A living statue was tossing ogres about as if they were stuffed with straw. Jack, with his arms outstretched and a candle in his pumpkin head, was making every ogre he approached scream in terror. The Scarecrow wielded a pitchfork while moaning and walking about like a zombie. The Tin Woodman laughed evilly, swinging his axe, careful to not actually hit anyone. Even Scraps got in on the fun, running along the ogres' heads, hopping from one to the next, while making horrifying wails. Others played their parts too. The magic beings had recognized the ogres' fear of them, and were using it to frighten them out of the Emerald City.

"Ogres!" yelled Citros. "This is a ruse! They will not harm you. Gather yourselves and remember who you are!"

Whether the ogres would have heeded him and pulled themselves together, no one can say, for at that exact moment, the Wizard of Oz, who had entered the Throne Room and opened the wall safe, clasped the Magic Belt around his waist, and magically turned all of the Orange Ogres into oranges with a single wish.

"That was fun!" exclaimed Jack, taking the candle out of his head.

"You were quite scary," said the Tin Woodman to the Straw Man. "If I could sleep, I'd have nightmares about you."

"I'm grateful I can't sleep, as I was not half as scary as you!" replied the Scarecrow.

The Wizard now appeared to tell them that they had regained possession of the palace, that the animals had freed everyone still imprisoned, and that Ozma had scheduled a meeting for the next morning with whatever advisors were currently in the Palace to decide what was to be done with the invaders.

The next morning, a motley crew had gathered, anxious to see what would become of the Orange Ogres.

"Why don't we just let them remain oranges?" suggested Scraps.

"Now that would be cruel," disagreed Ozma. "We would be ogres ourselves to do such a thing. I would prefer to return them to their rightful forms unless there is some very good reason not to." To determine this, Ozma invited the slaves who been brought there by the ogres into the meeting. The ogres' slaves were themselves awed by their surroundings and just as terrified by strange non-human inhabitants of Oz as their masters had been. To make them comfortable, Ozma dismissed everyone but the Wizard and her human councilors. Even so, the former slaves spoke reluctantly at first, as they were in awe of the people whose magic had defeated their masters so easily. As they talked and learned how warm and friendly Ozma and her companions were, they slowly started to feel more at ease, and eventually explained how the ogres had attacked and raided their homes, taking the strong men and women, and leaving the old and weak to care for the village children.

"Did they kill any of your people?" asked the Wizard.

"They always came at night," said one man named Liw, "so we could not mount a defense. The only ones who were killed were those who fought back, and Citros did not allow the ogres to kill helpless victims."

"It was the same in our village," explained a woman named Wallia. "I am no friend of ogres, but I did hear Citros instruct his army not to kill anyone they didn't absolutely have to. I also remember him telling our village apothecary to tend to our injured people."

"That's very interesting," said the Wizard. "Rather un-ogreish, really."

A bearded man in his thirties said, "Sir Wizard, and Your Highnesses, my name is Nol. I come from Arancia. I was taken from my two children by the ogres to be their slave. Make no mistake. These are cruel, heartless monsters. Perhaps they have not yet killed in cold blood, but how long before they desire a taste for human flesh? How long before they decide our children..." at that he paused, stricken by the very thought, "that our own children might serve as food for them."

This reminded them about the stories and reputation of ogres who consumed human flesh in fairy tales. While some of these tales were pure fantasy, the Ozites knew that many of them held considerable strains of truth.

"We cannot judge them by their reputation in such books," said Betsy wisely.

"No, we should judge others by their actions," said the Wizard. "I've heard of a few ogres in recent times who've not been very friendly. These do seem... different from those."

"What we do know suggests that they're willing to conquer and enslave, but only to kill in battle," said Dorothy. "I think Nol has a point. How long before they decide killing's not only justified, but the best way to handle their enemies?"

"Or maybe they have a strict code," suggested Trot. "The fact is we don't know much about them."

"Even though your country is not within my dominion," said Ozma to Nol and the former slaves, "you are right that I cannot send the ogres back to their former home as they were, where they would only continue enslaving people."

"It's a tricky one," Uncle Henry interjected. "You can't send 'em back to where they came from, but you can't just drop 'em anywhere, an' make 'em some other innocent folks' problem."

"Well, is there anything useful that the ogres could do?" inquired Em.

"They don't seem to be good at anything but pillaging," said another of the former slaves.

"Didn't you say something about the ogres having orange groves?" Dorothy asked.

"Yes, I had to work in them," replied one man. "They grow the finest oranges I've ever tasted."

"Do the ogres eat the oranges they grow?" asked Henry.

"Yes," replied Nol, "of course. What are you getting at?"

"Well then, why can't the ogres sell their oranges to nearby towns?" asked Betsy. "That way, they'll be useful to society, and won't be hurting anybody... that's if you can get them do that."

"I remind you we are speaking of *ogres*," said Nol heatedly. "They are not like you and your *gentle* folk. They are vicious, violent and oppressive creatures. They would never agree to work for a living, even if they feigned to do so to be free of their enchantment."

"I understand your concern, Nol," said Ozma, "but I ask you not to surrender to your fears. We have dealt with folk like these ogres before. I have a plan that will ensure that the Orange Ogres will be friends with your people forever."

"Impossible! You just said you wouldn't send them back!" Nol protested.

"I said I could not send them back as they were. I know it can be hard to believe, but you have my word that I will never allow the ogres to harm their neighbors again. Put your fears aside and trust me," Ozma said. "I will send you all back to your original homes and you will find that all you have lost has been restored. Tell your people that when they see the ogres again, they will come to trade, not to rob. I understand how you must feel, after all you and your people have suffered at their hands, but I ask you to release the hatred and bitterness from your hearts, forget the past and look instead to the future."

The men and women spoke amongst themselves briefly, and then a man who introduced himself as Amigus stepped forward to address the court. "I must admit that I worry your promises are too good to be true, but we have heard of Ozma of Oz, even in far Arancia, and every story we have heard says that what she promises, she does. On behalf of my people, I say that we will trust you to keep your word." He bowed respectfully.

Ozma nodded to acknowledge him, then touched the Magic Belt, spoke a few words that no one else could hear and the former slaves vanished from the room. An instant later they were back in their old homes reunited with their loved ones, with everything that the ogres had taken from them restored to the way it had been before their lives had been broken by the invaders.

Queen Ozma spoke quietly to the Wizard, Dorothy and Jellia, then used the Magic Belt to restore Citros and the nine other council heads to their proper forms. Ozma explained to the surprised bunch that she was going to send them back to their old homes on the condition that from now on they would no longer raid neighboring villages, but sell oranges to them. The Ogre King roared a refusal, demanding his right to the throne by virtue of conquest.

"An archaic notion," the Wizard said, "And actually, we re-conquered you. So, if that's your claim to the throne, you don't have much of a case."

"Tell me something, Citros," said Ozma. "Your former slaves have said you've never killed a man in cold blood. Is that true?"

"Of course it is!" the ogre answered angrily. "We do not take lives for sport. Nor have my people eaten infants, or is that what you think ogres do? I imagine that is what your stories say about us, that we are cold-hearted murderers. Perhaps that is how your people have justified your mistreatment of us."

"Stories, I've found, are a little like people," the Wizard answered. "Some you can trust, and some you can't, but the worst ones mix the two together, so that you don't know what to believe. But the good ones are worth the cost of sorting through the bad."

"Citros," Ozma interjected. "Your people once asked you to rule over them as their king, but you refused and chose to create the Council of Ten instead. Why did you decline the crown when it was freely offered to you?"

"I didn't want the burden of responsibility that a king must bear," he replied. "I had learned from the old legends exactly what kings do. Human, ogre, it does not matter; I did not seek to follow their example. Then I saw this city. Never had I dreamed of such beauty. As soon as I sat upon the throne, I knew I could never be content again. I think it must be a kind of sickness, an infection of the soul that can never be cured. Perhaps it *is* just lust for power and I have fallen victim to it, as my ancestors did of old. As the humans had. You will have to kill me if you wish to stop me from returning again and again to conquer this most beautiful of cities."

"That is not our way in Oz," the Wizard said.

"Your condition sounds very painful," Ozma said sympathetically. "Fortunately, we have a medicine that can heal you." She rose, stepped down from the throne, and offered her hand to lead Citros out into the palace grounds. They walked together a little while until they came to an alcove in the midst of a garden of begonias that constantly changed their color and shape. There, Jellia Jamb was waiting for them.

"Is that the drink I asked you to bring for my friend Citros?" Ozma asked

Jellia curtsied and answered. "It is, Your Highness."

Ozma took the glass of dark green liquid, then turned to offer it to the ogre. "It will not harm you. You have my word."

"There is no need to treat me as if I was a frightened ogreling, still weaning on his mother's teat. I threatened your rule and know well enough that death is the sole reward for those who try and fail to overthrow a kingdom. I am a warrior. I prefer a warrior's death, but if this is your way, I will abide."

After making this short speech, he lifted the glass to his lips and drained it without showing the least hesitation. "There," he said, handing the glass back to Ozma, "it is done."

He waited silently for death to gather him in, but nothing happened. Then a strange look settled on his face.

"How did you like it?" Ozma asked.

"It was sweet," said the would-be Ogre King, "almost as sweet as the juice of the oranges in the Arancine Valley. I will admit that you have delicious poisons here. How much time do I have left?"

"King Citros," the Wizard admonished. "You would do well not to suggest that Ozma of Oz is a liar. The Princess has said that you will come to no harm, and that is the end of the matter."

"Perhaps what you say is so, but I do feel different, somehow. If you have not poisoned me, then what have you done?"

"The glass contained Water of Truth," Ozma replied. "It comes from a pond here in Oz."

"What is its effect?" Citros asked.

"As the name suggests, it makes you speak the truth," Ozma answered.

The ogre frowned. "I have always been truthful," he protested.

"With others, perhaps, but maybe not always with yourself," said the Wizard. "Water from the Truth Pond ensures that those who drink from it can no longer live under falsehoods. You have blamed your human neighbors all your life for driving your people into the caves to hide, when deep down you knew this was not just. The people who had oppressed your ancestors were long dead. Yet, you used this anger as a reason to terrorize your human neighbors."

The ogre thought for a moment. "What you say has the ring of truth. Nevertheless, my people *were* oppressed! Has man changed so much over the years?"

"As I discovered myself, they have not," acknowledged the Wizard. "Yet, we are not all the same. And have you ever wondered why your people were so mistreated?"

"Our legends purport to tell us, but I refuse to believe they are true," Citros said. "They were designed by the Elders long ago to keep themselves in power and us in fear." The other members of the ogre council echoed agreement with this.

At that, the Wizard asked everyone to follow him into his quarters. Once everyone was situated, he pointed to a lantern that hung at the end of a long chain from the ceiling. "This unusual device is called a Magic Lantern. I reconstructed it not long ago. It shows the past, and is similar to some other devices I've made, but is considerably less dangerous and more useful.

"What you are about to see is from an ancient time long before our world was sundered from the Outside World," the wizard said. "I think you will find it rather interesting."

The Wizard then uttered a phrase in a strange-sounding language and made some mystical passes with his hands. Ozma, who knew that the Lantern responded to the user's request without the need for any spells, smiled in secret amusement at the old carnival showman's dramatics. "Show us the dawn of civilization!" the Wizard then exclaimed in English.

Suddenly an eerie light began to pulsate on and off in the Lantern. Then it started to rotate, slowly at first, but gradually growing faster. The light now settled on one place on a wall, and within it images began to appear. They were still images at first, but in a short time started to move much like the moving pictures in the outside world.

The tale that unfolded was that of an ancient land ruled by a cruel, violent and rapacious race of giants. Some were serpent-kings who used terrible magic to dominate the races they conquered. Bull-headed minotaurs, goat-shaped demons, and wicked humans served dark celestial beings who sent them to make war on their peaceful neighbors.

"The voice of the narrator that you hear is that of Tititi-Hoochoo," said the Wizard.

"I thought it was familiar," exclaimed Dorothy. "Did he help you make this? Are there more? This would be very helpful to me!"

"Questions for another time," said the Wizard.

"Who is this Tititi-Hoochoo?" asked Citros. "A human mage such as yourself?"

"Oh no," said the Wizard. "He and his sister are among the most powerful fairies in all the magical lands. They serve in the Land of An, a long way from here."

"I have heard of them from the old stories," Citros said.

"This device, and others like it, were created to establish the truth of the past... something that has not always been easy to discern."

The Wizard then directed the lantern to jump ahead, and it moved an unknown number of years. Now the images were of a wicked host gathered to battle the Great Ak.

"Show the ogres," the Wizard commanded harshly. After a momentary blurring of the picture, they saw creatures recognizable as ogres, although larger than the members of Citros' tribe. These ancient ogres were a fierce race who dwelt in the deep forests, or huddled at the feet of hills and lonely mountains, raiding, plundering, killing whoever they could catch, man or beast. One familiar scene that flashed by was that of a tiny man or child stealing magical boots from an ogre.

"So that particular fairy tale is true," said Dorothy fascinated. "And that earlier battle... those were the armies of awgwas?"

"Yes," the Wizard agreed, still watching the flickering images, "the awgwas, deadly relatives of the giants, goblins and ogres. If the Professor were here, he'd say that linguistically-speaking, orcs, ogres and awgwas all share the same root."

"That means they're likely branches off the same tree," added Dorothy, her brow furrowing as she pulled out a small notepad and began to write.

"These are the ancestors of my people," said Citros.

"Yes," said the Wizard. "But don't despair. Show us Citros's people," he commanded the Lantern.

After another series of flickers, the narrative jumped ahead again to follow a group of reddish-brown and orange colored ogres and ogresses as they found their way to the caves of Arancia where they made their home.

"So the legends *are* true! We descend from monsters who served evil beings and became like them," Citros said with a deep sigh. "Then I myself am guilty of this very thing when I took over the Emerald City, when I raided the neighboring villages and took men as slaves... I was merely repeating the ancient pattern."

"Your story is not that simple," said Ozma firmly. "Lantern: show us the oldest ancestors of the Orange Ogres." With that command, the lights flickered repeatedly, and the eerie glow settled upon an idyllic image of an ancient land, upon which moved graceful, elven beings within a magnificent park-like city built around stately trees. "As the Wizard said, your origins are complex. Your people also have the blood of these ancient ones running in your veins. In the oldest of days, some of these were corrupted by the dark powers. Foul bloodlines and dark magic transformed their offspring into half-beasts and monsters, who ruled as kings over men, such as you saw earlier. Yet, as the generations passed, different strains of beings emerged, and in the passage of many years and away from influences of evil overlords, some, such as your people, naturally returned to the behavior of your true forebears, and in this way too is evil undone."

Citros thought long and hard upon what he'd seen and heard. "You are saying that we are descended from these most ancient people. In this way, then, we have the bloodline of good and evil within us."

"As do most mortals," said Ozma. "You are all a true brotherhood."

"So you see," added the Wizard, "it was never power that you craved. The reason you became so enamored of the Emerald City is because you love beauty. This is how your people lived before the forces of darkness arrived to corrupt and destroy, and it is how you shall live again. We will help make your own home a place of beauty and pride."

"Why would you do this for us?" Citros asked. "Why would you help someone who invaded your land and tried to enslave you?"

"You have destroyed your enemy when you make him your friend," quoted Trot with a smile.

"There's a lovely tribe of goblins in Yartralia you should meet," offered Betsy. "They have a similar background as you, I believe."

"Oz even has a friendly troll," said Dorothy.

"And not a few friendly giants," added Trot.

"Kalidahs too!" reminded Betsy.

Scraps then spun around and burst into verse:

> "Silly ogres, don't you know?
>
> Love is the only way to go,
>
> Try it for yourselves and see,
>
> Forgiveness comes quite easily."

Ozma laughed. "She's right. You are no longer the evil creatures from the ancient past, neither orcs, nor even ogres anymore, but something new... You, Citros, and your benevolent people shall now be known as the Orange Ochres, so called because you cultivate the most delicious orange grove trees in Nonestica. If you wish, you can have a successful trade and abiding friendship with the villages around you, and because you are big and strong, you can protect them against anyone who would threaten them. More importantly, you can truly put aside the past and embrace a whole new and benevolent future for all of you"

Polp then spoke up, "Your words are as beautiful as your city, but the villagers are not as you are."

"We enslaved them," added Seads. "They will not forgive us so lightly."

"We've wronged them," said Peele. "They would be right to hate us."

Citros looked crestfallen. "Their numbers will grow, and the stories of our oppression will fill the ears of their children and their children's children, who will fear us and seek to wipe us out as they had in the olden days. If only I had understood the truth earlier, I could have established peace with them from the beginning, but alas it is too late. Rather than cause harm to another, we will leave our ancestral home, and the humans will have no one upon which to avenge themselves."

"There is no need," Ozma stated. "I've spoken with them, and they've already chosen to forgive. It *will* take time for trust and real friendship to grow, but if you are patient I know you will see it blossom."

"Patience may be another fruit we must learn to cultivate," added Peele.

Humbled by all they'd learned, yet eager to embark upon this new phase of their lives, the Council of Ten agreed as one upon this course, and pledged to forever be friends of Oz. The Wizard then took the ochres to look in the Magic Picture, where they watched in astonishment as a beautiful orange city spring up in the Orange River valley near the groves. It was designed in the aesthetic of their people and in harmony with the landscape, but was deliberately left unfinished for the ochres to apply their own personal touches.

It did not take long before the disenchanted ochres embraced their new home and lifestyle, but the very first thing they did was to visit the villages of their former slaves and apologize to them. Though some were wary, and some said they'd prefer to be left in peace, others were quick to forgive, and to the ochres' great surprise, some even gave them gifts of things they knew they liked.

Once their new homes were completed, the Council of Ten and their families made the journey back to Oz with the promised orange tree saplings to plant in the Emerald City, along the border of the Winkie and Quadling Countries, and in the gardens of Zim the Flying Sorcerer. The Ozites were only too happy to celebrate with them, and many foods and desserts sampled and taught them by Stovely the Chief Cook and his assistants from the Royal Kitchens.

They were joined by their new friends Dorothy, Toto, Billina, Omby Amby, Percy, Fanny, Trot, Robin, Betsy, Cap'n Bill, Eureka, Scraps, Bungle, Jack Pumpkinhead, Cowy, the Hungry Tiger, Spots, Carter Green, and numerous others. The Orange Ochres marveled at the friendship and diversity that existed amongst these varied people, and at last with many hearty goodbyes they were returned once again, contented, to their homes in the Arancine Cliffs.

The ochres tended their own orange groves, and every other week they traveled to a nearby village, but instead of raiding it as they once had, they brought oranges and orange products in exchange for services and goods. Upon seeing that Ozma's words had come true as promised, the villagers began to make friends with the ochres in earnest. For many years to come, the Orange Ochres protected the numerous villages from those who would otherwise harm them, and together they all prospered. Thus, the country to the south of Oz became a much more pleasant place to live.

QUIET VICTORY

by Marcus Mebes

I never understood why everyone was always so mean to the talking phonograph player, Victor Columbia Edison. You might recall he was brought to life by Dr. Pipt's Powder of Life, in The Patchwork Girl of Oz. *Since then, he's had a tough time making friends, which in Oz, is particularly unusual because we welcome all kinds!*

So, what was the problem with poor Victor? Well, people hated his music, which he has a tendency to want to play all the time. Of course, that's no reason to discriminate against him. As far as his music is concerned, I rather like it, but I've never been old-fashioned or narrow-minded like some people. Poor Victor has had quite a journey, and this story brought a smile to my face. I think it will for you too!

Trot Griffiths

The Musicker sat in blessed silence. He and Victor, the animated phonograph, had been quietly biding their time in his small cottage in a valley in the Quadling country, in the Land of Oz.

Allegro da Capo had been practicing his breathing exercises for years, and by meditating had learned to slow his metabolism to the point where he could take short, gentle breaths that barely made any sound at all. The reeds in his larynx wheezed gently and rhythmically, but almost too quietly to register.

Victor Columbia Edison had a difficult time, at first, settling into the Musicker's valley. The creature would amble and play about, romping around so much that the mechanics in his phonograph rattled and threatened to come apart.

Not wanting to compromise the integrity and entirety of his new companion, Allegro had impressed upon the animated furniture the benefits of calming oneself and practicing patience and self-control. Victor's old records had been so badly scratched and cracked that there was nothing musical about the noise that came from Victor's horn as his needle skipped about on the platter. The needle itself—diamond-tipped and fine at one point in history—was now badly worn down, and further added to the cacophony that vomited forth from Victor's speaker. Allegro had promptly removed the disc, tossed it into the fireplace, and secured Victor's needle arm to its stand with some strong wire.

Now, at last, the job was done. "It's a refreshing change," commented the live phonograph. He had remained motionless during the last few weeks as Allegro carefully had mended the loose screws in his table body. With gratitude, he realized just how much his body had suffered throughout the years, and he endured patiently as Allegro did his best to repair or replace components that were damaged.

"How you, ah, got about on this broken leg for so long is a wonder!" the Musicker had muttered in his thick accent. With precision learned from years of solitude and practice, Allego had cut a board to match the size and shape of Victor's three other legs. Though all four of Victor's appendages were damaged in one way or another, his left rear leg was barely holding together, and no amount of wood putty, screws, or dowels would keep it from falling apart like so many wood splinters.

Now, as the two companions sat in silence, reminiscing about their lives, Victor recalled how Allegro had carefully removed his badly damaged leg. If the creature had possessed a face, he would surely have smiled at the memory. As traumatic as losing the limb was, Victor felt no pain. Once the leg had been removed and the new one mounted in place, he could feel his life flow into the wood, and knew that the leg was part of him. The old leg—horrors!—had been thrown into the same fireplace as the broken record. Additional repairs were made in time, but the leg was, by far, the most prominent.

Thinking back further, Victor recalled the day that brought him to Allegro's valley.

The Red Jinn of Ev was very patient with him. Very accommodating. In fact, it seemed that—at first—the jolly

Red Jinn enjoyed Victor's company. Indeed, Jinnicky probably did, being such a jovial, rowdy and boisterous soul. As with everyone, however, Victor's... well, everything about Victor annoyed people. And being a sentient, living being, Victor had feelings. And feelings could be hurt.

Over the decades, Victor had done his best to maintain the appearance of being lackadaisical and not caring what others thought of him. But, truth be told, the phonograph was tired of being excluded, tired of being ostracized, tired of being banished and unwelcome. This feeling had gotten him into trouble, particularly when he ran into others, such as the Blue Bear Rug, who felt as neglected as he did, but that only got him banished to the middle of the Deadly Desert. After escaping from there, he'd met a young girl named Lacey who was determined to help him, and brought his plight to the attention of those at the Emerald City where he could at last fulfill Scraps' suggestion that he "find someone who is real wicked, and stay with him 'til he repents." Yet, after Lacey left to return to the Outside World, Victor grew restless again, and longed to meet others who would appreciate him for the single purpose for which he was invented: to play music.

"*Good grief!*" shouted the Jinn, covering his ears and dramatically gnashing his teeth. "Enough already, my good machine! There's patience, and then there's patience! You've worn down my last nerve!" The Jinn's ceramic lid juddered atop his jar body as his head vanished inside.

Victor had been dancing around, blaring loud, scratchy, poppy, and skipping music from his megaphone speaker. But at Jinnicky's admonition, he had stopped, frozen in place. Certainly he'd heard similar words before, but the Jinn's were the ones that finally made a difference.

His head slowly rising up, the Jinn peered out from under his lid. "That's a good fellow," said the Jinn. His retainers gathered around him, including his dear friend and servant of the magic dinner bell, Ginger. They'd all been touring the northern Gillikin Country when they ran into Victor, and though their initial interactions were amicable enough, the Jinn's brutal honesty interrupted the sojourn in the purple country.

"I've hurt your feelings, haven't I?" asked the Jinn, his head once again emerging from his jar. His face dropped in sadness. "I'm sorry, old chap. But here, here! Har har! There's a Musicker out thar!" Jinnicky spun about in a twirl of red clink and clankering. "Where was that fellow? Ginger! Koreander! Tommerick! That Musicker fellow. Where did we run into him?"

Allegro's wheezing brought Victor back to the present. "I have saved this for years," murmured the Musicker, doing his best to control the accordion bellows in his body. Very carefully, the man had arisen and gone into the house and re-emerged before Victor had even realized it. Very carefully, Allegro set a flat, black vinyl disc onto the phonograph's turntable, and unlatched and lifted the arm. Gently, he set the needle upon the record's outermost groove and leaned back.

A gentle tune wafted from Victor's horn.

"Control, my friend," encouraged the Musicker, holding out his hands toward the phonograph. Allegro sensed that Victor wanted to dance, but such jostling would damage the record, and loosen the joints so recently mended. "Just enjoy the music."

Victor remained motionless as the record spun on the turntable. A pleasant, sweet tune played, and in the course of time, several more followed. Upon the one side's completion, Allegro turned the disc over and they played the second side.

"It was serendipity that brought this little treasure to me one day, long, long ago," whispered the Musicker, smiling. "We make good use of it now, eh, my friend?"

With utmost control, Victor nodded his horn in assent. "One day soon we will go to see Ozma," suggested the phonograph. "I'm sure she will help you." Victor knew that Allegro longed to have the accordion bellows and harmonical larynx changed into those of a normal human's... or, at least, something not as invasively persistent.

"I have no doubt of that, my friend," spoke Allegro, carefully folding his hands across his stomach. He sighed, letting out a gentle melody that sounded much like a harmonica tune. Taking short, shallow breaths, the Musicker closed his eyes and relaxed upon his chair. "But we are doing well enough on our own, are we not?"

VANEEDA OF OZ

by Nathan M. DeHoff

This story features the daughters of two famous women in Oz history, the Wicked Witch of the East, and Jinjur, former general and would-be conqueror of Oz. (Jinjur's son Perry appears in another story we recently discovered.)

I'm intrigued by tales of those who had to overcome adversity to become the people they are. Vaneeda is a character you might judge based on who her mother was, but as you'll see, things are not always as they seem. This is true of Paella, as well, a cookywitch who runs a café in the Munchkin Country.

There is some intrigue regarding the history of the Munchkin Country, which this story shines some light on.

Betsy Bobbin

Eight miles from Toomuch Mountain, which is in the exact center of the Munchkin Country of Oz, rises a mountain of glass. On its top-most pinnacle lives Vaneeda, daughter of Lady Malvonia, better known as the Wicked Witch of the East.

A witch of no mean ability herself, she had assumed she would inherit the land after the death of her mother when a house fell on her. Instead, the Munchkins appointed a man named Froom, who claimed to be related to the previous king. This claim was later discovered to be spurious, and for some time the Munchkins chose to have no sovereign at all, save for Ozma, who ruled over all of Oz. This was odd for the Munchkin Country, which in the past had two rival royal houses, one in the north and one in the south. The southern kingdom had waned over time, leaving only the north to rule in actuality, but when King Cheeriobed went into mourning after the disappearance of his wife Queen Orin, no one had heard from him in years, and it was assumed that he was no longer acting as functioning ruler of the north. This left a power vacuum that Froom the Fraud, as they now called him, attempted to fill.

Following the ousting of Froom, Vaneeda again campaigned for the position of Queen of the Munchkin Country, promising to be a much better ruler than her mother had been, and while she did win some support—mainly from those who lived far from the reach of her mother's dominion, or from those who preferred authoritarian rulers, it was never enough to gain power.

Eventually, the north and south rose again. In the north, Queen Orin was found and Ozma re-appointed her and King Cheeriobed rulers of the Munchkin Country. Then, the son of the old Southern king, Prince Ree Ala Bad, was found, and Seebania was restored to him and his wife, Queen Isomere.

While still making appearances occasionally to maintain goodwill, Vaneeda grew more and more reclusive and despondent, choosing to spend almost all of her time on top of her glass mountain perfecting her glass magic.

Many years later, two girls were exploring the forests of the southern Munchkin Country, and were quite hungry. Fortunately, they came upon a small inn decorated with teacup turrets and a large pie in the middle of the roof. Entering the place, they were immediately greeted by a tall red-haired woman.

"Hello, and how are you children?" asked the woman. "Would you like to try one of our blueberry omelettes? They're on special today."

"I think we'd like to see a menu," replied the older girl, who did not find the sound of this dish to be particularly appealing.

"Well, certainly, honey! Why don't you two sit down right here, and I'll bring you some menus." The older girl, who was named Henrietta, had graceful features and was bespectacled, with plaited, dirty-blonde hair. The younger, Winnie, was pretty as well, with medium-length, wavy brown hair. When the waitress returned, Henrietta ordered pancakes and coffee, Winnie a cheese Danish. There were few other customers, although a few woodsmen sat a table on against the south wall, a woman with a copy of *Gozzip* magazine occasionally took a bite of a muffin on the table in front of her, and three bears were enjoying a meal of porridge.

"Want some more coffee, hon?" asked the red-haired woman, after the two girls had finished eating.

"Sure," replied Henrietta. "What about you, Winnie?"

"I don't drink coffee," replied the other girl at the table. "I'm only ten."

"Yes, but how many years have you been ten?"

This was not an unusual question in the Land of Oz, where, due to an enchantment that affected the entire land, aging was purely optional. While the lady poured a cup of coffee for Henrietta, a rather breathless paperboy came in the door.

"Extry! Extry!" called the boy. "Munchkin Royal Family turned into glass!"

"Turned into *glass*?" asked Winnie.

"Which Royal Family?" asked Henrietta.

"Yes, and the Northern Royals from the Ozure Isles!"

"Oh, the High Royals," stated Henrietta. "I'm sure it's just one of those joke papers, like the one that claimed the Wizard of Oz had secretly married the Good Witch of the North. Or maybe it's advertising a series of drinking glasses with the pictures of the royal family on them."

"No, miss," replied the paperboy, shaking his head. "They were genuinely turned to glass, sure as my name is Lanx."

"Have a copy of your birth certificate handy?" asked Henrietta. Winnie, however, inquired, "Couldn't Ozma just change them back?"

"No, according to the story, it's a form of magic she and Glinda ain't familiar with. They visited the castle last night, but haven't had any luck disenchanting them."

"Who would do such a thing?"

"Pretty much any two-ozzo magician in the country," replied Henrietta. "It's a general occupational hazard of being a ruler in Oz, as far as I can tell. Poor Queen Orin's already been enchanted once. They should see if Mombi's come back from the dead."

"Didn't you hear?" asked Winnie. "She's been alive for years."

"Has she?" exclaimed Henrietta. "Well, there's your culprit! Mystery solved."

"I don't know, honey," put in the waitress. "There aren't that many magicians who specialize in glass magic. I have to suspect it may have been Vaneeda's doing. She's been talking about campaigning for years."

"*Campaigning*? What's that?" asked Winnie.

"It's when you advertise to try to get selected for a high office. She always believed she was the rightful heiress to the Munchkin throne."

"So this Vaneeda is related to royalty?"

"Well, sorta. It's a bit of a story... Would you mind if I sat down?"

Both girls insisted she do so, anxious to learn more.

"My name is Paella. I'm an old friend of Vaneeda's. She's the daughter of the Witch of the East."

"You mean the *Wicked* Witch of the East? How awful! I can't imagine having a despot for a mother," declared Henrietta. "Um, no offense, Winnie."

At a confused look from Paella, Winnie explained. "I'm Jinjur's daughter. You might remember her as *General* Jinjur, who had once led a rebellion against the Emerald City, back when the Scarecrow ruled."

"Oh, well, one can't forget her!" said Paella with a laugh. "She's in all the history books."

"Thankfully, she leads a much less *exciting* lifestyle now. Mostly, she farms, gives me and my brother chores, well, back when he lived with us, and paints pictures."

"Incredibly realistic pictures," added Henrietta.

"She is quite talented," Winnie acknowledged.

"I can't say my mother was really much of a mother," the waitress admitted. "I'm sure she had her reasons, but she sent me away to boarding school as soon as I was old enough to go. I studied cookywitchery, like she had. That's where I became friends with Vaneeda, though she was studying more advanced magic. Her mother must have known she wasn't going to live forever, and intended Van to carry on in her footsteps. Big footsteps they were, too, as she could go anywhere in the world in three steps. Anyway, after she was hit with the house and the Munchkins selected Froom as their ruler, Vaneeda felt she was robbed."

"But the Witch herself was an illigi... illegi... *illegitimate* ruler," put in the paperboy.

"But what makes a ruler legitimate?" the waitress asked. "People will argue about rights of succession, but in the end the throne belongs to whoever is able to take it."

"That's what my mother always said, too," agreed Winnie.

"Yeah, but without the will of the people, then all you have is a tyranny," added Henrietta.

"Which is why Van tried to win over the sovereigns of the lesser kingdoms," Paella explained, "Keretaria, the Seven Blue Mountains, even Seebania here in the south, but it never worked. They all believed she'd be like her mother, and no one wanted another Wicked Witch dominating them."

"So Vaneeda *is* a wicked witch?" questioned Winnie.

"No, I wouldn't say that, but she's done some things I've found... morally questionable. I think I should go and have a talk with her about this latest development. Last I heard, she's still living on Glass Mountain." After a moment, Paella turned to the girls, and seeing the look of excitement in their eyes, she asked. "Do either of you feel like an adventure? I could sure use the company."

Henrietta sighed aloud. "I'd love to, but I have way too many chores to do. In fact, I've been already been away too long. Why don't you go, Winnie?"

"Do you think I can? asked Winnie excitedly.

"I don't see why not? It seems all you do is chores," Henrietta said.

"That's true," Winnie said. "I've been on the farm for most of my life. I never really get to have adventures. Mother's got enough help these days. I don't see that another day or so away will hurt anything."

"Then it's settled," declared Paella. "I'd better set the café to automatic." With that, she uttered a few complicated words and rapped a spatula on the counter, which produced a ringing noise from the direction of the kitchen.

"If anyone orders anything, the kitchen will take care of it," explained the Cookywitch. "Not the same as having the personal touch of me being here, but better than nothing in case any hungry travelers come along. Now then, shall we leave?"

Henrietta promised that on the way home she'd inform Winnie's mother of her whereabouts, and the two girls hugged goodbye. Winnie followed Paella outside, where the witch had taken a pie tin from her apron. At a word from her, it expanded to a size large enough to accommodate two passengers. With an amazed Winnie having taken her place inside it, Paella levitated it into the air. The young girl held tightly to the sides as the pie tin sailed off north over the blue forests and hills of the Munchkin Country. Eventually, Winnie relaxed and began to enjoy the ride. Soon enough, they arrived at a range of mountains where, hidden among the rocky peaks, stood one mountain made entirely of glass. At its top could be seen a cabin of frosted glass, and it was right next to this dwelling that the Cookywitch landed the pie tin. When she rang a glass chime, a woman in a long black dress, glass slippers, and white socks answered the door. Her skin was an unusually colored deep blue, her hair straight and black, and her nose somewhat hooked.

"Paella! What a pleasant surprise! I haven't seen you in years!" exclaimed the woman. "And who is your friend?"

"Hi," announced the girl, trying hard not to stare or appear nervous. "I'm Winnie, Jinjur's daughter."

"Jinjur?" Vaneeda exclaimed. "The woman who raised an army to conquer the Emerald City?" At Winnie's nod, she added, "I liked her style. Are you planning on becoming a conqueror yourself, Miss Winnie?"

"Oh, no," Winnie said. "Being a farmer is enough for me."

"Conquest is definitely not for everyone. So, come on in and make yourselves comfortable."

The interior was clean and contemporary, with angular accessories in various subtle hues, akin to the High Evian style found in the latter days of the reign of King Evardo. Intricate glass sculptures could be seen everywhere. Winnie and Paella remarked upon them.

"I'm glad you like them," Vaneeda said. "They're of my own design. So, what brings you here?"

"You mean you haven't heard the news yet?" inquired Paella, seating herself on a high-backed glass chair that looked like a mini-throne. Winnie followed suit, finding a smaller seat off to the side.

"I don't often get news here," Vaneeda said, seating herself on a similar looking mini-throne opposite her old friend. "None of the newsboys can climb the mountain, so it's only when the birds see fit to tell me something that I get to hear current events."

"So, you didn't know about this?" asked the Cookywitch, as she took a newspaper from her apron and unfolded it, pointing to the lead story.

"Oh, my shards! And you want me to see what I can do to restore them?"

"Don't play games with me, Van. We go back a long way. I came because I think you're the one who transformed them in the first place, and I think you should undo it before you get in serious trouble."

"Paella, I did no such thing! I'd never do a thing like that!"

"What about the time you trapped that poor boy in the mirror just for contradicting you…?"

"He was slandering Mother," Vaneeda explained. "Besides, that was ages ago! I let him back out. He kept insisting on playing chess, and then complaining long and loud when he lost, which was often. You know how it is when boys want you."

"I wouldn't know," said Winnie. "I'm still only ten."

"Well, I always liked the attention," said Paella.

"You *would*," Vaneeda teased. "Did you know he went on to actually invent a reverse cheese grater?"

"I could use that in my kitchen," Paella remarked. "All right, but what about Peter?"

"Peter?" Vaneeda said with a sound of disgust. "He was bad news. Trust me, turning him into a glass man was a service to the community. He'd have harmed someone sooner or later. I used to keep him in repair, but he was so vicious, I stopped."

"I hadn't realized that," Paella said, "But what about your father?"

Vaneeda sighed. "That's a harder one. Let's just say he wasn't much of a father. He can still talk, at least. I left him that much. The point is that all of those were personal. I might think the king is ineffective and out of touch, but I don't have anything against him personally. And he throws very good parties. You both should come the next time! Speaking of hosting parties, are either of you hungry or thirsty?"

"Thank you, no," said Winnie. "I just ate at the café before we arrived."

"Paella is quite a good cook," added Vaneeda, "even if her powers are wasted in a café."

Paella only shook her head and smiled. This was an old debate between them. "Well, I'm glad you didn't have anything to do with it. But what was it you were saying about breaking the enchantment? Queen Ozma and Glinda have tried and failed."

"That's because they don't know glass magic like I do," said Vaneeda, as she took the paper and read the article. "Oh, I see. They're keeping the glass statues in the Emerald City. I've never much liked that place. I'll go if I have to, though. Shall I take my broom?"

"I'll never understand why some witches love brooms," Paella quipped. "They're so small and uncomfortable."

"Don't listen to her, Winnie," Vaneeda smirked. "She never learned how to *correctly* fly them. They're the ultimate freedom. The broom itself is just a guide stick. It could be anything, really, a pitchfork, a hoe, but the broom is a symbol of the oppression we once suffered as slaves. That's what makes it so perfect."

"You and my mother would get along," laughed Winnie.

"That's all ancient history," said Paella. "Besides, in Oz, wasn't it *your* mother who was the oppressor?" Ignoring Vaneeda's glare, she added with a smile. "Come on, let's take my pie tin. I assure you it's *much* more comfortable, even if it is free of political statements."

Vaneeda conceded, and the small group flew from the mountain to the west, crossing over the central part of the Munchkin Country, with its fields and forests. Vaneeda agreed that the pie tin was an easy ride, though not quite as powerful as a broom or as intimidating to those it flew over.

Finally, they reached the brilliant green capital of Oz, and landed right outside the palace. The Soldier with Green Whiskers was on guard at the door, and he asked what their business was.

Whispering to Vaneeda to let her do the talking, Paella replied: "We're here to disenchant the Royal Munchkin Family."

"So you're magic-workers, eh? Never seen you before, though you look familiar, little one. Where are your magic licenses?"

"Ah, we must have left them at home," said Vaneeda.

"That's hardly proper protocol," Omby Amby said, growing more distrustful.

"So, are you going to let us help, or what? We don't have time to fly back and forth for your protocols!"

"Hmmm, I suppose so, but remember that the entire Army of Oz will be watching you!"

"That's hardly saying much," Vaneeda spat, "since you *are* the entire Army of Oz!"

"I've got my eye on you," the soldier said as he moved aside to allow the three visitors into the throne room, where Ozma, Glinda, the Wizard of Oz, and other celebrities were gathered around a set of three glass figures of people.

"Visitors," he announced. "They claim they're here to help disenchant the Munchkin Royals, but they've got no papers."

"Snitch," Vaneeda shot.

"Aren't you the daughter of the Wicked Witch of the East?" asked Dorothy, rather rudely pointing her finger at Vaneeda.

"What gave it away, the blue skin?" Vaneeda asked acerbically. "Let me guess. You're the one who killed my mother?" When Dorothy tried to say something, Vaneeda waved her hand and overrode her. "Yes, yes, I know. It wasn't your fault. The tornado did it. I do wonder sometimes, what are the odds of a house landing on her by *accident*." The sarcastic emphasis she gave the final word was unmistakable.

"Maybe it wasn't an accident," Dorothy conceded, "but if somebody arranged it, it wasn't me. My house was caught in a cyclone. It's not like I could steer it."

"If you insist. It's not like she was much of a mother anyway. Of course, you did have to go and lose her Silver Shoes."

"That was *definitely* an accident," she said. "The Shoes don't seem to travel to the Outside World."

"Women and their shoes," said the Wizard, trying to break the ice. "And who might you be? The daughter of the Wicked Witch of the West?"

"Not exactly," said Paella. "My name is Paella. I run a café in the Southern Munchkin Country."

"Paella? Isn't that a Spanish food?" asked Glinda.

"Yes, well, it was originally just Ella, but I made such good pies that everyone called me Piella. One of my friends pronounced it Paella, and the name just stuck."

"Oh, yes, I remember now," said Glinda. "You're the cookywitch?"

"Well, not *the* cookywitch," she clarified. "Just *a* cookywitch." She chose not to go any further with this line of thought. Thankfully she was spared any more questions when Winnie announced herself.

"Oh, of course!" said Ozma. "I thought I'd seen you before. How's your mother been?"

"Well, though the macaroon crop hasn't been doing too well this year and she hasn't been all that easy to be around. So I went with her intern Henrietta to explore the country a bit."

While the others were exchanging stories, Vaneeda walked over to the glass statues and asked, "Do you mind if I take a crack at this?"

"You're going to crack them?" asked Jack Pumpkinhead. "I don't think that would help."

"No, melonhead, that's just an expression. I happen to be an expert on glass magic."

"An expert on glass magic, huh?" repeated the Soldier with Green Whiskers, who had approached the group. "How do we know *you* didn't enchant them?"

"That does make sense," stated the Wizard of Oz. "I remember you trying to be declared the ruler of the Munchkins."

"What is this? I come to help, and you treat me like a criminal? Walloping windowpanes, even in the Outside World you're innocent until proven guilty!"

"As you are here," said Ozma, walking over. "I know how hard it can be to live down a mother's reputation."

"Yes, it can..." Vaneeda said, taken aback by Ozma's sympathy.

"I too was raised by a Wicked Witch," Ozma said.

"I'd forgotten that," Vaneeda replied after a moment. "They're not exactly the best mothers in the world."

"Perhaps not, but they were all we had. We should talk some time," Ozma said more quietly, "when you're ready."

"Do you think you can break this enchantment?" Glinda said, approaching Vaneeda.

"Hmm, let me see." Vaneeda took a monocle from her pocket and looked at the figure of the King, then at the Queen and their son. "No, I definitely can say I can't."

"I figured she'd be no help," declared Omby Amby.

"Let me finish, you trumped-up security guard. I can't disenchant them because these figures aren't enchanted. They're just plain old glass."

"I had suspected that, but I couldn't be sure," confirmed Glinda. "I'll have to check with my contacts to see if anyone had these made recently."

"But if *these* aren't the Royal Family, where are they?" questioned Jack.

"Don't ask me? You're the ones with the Magic Picture," replied Vaneeda. So Ozma led the way to her sitting room and drew the curtains covering the Magic Picture, which could show anyone and anything it was asked to.

Upon the queen's command, "Show us the Munchkins Royal Family," the picture faded and showed King Cheeriobed, Queen Orin, Prince Philador and young Prince Roderick. They were seated at a table on which stood a bowl of blue fruit and a vase of blue flowers, in full color and certainly not made of glass, but at the same time seemed quite flat and lifeless.

"They look awful stiff," declared Dorothy. "I hope they're not..." she left the word unsaid.

"That would be unlikely," Glinda said, dispelling her concern.

"Maybe their laundress used too much starch," suggested the Patchwork Girl. "I hate it when that happens to me."

"Actually, it kind of looks like they're in a painting," observed the Scarecrow.

"Of course it does! It's the Magic Picture!" said the Wizard testily.

"No, I mean a painting inside the painting."

"Actually, aside from the people, that looks an awful lot like a painting my mom did a long time ago," said Winnie.

"It *does* look like her style," remarked the Scarecrow. "And I've known Jinjur to paint a haystack so realistic that I could use it to re-stuff myself. So do you think it's at her house?"

"No, if it's the painting I'm thinking of, she gave it up years ago. Not sure who she gave it to, though."

A command from Ozma to show the wall where the painting was hanging revealed that it was right next to a portrait of a short man in a high blue silk hat, whose hair stuck out at odd angles. Upon seeing this picture, the Scarecrow exclaimed, "I remember him! That's King Froom!"

"You mean Froom the Fraud?" questioned Scraps.

"Yes, he took over the Munchkin throne after Dorothy killed... er, first arrived in Oz, but he was forced to abdicate when an anonymous tipster revealed that he wasn't a descendant of royalty."

"Right, an *anonymous* tipster," put in Paella, with a meaningful glance at her friend.

"Vaneeda was the tipster, but at least she's not a hipster!" called out the Patchwork Girl.

"A hipster? Is that one of those Quadling tribes in the mountains?" inquired Jack.

"I don't know. I just say whatever comes into my head. But it makes sense that our friend here spilt the beans. Then the throne would be available... for *her*!"

"Yes, that was me," said Vaneeda, "but you yourselves said he was a fraud, so consider it a public service! Besides, it didn't do me any good. The Munchkins didn't want a king or queen after that. The Northern king was believed to have abdicated after Orin's abduction and no one could find the Southern king's son."

"That's because Mombi had cut off the Northern Royals," Ozma said. "Froom knew this and took advantage of that fact, spreading the lie that King Cheeriobed abdicated because he was in mourning. We didn't find out the truth 'til much later."

"And the Southern house came down to a man named Stephen," added Glinda, "and he'd gone into hiding with his nephew."

"Stephen? Oh, you mean Unc Nunkie!" exclaimed Scraps. "Ojo was responsible for giving me my brains, you know!"

"I don't understand why there's still a Royal Family in the south," said Dorothy. "No other quadrant has two ruling houses. Seems to me Cheeriobed and Orin should be good enough, 'specially now that they're back in power."

"There's some truth to that," Glinda stated. "But it's a long story. The Munchkins were a divided people for many years, long before you or the Wizard arrived. The north and south would often provoke each other, and sometimes go to war. Things improved a good deal when Pastoria II came to rule Oz, and his grandfather, King Ozroar took over the Southern Munchkin throne, averting a civil war. Unfortunately, he lost it to Ree Alla Bad's father, Tibira Alla Bad, an unpleasant man and a worse king, who began calling himself King Knotso Bad."

"More like 'not so' funny if you ask me!" Scraps interjected.

"I remember him," sneered the Wizard. "He sent me the head of the Gump thinking that it would win me over. Poor Namyl was depressed for a long time after losing his body."

"The Seebanians were a fallen house ever after. Even when Ozroar retook the throne, it didn't help, and it wasn't five years before he too was abducted by Mombi and transformed by Mossolb, leaving Tibira to take over once again until his disappearance."

"Mombi again, no doubt," said Jack Pumpkinhead.

"No, not this time. It appears someone else got to him first," said Ozma.

"We assumed it was Mooj," said Glinda, "though he denies it."

"So *why* is there still a Royal House in the south?" asked Dorothy.

"When I came to the throne, the Southern Kingdom wanted to keep their royal status for ceremonial reasons more than anything else. For the sake of their dignity, I allowed that even if they're royal in name only."

"Besides," added the Wizard, "there were two royal houses in the Winkie Country not long before I arrived."

"True," said Glinda. "Gloma kept ruling even after the Wicked Witch took over. It wasn't until after Dorothy melted her that she went into hiding in the Black Forest."

"This has all been very fascinating," said the Scarecrow, "but we still don't know why the Munchkin royal family is stuck in a painting or how they got there!"

"Oh, that's obvious!" exclaimed Scraps. "It's because it's a still life."

"Technically, dear, it's a portrait," corrected the Wizard. "A still life—which *you* most definitely are not—is of inanimate objects."

"You learn something new every day," said Scraps in an exaggerated drawl, rolling her button eyes.

"So who put them there, and how do we get them out?" asked Dorothy. "Can we determine where the painting is?"

"I don't know yet," said Ozma. "Vaneeda, what do you... wait, where did she go?"

"She's gone, vanished, split, flown the coop!" shouted out Scraps.

And so she had. Vaneeda had whisked her two companions back into the pie plate and was now hovering high above the Emerald City.

"Why did you do that?" Winnie asked.

Vaneeda replied, "I know where the fraud lives, and by the time they're all done talking, he'll be long gone. Paella, get this thing moving."

"Are you sure that's the best idea when Glinda already suspects you of criminal activity?" asked the Cookywitch.

"Just do it, you foolish foodie!"

So Vaneeda directed the pie plate to a Munchkin village not far from where Dorothy's house had landed on her mother. They landed outside a large dome-shaped house with stained glass windows, which looked to be dark inside.

"I don't think anyone's home," said Paella, as she looked into the building.

"Good. Now we can look for the painting without interference," stated Vaneeda.

"Isn't that illegal?" asked Winnie.

"Oh, we won't break anything. We'll just be entering." With that, the witch pointed at the keyhole while chanting a spell, then easily opened the door. The others somewhat reluctantly followed her into the house, which was decorated with many paintings and statues.

"Wow, is that a Geodesi original?" asked Paella, as she looked at a painting of a house on a cloud.

"Froom had as much art as possible commissioned back when he was king," explained Vaneeda. "I'd say he was a supporter of the arts, but since he kept it all for himself that would be far too generous. He was more like a hoarder."

"This looks like one of Mom's," said Winnie, who was examining a picture of the Scarecrow riding the Sawhorse.

"We're getting closer."

Suddenly, a voice called out, "Vaneeda, is that you?" The girls turned to the direction from which the voice had come, but saw nothing but a window containing the image of a rather blue man. It was clear from his garments that he had been a man of some means. Had he not been in a window, he'd have been an imposing figure.

"Yes, Father, it's me. I forgot Froom ended up with the window I made you into."

"Any chance of letting me out?"

"Not until you've apologized for sending me to that wretched school for all those years!"

"Vaneeda, you know that was your mother's idea. Besides, I thought you wanted to be a witch."

"I did, but there must have been a better way to learn witchcraft than at *that* place! Don't you remember how Professor Woyar hit me with a broom handle until I learned the spell to turn mice into rats? And how the other students mocked me? And how I had to take summer classes with all the lousy fifth-rate hedge witches who didn't know a crystal ball from a croquet ball?"

"Do you think I had any choice in that?" her father argued. "She thought it would build character. And what was I going to do, argue with someone who could turn me into a cockroach and step on me?"

"She was more afraid of you than you realized. It was your connections, after all, that helped secure her claim to the throne."

"You don't know the full story. There's much more to it than that. Besides, she mustn't have been too upset after you enchanted me, since I'm still here."

"Oh, you think she knew about that?" Vaneeda said. "I told her you had taken up with a scullery maid from Ev."

"Well, that wasn't very nice! Look, Vaneeda, I don't like arguing."

"Well, that's part of the problem, isn't it?" she retorted.

"If you're not going to free me, which you should, could you at least give me someone to talk to? It gets very lonely around here. There was a nice family that stopped by the other day, royals by the look of them, but they've been silent ever since Froom ensnared them inside a picture."

"Wait, did you see how he got them into the painting?" asked Paella.

"Not so well, because I don't have much of a view from here. I think he used some kind of box, though."

"A box?" repeated Paella. "A camera of some sort?"

"If we could find it, we might be able to find a way to get them out," stated Winnie.

"Oh, you're an expert on magic all of a sudden?" shot Vaneeda.

"Don't be mean, Van," admonished Paella. "It was a good idea."

"Sorry, Winnie," Vaneeda apologized. "Father always brings out the worst in me."

"*That* comes from your mother's side of the family!"

Vaneeda ignored him and the companions continued their search of the house. At last, Winnie discovered the portrait in which the royals were trapped, but was unable to get them to speak. Paella found a receipt for glass sculptures inside a desk drawer. A thorough search revealed no sign of a box of any sort, however.

"He must have taken the box with him, wherever he went," decided Winnie.

"That would make sense," said Paella. "Too bad we don't know anything about magic cameras."

"Actually, come to think of it, I believe my son does," stated Vaneeda.

"*You have a son?* How have I known you for so many years and not been aware of this?"

"He was rather young when he moved away. Kids don't like living on inaccessible mountain tops, apparently. You do remember my husband, though?"

"I heard about the accident. I'm sorry," Paella said, kindly, recalling some kind of magical explosion. "I had wanted to come for the funeral, but when I found you weren't having one, I sent you a note by falcon."

"Yes, I received it; it was beautiful, thank you. We had our son some years before that happened. Kluuon, his name is."

"Cultured one," Paella sussed out, "that's a nice name."

"Where does he live now?" asked Winnie.

"Last I heard, somewhere near Seebania. I probably have his address somewhere." The witch drew a small book from her pocket, and then asked, "Where is Kluuon?" The pages magically turned to reveal an address: "11 Blue Jay Way, Nefton."

"Nefton. I know where that is," said Paella. "It's near the Threetine Forest, where I sometimes pick silverware."

So the travelers returned to the pie pan, Paella being careful to place the painting in her apron pocket first, and flew off to the south, landing in a heavily forested region near the Munchkin River. Vaneeda's son lived along a path in the woods, in a small but elegant dome-shaped house with onyx trim. On the roof stood a rotating dish and a sock on a pole.

At the witch's knock, a voice from inside called out, "Just a minute! I'm coming!" A man wearing goggles and holding a wrench answered, and said, "*Mother*! I haven't seen you in forever! If I'd known you were coming, I'd have prepared a meal."

"We need your help, Kluuon," explained Vaneeda. "Do you still have that magic camera?"

"Sorry, I lost that about a year ago. A rogue wind took it away. Anyway, come in. I'm afraid the place is a mess, though."

When the companions entered the house, they realized that Kluuon was being truthful. It had only one room, not counting the bathroom, and every available surface was covered with gadgets or mechanical components. In the center of the room stood a great wheel with colored lights around it, each one flashing on and off as a certain spoke of the wheel triggered it. Model airplanes and rockets hung from the ceiling, and a mess of pipes sat on the stove. Gears and sockets of many kinds covered a large brass bed. "I was just in the middle of a project to see if I could use milk as rocket fuel."

"Did it work?" questioned Winnie.

"Not really, but maybe I haven't gotten it to the right temperature. So what were we talking about? Oh, yes. The camera. I don't suppose you remember Mossolb, the sorcerer who used to live in a castle near here?"

"The one who enchanted Ozma's grandfather?" asked Vaneeda. "Or was it her great-grandfather?"

"Something like that. He used a camera to trap people in portraits. The principle always interested me, but he would never let me see it. Finally, when I heard he was transformed into plaster, I went to his old castle to see if it was still there. It was broken, but I fixed it up and made some adjustments to it in between other projects. It was dreadfully old-fashioned, but Mossolb never really got out much. And then, like I said, it was blown away sometime last year."

"Maybe Froom had the rogue wind take it to him," suggested Winnie.

"Froom? You mean that pretender who cost Mother the throne? I've certainly never heard of him having any weather powers. If so, he was just as incompetent a magician as he was a king."

"Could someone have been helping him?" Winnie asked. "Mrs. Vaneeda, you said Froom wanted to get revenge on you. Is there anyone else who might have wanted to do that?"

"The old King of Seebania wasn't too happy about her inspiring a revolt," recalled Kluuon, "but I don't think he's around anymore."

"A revolt in Seebania? Vaneeda, were you in league with Mooj?" asked Paella.

"Oh, no! I never would have dealt with anyone like him. He was even crazier than Mama."

"Actually, I knew him in his younger days, and he wasn't so bad," declared Kluuon. "He helped Father and me with some of our mechanical work. After his trip to Ev, though, he came back totally changed. He was obsessed with finding some kind of master timepiece, if I remember right."

"Yes, I remember that," Vaneeda said. "That was after I encouraged the neighboring lands to rebel against that horrible Tibira, and he really had very little power outside his own castle after that. His brother Stephen was trying to mend relations with the smaller countries, but when Mooj showed up looking for whatever it was, both of them disappeared. Haven't they been discovered yet?"

"Well, Prince Stephen came back, but the current king is Tibira's son Ree Alla Bad."

"Another scoundrel. Wait, doesn't his son have magic powers?" inquired Vaneeda. "You know, Prince Ojam or Mojo, or whatever his name is."

"You mean Ojo?" put in Winnie. "I've met him before. He's a friend of Ozma's. He wouldn't have stolen the camera."

"I suppose," said the glass witch. "Did you ever try to track it down?" she asked her son.

"I did, but I never had any luck finding it. Finding things has never been my strong point, I'm afraid. And since some of my work is *technically* illegal, I couldn't very well go to the government. I sent a message to the Wind-Satchel Man over on Valley Mountain to see if he knew of any rogue winds operating in the area, but he hasn't gotten back to me yet."

"You know, Mrs. Vaneeda, this picture should be enough to clear your name," stated Winnie. "We can take it back to the Emerald City and see if Glinda or the Wizard of Oz can find any way to get the Royal Family out. For that matter, my mother might be able to paint them out."

"Let me see that picture," said Kluuon. When Paella handed it to him, he took a look at it and said, "If this was done with the camera, I think finding it is your best bet. Mixing in any more magic could just make it worse."

"Maybe we just should fly back to my house," suggested Vaneeda. "I think I can locate Froom in my crystal ball. Besides, Kluuon, you really ought to visit your poor mother occasionally."

"You live on top of a glass mountain. Father had to use special shoes to get up there!"

"Yes, I admired his ingenuity. That's partly why I married him. But you have flying devices that can get you there, right?"

"I still haven't been able to make a vehicle that will fly up that high without exploding."

"Well, for now, we'll take the pie tin," stated Paella.

So the four ascended into the air, and flew toward the north. "We're getting a lot of wind resistance here," observed the Cookywitch. "We might need to wait until it dies down."

"Wait!" shouted Winnie. "*Wind* resistance? Could this be the wind we're looking for?"

"Good catch, Winnie!" praised Vaneeda. "It's probably trying to stop us. Hey, wind! Are you the one that stole my son's camera?" The only response to this was a bit of sinister, blustery laughter.

"If only I had some way to capture it," Vaneeda said quietly.

"Actually, I just might!" exclaimed Paella. "I have this sack that I use to store winds for wind pudding."

"Wind pudding?" asked Kluuon.

"And you just *happen* to be carrying it?" asked Vaneeda incredulously.

"Yes, and it's a Stratovanian dish. Not very satisfying to my tastes, but very popular with sky fairies, mist maidens and air sprites. I always bring it with me when I go out. You never know when you'll catch a good wind."

The Cookywitch withdrew the bag from her apron, and with some help from Winnie and her friend, managed to trap the offending wind. The wind tried to escape her grasp, but the bag was made for catching winds, and Paella was far too strong for it to wrench itself from her hands.

"Now talk!" ordered Vaneeda. "Are you in league with Froom?"

"You ought to treat me in a manner befitting a king," said a gusty voice from inside the bag.

"Don't be putting on airs!" chided Paella.

"A king? Are you King of the Winds?" asked Winnie.

"No, I am the King of Seebania, and by rights ruler of the Southern Munchkin Country until your blue-faced friend decided to foment a rebellion against me."

"*You're* the long-lost king?" questioned Vaneeda. "You're Tibira Alla Bad, formerly known as King Knotso? Ha! I thought Mooj destroyed you."

"That's what he would have wanted you to think!"

"Then how did you wind up… like *this*?" asked Paella.

"After her mother—*that witch*—reduced my dominion to practically the original forest that my ancestors had claimed, I spent most of my time hunting. One day, I came across a strange creature that I knew would make for an excellent trophy, so I shot it. Just my luck, it turned out to be some sort of Wind Demon, which cursed me to become wind myself."

"You deserved it," spat Vaneeda, but that just made the wind bag blow harder.

"I would have thought Seebania had enough meat crops that one wouldn't have to hunt," observed Winnie.

"It does," commented Paella. "It's hard to stop these wicked trophy hunters, especially when they're royals. He's the one who shot the gump."

"Yes, I sent its head to the Wizard," said the wind. "That old hag Mombi wasn't too happy about it and threatened me! Apparently, she used gump hairs in her spells, and dead gumps can't grow hair. I blamed it on Ozroar! Ten years later, she took care of him too! I assumed it was because of what I told her, but who knows why a witch does anything? After that, I regained my rightful place on the throne until that blasted wind demon cursed me! Say, aren't you a witch? Can you disenchant me?"

"I wouldn't even if I could," Vaneeda exulted.

"You're lucky I'm only a wind!" he said menacingly.

"I should warn you," started Kluoon, "that if you threaten my mother, I shall have no choice but to bring you before our Queen Ozma, and you know what she did with Mooj!"

"Turned him into a drop of water," added Paella, smiling in spite of herself. They all knew Ozma had later released Mooj from that punishment, but they weren't about to tell the rogue wind that.

"I was just letting off some steam," the former king said. "Ah, I do miss those days. Oz was wild and dangerous before that namby pamby fairy had to come and enchant everything. Before that, hunting was considered a fine manly sport. It was prohibited once all the animals started talking, but I always thought that just increased the challenge."

"And they called *our* mothers wicked," Vaneeda said to Paella. "As I recall, Ozma had to have a talk with your son about that, too. Apparently the rotten apple doesn't fall far from the tree; he was an outlaw for years."

"Oh ho ho," blowed the wind Tibira. "Your mother was no saint either! Caused me many problems."

"Good!" Vaneeda exclaimed.

"So where's Froom?" asked Winnie.

The wind-bag refused to reveal it unless they released him, but after Paella threatened to use him for her recipe, the former king let out a long sigh, and finally admitted, "He's probably hiding out in his magic-proof cave."

"Froom has a magic-proof cave?" asked Kluuon. "I didn't think he knew any magic."

"Don't be so literal, boy! When I say it's *his*, that's only in a manner of speaking. I believe the Witch of the East enchanted it years ago."

"Oh, *that* cave," said Vaneeda. "I remember it."

At Vaneeda's direction, Paella steered the pie tin to a cave in the ruins of an old Munchkin city at the eastern end of the Yellow Brick Road. With the witch leading the way, the companions rushed into this cave and along a narrow passageway, finally emerging in a large cavern where Froom sat reading a book.

"I believe that's *my* old book!" shouted Vaneeda.

"Oh, so you've finally found me, you rabble-rousing tyrant's daughter!" said Froom calmly, as he looked up from the book. "Well, why don't come closer and arrest me, or enchant, or whatever it is you witches do."

"Nice try," said Kluuon. "We know what you've been doing with my camera!"

"Do you now?" Froom laughed, pulling something out a sack sitting on the ground near him. Vaneeda suspected it was the camera and warned the others. "For one thing, it's not your camera. It belonged to Mossolb."

"He was out of the picture when I took that camera," corrected Kluuon.

"Well, if you're such a hero then, why don't you see if you can reach me before I can snap a picture? I figure you've got a fifty-fifty chance. Hmmm, not so brave now, are you?"

Vaneeda, Paella, and Kluuon all shrank back at his threat, but to their shock and horror, Winnie started walking forward. Her friends cried out to her to come back, but she ignored them and kept a steady pace. Had she been enchanted? Froom pressed the button on the camera. "Gotcha!" he exclaimed, but nothing happened. Winnie kept on walking towards him. He pressed the button several times more, but still nothing stopped her. As he confusedly checked the settings, concerned at what might have happened to the camera, the girl grabbed it away from him.

"What? Why didn't the camera work?" asked Froom.

"This is a magic-proof cave," she stated as if it was the most obvious thing in the world. "So why would a magic camera work here?"

Froom attempted to escape from the tunnel, but Kluuon tackled him and Vaneeda quickly shoved him into the bag with the rogue wind.

"Good job, everyone!" Paella applauded.

"You know, Winnie, I hadn't thought of that!" said Vaneeda.

"Well, you have to be a good listener when your mom is a former general," said Winnie.

"Or the dictator of a country," observed Vaneeda.

"Or a giantess who keeps people in jars," added Paella.

"You're a smart girl, and I like a good listener," Vaneeda said to Winnie. "How would you like to come back to my mountain and be my apprentice?"

"Thank you, Mrs. Vaneeda," Winnie said gratefully, "and perhaps one day I will, but my mom's farm should be enough excitement for another year or so."

"I don't blame you," said Kluuon. "That mountain is a terribly boring place."

"It's not that bad," said Vaneeda, shaking her head. "You're practically as isolated as I am. Why don't you come and live with me? All you need is your equipment. Besides, you'd be safer from prying eyes."

"Hmmm, you know you've got a point Mother," said Kluuon, "I hadn't thought of it that way."

"Well, starting thinking of it."

"We would need proper transportation up and down that mountain," he said. "I'd need to be able to leave when I wanted, or if I needed more supplies."

"I think that could be arranged," Vaneeda said with a hint of a smile. "Besides, now that we've caught two villains, I'd say Ozma and Glinda owe us a favor!"

"Don't count your Dorothys before they've been hatched," warned Paella. "I don't see Glinda as the forgiving type."

After leaving the cave, Kluuon took the camera from Winnie, and made the proper adjustments to it to reverse a picture. "It's an addition I made myself," explained the magician. "I believe in the Great Outside World, they call it shopping a photo. I don't know what it has to do with marketing, but they use all kinds of strange terms out there."

Soon, the family appeared on the ground in front of the small party, blinking their eyes and wondering what had happened. "Where's that man who captured us?" asked Prince Philador.

"Bad man," said the small child who was his brother.

"You know, I think I recognized him," commented Queen Orin. "He ruled the Munchkin Country for a little while, back when I was still the Good Witch of the North."

"You mean King Froom?" questioned King Cheeriobed. "Oh, merciful Munchkins! Who would have thought he'd show up again? I thought he was disgraced."

"He was," explained Vaneeda. "He reemerged so he could frame me."

"But you were the ones who were framed," added Winnie, pointing out the picture.

"So we were inside of a picture, eh?" asked King Cheeriobed. "I must say that's a first for me. Has that ever happened to you, my dear?"

"No. I fell out a prophetic window before, but I've never been inside a painting," replied Orin.

"My joints still feel stiff. What kind of painting was it, anyway?" asked King Cheeriobed. "Probably a still life," he joked. "No wonder we couldn't move."

Prince Roderick laughed, but Philador just rolled his eyes, accustomed to his father's sense of humor. "Miss, I hope you won't mind my asking," he inquired of Vaneeda, "but aren't you the Wicked Witch of the East's daughter?"

"Oh, yes, I remember you," said the King. "Are you still trying to take my throne?"

"Yes," admitted Vaneeda, "but I would only take it honestly. Trapping people in pictures is not my style."

"Well, as long as you keep it civil, I don't necessarily mind having a challenger. Keeps me on my toes, and makes me the best king I can be."

"Fortunately, the mark of a good king doesn't include whether or not you wear shoes," mentioned Orin, pointing out her husband's unshod stocking feet.

"I can't say as I had time to put them on. That wind outside the castle made me awfully dizzy."

"We captured the wind, too," stated Winnie. "Turns out he's the former King Knotso."

"That upstart!" exclaimed the king. "I should've known. Always causing problems, those Southerners!"

"Now, now," cautioned Orin. "That's all in the past. Let's not fall back on the misguided ways of our ancestors."

"Easy for you to say, wife. You're a Gillikin." And with that, he kissed her. Philador just rolled his eyes again while his brother laughed and repeated the word "Gillikin."

"Well, we'd better get back to the Emerald City," said Vaneeda. "I'm sure Ozma will be looking for all of us."

The companions returned to the pie tin, and after dropping off Kluuon at his house, hugging him goodbye, and promising to visit again soon to talk about his moving back to the Glass Mountain, Vaneeda led the way to the Emerald City and Ozma's palace.

"So, daughter of a witch, come to turn yourself in for resisting arrest and leaving in the middle of a conversation?" asked the Soldier with Green Whiskers.

"Is that even a crime?" asked Paella.

"It is in some parts of the Munchkin Country, where Governor Melanie Column ruled that politeness counts."

"Mrs. Vaneeda didn't have anything to do with the enchantment!" shouted Winnie. "We have Froom and his helper right here in this bag!"

Omby Amby shook his head at this story, but dutifully led the three companions back to the sitting room, where Ozma greeted them. "Where did you go?" asked the Royal Ruler. "Glinda heard back from her friend in Silica that Froom had ordered the glass sculptures there, but I have to say your behavior did come across as suspicious."

"We can explain," responded Winnie. As they were talking, the Munchkin Royal Family entered the room as well, confirming at least part of their story. After the witches and girls had sufficiently explained everything, with the king and queen corroborating, Ozma took the sack and released Froom from it. The wind tried to blow away, but Glinda quickly grabbed the sack and caught it again.

"I don't think you're going anywhere," Glinda said.

At Ozma's command, Froom explained how he had ordered the glass sculptures as a decoy, kidnapped the royals, and trapped them inside the painting with a magic camera that a wind had brought him. The wind explained his own role in the plot, and everyone present was surprised to learn that he was actually Ojo's grandfather. Deeming him too dangerous to be disenchanted just yet, Ozma sent him to the Wind-Satchel Man to keep in check.

Glinda suggested that Froom get a taste of his own medicine, and he was sentenced to sit in a painting for a few days to see how he liked it. As he was turned into a vase, he actually got to be in a still life. Afterwards, he'd be given sufficient water from the Forbidden Fountain, ensuring that he'd get a new, and hopefully better, start in life.

Ozma determined that Vaneeda had acted with good intentions, though Glinda reminded everyone that she still behaved improperly, particularly in using magic without a license. Vaneeda didn't say a word, nor did she or Winnie give away the fact that Paella had done the same thing. Glinda looked over at Paella, as if she wanted to say more, but the Cookywitch lowered her head, and Glinda let it go. Vaneeda was sentenced to a week in Tollydiggle's prison in the Emerald City, after which she'd be allowed to fulfil the requirements to get a license.

Paella returned to her café, and upon learning that Henrietta needed some primary sources for a Munchkin history report, brought her to Valley Mountain to talk with the captured wind that used to be the King of Seebania.

Winnie stayed at the prison with Vaneeda for a week of board games and conversation, which Vaneeda appreciated, though she was annoyed at first at having to be there despite all the good she'd done for Oz. In the end, Tollydiggle turned out to be wonderful company, and both Vaneeda and Winnie ended up having fun and learning a few things about the history of Oz. Even more significantly, Ozma visited with Vaneeda frequently, and as the two walked the Royal Gardens and enjoyed lunches by the ponds, they had time to talk about their experiences being raised by Wicked Witches, and in the end, they became real friends.

A date was set for Vaneeda's magic test, and Ozma promised that she'd have the Wizard install a magic elevator of some kind so that she and her son could easily ascend and descend the mountain. She also said she'd allow Paella to petition for a license. In the time she and Vaneeda had been out catching criminals, Glinda and she had discovered that Paella's mother was the infamous Cookywitch of the Preservatory, but that they determined not to hold it against her. Finally, at Ozma's gentle prompting, Vaneeda restored her father to his original flesh-and-blood self, and the two did their best to reconcile. Their conversations, along with the perspective she'd gotten from Ozma, caused Vaneeda to try and understand her mother more than she had in the past, and this led her on a search for answers.

But that is a story for another time...

INTERLUDE III

Dorothy, Trot and Betsy continued to talk for a long time after dinner. When Ozma had finished her official duties for the day, she asked Jellia Jamb if she knew where they were. The maid told Ozma that she had last seen the three girls in a private nook in an enclosed part of the palace gardens, and that is where she found them.

When they saw Ozma, the girls excitedly welcomed their friend. "Come join us," exclaimed Trot. "We've been reading these amazing stories from the Royal Library's Lost Histories section. We're in a few of them too!"

"They were just stocked too," added Betsy, "so I don't think anyone besides us has ever read them."

"I was doing research on my Oz project," explained Dorothy, "when these two came in with stacks of books!"

"We're just now comparing notes," added Trot.

"I wish you hadn't been so busy," said Dorothy.

"It's the rainy days when I get to catch up," said Ozma with a rueful smile. "Perhaps you could share some of these wonderful stories with me."

"Of course!" Dorothy exclaimed.

"You arrived at just the right time," Betsy added. "I was just starting to tell the girls about *this* story I found that has all four of us in it..."

"That *does* sound like fun," Ozma said.

"I suppose," said Betsy a little uncertainly. "There's a funny thing about it, though."

"Oh?" Ozma asked. "What is that, Betsy?"

"Well, I've only read part of it, but even though it's something that happened to all us," she answered, "I don't remember it happening, and I have a pretty good memory."

"You still might have forgotten it," Dorothy suggested. "We've all had so *many* adventures."

"*You* more than most!" teased Trot.

"I can't argue with that," Dorothy laughed. "But what I mean is, it's easy to lose track. If it wasn't for our Royal Historians, I wouldn't remember half of them!"

"Maybe," said Betsy, doubtfully. "Anyway, I couldn't finish it because it was time to meet up." Then more quietly, she added. "It's just a feeling, but something tells me that maybe we *shouldn't* read this story."

"Now that you said that, we have to hear it!" exclaimed Trot, with a mischievous grin.

"I'm with her," said Dorothy. "You know how much I love a good mystery."

Still pensive, Betsy replied, "Mysteries can be fun, but *secrets* are different, 'specially when they hide things people shouldn't have done and don't want coming out."

"I certainly wouldn't want everybody knowing all *my* secrets," said Trot. "I hope you haven't been going around repeating everything I ever told you, Betsy!"

"Of course I haven't," said Betsy, hotly. "That's not what I meant."

"What shameful secrets could you possibly have, Trot?" asked Dorothy, laughing. "You're an open book!"

"That's true... *mostly*," she said with a smirk. "But there are some things about me that only Betsy knows, and some only Cap'n Bill knows, and some only you and Ozma know, and if I want anybody else to know them, that should be *my* decision."

"I couldn't agree more!" said Ozma.

"Secrets are fine," Betsy conceded, "so long as they don't harm anyone."

"Well, I'm glad we settled that. Can we read the story now?" Trot asked impatiently.

"Betsy, since you're the one who found it, I think you should read it to us," said Ozma. "Besides, you have such a pretty speaking voice."

"Thank you, Ozma," Betsy said. "Well, it starts with us..."

THE PUPPET-MISTRESS OF OZ
by Andrew J. Heller

O n afternoons when the weather in the Emerald City was fine (and Oz being Oz, this was almost every day), and she was able to take time from her busy schedule of making the Land of Oz a better place for her subjects, Ozma enjoyed having tea parties in the garden behind the royal palace.

The parties were held in a secluded little grove of bubble trees in the Royal Gardens. These trees resembled nothing so much as ten-foot tall milkweeds after their seeds had been set adrift by a breeze or the puff of a child's breath. Ozma loved to watch as they extruded their enormous bubbles of red, green, orange and a hundred other colors out of the tops of the stems. The wind would then tug them from the plants, and the gleaming opalescent bubbles would float off into the sky.

The guest list for the royal teas was almost always the same: the three mortal girls, originally from America, who had found their separate ways to Oz and had eventually come to live there permanently. Their names were Trot Griffiths, Betsy Bobbin and Dorothy Gale, and they were Ozma's closest friends.

The tea was set up in the bubble tree grove on a table reserved exclusively for this purpose. In addition to the royal tea set (the pot, milk ewer, sugar bowl and eggshell-thin tea cups were carved out of whole emeralds), the table contained plates of cucumber sandwiches with the crusts carefully removed, lemon-drop cookies, and chocolate Oz-cakes. There was a strictly enforced dress code for these parties. All three guests were required to array themselves in the style of the Edwardian era, which was the general dress code in Oz. The girls all wore light billowy frocks, voluminous petticoats and huge, floppy sun-hats.

Even though they had lived in Oz for many years, because the magic of Oz permits its residents to remain the same age forever, Betsy, Trot and Dorothy still appeared to be the girls of ten to twelve years old, even though they had been born as mortals. But they were not just young in appearance. The three friends still retained the simple, charming innocence of the young girls they appeared to be.

As their hostess (and Ruler), Ozma claimed the right to choose the first topic of conversation. Today, she decided that she would like each girl tell the story of how she came to Oz for the first time. Trot was first. After she finished her tale, Ozma said, "It's your turn now, Dorothy."

"Do you really want to me to tell that old story again?" Dorothy asked. "I'm sure you all must have heard it a thousand times."

Ozma looked at her thoughtfully. Dorothy was her very best friend in the world. Ozma had made her a Princess of Oz, and spent as much of her free time with her as she could. But as she considered it, in all the time she had known her... "You know, Dorothy, I am very familiar with the story, but I don't believe I have ever heard *you* tell it."

"I haven't either," said Trot.

"Or me," added Betsy.

"I guess it just *feels* like I did then, maybe because I've told it so many times," Dorothy said. "Well anyway, here goes." She began. "I was living on a farm in Kansas with my Uncle Henry and Aunt Em...

"... I didn't know how I could still be alive after being carried away by a twister like that, and then when I came out of the house and looked around, I wasn't real sure I *was* still alive. For a second, when I saw how strange and beautiful everything was, I thought maybe I had died and gone to Heaven. Then I met the strange little people and the Good Witch of the North, and I found out I was in Oz. The Good Witch told the Munchkins not to be afraid of me, and showed me where the Wicked Witch of the East was lying crushed under the farmhouse..." she paused and shuddered at the memory, "... and told me to take the Silver Slippers. She said she didn't know how they worked, but she knew they must be very powerful, and she sent me off to the Wizard of Oz down the road of yellow brick to the Emerald City. I met the Scarecrow, the Tin Woodman and the Cowardly Lion on the way, and it was a good thing I did, too. I never would have reached Emerald City without them..."

"...and in the end, Glinda explained to me how the Silver Shoes could take me home. So I said goodbye to my friends, and then next thing I knew, I was back in Kansas again."

"There's something a little strange about that whole story when you think about it," Trot said, after a pause.

"Why, what do you mean?" Dorothy asked.

"Don't you think it was a little strange that Glinda didn't meet you sooner than she did?" Trot said.

"What makes you say that?" Ozma asked.

"Well, if the Good Witch knew about Dorothy's house landing on the Wicked Witch of the East, Glinda must have known about it too," Trot replied, looking around the table at her companions.

"I guess so," Dorothy answered doubtfully. "But what if she did?"

"The Witch of the North didn't know how the Silver Shoes worked, but Glinda sure did," Trot explained. "So why didn't *she* come to the Munchkin country, and explain it to you right then? You could have gone home right away, and you wouldn't have had to risk your life a half-dozen times for nothing. Why, you probably would have never even *seen* the Wicked Witch of the West."

"Maybe Glinda didn't know about Dorothy and her house falling on the Witch, after all," Ozma suggested. "The Book of Records didn't open for her until later."

"Even without it, she had magical ways of knowing things," Trot demanded. "So how could she *not* know that the Witch of the East was dead?"

"And there's another thing," Betsy said suddenly. "How *did* the Witch of the North learn about the death of the Wicked Witch so soon? She was there almost as soon as it happened, and she certainly didn't have the Book of Records. Did some messenger tell her? What kind of messenger could travel so quickly? A magic one, I'd say. Not even a bird could fly *that* fast. So who was the messenger working for?"

Ozma looked from one to the other of her friends in bewilderment. "All these things happened many years ago. Why are you suddenly so curious about it now?"

"I guess because we never really thought about it before," Trot said. "You have to admit some of the things that happened don't make much sense, Ozma."

"Well, what if Glinda *did* know about the house landing on the Wicked Witch, and she didn't come to the Munchkin Country?" Dorothy asked. "What does it mean? She could've been busy with other things."

"And come to think of it, doesn't *that* seem like a strange accident," Trot added, "a twister dropping a house *right* on top of the Witch? That sounds more like magic than an accident, to me. Do you suppose it wasn't an accident at all? It's almost as if someone had arranged for that house to fall on the Witch?"

"'Someone?'" Ozma repeated. "Who do you mean, Trot? The Good Witch of the North?"

"Maybe, and maybe not," Trot answered. "Just suppose the Good Witch was working for Glinda, and that Glinda..." she trailed off, closing her eyes and sinking back into the cushions of her chair, lost in her in thoughts. She sat up abruptly, opened her eyes wide, and as if talking to herself, said, "But she couldn't... she would never... no..." Trot shook her head, and fell silent again.

"Couldn't have *what,* Trot?" Dorothy and Ozma demanded together.

"And who is *she?*" Betsy asked.

Trot looked around the table at her companions, meeting their eyes one after the other before she answered. "Why *she* is Glinda, of course," she said at last. "It's almost as if... as if Glinda arranged the whole thing."

"*Glinda*? What do you mean, Trot?" Ozma asked in a strange voice, half-rising from her chair. Her face was flushed, her body tense. "What are you saying? *What* did she arrange?"

"Everything," Trot answered. "I think she might just have arranged every single thing that happened to Dorothy after the twister brought her house to Oz. Just think about it: First, the house smashes the Witch. Then, the Good Witch of the North shows up in the Munchkin country almost as soon as the house is on the ground, tells Dorothy to take the Silver Shoes, then disappears, just like she had been waiting around for an 'accident' she knew was about to happen. But who was powerful enough to control a twister? Not the little old Witch of the North. But what about Glinda? If anybody has that kind of powerful magic, she does. While she's there, the Good Witch makes sure that Dorothy takes the one thing the Wicked Witch of the West wants most in the world: the Silver Slippers. Then, she sends Dorothy on a journey which ends up at the Wicked Witch's castle, a trip she didn't have to go on at all, if Glinda had just told her how the shoes could take her home." She turned to Dorothy. "You didn't need to travel all over Oz, or meet a humbug Wizard, or tangle with the Wicked Witch and almost get yourself killed a half-dozen times, if Glinda had done that."

"No...no, I guess not," Dorothy admitted.

Ozma sank back into her chair. "I'm sure there is an explanation..." she began.

"I tell you, everything that happened after the house fell on the Witch of the East fits," Trot said.

Ozma looked as if she was on the verge of tears. "Trot, think about what you are saying about our friend Glinda, Glinda the *Good*, the wisest, kindest Sorceress who ever lived!" she demanded. "How could *she* have ever done such things? And *why*?"

"That's a good question, Ozma. Why?" Trot said. "What could she have possibly gained that was worth risking poor Dorothy's life? She would never have gone to so much trouble without a good reason."

"That's right, Trot," Ozma agreed quickly. "Glinda had no reason to play such a cruel trick on Dorothy. You agree with me, Dorothy, Trot, Betsy, don't you?" She turned to her friends, almost desperate for their support.

"I...I'm just not sure, Ozma," Dorothy answered hesitantly

"You look at it the way Trot explained it, and Glinda is behind everything," Betsy said. "But if you look at it another way..."

"I feel terrible. I wish I'd never brought this whole thing up, Ozma. It was just a dumb idea," Trot said earnestly. "Why don't we just all agree to forget everything we said in the last twenty minutes."

"I agree," chorused Dorothy and Betsy.

Ozma started to nod her head, then turned it into a shake. "We could agree not to ever speak of it again, but how could we not think about it?" she asked. "No, dear friends, we can't just leave things this way. If Glinda is innocent, it would not be fair to leave her under suspicion. But if she really was responsible, we have a duty to find that out, too. Either Glinda was behind everything that happened to Dorothy, or there is some other explanation."

They all fell silent for a long time after that, each lost in her own thoughts, as the colored shadows thrown by the great bubbles passed over them. For many minutes, the only sounds were the soft clinks of teacups meeting saucers, and the faint crunch of lemon drop cookies being chewed.

Dorothy was the first to speak. "What did my visit to Oz accomplish?" she asked, as she watched a bubble of a particularly trying shade of chartreuse detach itself from a stalk and sail away. "What did it change?" She immediately began to answer her own questions. "The Wizard was exposed as a humbug, the Wicked Witches were destroyed, the Scarecrow became..."

"There, you just said it!" Trot exclaimed. "The Wicked Witches were destroyed. That was the biggest thing that happened, and it wouldn't have if you hadn't come to Oz."

"Okay, Dorothy's house killed the Witch of the East, but Glinda didn't send her out to get the Witch of the West," Betsy objected. "The Wizard of Oz did that."

"That's right, Betsy," Dorothy said. "Oz sent me out after the Witch, and I might have easily been killed by her. That was a very cruel thing for him to do, and not like him at all. He was a humbug, but you all know he was... he *is*, a good and kind man. So, why would he have done such a thing?"

"Because he didn't want anyone to find out that he was a humbug wizard. At least, that's what he told you later." Trot answered. "But there must have been other ways to do that without risking the life of an innocent girl. For one thing, he could have just refused to see you. That would have been simple enough."

"Do you suppose somebody *made* him...?" Betsy began.

Ozma stood suddenly. "I think we will go see the great and powerful Wizard of Oz right now," she said with great decisiveness. "There are some questions he needs to answer for us."

As usual, the Wizard was in his magic laboratory, which was adjacent to his apartments in the palace. Although he had been a humbug wizard when he first came to Oz, after he returned he had become a true student of magic under the tutelage of Glinda the Good and was now a powerful magician in his own right. He had for many years been the Royal Wizard and Ozma's trusted advisor.

The Wizard of Oz was a little man with a shining, bald dome, a spry step and an ever-present smile. His face lit up when he saw the four girls enter his laboratory.

"Now what brings four such lovely ladies here to visit a lonely old man?" Before any of them could answer, he raised a hand, and said quickly, "No, no, don't tell me." He launched into a familiar, old routine, one that had never before failed to make his little friends laugh. He touched a hand to his forehead, closed his eyes and said, "You want a spell to turn cats into dogs and vice-versa?" He studied their faces expectantly. "No, no, that's not it. Ah! You need a way to keep your hair from frizzing in the rain? No, that's not right, either. You..." He ground to a halt when he saw that none of the four had so much as smiled.

"So," he said in a serious tone, "how can I help you, Your Majesty, girls?"

"I was hoping you could answer some questions for us," Ozma said.

They followed the Wizard to a table, where he selected a chair and sat down. Dorothy took the chair right next to him and pulled it up until she was knee to knee, facing the old man.

"Oscar, you played a dirty trick on me and my friends when I first met you," she began.

"Dorothy, you don't know how ashamed I am about what I did back then," the old man protested. "If I could only..."

She cut him short. "I forgave you a long time ago. You've made up for anything you did in the old days a hundred times over, and I can't count how many times you saved my life." She took one of his hands with both of hers. "You are my friend, and I am yours, and nothing can ever change that. You know that."

He smiled warmly. "I don't deserve to have a friend like you, Dorothy, but I'm very glad I do," he said.

She squeezed the captured hand and smiled back. "We need you to tell us the truth, no matter what it is. Will you help us?" she asked.

"If I can, my dear," he answered.

She caught his eye and held it. "Why did you send us, me and my friends, out to kill the Witch of the West?"

"Why, you know why I did that, Dorothy," he answered, evading her gaze. "I told you a long time ago. I didn't want anyone to find out I wasn't a real wizard."

"Look me straight in the eye and say it," Dorothy demanded sternly.

He met her eyes and said haltingly, "I didn't want... you to... I mean... I thought you... you would..." He stopped and turned his head away from her.

"I...I can't, Dorothy" he admitted.

"Why not?" she asked.

He reddened. "Because I can't lie to you when you're looking at me," he said. In a voice only a little louder than a whisper he added, "And it's not the truth."

"Then please tell us the truth, Oz," Ozma urged. "Whatever it may be, whatever your reasons, you are forgiven in advance in return for your many years of loyal service to me and to the people of Oz. Speak the truth, and do not be afraid."

He stared at his feet, holding his head in his hands. He spoke so softly that at first they could barely make out his words. "I was afraid. *She* knew I wasn't a real wizard, and she... she told me that if I helped her out from time to time, she would allow me continue to pretend I was a wizard and leave me in charge of the Emerald City. But if I didn't..." he shook his head. Then he straightened up to look at Dorothy. There were tears glittering in his eyes. "I was afraid, Dorothy. She was so powerful, and I was just a pretend wizard, do you understand? So, when she told me what to do after you arrived in the Emerald City, to grant you an audience, then send you out after the Witch, I did it. I was sure you would be killed, and I didn't want to do it, but I was *afraid...*" Now a tear flowed freely over his cheek.

Dorothy reached out to gently touch the old man's face with her fingertips. "It's all right, Oscar. I understand. But please tell us..." she hesitated, afraid that she already knew the answer, "...*who* told you to do that?"

The Wizard lowered his head again, and mumbled something inaudible.

"I couldn't hear you," Ozma said, stooping low over the Wizard. "Say it again, please, a little louder."

"Glinda," he said, his head still down, his face invisible. "Glinda told me what to do."

Ozma's face suddenly went pale. She pulled out a chair, and sat down heavily, as if her legs could no longer support her weight. "So it *is* true, then," she whispered.

"Yes Ozma, it's quite true," came a soprano voice from the doorway. They all spun around to see a familiar figure, a tall, composed woman with heartbreakingly lovely features, dressed in flowing robes of red, the Royal Sorceress, Glinda the Good. "Did you really believe that the peace in Oz was built without paying a price?" she asked. "Did you think that kindness and good intentions can conquer evil all by themselves?"

"Glinda..." Ozma began.

"Sometimes, a great good can only be accomplished at a terrible price," the Sorceress continued, as if Ozma had not spoken. "There are times when one must harden one's heart and sacrifice the one for the good of the many."

"What are you talking about?" Dorothy asked.

"You know that the Book of Records in my palace tells me of any event that happens anywhere in the world. I have other books that tell of other things," Glinda said. "One of those things was an ancient prophecy that Oz would be freed of the Wicked Witches by a mortal girl from America. But the prophecy was not self-fulfilling; it needed someone to take a hand in it, to set it on its course."

Her voice became softer, and she seemed to be looking at something far away that none of the others could see. "The first was a brave little girl from Iowa named Sarah Johnson. Many years ago, she destroyed the Wicked Witch of the North, but she died in the moment of victory. Long ago. Her name should be known and honored in every cottage in Oz, but she is forgotten by all but me. She will live on in my heart forever. After Sarah, there came bright-eyed, bold Emily, and then many years later, Anne the fearless, but they were not the ones prophesied in the Book. I made arrangements, planned events so that they would go out to conquer the Witches..." She paused, and her voice dropped. "I sent them out to die," she finished tonelessly.

"You were the fourth, Dorothy," Glinda said, her voice becoming clearer again. "So many years had passed since Anne that I had all but given up looking for the one who had been foretold. Then the tornado brought your house along at the just the right moment, and I was able to control it enough so that it fell directly on the Witch of the East. That was a good guess, Trot.

"After that, I was certain that Dorothy was the prophesied one. I sent the Good Witch of the North to meet you, and instructed her in what she was to tell you. I prepared everything so that you would eventually confront the Witch of the West, and I hoped that you were, at last, the one in the prophecy, so that no more mortal girls would have to die to free Oz of the Witches. I was very glad when you succeeded, and came through unharmed."

"You cannot be the Glinda I know," Ozma said. "You must have replaced the real one. My Glinda would never have sacrificed the lives of innocent little girls, not for a prophecy, not for any reason."

The Sorceress smiled sadly. "I'm afraid there is only one Glinda, and I am she. You only know one side of me, the side that I have chosen to show you. You have never seen the other side of me, my dear Ozma, and you never will."

"You *used* me and those other poor girls, too!" Dorothy burst out. "You used the Good Witch, and the Wizard. You moved us around like, like..." she paused, searching for the right word.

"Like puppets?" the Sorceress suggested. "Yes, I'm afraid I did, dear Dorothy. I did what I had to do to protect Oz, including pulling the strings of ones I love, even endangering their lives. And because I did those deeds, and because of other things I did, terrible things of which I shall not speak, because of that, Oz today is a paradise, a land of peace and happiness, a country without evil. I paid a bitter price for what I did, one that you will never know." Glinda spoke the last few words slowly, as if she was in pain. She fell silent momentarily. Her face, which had always appeared so ageless, fleetingly revealed the weariness of long years which lay beneath the surface.

Then her voice and face returned to normal. "But now, my dear children, I am afraid that our fascinating conversation must come to an end." Something about the way she said these words made a chill run up the spines of the four girls.

"What... what do you mean, Glinda?" Trot asked fearfully.

"Don't worry, Trot. I would never do anything to harm you. In spite of what you might think, I am not a monster," the Sorceress answered. She raised a gleaming silver wand high overhead. "Look up!" she said in a commanding voice. All four girls unwillingly raised their eyes to stare at the tip of the wand, which was now emitting bright green flashes. Glinda muttered the words of a magical formula under her breath, then extended her free arm straight out from her body, with her fingers clenched in a fist. She opened all her fingers at once, and cried out "Sharkuu!" There was an even brighter, blinding flash, and suddenly Ozma and her friends were gone.

"Back in their beds?" the Wizard asked. "Like the other times?"

Glinda nodded. "Yes. Tomorrow, none of them will remember a thing about what they did today, nor will they have the slightest interest in finding out what they have forgotten. It's a very tidy little spell. Covers its own tracks."

"I wish you would use that spell on me, oh mighty Puppet Mistress," the Wizard said. "I'm not a young man any longer, Glinda, and this is not the first time I've been through this. It gets harder every time."

The Sorceress made a face. "You think you're *old*? Please, Oscar. You're not even in your third century yet. Compared with me, you're a mere child, hardly older than those girls. Think: you know I can't use that memory-spell on you, as long as you have the anti-magic charm hanging around your neck, and you need its protection when you're working with those powerful spells in your laboratory," Glinda said. She saw that he was about to object, and quickly continued. "And don't tell me you'll remove it and put it back after I clean up your memory. It won't work."

"Why not?" He demanded. Then he answered his own question. "Oh, I remember now; I asked you the same thing last time. The charm will cancel out the memory-spell as soon as I put it back on, and I'll remember everything again. Well then, maybe I'll hang up my Wizard hat, and just retire from magic for good."

Glinda made a rude noise. "That'll be the day," she said. "Now why don't you stop talking nonsense, and show me that new weather device you've been working on?"

AFTERWARDS AND NOTES

The Great and Terrible Oz Mystery
Michael O. Riley

The idea for "The Great and Terrible Oz Mystery" was suggested to me by the question of how the Wizard maintained his illusion of great power and mystery with those people who worked and served him in the palace. It would have been impossible—and impossibly lonely—for the Wizard to live there so long without contact with anyone. I structured the story as a mystery because that's my favorite genre for pleasure reading, and I wanted to pay a small tribute to the mysteries Baum incorporated into his juvenile fiction. I continue to be fascinated by the detective story form, and I'm now completing my second murder mystery novel—no connection to Oz this time.

Editor's Notes

The Phanfasms are Erbs, along with the Mimics and other entities that Baum calls "evil spirits." The Erbs appear in a number of stories, including the following:

The Emerald City of Oz, by L. Frank Baum
The Carnevillans of Oz, by John Bardy
The Magical Mimics of Oz, by Jack Snow
The Royal Explorers of Oz: Book 3, by Marcus Mebes, Jeff Rester & Jared Davis
The Law of Oz and Other Stories, by Paul Dana
The Magic Umbrella of Oz, by Paul Dana
The Living House of Oz, by Edward Einhorn

The Witch's Mother in Oz
Paul Dana

The idea that Mombi might be a Yookoohoo came to me during a reread of Baum's *The Marvelous Land of Oz*. In Chapter Twenty-Two the cornered Mombi suddenly reveals that she can transform herself quickly and easily, with no tools or ceremonies or incantations, an ability that she has not used hitherto and that she shares with very few characters in Baum's books. The best transformers in the series are Kiki Aru, who must utter a magic word, and the Nome King, who must use his Magic Belt—and the two Yookoohoos, Mrs. Yoop and Red Reera. Mrs. Yoop, to be sure, uses a magic apron that she herself has made for this purpose, but it is not much of a stretch to imagine Mombi wearing a similar sort of talisman. A knottier problem is the fact that Mombi makes no use of this simple magic until she absolutely must, preferring instead to work with complex and time-consuming formulas whose effects are often illusory. "The Witch's Mother" is my attempt to solve this problem.

Editor's Notes

This story takes place during Chapter 21 of *The Marvelous Land of Oz* (after page 252 if you have one of the original or facsimile editions), where Mombi first debuted.

Although Mombi's fingerprints are all over the Oz series, such as in *The Giant Horse of Oz*, *The Blue Emperor of Oz* and *The Seven Blue Mountains of Oz* trilogy), she herself plays a significant role in several stories, including the following:

"The Gillikin Witches of Oz," by Paul Dana (forthcoming)

How the Wizard Saved Oz, by Donald Abbott

"Witches of the West," by Darrell Spradlyn & Marcus Mebes (*Oziana 2013*)

Oz and the Three Witches, by Hugh Pendexter III (*Oz-story Magazine #6*)

"Sunday Visits," by Michael Pickens (*Oz-story Magazine #4*)

Dorothy and the Magic Belt, by Susan Saunders

The Ork in Oz, by Jack and Larry Brenton

The Lost King of Oz, by Ruth Plumly Thompson

"Mombi's Pink Polkadot Vest," by Fred E. Otto (*Oziana 1985*)

Bucketheads in Oz, by Chris Dulabone and other authors

"Executive Decisions," by David Tai (*Oziana 38*)

"Thy Fearful Symmetry," by Jeff Rester (*Oziana 38*)

"Jenny Jump's Adventures in Time and Space," by Nathan M. DeHoff (*www.oztimeline.net*)

"The Malevolent Mannequin of Oz," by Joe Bongiorno (*Oziana 2015*)

The Trade: A Langwidere Story
Mike Conway

"The Trade" came from a desire to see more of Princess Langwidere, who has so much potential and who has seen so little time on the page. I like taking underused characters and doing something different with them. I also like stories where characters surprise you. Princess Langwidere is an anomaly, but she wasn't as coldhearted as one might think, and you can see this in the way she handled Cari. This short story was turned into an interactive visual novel. I adapted and programmed it, and my son did the character art. You can find it at: https://forestmaster.itch.io/langwidere-the-trade.

The Lost Tales of Oz

Editor's Notes

Princess Langwidere was first written about in *Ozma of Oz*, by L. Frank Baum, and has remained a bit of a mystery, as she possesses the ability to live without a head, and to put on other heads that have been chopped off of other women. Langwidere's disposition changes with each head, but she remains Princess Langwidere and does not become the persons who formerly had their heads. This is reminiscent of the monarch and royal family of Mo (from Baum's *The Magical Monarch of Mo*), who are able to switch heads and lose limbs without pain or loss of life. For more of the life of Princess Langwidere, see: "The Princess of Ev," by Joanna Payne. An anthology is forthcoming which will explore the mystery of Princess Langwidere in greater depth.

Ojo and the Woozy
J.L. Bell

The seed for "Ojo and the Woozy" was the idea of more *Little Wizard Stories*. In each of those tales, L. Frank Baum sent a couple of his recurring characters off on a brief adventure. Ojo and the Woozy seemed like a natural pairing. They're already friends, but their personalities contrast: Ojo's moods highlight the Woozy's equanimity. When I sat down to find what trouble those two could walk into, however, I realized that their biggest challenge at the end of *The Patchwork Girl of Oz* is adjusting to life in the Emerald City. After years of isolation in the Munchkin forests, they have to follow new rules, learn new customs, make new friends. I could remember how those problems felt. Sometimes, I recalled, the hardest struggles happen close to home.

Acknowledgements and Notes

Editor's Notes

Ojo Alla Bad has had many adventures since his first one in *The Patchwork Girl of Oz*, including becoming Ozma's first human prisoner, discovering that he's the son of a prince, and his accidental consumption of a magic Phoenix egg. The stories in which Ojo plays a significant role include:

"The Great and Terrible Oz Mystery," by Michael O'Riley (included in this collection)

"The Cookywitch Coven: The Adventures of Ojo, Unc Nunkie, and Dr. Pipt" (included in this collection)

"Unc Nunkie and the White King of Oz," by Greg Hunter (from *Two Terrific Tales of Oz*)

Ojo in Oz, by Ruth Plumly Thompson

The Magic Bowls of Oz, by Ryan Gannaway & Peter Schulenburg

The Law of Oz and Other Stories, by Paul Dana

The Magic Umbrella of Oz, by Paul Dana

Yookoohoos of Oz, by Paul Dana

The Immortal Longings of Oz, by Paul Dana (forthcoming)

The Woozy first appeared in *The Patchwork Girl of Oz*. The stories in which the Woozy plays a significant role include:

"A Trip Down Memory Lane, or How the Woozy Came to Oz," by Edmund Zebrowsky (*The Emerald City Mirror #7*)

The Emerald City Mirror, issues #49-55, by David Hulan

"The Woozy's Tale," by Gili Bar-Hillel (*Oziana 1992*)

"The Threat of Civil-Oz-Ation," by Dan Cox (*Oziana 1975*)

"The Year of the Woozy," by Seraphim J. Sigrist (included in *In Other Lands than Oz*)

A Refugee in Oz, by Kim McFarland

The Other Searches for the Lost Princess
Nathan DeHoff

Continuity Notes

- These stories take place after Chapter 5 of *The Lost Princess of Oz,* and before Chapter 26.
- The dialogue in Betsy's introduction comes from J.L. Bell, which he wrote in the BCF Pumperdink forum discussion of *The Lost Princess of Oz*, after fellow author David Hulan *(The Glass Cat of Oz)* commented that people might have been pestering Glinda while she was trying to work out the best way to save Ozma.
- I used a thesaurus to get some of the names in the Bunkum Hill section, although I thought of quite a few of them on my own. *The Book of Bunkum* is a reference to *The Bunkum Book*, by Aubrey Hopwood.
- According to a letter from L. Frank Baum, the Marshmallow Twins were supposed to appear both in a chapter of *The Patchwork Girl of Oz* (to replace the excised Garden of Meats episode) and another book. They never appeared at all as far as I know, so I used them here.
- The Candy Country and its Giant Royal Marshmallow are from Roger Baum's *Dorothy of Oz*. The film version, *Legend of Oz: Dorothy's Return*, has the character Marshal Mallow fall in love with the China Princess. While there were some major missteps in the film, I liked that element, so I tried to adapt it here.
- Prezumba was simply a place I made up for the yak's story, but that isn't to say I might not develop it further in a later tale.

Acknowledgements and Notes

- I wanted to keep these stories fairly short, but the book indicates that the other search parties were gone for as long as Dorothy's or longer, and their adventure took place over more than a week. As such, I indicated that the parties each had more time searching after the experiences they had here.

- The subject of Mombi's pigs was brought up in a list of story suggestions before, perhaps by Fred Meyer. The idea there was that they might have been enchanted people, but I instead made them pigs who were altered in punny ways by Mombi's magic.

- Jellia's father Jimb Jamb is named and established as Mombi's closest neighbor in Onyx Madden's *The Mysterious Chronicles of Oz*.

- The boar who steals books from Mombi is a major character in Greg Gick's *Bungle and the Magic Lantern of Oz*.

- The name Tattypoo for the Good Witch of the North and her dragon companion Agnes are from Ruth Plumly Thompson's *The Giant Horse of Oz*.

- Mycroft Mason's "Four Views of General Jinjur" establishes that Jinjur's husband left her (other sources suggest he eventually returned) and that the King of the Munchkins from *Ozma* was a pretender.

- Ogoshen, Herville and Brigadier General Tanjrine are introduced in Phyllis Ann Karr's *Hollyhock Dolls*.

- The Imperial Squawmos and the concept of a cookywitch derive from Thompson's *The Cowardly Lion of Oz*.

- Paella and her café appear in another story of mine, "Vaneeda of Oz," which appears in this collection.

- The reason why Unc Nunkie is nervous about searching the southern Munchkin Country, and indeed his and Ojo's back story in general, is revealed in Thompson's *Ojo in Oz*.
- Henry Blossom's *Blue Emperor of Oz* gives more detail on that character, and why no one remembers him very well. The same book also visits Wam's workshop on Old Smokey, although the character of Wam was previously mentioned in *The Cowardly Lion of Oz* and *The Wishing Horse of Oz*. His fate is revealed in Melody Grandy's *The Seven Blue Mountains of Oz* trilogy.
- The name Obediah for the former King of the Munchkins is from March Laumer.
- Sugarene of Overhill is from Fred Otto's "The Wogglebug's New Clothes," from *Oziana 1987*.
- Cinnamon City and Floss Confection appeared in a collaborative story called *The Ruby Ring of Oz* on the old International Wizard of Oz Club forums. Jared Davis came up with Floss's name, but the city was my idea.
- Thompson's advertising pamphlet *Billy in Bunbury* refers to Devils Food as King Hun Bun's magician. I decided to give him a bit of an origin story.

Chop
Eric Shanower

"Chop" began as a response to a call for contributions to an anthology of dark Oz stories. I don't remember how the idea came to me, but it seemed like a logical continuation of the relationship between Chopfyt and Nimmie Amee in Baum's *The Tin Woodman of Oz*. Although I didn't complete "Chop" by the anthology's submission deadline, eventually I reached the point where I considered the story finished. It was collecting rejections from the fantasy market when editor Joe Bongiorno asked whether I had a story I might submit to *The Lost Tales of Oz*. I thought "Chop" was far too grim and out of continuity. But I guess I was wrong. Joe accepted the story for publication.

Editor's Notes

Nimmie Aimee and Chopfyt were first introduced in L. Frank Baum's *The Tin Woodman of Oz*. They later appeared in Phillip Lewin's *The Master Crafters of Oz*, and Melody Grandy's *Forever in Oz*.

Button Bright was first introduced in L. Frank Baum's *The Road to Oz*. He made a surprising return in Baum's *Sky Island* and *The Scarecrow of Oz*. Since then, he's appeared in numerous stories, including significant roles in the following:

"Twin Properties," by Aurilly *(oztimeline.net)*
The Lost Princess of Oz, by L. Frank Baum
"Button-Bright and the Knit-Wits of Oz," by Jim Vander Noot *(Oziana 1987)*
"The Adventure of the Cat that Did Not Meow in the Night," by Jay Delkin & Eric Shanower *(Oziana 1976)*
Button Bright of Oz, by Harry Mongold
"The Ransom of Button Bright," by J.L. Bell *(Oziana 2009)*
The Magic Bowls of Oz, by Ryan Gannaway & Peter Schulenburg
A Promise Kept in Oz, by Dennis Anfuso
"Ozma Fights the Sniffles," by J.L. Bell *(Oziana 2000)*
The Law of Oz and Other Stories, by Paul Dana
The Magic Umbrella of Oz, by Paul Dana

The Lost Tales of Oz

In Flesh of Burnished Tin
Jeff Rester

My inspiration for writing "In Flesh of Burnished Tin" was a longing to see an Oz story that spelled out the various things that happened to the Tin Woodman on his way to becoming who we know today. As Baum and other authors wrote more and more Oz books, certain characters like Nick Chopper had more backstory created for them. With a longing to see the continuity of such backstories harmonized, I began my little project with "Dreaming in A Scarlet Slumber" and continued with "In Flesh of Burnished Tin."

As I began "In Flesh...," I became more keenly aware of Nimee Aimee and what she must have suffered at the hands of the Eastern Witch. That is how I started the story, and how it unfolded with Nick himself having been through his own heartache and loss. It was their mutual pain, and a longing for something more...something better...that began the story of their intertwined destinies. And this in turn led to the hope that would be the Oz we all know and love today.

Diplomatic Immunity
David Tai

Diplomatic Immunity was written from a desire to see what happened to Sky Island, as well as to look at the things that make Betsy different from Trot or Dorothy. How does Betsy feel about being the only non-royal of her female Oz friends? And once I got that background set, Betsy and Trot wouldn't shut up telling me *their* side of things! Teenagers. What can you do?

Editor's Notes

Betsy Bobbin first appeared in L. Frank Baum's *Tik-Tok of Oz*. Mayre "Trot" Griffiths first appeared in L. Frank Baum's book *The Sea Fairies*. She became a princess in the sequel *Sky Island*, and later came to Oz in Baum's *The Scarecrow of Oz*. Both girls moved to the Emerald City and have appeared in numerous stories since, including several in this collection, and significant roles in the following books and short stories:

The Lost Princess of Oz, by L. Frank Baum
The Witch Queen of Oz, by Philip John Lewin
The Magic of Oz, by L. Frank Baum
Masquerade in Oz, by Bill Campbell & Irwin Terry
The Master Crafters of Oz, by Philip John Lewin
The Hungry Tiger of Oz, by Ruth Plumly Thompson
The Giant Horse of Oz, by Ruth Plumly Thompson
"Betsy Bobbin of Oz," by Greg Hunter (from *Two Terrific Tales of Oz*)
The Red Jinn in Oz, by Mildred L. Palmer
"A Princess of Oz," by David Hulan (*Oziana 1995*)

The Scrap Bag Circus of Oz
M.A. Berg

It was a cold and wintery night. The snow had begun to fall just as I finished my manuscript *Blue Dog and the Wizard of Oz*. I put it in a stamped envelope addressed to *Oziana*, pulled on my boots, and prepared to run to the mail box. Suddenly I heard the ringing-ting-linging of sleigh bells and the neigh of a horse. Guests, at this hour? But when I opened the front door all I could see was blowing snow.

I made a hurried trip to the mail box. Already the tracks of the sleigh's runners were being covered by snow. I pulled up the red flag on the mail box to alert the rural mail carrier there was outgoing mail. There in the back of the box was a manila envelope addressed to me, and sealed with green wax and the imprint of a small horse shoe and the initials O.Z. The Sawhorse! But how could he write to me? And why?

Reasoning that he had help from someone with fingers, I returned to my warm fire and opened the large envelope. I pulled out a manuscript and a letter. The brief letter asked me to submit the enclosed story from *50,000 Miles on the Back Roads of Oz* to *Oziana* magazine, but under the pseudonym, Deciduous Equine. The author wished the story to be published on its merit alone, and not as a favor to a famous celebrity and palace favorite. He asked that I edit the story to remove all first person references. He thanked me in advance and wished me a happy holiday.

The Wizard in New York
& Ali Cat in Oz
Sam Sackett

The Wizard in New York is dedicated to my wife, Suwapee. The story was first conceived to answer a fan question regarding how Stan and Ollie wound up in Oogaboo in my book *Adolf Hitler in Oz*. I feel the details of the 1939 World's Fair may drag it down, but I hope you'll enjoy it nonetheless. By the way, the kid standing in line at the RCA Building is me. My mother drove me to New York from California in her 1930 Chevrolet to meet her family and visit the fair. I was 11 at the time. The only part of the fair I really remember is the television exhibit. My mother would never have been so snippy to Oscar.

The Lost Tales of Oz

Ali Cat in Oz is for Rob and John, to whom I used to read the Oz books when they were little. Ali was modeled on my cat, BrooTwo, who died last year at the age of 14 (in 2015). To the extent that the story has a basic premise, it is that doing nice things for people will bring unexpected rewards. If *Adolf Hitler in Oz* was about good vs. evil, overcoming obstacles is what this is about. The Fussbudget section was meant to be funny, but writing comedy is always risky. As Eddie Cantor once said, "One man's gag gags another man."

Editor's Notes

Those who've only seen the MGM film version may not be aware that, like Dorothy, the Wizard came back to stay in Oz. He features in numerous stories. The following list includes his adventures while he lived in the outside world, as well as his early years as ruler of Oz until the time he returned to learn real magic from Glinda:

How the Wizard Came to Oz: The True Origin of the Wizard of Oz, by Donald Abbott (forthcoming)
The Wonderful Wizard of Oz, by L. Frank Baum
"The Wizard of Aurissau," by Nathan M. DeHoff (www.oztimeline.net)
Buffalo Dreams, by Jane Mailander
"The Adventure of the Sinister Chinaman," by Barbara Hambly (from *Sherlock Holmes: The Crossovers Casebook*)
Dorothy and the Wizard in Oz, by L. Frank Baum
Oz and the Three Witches, by Hugh Pendexter III (*Oz-story Magazine #6*)
"The Mysterious Palace of Voe," by Jay Delkin *(Oziana 1974)*

Acknowledgements and Notes

Lurline and the Talking Animals of Oz
Joe Bongiorno

I wrote *Lurline and the Talking Animals in Oz* in order to better understand the crucial time period in which Lurline gave the animals in Oz speech. Paul Dana had given us a wonderful glimpse of the enchantment in his book *The Law of Oz and Other Stories*, and I built from there, only from the perspective of an ordinary family and the impact the changes had on a farming town that drew its sustenance (financially and otherwise) from animals. The story was initially much longer, and some of that ended up in the supplemental booklet *Lost Histories from the Royal Librarian of Oz*. There is considerably more to tell about Lurline's journey, but I leave those adventures for the sequel anthology.

Editor's Notes

The Fairy Queen Lurline and her enchantment of Oz were first mentioned in *The Tin Woodman of Oz*. Since then she's been mentioned or appeared in several stories, including:

"The Banishment of Faleero," by Nathan M. DeHoff
(www.oztimeline.net)
The Mysterious Chronicles of Oz, by Onyx Madden
The Witch Queen of Oz, by Philip John Lewin
Glinda of Oz, by L. Frank Baum
The Master Crafters of Oz, by Philip John Lewin
The Magical Mimics in Oz, by Jack Snow
The Law of Oz and Other Stories, by Paul Dana
The Magic Umbrella of Oz, by Paul Dana
Lurline and the White Ravens of Oz, by Marcus Mebes
The Seven Blue Mountains of Oz, Book 2, by Melody Grandy

The Lost Tales of Oz

The Royal Explorers of Oz: Books 1-4, by Marcus Mebes,
Jared Davis, and Jeff Rester
Paradox in Oz, by Edward Einhorn
Lurline and the First Fairy Queen of Oz, by Joe Bongiorno
(from *Lost Histories from the Royal Librarian of Oz*)

Tommy Kwikstep and the Magpie
Jared Davis

Writing "Tommy Kwikstep and the Magpie" was a process.
Early on, I had an idea to create a story that addressed Ozma
bringing several people to live in the palace, the idea being that
this is her surrogate family. However, the early draft was fairly
flat and uninteresting. So, I added someone to become an
antagonist, eventually deciding on Tommy Kwikstep. Yet it just
didn't feel right to have Tommy as the "villain" of the piece.

It was about that time the Scottish comedian Limmy posted a
video in which he spots a magpie in a park and tries to quote
the Magpie rhyme, having trouble remembering it all. I'd heard
the first seven lines in the song "Magpie" by Patrick Wolf.
Listening to the song a few more times, I had the inspiration to
make a story not about Ozma, but about Tommy.

Corina the Magpie was inspired by looking up different types
of magpies, and seeing how colorful this bird was, I knew it
existed in Oz. The Good Witch of the North was a character I
wanted to see back in Oz stories after Ruth Plumly
Thompson wrote her out in *The Giant Horse of Oz*. Having
her run a music hall and serve drinks felt a little unusual for
a new career for a Good Witch of Oz, but the quirkiness of it
just felt right for Baum's world.

Acknowledgements and Notes

Perry had been invented for a round robin story I'd begun online long ago titled "The Ruby Ring of Oz." Making him and Tommy fall in love was inspired by Wolf's song, particularly the lyrics "You can run on, run along and make a home between the knees of her, or among the brackens and the ferns and the boy who has a name."

There's a real lack of LGBT Oz characters. A number of them lend themselves to queer interpretations, but none are openly LGBT. Making Tommy having a male love interest might be a stretch for some readers as he's an original Baum character, but he's a Baum character who appeared in only one chapter of *The Tin Woodman of Oz*, so there was very little about him. I won't argue that Baum would have given him this story, but if it's a problem for you, simply see it as my separate interpretation of Oz canon.

The bigger issue with having an LGBT relationship in Oz is that it didn't feel right to use the terms "gay," "bisexual" or anything else. While these terms describe valid identities, they exist because society requires us to point out a difference. In Oz, I can't believe that it would be an issue to love who you'd want, particularly when no one dies, so it feels like the people of Oz would adopt a "live and let live" stance on this. The idea of having Dorothy question a same sex relationship when the term "friend of Dorothy" exists was too much fun not to touch on.

In the end, this story brought up a lot of interesting concepts as I developed it. But I'm very pleased with how it turned out and I hope others enjoy it.

The Lost Tales of Oz

Editor's Notes

Tommy Kwikstep made his first appearance in L. Frank Baum's *The Tin Woodman of Oz*. He and Perry appear again in the forthcoming book, *The Haunted Castle of Oz*, by Marcus Mebes.

Ozma and the Orange Ogres in Oz
Nathan M. DeHoff & Joe Bongiorno

I wrote the first draft of "The Orange Ogres in Oz" over twenty years ago. I think it mostly had to do with how orange was one of the major colors not represented in a country in the Oz series. I know I'm not the first person to come up with my own orange land. March Laumer had Unnikegwick, and Fred Otto the Amber City. I didn't know about either of these when I wrote my story, though. And then I guess I just did some word association to come up with Orange Ogres.

~Nathan M. DeHoff

Nathan's stories always fire up my imagination and he's been kind enough to put up with my out-of-control impulses! When I first met Citros, he struck me as someone frustrated with a situation that started long before he was born. His intentions weren't bad, but he was going about things in the wrong way. Still, I knew that Ozma would see in him a kind of nobility. The beautiful thing about Oz is how magnanimous in spirit its rulers are, how they have no agenda other than to help and heal others, even those who appear threatening. It's quite a rare thing, and something we could use more of in the outside world.

~Joe Bongiorno

Acknowledgements and Notes

Quiet Victory
Marcus Mebes

The story of the Musicker and Victor Columbia Edison came to me in a stroke of inspiration. I had not planned to write the story; rather, it seems like it just evolved naturally.

Oz is a land of happiness and peace, and I can't imagine anyone—natural or magicked to life—existing in a state of unhappiness or perpetual annoyance. Or a being that causes perpetual annoyance. Victor Columbia Edison is portrayed as a character who annoys people, and as a character with some staying power, I'd like to think that Ozma would at some point or another help the guy out. Since that hasn't happened, perhaps circumstances would lead to him eventually getting tired of being ostracized, and wanting to change. So, as an opportune circumstance, the annoying creature finally encounters someone who not only understands him, but empathizes with him, and knows a way to help.

On top of that, I thought it was high time the world heard from these two obscure characters again.

The concept of achieving peace and enlightenment through meditation might not be an enchantingly amiable and cozy story that Baum or his successors might have written, but it's definitely something that our fast-paced world of instant gratification, self-centered entitlement, and discourtesy needs more of. Hopefully the story will inspire peace and calm in an otherwise frenzied world.

The Lost Tales of Oz

Editor's Notes

The Musicker is from *The Road to Oz*. Victor Columbia Edison first appeared in *The Patchwork Girl of Oz*, and has had several further adventures here:

"Unk Nunkie and the White King of Oz," by Greg Hunter
Bungle and the Magic Lantern of Oz, by Greg Gick
The Astonishing Tale of the Gump in Oz, by Dennis Anfuso
The Lonely Phonograph of Oz, by Debbie Bumstead
Bungle of Oz, by Carrie Bailey

Vaneeda of Oz
Nathan M. DeHoff

In an interview with Ruth Plumly Thompson, she gave an example of an opening paragraph for an Oz story that she never wrote, proposing the existence of a daughter of the Wicked Witch of the East named Vaneeda. (She might have said West, due to her typical mix-up of directions, but it mentions the Munchkin Country). I decided I should tell her story, and added in a bit about the Munchkin King mentioned in "Ozma of Oz" who seemingly disappears prior to *The Giant Horse of Oz*. Jared Davis came up with Winnie, Jinjur's daughter, and since he was writing about Jinjur's son, he suggested I use Winnie.

Editor's Notes

Paella appeared earlier in the story "The Cookywitch's Coven," the third entry in *The Other Searches for the Lost Princess*, available in this collection.

Acknowledgements and Notes

The Puppet Mistress of Oz
Andrew Heller

"The Puppet Mistress of Oz" is the result of many years of my gradually increasing suspicion that all was not as it seemed in Oz. After watching the 1939 MGM adaptation of *The Wonderful Wizard of Oz* for perhaps the fifteenth time, it occurred to me that Glinda could have easily sent Dorothy home by simply explaining how the Ruby Slippers (Silver Shoes in the original) worked, and could have done so any time after the house had crushed the Witch. Glinda's explanation, that there was no point in telling Dorothy until she learned what she really wanted, was patently bogus. All Dorothy did the whole time in Oz was tell everyone how much she wanted to go home.

The fact that in the original novel, Dorothy is met by the Witch of the North (who, oddly enough, never appears again), doesn't change much. For the reasons I set forth in the story, Glinda had to know what was going on. For additional evidence, I point to the Sorceress' reaction to Ozma when the latter proposes to stop the war between the Skeezers and the Flatheads, in *Glinda of Oz*. Glinda tells Ozma that it is none of their business.

Clearly Glinda has a much more realistic view of life than Ozma, and she is far more willing to use whatever means necessary to protect Oz. Once I was able to reason this far, the story almost wrote itself.

BIOGRAPHIES

Joe Bongiorno is the creator of The Royal Publisher of Oz (www.theroyalpublisherofoz.com), which publishes stories in the universe begun by L. Frank Baum. Joe maintains The Royal Timeline of Oz (www.oztimeline.net), the Star Wars Expanded Universe Timeline (www.starwarstimeline.net), and the X-Files Chronology (www.xfilestimeline.net). Joe has written the book series *Black Sabbath: The Illustrated Lyrics,* co-edited the *Cyberpunk Nexus: Exploring the Blade Runner Universe,* and has written short stories and essays for *Oziana* magazine, *Star Wars Gamer* magazine, and several anthologies for Sequart Books.

Michael O. Riley is the author of *Oz and Beyond: The Fantasy World of L. Frank Baum* (University Press of Kansas, 1997) and *A Bookbinder's Analysis of the First Edition of The Wonderful Wizard of Oz* (Book Club of California, 2011). He is the owner, printer, and bookbinder of The Pamami Press, which has produced several deluxe books based on the rare works of L. Frank Baum. He is also Professor Emeritus of English at Georgia College where he taught Children's Literature and British and German Romanticism.

Paul Dana is the author of *The Law of Oz, and Other Stories, The Magic Umbrella of Oz, Yookoohoos of Oz,* and the upcoming *Immortal Longings of Oz,* all published by The Royal Publisher of Oz. He is also a past winner of the Winkies Award for Fiction, for "Gillikin Witches of Oz."

Mike Conway is the CEO and Founder of Darkstar Eclectic Media, a company dedicated to producing the best in games and fiction. Mike also runs a hobby business called Forestmaster Games, to distribute visual novels His current projects include: *Heroes of Oz* RPG: The tabletop roleplaying game based on the famous Wizard of Oz books by L. Frank Baum using the Fudge System, the Darkstar Universe, an open-source superhero, fantasy, and sci-fi universe made available under a generous Creative Commons license.

J. L. Bell has written fiction and verse for *Oziana, Oz-story Magazine*, and the *OzCon* program booklet. His articles for *The Baum Bugle* include the first detailed study of an L. Frank Baum manuscript and analyses of *The Enchanted Island of Yew, John Dough and the Cherub, Dorothy and the Wizard of Oz*, and other books. He lives outside Boston, researching local history, and his non-Oz writing includes *The Road to Concord: How Four Stolen Cannon Ignited the Revolutionary War*.

Nathan DeHoff is a long-time fan of Oz who's written numerous stories and essays on the fairyland over the years, largely concentrating on Oz from an in-universe perspective. You can check out his blog at: http://vovatia.wordpress.com. He currently lives in Brooklyn with his wife Beth and two cats, and a Library Science degree he hasn't been able to put to much use as of yet.

Eric Shanower is the award-winning illustrator of the graphic novel series *Age of Bronze* (www.age-of-bronze.com), retelling the story of the Trojan War. With cartoonist Skottie Young, he adapted six of L. Frank Baum's Oz books to a Marvel Comics series of *New York Times* best-selling graphic novels. He wrote the Eisner Award-winning comics series *Little Nemo: Return to Slumberland* with art by Gabriel Rodriguez. Shanower's past work includes his own graphic novel series, available as *Adventures in Oz* (IDW), the story "Happily Ever After" included in the Lambda Literary Award finalist *How Beautiful the Ordinary*, and art for *An Accidental Death* by Ed Brubaker, *The Elsewhere Prince* by Moebius and R-JM Lofficier, and Harlan Ellison's *Dream Corridor*. He was co-publisher of Hungry Tiger Press, which specializes in books and cds reprinting and continuing the works of L. Frank Baum. Shanower's illustrated books include *The Rundelstone of Oz* by Eloise McGraw, *The Wicked Witch of Oz* by Rachel Cosgrove Payes, and *The Runaway in Oz* by John R. Neill. He wrote and illustrated *The Giant Garden of Oz* and *The Salt Sorcerer of Oz and Other Stories*. His work has appeared on television, in magazines, and in children's books, as well as several documentaries, including *The Origins of Oz* (BBC), and "Because of the Wonderful Things It Does" on the video release of the 1939 MGM *The Wizard of Oz*. He lives in Portland, Oregon, with his partner, David Maxine.

Jeff Rester was born and raised in Mobile, Alabama, where his love for Oz started with the annual viewing of MGM's *The Wizard of Oz* that came on each spring on CBS. Like most all other children of that time, he was surprised to learn there was more than one Oz book and that Dorothy went back to live forever in Oz with her aunt and uncle. Jeff enjoyed reading and writing as a child, and especially loved creative writing. All of that was the beginning of writing his own Oz stories, some published in *Oziana* magazine and *The Royal Explorers of Oz* book series. His grand opus *Death Comes to Oz* is forthcoming.

The Lost Tales of Oz

David Tai got involved with Oz writing via Marcus Mebes while reading the various Oz books. He began editing after suggesting fixes for Oz stories that Marcus was doing for *Oziana* magazine. After speaking with Oz author, Jared David, he wrote "Executive Decisions" (Oziana #38) as has since then written new short stories revolving around "Whatever happened to..." to satisfy his ever-curious investigations of Betsy and Trot. He is currently at work on *The Thirty Heads of Princess Langwidere in Ev*.

Margaret Berg was born in Fort Wayne, Indiana, on April 6, 1927. She became a library coordinator, and as a member of the International Wizard of Oz Club, went on to review more than thirty titles for "The Oz Bookshelf" column of *The Baum Bugle*. An active member of the Quakers, who enjoyed corresponding with friends and family, Margaret went on to write Oz books and short stories, including "New Moon Over Oz," in *Oziana 1994* and *Ozallooning in Oz*. Margaret died peacefully at home on January 20, 2016. Her additional works are forthcoming from The Royal Publisher of Oz.

Sam Sackett was born in southern California and very early was put on a diet of Oz books for birthdays and Christmases. Burned out on university teaching after 23 years, Sam went into journalism, then advertising, then public relations, and finally career management. Retired, spent six years in Thailand, then back in the US. He's written four novels, *Adolf Hitler in Oz*, *Sweet Betsy from Pike*, *The Robin Hood Chronicles*, and *Huckleberry Finn Grows Up*, as well as three books of short stories: *Through Farang Eyes, Snapshots of Thailand, and Chamberlain Stories*. Sam passed away on March 29, 2018. His final works are included in this volume.

Biographies

Jared Davis ("Jay" to his friends) was born and raised in the American Ozarks. A lifelong love of literature, his early relationship with Oz was rocky. Finally, he returned to it and began The Royal Blog of Oz in 2005, followed by the Royal Podcast of Oz in 2009. He finally broke into writing Oz literature with his own book *Outsiders from Oz* in 2012, "The Way of a Lion," (*Oziana 2013*), "How the Adventurers Returned Home," "Roselawn" and others. In addition to his writing, he also assists with the *Baum Bugle*, the journal of the International Wizard of Oz Club and chaired the 2018 OzCon International. He lives in Springfield, Missouri with his two cats, Phantom and Suzanne.

Marcus Mebes is a graphic designer living in Louisiana. He is a lifelong fan of literature, having read an abridgment of *The Wizard of Oz* as a toddler, then delving into the series in the mid- to late-80s when Del Rey reprinted the majority of them and Eric Shanower's graphic novels hit the market. His favorite Oz author is Thompson. He is the creator of Pumpernickel Pickle, which has published the works of March Laumer. His own recent titles include *The Mysterious Caverns of Oz, Shipwrecked in Oz, The Bashful Baker of Oz*, and the epic four-part series *The Royal Explorers of Oz. The Haunted Castle of Oz* is forthcoming.

Andrew Heller is the author of several Oz books, including *The Giant Chincilla of Oz* and *King Rinkitink* (with help from L. Frank Baum). He has also written several alternate histories, including a novel about the Great War (*Gray Tide in the East*) and one about the American Civil War (*If the North Had Won the Civil War*). He is the father of two children and a chinchilla, and lives quietly with his wife in suburban Philadelphia, where he indulges in the hobbies of stamp collecting and the production of giant robots in his basement library.

NEED MORE ADVENTURE IN YOUR LIFE?

BUTTON-BRIGHT & OJO'S ADVENTURES IN OZ TRILOGY

CONTINUING THE FAMOUS OZ STORIES BEGUN BY L. FRANK BAUM

AVAILABLE ON AMAZON.COM & EBAY

DELUXE HARDCOVER EDITIONS ON LULU.COM

MYSTERY AND INTRIGUE IN
OOGABOO

QUEEN ANN IN OZ AND ADOLF HITLER IN OZ ARE AVAILABLE ON
AMAZON.COM & EBAY
DELUXE HARDCOVER EDITIONS AVAILABLE ON LULU.COM

FOR OZ-BOOKS, ERIC SHANOWER ART, AND SO MUCH MORE!

Welcome to
HUNGRY TIGER PRESS

http://www.hungrytigerpress.com

Explore Oz!

The International Wizard of Oz Club

Membership brings rewards:

1. Three issues of the Club's premier journal *The Baum Bugle*, fully-illustrated with rare photographs and drawings, popular and scholarly articles on every aspect of the Oz phenomenon.
2. News in the world of Oz, including annual issues of *Oziana*, magazine featuring new Oz stories, and invites to upcoming conventions where you can meet fellow Oz fans, authors, and dealers.
3. Discounts on Club publications

Join online at: www.ozclub.org

Or write: The International Wizard of Oz Club, Inc.
PO Box 721129
Berkley, MI 48072-9998
USA

RINKITINK IN OZ
AS IT *SHOULD* HAVE BEEN!

WINNER OF THE 100TH ANNIVERSARY
INTERNATIONAL WIZARD OF OZ CLUB CONTEST

ANDREW HELLER & L. FRANK BAUM
REVEAL THE TRUE STORY OF KING RINKITINK,
PRING INGA AND THE IRASCIBLE GOAT BILBIL!

AVAILABLE ON AMAZON.COM
DELUXE HARDCOVER EDITION AVAILABLE ON LULU.COM

www.ingramcontent.com/pod-product-compliance
Lightning Source LLC
Chambersburg PA
CBHW030921020726
47498CB00001B/59